ALL THE RIGHT THINGS

LINDA SHANTZ

ALL THE RIGHT THINGS

eBook edition ISBN: 978-1-990436-32-1

Paperback ISBN: 978-1-990436-33-8

Hardcover ISBN: 978-1-990436-34-5

ALSO BY LINDA SHANTZ

The Good Things Come Series:

Bright, Broken Things (a prequel)

Good Things Come (Book 1)

All The Little Things (Book 2)

All Good Things (Book 3)

This Good Thing (Book 4)

Merry Little Things (Book 5)

All The Best Things (Book 6)

Horse of the Year (Book 7)

Shiny Little Things (Book 8)

All The Right Things (Book 9)

Good Things Come Series: Books 1-3 Box Set

Good Things Come Series: Books 4-6 Box Set

Sign up for my newsletter at:

https://www.lindashantz.com/writes

Join my Patreon to read as I write!

https://bit.ly/patreon-Linda-Shantz

*For my grandmother, Anna Caroline McIlraith, who loved
fiercely and was not afraid to speak her mind*

A NOTE TO THE READER

All The Right Things takes place immediately after *Horse Of The Year*, but may be read as a standalone.

The Good Things Come Series is set in the world of North American Thoroughbred racing, which has its own vocabulary. If you're unfamiliar with this world, there's a glossary of terms at the end of the book. Feel free to point out any that I'm missing!

In 2023, following the death of Queen Elizabeth II in September 2022, the Queen's Plate returned to being called the King's Plate to reflect the new British Monarch, King Charles III.

CHAPTER ONE

THE SUN RISING above the jagged skyline was a welcome sight, a ball of fire in a lightening blue sky casting long shadows on the training track. April's early morning air had a bite, frosting the fringe of grass surrounding the dirt oval and rimming the flossy puffs of breath from the horses' nostrils with gold, like dragon fire as they galloped past. Jet planes roared above the constant drone of the nearby highway, but all Dean Taylor heard was the rhythmic thrum of hooves, the flutter of nostrils, and the steady beat of his heart.

Fifteen years, and he still thought of his late father every time he stepped up to this rail. His feet didn't quite fit in the imprints left there, but every new racing season, he had fresh hope that he'd measure up.

The outrider's pony dozed with one hind leg cocked, soaking up the rising sun's warmth with hooded eyes and droopy lower lip. Long legs draped his barrel in chaps as weathered as the shack behind him, leather the colour of warm ochre matching the patches on the pony's coat. A tall to-go cup with a recognizable green logo was propped on the horn by a cowhide-gloved hand as Gord, the outrider, scanned the training track for trouble. He wouldn't have looked out of place on the plains of Montana, surveying a herd of grazing cattle, except for the helmet the rules of the backstretch required him to wear. *Yellowstone meets Seabiscuit.*

"'Morning, Dean. Ready for opening day?"

Dean glanced up, smiling. "More than ready." After the long stretch without racing from December to April, the coffers were running low.

"How many two-year-olds you got?"

"Three. They're like triplets, all of them dark bay. I have to scan their microchips every day to tell them apart."

Gord laughed, his eyes never leaving the scene before him. Dean didn't actually have any difficulty identifying the three juveniles as long as he could see their faces, though as familiar as he was with each one, sometimes even he did a double take if two of them were out of their stalls at the same time.

His charge progressed around the turn at a choppy, uninspired trot, just another dark shape backlit by the sunrise amid the hurly-burly of the track. The exercise rider pulled the colt up and turned him to face the infield, hesitating only briefly before she wheeled him to the right and set off at a gallop. At least that's what the colt was supposed to be doing. It looked more like a hobby-horse canter. *Ba-dum, ba-dum, ba-dum.*

"That your good two-year-old?"

The voice — not Gord's — pulled Dean's gaze from the colt's balky bounce, and he eyed the older man shuffling up next to him with a wry twist of his lips. Len was as sharp as the nails that tacked shoes to the horses' feet. He didn't miss a thing around here.

"That's Cruze, my homebred," Dean said, as if Len didn't already know.

"The half-brother to your big horse?" Len asked.

"The very one. He's got some big shoes to fill and doesn't seem in any hurry to do it." Cruze wasn't excited about anything but napping and regular meals.

Len chuckled. "It's early days, yet."

The colt came around the turn in the middle of the racetrack. Even with the challenging visibility, Dean could see his ears up, his stride sticky. Nothing about the horses breezing on the rail engaged him. Sure, it was early days, but could he not show just a little interest in running?

"Your father's been nominated for the Hall of Fame this year," Len said casually.

Dean shot Len a look. "That's great," he responded, a beat too late to be convincing.

Not really a surprise, was it? A car accident had cut Ed Taylor's career short, but no one would debate that his accomplishments merited the honour. The prospect just hadn't been on Dean's radar, and it caught him off guard. Another reminder he'd fallen short. Fifteen years. Flashes of success, but nothing enduring.

Len met his eyes, nodded like he saw all of it. Dean had known Len since he was a kid hanging around the barn. He'd inherited the aged trainer's friendship along with Ed Taylor's business after his father's death. Len was more than someone he could count on for a good story; he'd become a mentor when Dean needed one most, a steady presence as he assumed the position he'd always wanted — just not the way it came to pass.

Dean noticed the pony first — woken in an instant from his slumber, on his toes, rocking in place — before the warning met Dean's ears.

"Loose horse!"

Stirrup leathers and reins flapping, the runaway barrelled toward them, downed rider rising slowly from the dirt. Dean groaned. He recognized that dark bay face with the squiggle of white on his forehead. Cruze zoomed past, Gord driving his pony in hot pursuit.

"Maybe he can run a bit after all!" Len chortled.

The outrider snagged the delinquent before he reached the next turn. Only then did Dean turn back to his exercise rider, stomping through the deep, sandy track.

"You all right?" he asked with a twinge of guilt for putting his concern for the horse before her well-being.

Crystal glared. "I'm fine. Eff my life with that horse. Eff those effing geese."

He tightened his jaw so he didn't smile. Canada Geese were as common as pigeons around the racetrack; Dean hadn't even registered them. But Cruze had. The colt would nap through the rat-a-tat of a shockwave treatment on the other side of the barn, but lit up for waterfowl.

"I'll grab him," he said.

"No, it's fine," Crystal snapped, marching past.

At least the colt hadn't ducked out the on-gap and clattered back to the barn. Dean owed Gord a bottle of bourbon.

A trio of horses snorted and skittered across the stonedust on the horse path, still agitated by the commotion. Gord jogged his pony toward them, Cruze bright-eyed and looking pleased with himself as Crystal reached for the colt, grabbing him close to the bit. Her lips moved as she nattered at him and scrubbed him on the neck.

"See you later, Len," Dean called over his shoulder, sure the older man would update him on all the backstretch news at the end of the morning — and hoping Cruze wouldn't be the top story. He met Crystal at the gap.

"I'll leg you up. Save you the walk of shame." He couldn't help a grin as he lifted her into the tack.

Crystal picked up the lines, but not her irons. "Are you going to make me take him around again?"

"No. I think that two-minute-lick he did once he was rid of you is enough for today."

Crystal rolled her eyes, her legs dangling at the colt's sides, apparently convinced the threat of errant birds was gone. Dean wasn't sure he'd be so relaxed after being dumped in the dirt, but that's why he stayed on the ground.

When they reached the barn, Dean's assistant rushed over, snatching the colt's halter and a shank from the rail.

"Why are you back so soon? I'm not even done the stall yet!" Nikki said with red hair flying, following as Crystal directed the colt into the cinder block box.

Dean paused in front of the end stall, staying clear as Crystal expounded on the *effing geese*. Ride The Wave stood in the doorway, a thick bed of golden straw sprouting around his dark legs, tufts of pale green pulled from his overstuffed haynet. The big horse stretched as far as the stall yoke would allow, the reach of his lips like a stubbier version of an elephant's trunk.

"If only, eh buddy?" Dean said as he dug the expected peppermint from his pocket. "A trunk would be handy, wouldn't it? You could hold hotwalkers hostage and demand treats as ransom."

Ride The Wave was Dean's constant, the one who, by winning the Queen's Plate two years ago, had given him a glimmer of hope that he was finally worthy of being Ed Taylor's son. The colt's four-year-old season had been lacklustre but ended on a positive note with a win in the marathon Valedictory Stakes on closing day. This year would be better. The Wave had been training like a bear since shipping in at the end of February. Dean was counting on him and old Fargo — who'd won on opening day for three straight years — to bring some money in early and take the pressure off his strained bank account.

"You'll buy your little brother some time," he said, giving The Wave a light slap. "He's going to need it."

Crystal stalked past on her way to the last horse, arms full with saddle, pads, bridle and martingale. Nikki barged from the stall with Cruze, the colt diving for his water bucket as if he'd completed an Ironman.

"I'll walk him," Dean said, easing the long leather lead shank from Nikki's grip. It was too cold for baths this morning. "You finish the stall. Tell Brenda to take her time with Fox. I've got this guy."

He'd never minded walking, the lowest of all backstretch occupations. There was a welcome mindlessness to it that allowed for wandering thoughts, at least as long as he wasn't expected to maintain a conversation with someone else touring the shed. It let him run with the possibility that carried him this time of year. Anything could happen.

The good two-year-old Len mentioned could turn out to be something big.

The Wave could regain his championship form.

The three-year-old filly might grow into herself in time to run in the Oaks.

It's what kept him coming back every season, got him out of bed before dawn each day. This place, these people, those horses. Forty years from now, he wanted to be like Len, still standing at the rail, watching the dragons fly by.

Brenda's voice cut into his reverie. "I'll finish him up. Nikki wants you for something."

Dean glanced at his watch. He'd lost track of time, going round and round. "Another turn, then he can have some grass." Such that it was, this time of year. He passed Cruze to the hotwalker and called, "Where are you, Nikki?"

Her response came from the end of the shed. "The Wave's stall."

He sauntered down and poked his head in the doorway, greeted by his big horse's powerful hindquarters, The Wave's head tethered to a ring on the stall's back wall by a sturdy rubber bungee.

"What's up?" he asked.

Nikki paused, brush in one hand, rub rag in the other, and frowned. "I think you'd better have a look at his tendon."

CHAPTER TWO

"I'm sorry, Dean. It's always the good ones."

Dean pulled a peppermint from his pocket and offered it to The Wave, not really watching as the big bay inhaled the treat. "Thanks, Jake," he said, forcing himself to focus as the veterinarian closed the ultrasound unit that had assisted in the diagnosis.

Jake nodded, and Dean returned his gaze to The Wave instead of following the vet to his SUV, parked outside the long barn.

"All right, buddy," he said, backing the horse a few steps so he could steer him into the stall. The Wave followed like an overgrown puppy. "Let's get you done up."

He took his time smoothing thick grey mud over the horse's left tendon because it would delay the inevitable call to his partner. Dean shook his head. The injury was barely even visible — only a trained eye would notice it, feel the slight temperature difference — but that subtle thickening of tissue, slightly below the horse's knee, was a twenty percent tear. It didn't have to mean retirement, but the older a horse got, the harder it was to bring them back, and what was the point if The Wave would only ever be another two-bit claimer? He deserved better.

Dean straightened, leaving streaks of mud down his thighs as he wiped his hands on his jeans, assessing the finished job, a standing bandage set over the paper-covered poultice. He pulled off the halter, letting The Wave rub his head against his arm. As Dean leaned into it, he heard his father's voice.

Your heart's too big for this game.

He pushed away the emotions along with the horse's head. It was the end of The Wave's career, not the end of the world. "Not that it matters to you. You'll love retirement. Especially if we can find you some mares."

The barn was quiet, shedrow neatly raked, his help sent home while he stayed for Jake. Dean waited until he was in his cramped office to bring up the number, feet resting on an old milk crate as he leaned back in the creaking office chair. Ride The Wave's framed Queen's Plate win photo dominated amid more ordinary victories.

His thumb hovered over the screen, then punched the call icon with resignation. "Andy? Hi, it's Dean. I've got some bad news. Ride The Wave's bowed."

A muffled curse met his disclosure, and Dean imagined the big man parked behind a massive desk in a corner office high in some downtown skyscraper.

"He's going to the farm." Dean didn't say the rest of it, assuming it was self-explanatory. *He's done.*

"I think we need to be realistic here, don't you?" Andy said.

"How so, Andy?"

"He's five now. He had a great three-year-old season, but last year was disappointing. And I don't know about yours, but my phone sure hasn't been ringing off the hook with people interested in standing him at stud."

There was no comeback to that truth. Dean drew in a breath, releasing it slowly. "What are you saying, Andy?"

"It's time to let him go. Drop him in. Lose him."

Dean pulled the phone from his ear and stared. It wasn't the first time Andy had opposed him, and Dean wasn't violent, but this conversation made him want to throw the device against the wall. "I'm not doing that, Andy. This horse won us the Plate."

"He's not winning anything right now, is he? It's time to cut our losses while we can still get something for him."

Making himself breathe, Dean scanned the walls again. Ed Taylor had trained Ride The Wave's sire, Catch The Joy, to victory in the Canadian Triple Crown and the win photo from the third jewel hung not far from The Wave's Plate memento. Dean had pulled The Wave from his momma on the family's farm, watched him take his first breath, steadied him as he took his first steps.

His father stared back at him from that winner's circle shot, all smiles in that moment of victory, and Dean wondered if he'd approve of what Dean was about to do. With a sigh, he said, "So what were you thinking we should run him for?"

Andy exhaled like he thought Dean had come to his senses. "Someone would take him for forty, don't you think?"

"I'll buy you out then."

The line went so quiet, Dean thought he'd lost the connection.

"What?" His partner sounded more surprised than angry.

"He won't win, Andy. He'll blow that tendon and won't be good for anything more than mowing the lawn. This way you still get your money." *And the horse doesn't end up crippled.*

"Fine," came the growl on the other end. "If that's what you want to do."

Want to? No. Had to? Absolutely.

Dean locked the office and took one last wander down the shedrow to check on his charges. The Wave munched his hay — oblivious to Dean's discord — pausing long enough to inhale another peppermint. He owed this horse so much, and The Wave didn't owe him a thing. But twenty thousand dollars. Like he had that at his disposal.

Next door, Cruze lay flat out — the two-year-old's second-favourite position, after eyeballs-deep in a feed tub. The colt's ear twitched and his legs rustled the straw. Dreaming big dreams, Dean could only hope. He wished he could've given Andy half of him instead of cash, but Cruze hadn't shown enough potential to be worth it. No one would value a piece of this baby at twenty thousand. Not yet. Maybe not ever.

The second of the dark bay triplets, owned by Andy, dozed at the back of his stall. The third was the good two-year-old Len had talked about. With not even a thumbprint of white on his dark body, Fox was the kind of plain brown wrapper people walked right past — and most had last fall at the local mixed sale, letting Dean scoop him up for a modest bid as agent for a new client, keeping only a quarter interest for himself. Mitigated risk, minimized return. The trade-off that let him play a game he couldn't otherwise afford. What had drawn him to the colt wasn't some magical connection; Dean had liked something about his eye, something about his walk. Fox had developed over the winter and started turning heads as a two-year-old this spring. Dean's friends joked he was always high on his horses, but everyone knew he was right about this one. In a couple of weeks, he'd prove it.

The colt was everything Cruze was not.

Dean offered his hand, and Fox lipped the peppermint before getting it on his tongue, then to his molars, still mastering the art of candy consumption.

"I'm counting on you to get me out of this mess."

The grip on the wheel of his Chevy truck didn't ease until he left the concrete jungle of Vaughan behind. Each year, it seemed to take longer for the grey of factories, warehouses and new housing developments to yield to trees and rolling hills. He used the forty-minute drive to regroup. Triple Stripe Stables stood two of Canada's top stallions and was a stone's throw from the Taylor's Northwest Farm. He'd talk to the owner's daughter, Liv, about The Wave; see if they could arrange something. They were friends, after all, and when she'd still been a jockey, Liv had ridden The Wave a few times and always loved him. It was still a big ask, and it wouldn't be free — stallions cost a lot to feed and manage — but if he didn't try, he'd never know.

King City was Canada's Thoroughbred horse country — smaller and younger than Lexington, Kentucky, the heart of the breeding industry. The area hadn't been excepted from urban sprawl. Many of the bigger farms had been sold, turned into golf courses or two-acre estate homes. Sometimes, Dean felt like the last of a dying breed, the next generation stepping up and trying to make a go of this tough business. Days like today, it was harder than others.

He pulled into the strip mall along the town's main drag, slipping the Chevy into park and not bothering to lock it when he hopped out. It was old enough now, it probably wasn't worth stealing, and all anyone would find if they ransacked it was a layer of dust and old racing forms and condition books.

Dean barely noticed the tinkle of the little bell that announced his arrival in the shop, but the rich smells of fresh-ground coffee beans and baking couldn't be ignored, no matter how many times he came through that door.

"I don't know why you don't just text on your way. I could have it ready for you."

The sight of the tall, blond woman who appeared from the kitchen lifted the corners of his lips and the weight of the morning's woes from his shoulders. He wasn't bold enough to text her, of course. When it came to women, he wasn't bold at all, which was why he was thirty-eight, single, and nursing a crush on his sister's employee. Besides, it wasn't as if he minded the wait, when it gave him an excuse to be around her longer.

"Thanks, Monique," he said when she presented the small espresso cup with its perfect caramel-coloured crema. He insisted on not using a to-go cup. For the time it took him to drink it, it was worth saving a paper vessel, not just for the environment, but for the bottom line of his sister's business.

"Faye's not here," Monique said. "She and Will went to look at a house."

It was cute she thought he was here to see his sister. He didn't stop by every day. That would make his feelings too obvious. He wasn't ready to act on them quite yet.

Today, though, he did need to talk to Faye. She wouldn't be pleased about his impetuousness. "I'll see her at home."

Monique set a plate next to the cup, one of the café's famous butter tarts waiting for him. The hair piled on her head in a neat bun was under a hairnet — she'd probably been baking and forgotten to remove it when she came to the front. An apron covered her outfit and most of her shape. She liked to dress in black.

Dean appreciated that Monique didn't try to talk about horses. Even though Faye wasn't hands-on with the farm, she'd been raised around them. With a father who had been a top trainer, she couldn't help but know things, even when she professed to be clueless. Monique truly was clueless.

She talked about other things. Some he didn't care about,

like celebrity gossip or whatever was trending on social media. But she was smart, too. Smart about food, and smart about music, and smart about current events. Their conversations were never lengthy — he could only milk an espresso and butter tart so long — but they always found something to discuss.

A customer came in, and Dean excused himself, setting the cup and plate in the plastic bin to the side. He gave Monique an unseen wave and departed.

The maple trees flanking the entrance to Northwest's short laneway were unfolding their leaves, the lawn around the small red brick farmhouse greening up. Gravel crunched under the truck's thick tires as Dean tried to avoid the potholes left from a winter of abuse — just one of the things on his list of what needed to be fixed. The mare in the paddock across from the house stuck her neck through the fence rails, reaching for the blades spouting there, because, the grass was always greener, wasn't it? She'd popped a board on one end. Dean put that repair at the top of his list.

Faye's old Corolla was parked at the side of their century home, but that didn't mean she was inside. She and Will might have gone to look at the house in Will's car. Gus bounded up to him as he entered through the screen door off the back deck, tongue lolling in his goofy Golden Retriever grin. Dean scratched the silken ears before removing his shoes, straightening them on the rubber mat behind the door, and noticed Faye's slip-ons. Her purse was propped on the kitchen table. She must be here after all.

The dog tore off, returning with his ratty old tug toy. Dean gave it a couple of half-hearted pulls before gravitating to the counter. The coffee pot was warm and recently brewed, Faye's favourite mug next to it. Dean poured himself a cup. His stop at the café wasn't about the caffeine pickup.

"You want coffee?" he called.

"Yeah, thanks." Faye wasn't fussy when she was working on the books.

She was at the computer, spreadsheet open, her back to the door, long dark hair in a messy bun. Nostalgia was hitting him hard today. Faye looked just like their mother had as she'd done the same task, all those years ago. It never went away, the grief. They'd just learned to work around it.

Save for a more current stack of *The Blood-Horse* and a smattering of best-sellers within the wall of books, the office was virtually untouched from the day Dean had returned, leaving university to be with a teenage Faye after he'd learned of the crash that had taken both their parents and middle brother, Shawn. Their mother's reading chair remained angled by the window, and framed images of Ed Taylor's greatest victories still presided above the desk. Dean kept his at the track — they weren't worthy of sharing this space.

A family portrait from when Faye was tiny enough to be in their father's arms rested beneath a lamp on a side table. In it, Shawn shoved an elbow into Dean's side with unrestrained mischief, while Dean ignored him with a responsible big brother expression. He still remembered the two of them exploding into a tussle of dust a beat after the shutter release, ruining their good clothes and promptly ending the shoot. Their mother had never been very successful at getting them to behave for formal pictures, and once Faye started walking, she gave up and accepted that the winner's circle images from the races her husband won were the best she'd get.

Dean wished now they'd been more cooperative. He set the cup next to Faye.

"Thanks." She glanced up, smiling before her focus returned to the screen, lips pressed together. "It's time you increased your day rate. The cost of everything is up this year. It's not sustainable."

Dean sank into the overstuffed chair, feeling like a child avoiding his mother's reproach as he stared out at the mare, still stretching through the fence boards, her foal nearby, nibbling new shoots of grass. "That won't go over well with Andy," he muttered.

Faye swivelled toward him. "So? He can afford it. *You* can't afford to go on like this."

"What I can't afford is for him to decide he wants someone with a higher win percentage to train his horses." Andy could be a pain, but he'd remained loyal when their father's other clients had fallen by the wayside, one by one.

"Andy's not going anywhere. It's time you realized your worth." Lecture over, Faye spun back to the computer, reaching automatically for her coffee. "How'd it go today?"

If she'd asked that first, he might have told her how well Fox was training, how Fargo looked ready to continue his opening-day win streak, or about Cruze's altercation with the Canada Geese. They could have laughed about that. But as they were already talking money, he might as well get it over with.

"The Wave's got a tendon."

Faye caught his eyes, brows raised. "How bad?"

"Bad enough. Twenty percent tear."

"So what does that mean?"

"It means he's retired."

She frowned. "What did Andy say?"

"He wants me to drop him and lose him."

"He should know better," she said, scowling. "Even if it was totally not the right thing to do by the horse, you'd never live it down."

"He doesn't see it that way." Dean rubbed his forehead and took a sip of coffee. "I told him I'd buy him out."

Faye's stare said it all, but to her credit, she didn't protest. She straightened, squaring her shoulders. "I know you set aside some money from The Wave's win in the Valedictory for the wedding. Use that."

A lump rose in his throat. "You keep it, Faye. You deserve to have a nice wedding."

"Between Will and I, we have enough connections that it won't be that expensive. And the shop is doing well. If we can get the online ordering for the website, it should do even better."

Dean shook his head. "We've always gotten by. We'll be racing soon. It'll take care of itself."

"We've been surviving," Faye countered. She swung back to the computer. "You're a good trainer, Dean. Stop comparing yourself to Dad. I'll write a letter about the increase and put it in with this month's bills."

He didn't argue with her. There wasn't much point, with Faye. Dean drained his cup and rose. He'd better not put off fixing the fence board any longer or the foal would see it as an escape route.

"Hey," he said, remembering. "How was the house?"

Each time Faye and Will returned from a viewing shaking their heads, Dean kept his pleasure to himself. Since their Christmas engagement, he'd known it would happen eventually, but he wasn't ready for Faye to leave, and he liked Will, too. The house was small, but it would be empty without them around.

Faye shrugged, eyes remaining on the screen. "Not the one."

Dean breathed a sigh of relief.

CHAPTER THREE

"He ready, Nikki?"

Nikki ducked out of the stall and slipped past Dean, her jumble of tight, terracotta-coloured curls bouncing as she went. "Just grabbing a shank."

Dean took the bridle hanging on the door and had it on the dark bay two-year-old before Nikki returned moments later. "I'll walk him until Nate gets here so you can start mucking. Then you'll have time to come out and watch, if you want."

"Thanks, Dean!"

There weren't many other horses on the shed this late in the morning, so Dean let Fox play, holding the shank loose so it bounced with the colt's antics as they travelled the entire way around the barn instead of cutting through the gap in the middle of the long block of back-to-back stalls. The two-year-old wore Dean's expectations like a cloak of promise — he looked good, felt good — and Dean was happy to have the time to let the young horse limber up while he waited for the rider to arrive. Jockeys were always in a hurry, rushing from barn to barn. As soon as they graced you with their presence, you tossed them up and headed straight out.

Grooms ducked out of his way with buckets and bandages, Fox interrupting their duties and conversations. When Dean came around to his side again, Nate Miller was there — not just on time, but early — ready to go, in boots and faded jeans, the navy safety vest encasing his torso matching his red-and-navy-covered helmet. He stood in front of Ride The Wave's stall, mock-boxing with the horse, the two of them bobbing.

Nate noticed Dean and stopped — then The Wave gave his shoulder a shove, knocking him off balance.

"You won that round," Nate said to the horse, grinning. The Wave tossed his head in triumph.

Dean stopped Fox in front of them and tried not to make comparisons. The Wave: tall, rangy, mature. Fox: smaller, more compact. The Wave, over. Fox, just beginning.

"How's the big horse?" Nate asked. When Dean frowned, Nate's smile disappeared. "You find something?"

"Tendon. He's going to the farm today."

Nate turned to The Wave and ran a hand over the horse's powerful neck. "I'm really sorry to hear that."

Dean didn't doubt the condolences were genuine. Nate had been on The Wave for that Queen's Plate win, after all.

"Can we move things along? I got a hot horse here."

Both Dean and Nate did little more than glance at the cranky voice. The hotwalker was just being contrary — Dean had seen the neighbouring trainer's horse walking long enough to be cooled out by now. Nate stepped up to Fox, taking the time to look over the tack on both sides before accepting Dean's leg up.

Dean led them out to the track, the colt alert, dancing in anticipation, tugging on the bit. He'd breezed enough times to know the signs. Both men were silent. Dean didn't feel the need to make polite conversation with Nate Miller. All the things that came to his mind to mention, Nate would already know. Faye's fiancé was Nate's best friend, so he'd be up to date on their house hunt. Nate now knew about Ride The Wave's diagnosis. What were they going to talk about, the weather? Nate had done the task set before him more times than Dean had, so Dean wasn't about to tell him how to do his job.

At the tunnel to the main track, Dean called the colt in to the clocker before walking them through and up the grade to the oval. He turned horse and rider loose and took his post at the rail. Len was already there, as reliable as if Dean had sent out an invitation. Nate jogged the colt off. Dean watched until they were out of view.

Len squinted under the bill of his dusty old ball cap. "That the one?"

"That's him," Dean confirmed, as if he needed to, because Len knew.

He could almost see the ears around them prick like he'd just told a pack of dogs he had a pocket full of treats. He wasn't good at playing coy, but at that moment, he wished he were because anyone who hadn't seen Fox before would be watching now. But it wasn't as if he could train the colt in secret. And what would be the point? Dean wasn't much of a bettor. Being part of this business was gamble enough.

"He must be ready to run," Len said.

Dean nodded, responding, "Sunday. He'll get his gate card today," and wondered if his tone had been low enough for the eavesdroppers not to hear. Everyone would know as soon as entry day arrived, anyway.

When Fox galloped past, he looked like any other unknown on the racetrack. Average looks, average height, average stride. Nate brought the colt to the gate, set in the chute off the main track oval, and the crew loaded Fox next to two other youngsters seeking their gate cards today. A formality for his talented colt, another box to tick. Fox felt like something Dean could count on in a business where there was no such thing as a sure thing.

Fox broke sharp, one of his workmates with him, the other, a big grey, popping out sluggishly. As they sprinted past, Fox's stride, unremarkable when he galloped, became a thing of beauty as he breezed, hooves skimming the track's surface. He settled nicely just off his company once they were out of the chute, the grey still trailing. Dean followed them as best he could with the infield obstructions — the shrubs, the flagpoles, the tote board — and was sure his colt was a neck up at the wire. It didn't matter. Today wasn't about winning. That would come.

He said goodbye to Len, feeling the buzz he left in his wake. The clocker gave him the colt's time, and Dean met Nate, glancing up at him as they walked back to the barn, Dean stepping in time with the rhythm of the colt's quick breaths.

"He's nice, Dean," Nate said. "But you know that."

Dean didn't bother to respond. True enough. He didn't need the jock's assurances, but appreciated it, nonetheless.

The vibe between the two of them wasn't awkwardness or antagonism, though the last traces of tension might linger. Maybe only Dean felt it. Personal feelings about Nate Miller aside, he wasn't about to let them affect business. If the connections between them gave Dean first call from one of the top riders at Woodbine, he'd take it. A middle-of-the-road trainer like him needed every advantage he could get.

Northwest's gooseneck trailer waited outside the barn, Ride The Wave's lift to the farm. Dean's manager, Stacy, chatted to Nikki in front of the horse's stall, her strawberry-blonde ponytail swinging as her arms waved with whatever tale she was relating. It made Dean's job easier that the two women got along. They didn't see a lot of each other, but communicated about the comings and goings between farm and track often.

He sent Stacy and The Wave on their way, then picked up a pitchfork and started going through the stall, wondering how he was going to fill it. Unlike some of his colleagues, he didn't have an endless supply of horses waiting at a training centre for a turn. At least the call he'd make today was better news than yesterday's conversation with Andy. And for a more agreeable owner.

Jacob Cheng was a tech whiz whose family owned racehorses in Hong Kong. For someone who'd shown a high risk tolerance with his business — he'd made his first million before the age of thirty — Jacob had been far more cautious with his foray into ownership, going partners with Dean on the modestly priced yearling. He was a breath of fresh air after Andy, who constantly asked Dean why he didn't try this or that latest thing, always questioning, always pushing, pushing, pushing.

He needed more owners like Jacob and fewer like Andy.

A light tapping on the metal doorframe pulled him from his thoughts. Dean grinned at the young woman standing there, dark hair pulled into a ponytail, her smile always a guaranteed pickup.

"Hey, Em. What are you doing in here today?"

"One of our exercise riders needed the morning off, so I filled in. Why was Stacy here with the trailer?"

"She was picking up The Wave."

"I heard about his injury. I'm sorry. It sucks so early in the season."

"It does," Dean agreed.

"What are you going to do with him?"

Dean piled the salvageable straw in a back corner. "The

priority will be rehabbing his tendon, but I'm going to talk to your sister. Maybe we can work something out."

"If he comes to our place, can I get on him? He'll need something to do during the off-season." She grinned.

Dean didn't say it, but if Liv did agree to some sort of arrangement to stand Ride The Wave at stud, Dean would bring him home for the off-season. He couldn't justify the expense of keeping him on someone else's farm when he wasn't on active duty.

"You going to turn him into a dressage horse?" he asked wryly.

"Why not?" Her lips twisted, blue eyes bright. "Cross-training is good for horses too. It worked out for Just Jay, didn't it?"

It certainly had. Emilie had started riding Just Jay after he'd recovered from an injury, training him up like she might have a future event horse. He'd looked so good, Liv had put him back in training. The rest was literally history. Dubai. Royal Ascot. Breeders' Cup. And a hefty stallion deal at one of the top farms in Kentucky. The difference was, Ride The Wave wasn't quite as well bred as Just Jay. Dean dragged the muck bucket from the stall and leaned the pitchfork against the cinder-block wall.

"How's old Fargo doing?" Emilie asked.

If she'd watched the gelding's race on opening day, she'd have seen for herself. Fargo had kept up his win streak, but it hadn't been as easy as years past.

"He came out of the race well," Dean hedged.

"I've got someone he'd be perfect for, if you think he's ready to do something new."

Rehoming retired racehorses was Emilie's pet project. She split her time between her physiotherapy job, galloping a few days a week for Liv at the track, and training retirees for the next phase of their lives. Emilie was one of a few people around the backstretch who kept an eye out for horses whose performance was starting to taper, ready to intercede. It was too soon for her to nudge him about Fargo.

"We're not there yet," he said, "but you'll be the first to know."

"Wouldn't it be nice for him to end his career on a winning note?" she said. "He's been good to you."

"He has," Dean said, pushing away pangs of conscience. "He'll tell me when he's done, Em."

For now, he needed Fargo in that stall.

CHAPTER FOUR

Neck bowed against Nikki's grip, Fox grew two inches, lick of mane floating, game face on. This colt looked like he knew he was going places. Dean accompanied Fox to the paddock, holding a lead attached to the bit on the off side. Not that Nikki wasn't capable, but he wasn't taking chances with this one.

Every step of the long trek from the backstretch to the path up to the grandstand saddling enclosure, he was aware of being observed, those heads Fox had been turning for weeks in the mornings here to see if he was the real thing. Dean felt in his bones the two-year-old was worthy of the hype. What was the point of being in this business if he didn't believe it?

When they reached their destination, he let Nikki continue on her own to the identifier who would scan the colt's microchip to make sure he was who the program said he was: Silent Fox. The paddock judge's call rang through the enclosure.

"Put them in, please!"

Nikki wheeled Fox into the saddling stall to face the spectators. Dean placed a hand lightly on the colt's neck. Cool and dry. Fox stood relaxed but interested in his surroundings as Dean and the valet secured the saddle.

"He looks like he's handling it well," Nate said, shaking Dean's hand as Nikki led the colt away. The hollow footfalls on the rubber paving stones and the low hum of voices reverberated around them.

"He's the whole package," Dean said.

He legged Nate up, and his job — for the next ten minutes, at least — was over. Escalators carried him to the second level of the grandstand, and he weaved through the weekend crowd — if he could call it a crowd — to the outdoor portion of the seating. He was used to watching his horses run alone. Nikki preferred to view trackside with the other grooms. Faye was busy at the café, likely dealing with the Sunday after-church crowd. Business in San Francisco prevented Jacob from seeing his horse run. Someone claimed the seat next to him as the field entered the track — irritating, when there were plenty of vacant spots — until with a glance, he realized it was Liv.

"Good afternoon," he said, dropping his binoculars to his lap.

Liv's lips twisted with the hint of a smile. "'Afternoon, Dean."

"Are you clocking my horse?"

"Isn't everyone?" The twist became more pronounced. "At least one of us has a precocious two-year-old this year."

Dean didn't let his gaze linger long — just enough to note the way her dark hair was pulled back from her delicate features, a few strands that had worked loose lifting in the westerly breeze. She always dressed conservatively in dark colours. Black jeans, a short navy jacket, a white blouse open at the neck. When his eyes fell to the small pendant resting between her collarbones, it was time to look back to his horse.

He couldn't even think of Liv as the one who'd gotten away,

because he'd never actually chased her. Instead, he'd watched her story play out with another leading man while he remained an extra, a member of the supporting cast, secretly pining. What a tiring role.

Liv shared his silence as they followed the proceedings, from post parade to warm-up to loading in the gate. The two of them poised on the edges of their seats, frozen, waiting for the barrier to release its captives.

The doors flew open, seven two-year-olds erupting in a wave of chaos and colour. Fox broke clean. Dean's heart raced with the colt, hope and expectation carried on the dark bay's firing legs and bunching muscles. Nate kept him clear, sitting third just behind the battling frontrunners, setting a snappy pace.

The field flowed around the turn, and Fox was poised, ready. When Nate sent him at the head of the stretch, the hairs raised over Dean's entire body, giving him goosebumps. Fox swept around the outside, vanquishing the leaders with a stride that took his breath away. Morning whispers became the roar of *I told you so*. Clear of the field, the colt's advantage lengthened down the lane with every pump of Nate's arms.

Dean didn't realize he was standing, only the dryness of his throat letting him know his had been one of the screaming voices, forgetting he wasn't alone until Liv gave him a squeeze. He crushed her in a hug, catching his breath like he'd ridden the race himself.

It was true. Fox was all of it, and more.

"Congratulations!" Liv laughed.

She stepped out of the way so he could pass. Dean sprang down the steps to the apron, waylaid by handshakes and thumps on the back before Nikki met him with a high-five. In the distance near the clubhouse turn, Fox trotted toward them with a spring in his step.

As Nikki and Fox headed to the backstretch after posing for the win photo — an exclusive affair, with just the two of them and Nate — Dean left the winner's circle, his phone ringing before he'd extracted it to call Jacob. He glanced at the number, the New York City exchange making his eyebrows arch, but didn't stop walking. After a beat, he hit decline. He had a horse to check on. That came first.

Before he reached the parking lot, it rang again.

Los Angeles.

Dean stopped, staring at the line of vehicles in the lot, and only then remembered he'd walked over with Nikki and Fox. Sighing, he put the phone on silent and tucked it away, resigning himself to the hike back.

Before he made it far, the patter of running feet and the sound of his name stopped him.

"Wait up!" Liv wasn't the least bit out of breath when she reached him. "I tried to call you. I saw you'd walked over and wondered if you wanted a ride."

"Yes. Please." He grinned. "I turned my phone off."

"Was it blowing up?" she asked with a sideways glance, leading the way to Nate's sleek, dusky-blue Porsche Carrera.

"It was."

Liv unlocked the doors, and when she settled behind the wheel, she looked perfectly in her element.

"Finally, I get to ride in the Porsche," Dean said. He slouched and shifted, trying to get comfortable. There wasn't a lot of headroom.

Liv flashed a smile as the engine rumbled to life. "It's the real reason I married Nate."

She was joking—because it had taken much more than a flashy car to win over Liv Lachance — but it reminded Dean that he would never make the kind of money Woodbine's leading rider did.

"Thanks for the lift," he said when Liv pulled up outside the test barn. He paused, hand resting on the door handle. "I want to talk to you about Ride The Wave."

Liv nodded. "All right. I'd love you to come see a set go on the gallop at the farm. Maybe you could come over?"

"Sounds good. I'll send you a text sometime soon."

He was careful to duck as he climbed out, rolling his shoulders as he strode to the test barn, a cinderblock building behind a tall chain link fence. Nikki assured him all was well, and he stood with her, watching Fox for a few turns, before walking to his barn.

The shed was quiet except for the soothing sounds of the horses munching hay. Fargo dozed, hindquarters facing the door. Cruze napped, flat out. Occasionally, the crackle of the old PA system disrupted the peace.

Get them ready.

Bring them over.

The winner of ...

The winner of the third race was a name Dean would never forget, like someone he'd met at a party — when he wasn't even sure what he was doing there. He went to his office and turned his phone back on, pen and paper at the ready to record the names and numbers he was sure by now filled up his voice mailbox.

By the end of training the next morning, the deal was finalized. A quarter of a million dollars.

Two. Five. Zero. Three more zeroes.

Dean went over the oval digits with his black gel pen, again and again, then gave the last two pupils and eyebrows. He paused, because a big smiley face just didn't fit the emotions that dollar figure gave him.

Everyone in horse racing knew when someone offered that kind of change for a two-year-old — especially one you'd grabbed for peanuts at the local sale last fall — you took the money and ran. If you didn't, the day after you turned it down, the horse colicked, or kicked the wall of its stall and smashed a sesamoid, or dropped the rider in the morning and crashed through the outer rail. There were a million ways a young horse might find to die.

The remnants of the victory spread Nate's agent had dropped off that morning sat on Dean's desk. It was probably why Nate was so popular — when he won races, he always ordered the traditional next-day treat for the winning barn from Faye's café. No pizza or Tim Horton's coffee from this guy. Dean grabbed a half-eaten croissant and left the office.

Cruze, actually awake, stretched over his screen, lips flapping. Dean pulled off a piece of the pastry and offered it to the colt. He didn't expect Cruze to take it, but it vanished from Dean's palm. The colt's jaw worked, and instead of spitting it out, Cruze nudged Dean's arm, looking for more.

"Champagne taste on a beer budget, buddy," Dean said. "You'd better start working a little harder if you want to live that kind of life."

Why did it suddenly feel like his future was resting on a two-year-old with all the enthusiasm of a garden gnome? A penchant for pranks, a dash of whimsy — and zero desire to be a racehorse.

CHAPTER FIVE

THE FOUR WOMEN clustered at the fence, the curious foal in his glory as the centre of attention. Will flipped burgers, and Faye emerged from the house with more food, setting platters on the deck's table. Then she found her wine glass and planted herself next to Dean.

"You were very generous," she said.

At least she didn't say *too* generous. He'd given them each something. His assistant, Nikki; the exercise rider, Crystal; the hotwalker, Brenda.... even his other groom, grouchy old Squeak. Stacy, his farm manager, too. And Faye, who had protested, but Dean insisted she was part of the team.

It felt right to reward his staff for their hard work with a bonus, over and above their usual stake money — especially considering they didn't win many races. How often did he get to do that? Not since The Wave had won the Plate, two years ago. Dean paid them fairly, but their salaries were still modest considering the skill and workload involved in their jobs. With good help so hard to come by these days, he was grateful he'd had the same crew for a few years now. There was no taking that for granted.

And now, they were all here on the farm for a celebration — except for Squeak, who didn't drive but had turned down a ride. No surprise — Squeak complained daily about working with a bunch of women and would rather spend the afternoon drinking with his buddies than spending more time with them.

"Is Jacob going to buy something?" Faye asked. "Or maybe claim a horse?"

Fox's departure and The Wave's retirement brought the empty stall count at the track to two. It was a common misconception that trainers rented stalls at the track. They didn't. Stalls were assigned with the understanding they enter horses to fill races. The tracks made their money on gambling, and bettors wanted full fields. Dean needed horses — horses that could run — to keep in the good graces of the stall man. *Use 'em or lose 'em.*

"He said he wants to wait for the sale. He likes the idea of a fresh slate." Claiming was always a bit of a crapshoot; you never knew what you were inheriting. "I wish I had something I could sell him half of, but Cruze isn't exactly inspiring at the moment."

"You didn't even have The Wave at the track as a two-year-old. They *are* half-brothers," Faye reminded.

Dean grinned at her. "When are you going to stop denying you don't pay attention to this stuff?"

"I'm not sure why I bother."

"I think I just need to breeze him and see if it wakes him up. If it doesn't, I'll bring him back here for the summer." Except that would be another empty stall he couldn't fill.

"Burgers are ready!" Will yelled in a camp counsellor voice so convincing it made Dean wonder if he'd ever been one.

The women turned from the foal, leaving the colt with his

head stuck through the boards, stumpy tail flapping uselessly at flies. With a snort he stepped free of the fence and wandered to his mother, lining himself up to nurse.

Dean was content to listen, enjoying the beautiful May afternoon and the group's camaraderie. Brenda, the retired woman who walked hots for him because she wanted to stay fit and busy, regaled Faye with tales of her grandchildren. Crystal talked music with Will. Stacy and Nikki had their heads together at the picnic table set in the shade of a tall, leafy maple. From Stacy's animation, hands flying around, Dean would bet she was telling Nikki about the foal's never-ending antics, both of them laughing — and knowing in a couple of years, that bratty colt would be Nikki's nightmare two-year-old at the racetrack.

"Dean?" Stacy called. "Can we talk to you?"

Gus raced ahead of him as he sauntered over, the Golden thrilled for a new cleanup assignment. The dog snuffled through the grass under the table's weathered wooden slats as Dean slid onto the seat next to Nikki.

"What's up?" he asked. They probably wanted to discuss an article they'd read about something that would save time or money or improve the horses' lives. It was just another part of what made them such great employees. They were always reading, always learning.

"This is great, thank you," Nikki said, Stacy nodding enthusiastically.

"You're welcome, but thank you. You two let me sleep at night."

They glanced at each other, and the look they exchanged gave Dean a queasy feeling.

Nikki's eyes flicked to his. "We love our jobs. You're the best boss, and giving us a bonus when you sold Fox was just so generous." She swallowed, fingers wrapping and unwrapping around the base of her vodka cooler. "Maybe it's a bit ironic that's what's letting us do this."

"Do... what?" Dean said. *Just spit it out.*

"We've both always wanted to go to Australia, and not just to visit," Stacy began. "I've been researching it for years, and then last week, the perfect opportunity showed up. See, I've made a couple of friends online who work in the racehorse business over there, and they said they could totally find us jobs. It's perfect. We'll get our trip of a lifetime, and it'll pay for itself! We've both been saving for the flight and were thinking maybe next year. But thanks to you, we can do it now!"

"Everything just came together!" Nikki jumped in, oozing excitement before she caught herself. "We feel terrible about leaving you, really we do, but the timing is just so right. And it's only for twelve weeks."

Stacy took over. "You'll have no trouble finding summer help, with kids off school. Guelph has that employment program — they'll even give you money to hire someone. My little sister is in it. I'll bring her in to meet you. She hasn't found a placement yet."

Dean looked from one animated face to the other. "Both of you?" he croaked.

He wanted to say, *I can't guarantee your jobs will still be here—* like there weren't more desperate employers in all facets of the horse business than people were willing to work. He'd always counted himself lucky because his staff was perennially steady. People liked to work with him. They might not win as many races as some outfits, but he was fair, and he pitched in. Hadn't these two just confirmed that?

"Now's the time to do this, while we're still young," Stacy said. "You understand, you know you do."

He did. It wasn't their fault he'd never felt he had that freedom. But he'd never wanted it, either. Not that he was averse to travel, if was with a big horse that took him across the ocean like Just Jay had done for Liv and Nate in the past year, but otherwise, everything Dean wanted was here.

He wasn't a workaholic. He took a ski trip at the end of every racing season, and the odd day off in the summer to mountain bike or visit Saratoga. But journeying to places like Australia... he just wasn't the guy that needed to see the world. He was a homebody — and the farm was home.

"It sounds like a great opportunity," he conceded, trying to hide that he was *not* happy about this. How could they expect him to be? But Stacy and Nikki were thrilled. They were going to Australia, both of them. And he had bought their tickets.

Faye, picking up used plates and stacking them on a tray, caught his eye when he returned to the deck.

"What was that about?" she asked, quietly enough no one else was likely to hear.

Dean tried to unlock his jaw and muttered, "I'll tell you later."

———————————

Faye practically jumped up from the couch, her mouth dropping open. She snapped it shut and blinked. "Australia? Both of them? How can they do that?"

From the kitchen, plates clinked as Will filled the dishwasher, letting them talk. Dean rotated the wine glass she'd poured him, but didn't touch the contents. He pressed his lips into a line. "Easily enough, thanks to my generosity, apparently."

"When are they leaving? I hope they're giving you some notice."

Dean rubbed his fingers over the lines on his forehead as if that could smooth all this out. "They said they would, if I needed them to."

"You need them to, Dean! It's common courtesy. For as long as they've both been with you, it's the least they can do."

Faye rarely got sharp with him, and it felt like a slap. He couldn't believe they were having this conversation — that his two most loyal employees would abandon him like that. But what was he supposed to say? They'd earned the adventure of their dreams. Why did it have to be at his expense? Hiring new employees was a nightmare. It was becoming impossible to find people who weren't afraid of hard work and didn't whine about no weekends off or starting before dawn.

"It'll be all right, Faye. We're down two horses at the track anyway." Had that become a plus? "I can take over Nikki's until I find a groom. I might not even need one."

He thought she'd push back on that, but Faye could do the math. The income lost approximated Nikki's salary. He wouldn't have to pay a new groom as much as an assistant, but it still didn't balance out without horses in those stalls.

"And the farm?"

"I'll feed and turn out before I go into the track, and I can muck out when I come home."

"And on race days?"

Each point she made pricked like a pin going into their mother's old tomato-shaped pincushion. "It's not forever, Faye. It's just until I find someone. Stacy says her sister just finished that program at the university. She's looking for a placement."

"You think a kid who's done a six-week course online is going to be able to handle that job?" Faye shook her head and took a swig of wine. "Remember, I can't clean a stall to save my life. And don't you dare ask me to handle any of the horses. I'm not going anywhere close to that devil spawn colt of yours."

Dean chuckled, despite his mood. "I wouldn't do that to you."

Faye may have been raised on the farm, but she had a healthy fear of the creatures that inhabited it. It wasn't about not wanting to get her hands dirty — she was right, she did a terrible job on the stalls, but she'd pitch in if needed — she was afraid of them. It had horrified their father. Ed Taylor had never understood that his daughter wouldn't ever be hands-on in the life he'd worked so hard for, even if nearly losing a finger to a crotchety old broodmare when she was little likely justified her aversion.

"Speaking of foals, when's that last mare due?" she asked.

"Two weeks."

"You have to find someone *yesterday* then, don't you? You can't nightwatch on top of everything else. You have to sleep, Dean."

An inconvenient fact. "It's Cherry. She's my old reliable. I'll only need to watch her for a night or two."

Watching was non-negotiable. If he hadn't been there for the mare whose baby had died during foaling back in February, he would have lost her, too. The farm couldn't afford another blow like that.

The frown hadn't left Faye's face. "I hope you're right."

"It'll all work out."

If he repeated it often enough, he'd start to believe it. Because one way or another, it would.

CHAPTER SIX

"DEAN!"

Cruze shifted on three legs as Dean flinched at the familiar bellow. He finished with the foot in his hand and contemplated seeing how long he could hide in the stall before someone tipped Andy off, deciding he could finish picking out the two-year-old's last hoof before emerging.

"Morning, Andy," he said as he secured the stall gate behind him. "This is a surprise." He hoped his tone didn't betray that it was never a *pleasant* surprise to see Andy.

The barrel-chested owner was not a tall man, but most people were shorter than Dean. Andy's thinning hair — always neatly trimmed — never failed to make Dean aware that he needed a haircut himself. He reflexively ran his fingers through the thatch sticking to his forehead, still clutching the hoof pick in his other hand.

"I was nearby," Andy said. Not that he needed to explain why he was here, except that he didn't come to the backstretch very often. "Is that my two-year-old?"

Dean glanced over his shoulder at Cruze, who poked his

head over the yoke with a mouthful of the second cut hay Dean had tossed on his mat. "No, that one's mine."

He didn't remind Andy of the colt's heritage because so far, the fact that Cruze was a half-brother to Ride The Wave was just about names on his foal papers. Nothing about him impressed anyone, except his ability to sleep through an explosion and his taste for expensive French pastry.

"Gastronomy's down here with Squeak." Dean led the way.

"How is he doing? I haven't seen him on the worksheet yet. My colt hasn't even breezed, and you already got Jacob's horse to the races. And sold him for a tidy sum, I hear."

Dean's eyes shifted sharply to the owner, though it shouldn't have caught him off guard. Word always travelled at lightning speed on the backstretch, and Andy had been in the business long enough to have a well-branched grapevine.

"He's coming along nicely," Dean said, because there was no point reminding Andy that these were living, breathing, animals, not robots. Jacob's colt had been an anomaly. That kind of precocity didn't land itself at Dean's feet very often.

"When's he going to breeze?" Andy persisted. "These horses need to be running, not standing in stalls."

"I'm entering Epicurean Elegance tomorrow for the weekend," Dean said to mollify the owner, pronouncing the name carefully. The ones Andy picked were always a mouthful. Dean just called the three-year-old filly Epi. "And there's a race for Sun and Stars next weekend." At least Sunny, the four-year-old gelding they owned in partnership, Dean had named before Andy had bought in.

"I've been paying a day rate for that two-year-old for three months," Andy went on, hammering on the subject of Gastronomy like he was pounding a nail into a wall. "He must be ready to do something by now."

"I'll have Crystal gallop him along soon. If he handles that all right, maybe next week he can breeze a quarter," Dean said, relieved that Andy seemed to be on his way out. He'd been here all of ten minutes, but it felt like an eternity.

Andy turned to face Dean at the end of the barn. "My friend Tony said his trainer put his two-year-old on some new supplement that's really picked the horse's head up. Expects him to be running by the end of the month. You should look into it. I'll find out what it is and send you the information."

Sure, Andy. Because some supplement was going to replace another month's training.

But it wouldn't hurt Gastronomy to have a little two-minute lick. Maybe *that* would pick the colt's head up and Dean wouldn't need to entertain some trendy nutraceutical. Though if Andy was convinced they should try it, it wouldn't come out of Dean's pocket, so there wasn't much point in fighting him about it. Dean had bigger struggles — like Nikki and Stacy's impending departure.

At the end of the morning, he put on a clean change of clothes. His best black jeans were just old enough to be worn in without being faded or thinned out. He tucked in a crisp white shirt and rolled up the sleeves, notched his belt, and ran a hand through his hair. Faye kept offering to cut it — with not-so-subtle hints — and he should probably agree. He might even let her take him shopping. If he was going to break out of the mid-level trainer rank he'd been stuck in for most of his career, it was time to step up his image. Within reason, of course.

"Ooh, boss! Looking sharp!" Nikki stopped in her tracks when she saw him. "Got a hot lunch date?"

Dean tucked his fingers into his pockets, still not believing that in twenty-four hours, she'd be gone. "I'm courting potential employees," he said dryly. That might be what it came down to, the way things were now: wining and dining prospective staff as if he were recruiting for a major corporation. "It's going to be tough, finding someone to replace you."

"*Don't* replace me," she quipped. "Hire someone just good enough to get you through. I'm coming back."

Dean bit his tongue. *She'd better*. He freed his hands and made an awkward gesture toward her. "I guess this is it, then. Have a great time." The words felt like a mouthful of dust.

Before he could avoid it, Nikki threw her arms around him. "I mean it, about my job. Don't hire anyone really good."

He should be so lucky. Dean patted her on the back self-consciously, then stepped aside. "I'm not making any promises."

Nikki swatted him with one hand, brushing away a tear with the other. He'd have to go through the whole thing again with Stacy at the farm this afternoon. One of the good things about having a sister, he wasn't uncomfortable seeing a woman cry. Nikki put away her rake and gave all the horses kisses before dashing away, chattering about still needing to finish packing, leaving Dean alone on the shed, making his last check before heading out.

He planned to stop by the café on his way to see Liv about The Wave — picking up a cappuccino for her was a good excuse. It wouldn't hurt for Monique to see him cleaned up, because, what was he waiting for? This was going to be his breakout year. He envisioned her beside him in the infield winner's circle after the Plate — it would have to be next year because he didn't even have a horse nominated this year. Gastronomy? Cruze? He snorted. This *was* a fantasy. Almost as tall as him in heels, Monique would be dressed in her finery, giving Faye a run for her money.

There was the age difference, but he gathered Monique had a history with such things. Coming to work for Faye at Christmas had been her way of escaping a toxic relationship with someone much older than Dean. They'd had the chance to get to know each other when she'd lived at the farmhouse for a few weeks until she'd found a place in town. It wouldn't have been appropriate to suggest anything when they'd been under the same roof.

He'd learned his lesson with Liv, waiting for years before speaking up — too little, too late. Today could be the day. It felt right. Though it had been so long since he'd asked a woman out, he wasn't sure he remembered how to do it.

Could I take you out sometime?

What would you think of grabbing a bite?

He stopped in front of Cruze and crossed his arms. "What do you think, buddy? Any advice?" This two-year-old colt had more charm than he did.

The local jazz station filtered through the truck's speakers as he drove. On impulse, he switched the sound system to auxiliary at a light and hit play on an old Dave Matthews Band album. Faye had gotten him back into listening to them, after that concert she'd dragged him to three years ago. That was the first time he'd met Monique. She'd been with Will, and both he and Faye had assumed — wrongly, as it turned out — that Monique and Will were an item.

By the time he'd pulled into a spot in front of the café, Dean had decided on *Would you like to have dinner sometime?* He slid out of the truck, not recognizing any of the other vehicles in the lot. That was good. Having Nate, or Will, or Emilie there would ruin his plan.

The bell on the door announced his arrival, tantalizing aromas piquing his sense of smell. Monique stood behind the counter, her head inclined, talking to someone. A man leaned toward her, a hand resting casually on the edge of the surface, and Dean had the distinct impression he was interrupting something.

Monique straightened, peeking around the man. She wasn't wearing her apron over her smooth black outfit or a hairnet over her neat blonde bun. "Hi Dean!"

He took a couple of hesitant steps from where he'd stopped on the mat inside the doorway, feeling vaguely stricken, saying cautiously, "Hi Monique. How are you today?" He sounded like he was addressing a primary school teacher.

"Have you met Rory yet?" Monique asked, waving a hand toward the man turning partway toward Dean. "Rory just started working for Liv and Nate on the farm."

He'd heard about Liv's new hire, someone she'd met last summer when she'd spent a few weeks in England. Rory wasn't as tall as Dean, but definitely younger, probably in his mid-twenties — a more appropriate age for someone like Monique. He wore short boots not unlike Dean's, but Rory's looked lived in, like he actually rode in them, which he probably did. His dimpled smile reminded Dean of someone, dark eyes bright with mischief under a mass of loose black curls.

Cruze. That was it. Rory reminded Dean of his cheeky two-year-old.

He approached and offered a hand, pulling up the congenial smile he'd practiced often in his line of work. "Good to meet you, Rory. How are you liking Canada?"

"So far, so good," Rory responded, with a quick glance and fresh grin for Monique, his words laced with a Scottish accent. He rubbed his hands on his thighs and gave Dean a nod. "Right then. I'd better be going." Rory slipped around Dean and then walked backwards a few steps, sticking out his thumb and little finger at the side of his face. "I'll call you, Monique."

Dean sighed, unable to keep himself from watching Rory leave, taking time to reframe his mind before he turned back to Monique. Her face was flushed. She'd never smiled at *him* like that. It seemed to take her a beat to focus on him.

"Let me guess. The usual?" she asked, her cheer sounding artificial.

"And a cappuccino, please. To go," he said. "I'm on my way to see Liv." Thank goodness he didn't have to come up with an excuse not to linger.

She prepared the coffee, and he didn't enjoy the smell of it streaming through the filter as much as he usually did. The squeal of the steamer pierced his ears.

Once the plastic lids were secure, Monique slipped them into insulating sleeves and set them next to the register. "Anything else?"

"I can't very well come in here without getting some butter tarts," he said. He didn't think taking Liv sweet pastry would improve his chances of working something out for The Wave, but it couldn't hurt. "Half a dozen, please."

Monique put the plastic wrap-covered tray of tarts into a bag, and Dean handed her cash, telling her to keep the change.

When he was back in the truck he turned off the stereo. He'd waited too long — again. The strong, silent type might work in the movies, but in real life, he was the guy who ended up alone.

Turned out slow and steady didn't always win the race.

CHAPTER SEVEN

Dean punched the passcode Liv had texted him into the keypad, glancing at the camera mounted on one of the stone pillars flanking the paved driveway. This was the first time he'd encountered the new gates at Triple Stripe Stables, installed this spring. Liv's life had certainly changed in the last year, thanks to Just Jay, a big horse that made Ride The Wave seem common. Liv hadn't changed, though, and now that Dean's miscalculation at the Plate Ball two years ago was far enough in the past to dismiss it as an awkward anecdote, he could accept they were better off as friends. She'd help if she could.

The gates swung closed automatically in his rearview mirror. Maples lined the drive on either side, majestic things arching overhead, more abundant than those on his own farm. He followed the lane, making a left where it forked behind the main house, and pulled up outside the training barn. Inside, he found Liv and Jillian, one of the farm's exercise riders.

"Perfect timing," Liv said. "We're just about to head out."

Again there was no sign of Nate, and Dean relaxed. He'd always felt Liv got him because they were so much alike, and the dynamic changed when Miller was around. But while similarity worked well for friendships, opposites attracted when it came to romance, it seemed. Liv and Nate. Emilie and Tim. Well, Faye and Will weren't really opposites, so there went that theory. Generalizations were never a good thing. He handed Liv the cappuccino.

"Thanks." She smiled, allowing herself a moment to take a sip.

"Sorry, Jillian. I should have brought you something," Dean apologized. "Will you settle for a butter tart?"

"That's a pretty good consolation prize," the tall, willowy young woman said, her boots scuffing the barn aisle as she skittered over and reached into the paper bag Dean proffered. He'd opened the package and eaten one on the way

"The gate looks good," he said.

Liv scowled. "An unfortunate sign of the times. Seems absurd when the horse who inspired and paid for it lives in Kentucky now."

That didn't mean the potential threat was gone for Liv or the horses on her farm. A disgruntled former employee had harboured enough resentment to sabotage Just Jay in an attempt to smear Liv's reputation, so precautions needed to be taken in the name of safety. It was the price of her success. At least Dean didn't need to worry about such things. There was no one around who was out to get him. At least, not anymore.

"Where's your new exercise rider?" he asked.

"Rory?" Liv set the coffee cup on a foot locker and reached for a bridle. "He's off today."

That was a relief, too. After meeting him at the café, Dean was grateful not to have another reminder that things were over with Monique before they'd ever started.

"Rory is making clichés of all of us," Jillian said with a laugh as she pulled a chestnut from the next stall. "That curly hair, the dark eyes, and the *piece de resistance,* a Scottish accent?" She fanned her face with her free hand. "Swoon!"

"Not me," Liv said, waiting for Jillian to go by before leading out a dark bay with a smattering of interesting white markings. "I never got the accent thing."

"Because you have one?" Jillian teased.

"I do not."

Dean remembered when Liv did. The first time Faye had brought her to their farm, she'd been freshly moved from Montreal. High school in Ontario seemed a strong motivator to train it out of herself. The only time Dean noticed the accent surfacing now was when she pronounced certain words or the French names of some of the Triple Stripe horses.

"If the accent doesn't do it for you, you've got to admit he's got a nice butt." Jillian flashed a grin over her shoulder.

Dean's gaze dropped to the asphalt of the barn aisle as he followed them outside. He should be used to hearing women talk like that, because his sister had, before she'd settled down. Faye had been a bit of a wild child in her teens and early twenties. It still made him uncomfortable, though. He legged up the two riders and walked next to them along a stonedust path between lines of evergreens.

"Are these your non-precocious two-year-olds?" he asked, running his eyes over the youngsters. Both were well-developed and looked closer to running than Cruze and Gastronomy.

Liv laughed. "Yes. This is a full sister to Chique, and that's a full brother to Just Jay. You'd think they'd be on the program, but they are not."

"Or, is it more accurate to say *you* are not?" Dean peered up at her.

She dropped him a glance. "Maybe a little of that. But I'm not against racing two-year-olds, I just don't believe the world will end if they don't make it to the races till three."

"Some owners think that way," Dean muttered. "Did you ever give your dad that unicorn t-shirt?"

Liv snorted. "I didn't. I'll have to work on that for Father's Day."

Ed Taylor and Liv's dad would have butted heads if they'd had an owner-trainer relationship. Training racehorses was a business, not a passion, his father had reminded Dean time and again. That's why he'd been driven away when he'd begged to stay on at the track after high school. University had been non-negotiable. *Your heart's too big for this game.*

No wonder Andy wasn't happy. He kept expecting Dean to be like his father.

His eyes flicked to Liv again. "After what happened with Fox, Andy's pushing about his two-year-old."

She didn't look surprised. "I want to take these two into Woodbine soon and let them do a little something. We could go in company with yours. Put Nate on Andy's colt, make Andy think he's attracted the attention of a rider."

Dean smirked. "I like that. Let's do it."

They reached a hay field, lush, green timothy dominating darker, leafy alfalfa. Someone had built a bench out of old straw bales and a board, but Dean didn't sit, watching the two-year-olds jog off up the incline, a path about fourteen feet wide around the perimeter. They did a full circuit before breaking into an easy gallop, then surprised him by slowing, turning, and going the other way. At the track, they always trained and raced in the same direction. He'd never questioned it; that's just how it was done.

"Is that it?" he asked when they pulled up not far from him and turned to face across the field.

"Every day's not this easy," Liv said. "We bring them out here a couple of times a week. They go to the training track three days and gallop along on one of them. They get a day off."

She dropped her feet from the irons, letting them hang at the filly's sides. "I'm not sure I know what I'm doing, but they seem happy. That's good enough for now."

When the two-year-olds were taken care of and the tack put away, Liv removed her helmet and kerchief. She pulled her dark hair free of its ponytail, running her fingers through it before taming it again with the elastic.

"So, The Wave," she said, leaving the barn for the sunshine outside.

Dean nodded. "I want your opinion. I think he deserves a shot at stud. He's got a solid pedigree, good conformation, a respectable race record. I know you like him."

She stopped and turned, her expression all business. "I love him, but that doesn't matter. It's going to be a hard sell. He's not a speed horse, he's a marathon horse. He might be what racing needs more of, but he's not what breeders want. They want sales yearlings that give them a quick ROI. And neither you nor I have the number of mares it would take to support him."

She wasn't telling Dean anything he didn't already know, but it deflated him just the same.

"But I'll talk it over with my father and Kerrie," she continued. "We have room. At the very least, we can assess his fertility. Do you have anything to breed him to? I've got a nurse mare we have to cover that we could use as a test mare. We're just running out of season. It's almost June."

Just that little bit of hope lifted his heart. Dean wanted to hug her. "I've got one mare left to foal who might time out right for him."

"I'll see what I can do."

What a rollercoaster of a day, too many ups and downs packed into too few hours. He left Triple Stripe, ready to make himself some lunch before seeing how things were going with Stacy's sister, Kimmy, who'd come for a few days to learn the routine. Dean still wasn't sold on her. She was so young and inexperienced, but he felt obligated to give her a shot — plus, the employment program offered a tidy financial incentive to subsidize her wages.

He brewed a pot of coffee and tossed Gus a sliver of ham from his sandwich, hearing Faye's voice in his head, scolding him for indulging the dog. The Golden stared at him hopefully until the crunch of tires grabbed his attention, sending him dashing for the door in a cyclone of flying yellow hair. Faye fussed over him before kicking off her shoes and dropping her purse and an information sheet for another house on the kitchen table.

"Any luck?" Dean asked.

She shook her head, grabbing a cup of coffee and joining him.

"Sorry," he said, even though he wasn't. He tossed Gus the last piece of crust from his sandwich and wondered how much longer he'd get to see Faye scowl at him like that. "I met Liv's new hire today at the café."

Faye's look said it all: guilt laced with sympathy. She had to know Rory had been chatting up Monique.

"He's a charmer." She met his eyes. "I don't know what to tell you, Dean."

She didn't have to tell him anything. It was Liv all over again. Had he really thought someone like Monique had been just waiting for him to ask her out? Why couldn't Rory have felt his calling was at the track instead of out here, interfering with Dean's plans just when he'd mustered the resolve? Well, if there was one thing he was good at, it was moving on.

"You need to put yourself out there and not keep expecting a girlfriend to fall into your lap."

"Don't start, Faye."

"I'm dead serious. After Liv, you just transferred your

pining to someone new. Do you know how long I wanted to give you a shove, seeing how you looked at Monique? How, since she moved out, all of a sudden you were stopping by the shop a few times a week?"

Why was it that the objects of his adoration were always oblivious, but his sister seemed to know even before he knew himself?

"Our estate agent was telling me about this dating app." Faye continued, undeterred. "She and all her friends have found great matches there. The reviews are phenomenal. Let me set up a profile for you."

A strangled laugh escaped from his mouth. Just the thought made his chest tighten. "I don't think that's necessary, Faye."

"I think it is. There's no shame in it, Dean. It's how everyone's finding their partners these days. Especially people like you."

Busy, self-sufficient, socially inept? It was a magical combination. Dean leaned back and crossed his arms, a wrinkle between his brows.

"Don't you trust me?" she said.

Dean snorted. "Not really, no!"

She glanced at the time and popped to her feet. "Gotta go. Think about it."

Dean listened as her car departed. It could have been worse. Faye could've secretly nominated him for that *Farmers In Love* show he'd seen advertised. What was the harm? It might be good for a lark, a diversion from his business stress. How hard could dating be? It was like riding a bike, you didn't forget.

Except he could ride a bike, but he'd never really learned how to date.

CHAPTER EIGHT

THE FIRST MORNING WITHOUT NIKKI, Dean felt as if he was missing his left arm. He stayed in the barn to keep an eye on the new groom Squeak had found — sending Crystal out to the track on her own — because he wasn't entirely sure about the guy. The only exception he made was for Andy's two-year-old. He'd instructed Crystal to let the colt gallop along down the lane and wanted to see him go.

Gastronomy looked all right. He'd be ready to breeze in company next week with the Triple Stripe two-year-olds. Cruze was another matter. Since that day the geese had scared him, he hadn't shown a lick of speed.

In Dean's absence, the shed didn't implode. The new groom puttered along between frequent smoke breaks. Squeak appeared strangely content — probably happy Nikki was gone. One less woman around.

Crystal was out forever with the last horse, but it was Cruze so Dean wasn't surprised. Suddenly the new groom was in a hurry. He paced on the apron in front of the barn, pulling on a cigarette. Apparently, the guy couldn't smoke and fill buckets with bathwater at the same time.

He skulked back into the shed once his cigarette was finished. "Look, I got a dentist appointment. My buddy's picking me up at ten. I gotta go, man."

Dean tried to keep his face from distorting. "All right. Go ahead. See you tomorrow."

But the guy remained in front of him, shifting from one foot to the other.

"Was there something else?" Dean asked, conjuring patience.

"I was hoping," the groom began, eyes shifting. "You could pay me for today."

Again, Dean controlled his face, smiling benignly instead of frowning. "You'll get paid every Friday." *By cheque.*

"It's just, well... I was wondering if this week I could get an advance. Dentists, they're expensive, you know."

The state of the guy's teeth made Dean think it had been a while since he'd seen a dentist, but Dean couldn't exactly accuse him of wanting the money to buy booze, even if he looked a little shaky. Dean needed him to come back tomorrow.

He pulled cash from his pocket and counted off some bills — not quite what he'd pay for a day's work, because he had to give the guy a reason to return. "Will this do? That's all I've got."

The groom didn't waste time snatching the money from Dean's fingers. "Thanks, boss."

He was gone before Dean said, "Thank you," which wasn't a sentiment he was feeling at the moment anyway. The guy hadn't even done up any of his horses. Dean picked up Nikki's grooming kit and set to work, and had the first of the halters cleaned and hung on the door by the time Cruze finally sauntered onto the shed, Crystal slouched on his back.

"I was ready to send out a search party," Dean quipped. "Thought maybe you'd been abducted by aliens."

"Because they would certainly want this fine specimen of a racehorse!" Crystal said, reining him to a halt. "I took him to the gate. Might as well do something productive with him. Not getting excited about anything is his superpower."

Anything except Canada Geese. "How'd he do?"

"Oh, he'll stand in there all day, calm as can be. I think he likes it in there too much, because he's in no hurry to come out. He might need a carrot on a stick to inspire him. Think we could rig something up?"

Maybe he should just let Emilie have Cruze now. Except that would leave yet another empty stall. It was only June — too early to give up on the colt.

"We're going to, ah..." Dean hesitated, anticipating how this announcement would go over with his exercise rider, "...breeze the two-year-olds with a couple of Liv's one day next week. Nate's going to get on Andy's colt. Think Cruze will go?"

Crystal's eyebrows arched under the peak of her pink helmet cover. "You're making *me* breeze him? You should be nicer to me, Dean."

She grinned and directed the colt into his stall, Dean following with the halter. Crystal hopped off and ran up the near-side iron before unbuckling the girth.

"I don't think he needs a bath or a walk," Dean observed.

"Nope!" Crystal agreed. "He's all cooled out."

Dean tied the colt up to pick his feet and brush away the saddle mark, then pulled off his halter. Cruze was probably ready for his nap — after Dean fed him his lunch, of course.

"What do you think, Brenda?" he asked, rubbing a soapy sponge over the leather as she dragged the hose onto the shed and topped up the waters. "Day One of the new normal is in the books." He wasn't going to let himself count how many more there were between now and the end of summer, when Stacy and Nikki returned.

Brenda smiled her grandmotherly smile. "We'll get by."

Let's hope so. Dean positioned the clean halter on its hook. Time to feed lunch, then go home and see how the farm had made out. He wasn't happy about asking Squeak to feed two days in a row, but he'd promised the old groom would see a little something extra on his paycheque this week. He had no illusions that Squeak's benevolence came for free.

The red flag beckoned from the mailbox when he pulled into the driveway at home. Dean braked and shifted into park. As much as he'd hated replacing the pretty metal box his mother had created all those years ago, with its iron racehorse galloping on top, the sturdy green and grey moulded plastic receptacle wasn't as enticing to teenagers who had nothing better to do on a Friday night than drive around with a baseball bat. No kid was taking out this thing. The snowplow in winter was another matter.

A plain white envelope hid amid the usual flyers, *The Taylors* scrawled in neat cursive. Curiosity got the better of him, though without an address or a stamp, it was unlikely to be news of an inheritance from a long-lost relative or some rebate he'd forgotten about. He tore the envelope open.

If the price is to your satisfaction, would you consider selling? If so, would you please give us a call? Thank you.

Dean recognized the name of the real estate agent; he saw her signs all over the place. He tossed it on the passenger seat with the flyers. Property values were soaring in the area. It was why Faye and Will were having such a hard time finding something in their budget — and why Dean still hoped they'd reconsider and stay here. It could work. They could build an addition.

Across from the house, the foal snoozed in the sun a few

feet from his mother, his inadequate tail thumping sporadically at the flies. Dean parked his truck and climbed the steps to the deck, opening the door without going inside.

"C'mon Gus. Let's go see how our newbie is doing."

Gus bounced in front of him as he headed to the barnyard. Just a quick check on Kimmy then, unless she needed him for something, he'd get out of her way for a few more hours. He'd help her bring in because she didn't know which horse went where yet. Once she went home, he'd walk The Wave and cold-hose that tendon. He certainly wasn't letting her handle his big horse.

The barn was dark. Dean checked his watch. Maybe it had taken Kimmy longer than expected to do the morning chores and she was having a late lunch — Stacy sometimes popped into town to grab something and would've told her sister what was available. He flipped on the lights and walked down the aisle.

The stalls hadn't been touched, the water buckets still varying degrees of full, shavings strewn with hay and manure. The Wave's shrill whinny beckoned from the stall next to the feed room, his net picked clean.

What happened? Did her car break down? Was she sick? She could have called... texted... but there was nothing. Not a word. Dean hadn't even realized her vehicle hadn't been there when he'd pulled in. He hoped she was okay. He sent her a text then picked up a pitchfork and started mucking out.

Dean was the first to admit he wasn't the best at stalls. Stacy got furious with him when he tried to help her, but today, he didn't have time to care — and no one was watching him. He prayed Kimmy only had a twenty-four-hour bug and felt too ill to contact him — or too embarrassed because it was her first solo day. *Don't feel bad, kid! Come back, it's all right.* He wasn't in a position to be angry with anyone.

So maybe The Wave got a shorter walk than usual and wasn't hosed as long, and hey, that tendon didn't look so bad; perhaps he'd leave it open and see how it was tomorrow. It wasn't as if The Wave was returning to the races or headed to the show ring. Dean had seen far worse bows on horses who were still running.

By the time he'd swept up, he'd had lost track of time. Gus dozed, bored, down by the stack of hay.

"Let's go, buddy. I'm starving. Maybe Faye or Will will take you for a proper walk later."

His truck was still the only vehicle parked beside the house. Dean tramped up the steps to the deck, two feeling like twelve. Inside, Gus bounded to his water and lapped his bowl dry, layering guilt on top of Dean's fatigue.

"Sorry. If I'd known we'd be that long, I would have brought some with us."

He heated leftovers in the microwave and ate in front of the television, feet propped on the coffee table, calculating how long he had before he needed to water off. The last time he'd cleaned that many stalls he'd probably been a teenager. So much for being fit. His legs were fine from plenty of walking and the bike rides he squeezed in whenever he could, but his shoulders and triceps ached, and his neck was stiff from using the fork on the same side the entire time. He couldn't hold it to the right any more than he could shoot a hockey puck that way.

There was time for a brief nap — then night check, and bed, because four AM came early. As if to support the decision, Gus flopped at the foot of the couch with an audible exhale, like air being pushed out of a balloon.

"Yo, Dean, you here?"

Dean sat bolt upright, disoriented. He blinked and squinted around the living room. It was dusk. Had that been Will's voice for real, or in a dream? His future brother-in-law appeared in the doorway — the real Will, not a mirage.

"Have you fed Gus? He's staring at me like he hasn't eaten in days, but I know better than to take him at his word."

Dean shook his head in answer, trying to dislodge the sleepiness. He felt drunk, the way it lingered. The muscles that had ached earlier had tightened into an overall soreness.

"He had a big drink when I got in from the barn. I wanted to wait a bit. Faye's always warning me about kibble and the risk of gastric torsion if he drinks around the same time as eating."

"Gastric what?"

"Never mind. I'm sure if you haven't heard it from her yet, you will." Dean climbed to his feet, swaying slightly.

"You all right, man?" Will asked, glancing around as if he expected to see a line of beer bottles.

"Tired, that's all." Dean lumbered to the kitchen and looked at the clock. It had been a couple of hours; it would be safe to give Gus his meal now. Dean scooped the Golden's ration from the food container and placed the bowl on the floor. It was gone almost before he pulled his hand away. Remembering that big drink, he let Gus out the back door, following. The Golden raced off the deck to the nearest tree, his eyes half-closed in relief as he lifted his leg.

"How'd it go today, with the new manager?" Will asked, slipping out behind him, hands in pockets.

Dean laughed, but there was no humour in it. "Just dandy. She didn't show up. I came home and nothing had been done."

"Really? She didn't call or anything?"

"I hope she's okay," Dean said. "I haven't heard from her."

"Wow. What are you going to do about tomorrow?"

"Hope it was a one-off, and that she comes, but assume she won't just in case."

The flash of headlights interrupted them, and Faye pulled in next to Will's Camaro. Once they were all in the kitchen, Dean recounted his tale of woe.

He sighed. "I'd better go do night check."

"Do you want me to do it for you?" Will asked. "I'd help tomorrow if I could, but I've got to be in the city."

"That's all right. Thanks for offering, though."

"It's not a problem. Go to bed. Gus and I have this covered."

"Well. Thank you, Will."

"Gotta take care of my favourite brother-in-law, right?"

Dean mustered a smile. Will was an only child.

Faye poured herself a glass of wine. "I'll put up a couple of ads on the job sites for the position," she said. "Leave it to me. You focus on the track, and I'll be your HR person."

"I guess there's no harm in that."

"Now, if you'd just let me manage your love life, you'd be all set." She grinned.

"Fine."

Faye brightened. "Really?"

What did he have to lose? Right now he was too tired to care. It took the last of his energy to climb the stairs — they were steep and narrow in the old house. He showered and collapsed into bed, his head like lead, sinking into the pillow with a lingering sense of dread that tomorrow wouldn't be any better than today.

CHAPTER NINE

WHEN DEAN ARRIVED at the track the next morning — fifteen minutes later than he'd hoped, because, sure enough, Kimmy was a no-show — the shedrow was lit up. At a glance, he saw Squeak's end was business as usual: all his horses tied to the wall, feed tubs cleaned and snapped to eyehooks on the doors, water buckets hung on respective posts across from each stall. What Squeak lacked in personality, he made up for in work ethic.

At the other end, it was a different story. Dark eyes and expectant faces followed Dean as he trudged into the barn. Cruze rattled his empty feed tub like he thought it might get him a second breakfast.

"No sign of Rocket Man?" Dean asked, not bothering to hold back on the sarcasm as Squeak trundled down the shed on the way to the disposal bin with a fully loaded pitchfork. He always had his stalls mucked before his horses trained; bless his cold, dark soul.

Squeak grunted. "Nope."

Dean walked straight to the whiteboard and wrote a big,

block-letter "W" next to each horse's name. "I take back every terrible thing I've ever said about you, Squeak."

"You've said terrible things about me?" Squeak looked stern, pausing with his now-empty fork. Then he gave a rare, raspy laugh, and returned to work.

"I'll get that horse out of the stall for you. You can let me know if you want a break. I can muck a few."

"I'm good," Squeak said, hoisting a newly loaded fork.

With all the stalls Dean had mucked at the farm yesterday and the prospect of doing it all over again today, those words were a relief. As he started walking the first horse, he called Crystal. It was early enough he'd catch her before she left home. She might as well have the day off.

"Are you sure I can't convince you to groom, Brenda?" he pleaded when she arrived. A hotwalker was easier to find. "Just until Nikki gets back?"

The older woman laughed like he'd told her a hilarious joke. "Sorry, Dean. My body wouldn't hold up to all the work a groom needs to do!"

Nikki's charges — poor, abandoned children — got their hooves picked at the end of the morning and that was it. Missing one day of grooming wouldn't hurt them, but Dean couldn't afford to skip many more training days. He told Squeak he'd feed — thanks to a text from Emilie offering to do stalls at the farm because Faye had told her about the situation. He had to wait around for the vet and blacksmith anyway.

Dean thanked Squeak for being a good sport and promised to pick up doughnuts tomorrow on his way in; Squeak didn't get excited about the fancy pastries from the café like the women did. After the vet left, he wandered down to visit Len while he waited for the blacksmith.

"Where you been?" the old man asked, as if Dean were only visible when he went to the track.

Len kneeled at the front end of one of his horses, rubbing liniment into a leg. Good thing they all stood quietly, because when Len rose, using the horse's leg for support like he was climbing a rope, Dean could practically hear the older man's joints creak. He feared one day he'd come to find Len trampled into the straw.

"The groom I hired yesterday lasted a day."

"Was that Splinter?" Len asked. "I coulda told you he was no good. But he'll show up on payday, you can be sure of that. Probably wanting cash. You watch."

Dean had to laugh. "My first mistake was giving him cash when he asked before he left yesterday — early, I might add. I don't expect I'll see him again. If you hear of anyone decent looking for work, let me know."

"They're a dying breed, Dean. S'why I do my own. Can't trust 'em anymore."

As he held Andy's two-year-old while the shoer put on training plates, Dean received a text from Stacy, profusely apologizing for her sister bailing on him. Kimmy had changed her mind, apparently.

I'm sorry, my sister is a flake. Stacy's message was followed by a string of emojis. Dean had never hated those little yellow icons more.

He texted her back. *You knew this already?* It was tempting to add a few of those ridiculous emoticons himself — or at least some additional punctuation marks.

She's my sister. Of course I knew.

But she'd still sent Kimmy his way.

She went on about how she'd thought school might help Kimmy grow up, that she'd love working for Dean as much as Stacy did and that the job would turn her life around and make her responsible.

It sounded like a lot to expect from someone Kimmy's age

taking a short-term summer placement. Besides, if Stacy loved working for him so much, why had she left?

Gastronomy dozed as if the colt was tuning out the blacksmith as much as Dean was, Clay grumbling about trainers trying to tell him how to do his job and ill-mannered horses. It wasn't until he was trimming the hinds that he asked Dean how things were going.

"I know a guy who might be interested in the farm," Clay said after Dean told him about the staffing issues. "There's an apartment, right? I'll give you his number."

Dean called before Clay was even off the shed. The man said he'd come out later that afternoon and assured Dean he could start immediately.

Dean hired him on the spot.

And fired him the next day when he found the man smoking in the barn. The stalls were done, anyway. He walked and cold-hosed The Wave, turned the horses in and fed, and took Gus for a walk before parking himself in front of the television with a cold drink.

Back to square one.

At least when he talked to the director of the employment program to tell her about Kimmy, she said she had a graduate who wanted to work at the track, would Dean be interested in that? He expected he'd have to teach them from scratch, but that might not be a terrible thing. At least then — hopefully — they'd learn how to do things properly right from the start. Len said good grooms were a dying breed, but Dean wasn't ready to believe it. They just needed to be willing to learn.

Gus raced to the back door at the sound of footsteps on the deck, and Faye called, "Hello!" in a sing-song Dean barely recognized.

He waited until she appeared in the doorway to offer his return greeting, catching a glimpse of the bottle of wine she'd set on the kitchen counter. Faye swept into the living room, bending to squeeze his shoulders and kiss him on the cheek before flopping onto the opposite end of the couch.

It took a conscious effort to keep his muscles from tensing, feeling a sense of impending doom. "Well?"

Faye's face was flushed, her eyes bright. She rested her head against the high back, one elbow draped over the armrest, and crossed her legs. "We found it! The agent's putting together our offer as we speak."

"That's great news," he said with all the enthusiasm he could muster.

"It needs a lot of work," Faye continued. "That's the only way we could afford to stay in the area. So don't worry, you won't be rid of us quite yet." She beamed, clearly already making plans for the renovations.

Dean's mouth moved, but he stopped himself from speaking. Will was many things — a talented musician, a self-taught but skilled pastry chef, an entrepreneur with a budding catering business — but was he handy? Could he frame and do drywall?

"Tell me more," he finally managed.

"It's only about ten minutes away. Do you remember the old Craven place, just west of here? The school bus used to go past it."

Dean nodded. He could picture the farmhouse, not unlike their own. The design had been popular in the late eighteen-hundreds. He'd read up on them once, amused to discover they were literally known as "A Cheap Farmhouse."

"It's been vacant for a long time, so our closing is super short, but it's going to be a while before we have it ready to move in."

He was happy for her, really he was. Faye had struggled for years after the accident. She'd been closer to their middle brother, Shawn, than Dean had. She deserved everything she was getting — the thriving business, the new house project, the partner for life.

Everyone was pairing off — Liv and Nate, Faye and Will, Emilie and Tim — leaving him behind.

Faye sprang to her feet. "I hope you don't have plans tonight, because we're celebrating!"

It was a good thing someone around here had something to celebrate.

Dean excused himself, leaving Faye and Will at the kitchen table. As they ate, Faye had said things like "the house has character," and "it's got good bones." This project would be her passion for the next months. She might not be moving out yet, but between that and the upcoming wedding, she'd hardly be present.

Amid the familiarity of the office, he settled in front of the computer. Faye had left a sticky note with the username and password for the job site. He typed into the boxes on the screen and got an error message. Then he noticed the other open tab, and clicked on it.

The site that popped up was slick, with images and videos of happy — and surely fake — couples, and promises of finding true love. *These places are meant for people like you*, Faye had said. But maybe she was right. If he was going to meet someone at the racetrack, it would have happened by now. And where else did he go? The grocery store. Apparently it could happen, but it would probably require eye contact. All he'd ever wanted was to meet someone naturally, no artificial intelligence matchmaking involved. But that was probably narrow-minded of him. This was the new world. Adapt or die... alone.

He wasn't sure he could do it. It felt as if he was looking through a catalogue before the yearling sales, trying to earmark the ones he wanted to examine. Except these were women. And there were pictures. That was just uncomfortable.

Nope, nope, nope. He pushed his chair back, and Gus scrambled out of the way.

"It'll be just you and me, buddy," he said. "That'll be fine. Unless you can help. How good is your nose? Can you sniff them out for me?" That would be useful.

You're just weird, Dean.

He told himself they were people who were just like him, trying to navigate this new way of doing things. And while on one hand, it felt risky, on the other there was a safety to it, the barrier of the interface, a way to filter the interactions. Assuming everyone was as honest as he was. Was he honest? He'd let his sister create the profile.

There were already messages in the inbox, and he sucked in a breath and clicked on the most recent one.

Huh. She'd gone to the same university as him, had a science degree, and worked in the pharmaceutical industry. She liked to read, and cook, and spend time with her eight-year-old daughter.

A child. What about that? He'd be okay with a kid. Or without one. Not a dealbreaker.

He inhaled, and blew the air out long and slow, and then responded to the message, not even bothering to look at the woman's profile. Her avatar was too small to tell him much, and photos lied anyway. Look at his. Faye had chosen one of him dressed up at the Queen's Plate the year Ride The Wave had won. That wasn't the real him.

Gus whined, and Dean gave him a sideways look. "Yes, I'm worried about me too. But here goes nothing."

Be yourself. As if he knew how to be anyone else.

When he finished, he had to move. He'd almost forgotten about the job site, but was too unsettled now to give resumés proper attention. His heart raced, a warm sweat breaking out over his body.

He'd done it. He'd put himself out there.

Before he even got out of the room, the computer chimed. Dean crept back slowly. There was a message. Grasping the mouse, he hesitated, feeling like, if he clicked, he would be lighting a... match. *Clever*.

Some part of him wanted to believe it could be as easy as that, that finally, *The One*, the reason why it hadn't been his university girlfriend, or Liv, or Monique, was because whoever was on the other side of those words had been there all along, waiting for him.

CHAPTER TEN

THE FIGURES ZIPPING around on the big-screen TV were a blur. Caroline knew all the players, knew the rules, and even knew when to yell at the refs for a bad call, but she hated hockey — more so now than ever. She'd only followed the game because her husband had been a huge fan. Still was a huge fan; he just wasn't her husband anymore.

There was something wrong about the NHL hockey play-offs still going on when it was practically summer. She stared intently at the game, determined to ignore the curious gazes of the men in the room. Tipping back her glass she gulped, barely tasting the clear liquid as it went down. Bars were so depressing — yet here she was.

"Since when do you drink gin?"

Caroline felt the arms thrown around her before she'd even fully turned to see Jess, that same old wide grin, same mousy-brown, wavy hair. She clung to Jess tighter than she'd meant to. Jess, who hadn't given up on her when she'd had every right to.

"I've moved up," Caroline quipped dryly, swivelling back toward the bar.

"If you'd like to call it that, okay." Jess slipped onto the stool next to her.

"What do you want?" Caroline lifted her now-empty tumbler, trying to get the bartender's attention.

"I haven't eaten since breakfast. I'd better have a Caesar."

Caroline's lips curved up. It was seven PM. More evidence Jess hadn't changed, using the classic Canadian cocktail as a meal. If prompted, Jess would go on about the health benefits of clamato juice, which had a tomato base, expounding on the antioxidants it contained.

The bartender glided over, capturing the glass in a practiced sweep and tipping his ear toward them to hear their order before swooping away just as quickly.

"We're going to get a table, right?" Jess asked. "Caesar or no Caesar, I need to eat something."

"Oh, yes. I can't take sitting at the bar any longer."

Caroline let the bartender know their plan when he plunked glasses in front of them. The place was dead — Tuesday night — so they easily found a booth. A server appeared, sliding menus onto the table and promising to return to take their meal orders before disappearing again.

"I think we need comfort food," Jess declared, opening the laminated list of the bar's offerings. "Greasy appetizers should do the trick."

Caroline certainly hadn't been eating anything remotely healthy of late, so it sounded like a perfect plan. When the server came back, Caroline looked up. "I'm going to have a beer. What do you have on tap?"

Jess was nursing her Caesar and requested water — ever the responsible one.

"Your hair looks good short," Jess said, smiling, though her eyes suggested she was thinking, *what did you do?*

Caroline ran her fingers through the almost spiky strands,

still not used to the new cut and conscious it was a lighter shade of blond than the last time Jess had seen her.

"Thanks," she said, when they both understood exactly what it had been: a breakup makeover.

"So..." Jess cast an almost subtle glance at Caroline's glass of beer, already relieved of half its contents. "Is this for real? You're back?"

Caroline looked theatrically over one shoulder, then the other, even though the place they'd agreed to meet wasn't a racetrack hangout. "Looks that way."

"What happened?"

How did she neatly summarize the last ten years?

At what seemed to be the height of a promising career, she'd abruptly given up training racehorses and moved to Saskatchewan — of all places — not long after marrying her extremely wealthy client, Bryce Harrington. Getting out of racing. Getting out of horses.

Caroline sighed. She'd kept so much from Jess, not wanting to dump the truth on her friend after making such a dramatic exit for what was supposed to be a better life. Sure, they'd kept in touch. *Merry Christmas. Happy Birthday. We're good.* Superficial shit.

Long story short, she decided. "His high school girlfriend resurfaced."

Jess eyeballed her, remaining silent, reminding Caroline how close they'd once been. Of course, there was more, but even back before she'd left, Jess hadn't known the half of what was going on.

Caroline drew in a deep breath. "She showed up with a kid. Can you guess where this is going?"

Jess's eyes shot up. "No! Oh, Caroline."

There was something liberating about finally sharing it with someone who would be on her side. "At first she said she wasn't expecting him to be involved. But it was only a matter of time. Bryce always wanted kids, and when we found out that wasn't in the cards for me..." Her throat constricted; her gaze, which she'd kept fixed on the plate between them, flitting up to Jess. *Yeah, some things you don't know until you try.* She couldn't help thinking how much money she'd wasted on birth control. "Let's just say, it wasn't a real surprise when I caught them together."

Jess gasped. Caroline wished she could say *it was good while it lasted,* but it hadn't even been that.

"Honestly, Caroline," Jess finally spoke. "I know it hurts like hell, but I'm sorry to say — well, no I'm not, you just probably don't want to hear it — you're *so* better off without him. You deserve more."

The thing was, did she really? Deserve better? Call it karma, providence, reaping what you sow...she'd made her bed.

"Enough about me," she said, because what more was there? "How are things with you?"

"As boring as ever," Jess said.

Jess gave her a brief rundown, but there wasn't anything Caroline didn't know. Her friend had gone back to school in her thirties and was now in a Master's program. The update reminded Caroline what field Jess was in, though what the end goal was, she had no clue. Maybe Jess would be one of those career students. She was even dating a guy who'd been the teaching assistant for one of her undergrad courses. It *was* boring, but after the last ten years of her own life, Caroline understood the appeal.

"So, do you have a plan?" Jess asked cautiously.

Caroline grunted and peered at the foamy residue in her glass. "First things first: another one of these."

Caroline sat up, trying to pry open her eyes, but they seemed stuck together. Much like her mouth, which had a fuzzy, parched feeling, a telltale sign of dehydration from having drunk too much and passing out before proper oral hygiene. Her head pounded with a vengeance. When she finally managed to grind her lids apart, she peered around, vaguely recalling how last night had ended.

Once her eyes adjusted to the darkness, she dimly made out the familiar surroundings. Jess's place hadn't changed any more in the last ten years than Jess had. Caroline kicked free from the quilt tangled around her legs and pushed up from the worn couch. What time was it? Where was the light? She needed to pee. Clue number three she'd had too much alcohol.

She found her phone on the coffee table —four AM —then made her way to the powder room with the help of the flashlight. A bottle of extra-strength ibuprofen liquid-gels waited next to the sink — *thank you, Jess* — and the softened water she washed two of them down with wasn't as gross as it might have been under normal circumstances. Her toothbrush was in her car, and she guessed her car was still at the bar. In a stroke of luck, she found a bottle of mouthwash under the sink and poured some into the cap, tossing it back without letting her lips come in contact with the edge. It stung as she swished it around before gargling and spitting it out.

Using some tissue to wipe off her smudged makeup and splashing water on her face, she cleaned herself up as best she could. Once the anti-inflammatories kicked in, she might feel human again. She padded her way back to the sofa and, melting into the cushions, drifted off again.

A weird dream buzzed around her slumbering brain, one where she felt almost conscious. It was too real, and she willed herself to wake up. She was on one of the good racehorses she'd trained, breezing down the homestretch. The mare finished the work well in her usual minute flat. That was when she blacked out, waking up to —

A dog licking her nose. Caroline's eyes snapped open and she yelped, sitting up with a start. A red and white Border Collie hopped up beside her nonchalantly, pressing against her with a big grin before lavishing her with more kisses.

She laughed, shoving him away, her pounding heart settling back to normal. "Good to meet you, too, Callum." *Or maybe good to be conscious of meeting you.*

Jess peered around the fridge door from the adjoining kitchen with a milk jug in her hand. "Just tell him to get down if you don't want the royal greeting. Do you want a coffee?"

Caroline extracted herself from the couch, Callum hopping down after her and following. "Coffee sounds good." The ibuprofen had done its job — she felt much better than she had two hours ago — but caffeine could only help.

Jess poured a mug from a pot on the counter and handed it to her. "I have to go feed and turn out. Make yourself at home. C'mon Callum!"

She should put on her shoes and go too. It wasn't as if she was going back to sleep. Outside, the sun was nudging over a line of trees on the east end of a fenced field, dew clinging to the grass and condensing on Jess's truck. How could Jess stand living out here, in the middle of nowhere, all by herself? Instead, she poured another cup of coffee and wished she knew what she was going to do with the rest of her life.

Caroline didn't notice how long Jess was gone — time passed in a haze right now. Callum bounded into the kitchen and lapped at his water bowl, Jess in his wake.

"Do you have any idea what you want to do?" Jess asked, stuffing things into a backpack Caroline was sure she'd had since high school.

"Get a job, I guess. Find a place to live."

"You know you can stay here as long as you like, right?"

"Thanks, Jess." But she didn't want to take advantage of her friend's generosity too long.

"I hate to bring this up, but Bryce is loaded. You're getting money, right?"

"Settlements take time." And of course she'd signed a prenup.

"He'd better be generous, after what he did. Why is he not giving you something now? That would be the right thing to do."

"There's a reason men like him are rich. Bryce is only generous if he's getting a charitable tax receipt." She didn't tell Jess she'd ignored Bryce's texts and calls after waiting out a year to apply for divorce. She just couldn't deal with him right now. Besides, all those years she'd had money, it hadn't made her any happier.

Jess pulled a laptop from her bag, sitting next to Caroline and opening it on the counter. Caroline recognized the job site she'd checked sporadically, as if the perfect opportunity would magically present itself. Each visit just made her mood darker.

"Wait — did you see this?" Jess turned the screen toward Caroline. "It's a farm job."

She didn't remember that one, no. "Farm? You know how I feel about farms."

"Yeah, yeah. Farm is a four-letter word. But it comes with an apartment. And they're just looking for someone for the summer, so you wouldn't be, you know, selling your soul or whatever you think it would take to lower your standards to that level." Jess rolled her eyes, then scanned the posting again. "Northwest Farm. Isn't that the Taylors?"

Caroline straightened, her heart skipping a beat. "What?"

"Northwest. Ed Taylor, the trainer who died in that

horrible car accident with his wife and son. You remember his other son, don't you? Dean?"

Oh, Caroline remembered Dean Taylor.

"I've never heard anything bad about him, anyway." Jess got up, followed by a scramble of Border Collie claws on tile. She opened the fridge and took out a jug of water. "He used to be a nice guy, at least." She poured glasses for both of them, eying Caroline suspiciously.

Caroline kept her mouth shut, ducking Jess's gaze but as Jess settled in the stool again, a scary look of enlightenment came over her face. Caroline refused to look at her.

"It's all coming back to me now," Jess said slowly with a gleeful smile. "That first summer we worked at the track. At the end, before we went back to school. Vicki dared you to kiss him at that party."

Caroline pressed her face into her hands. "We were so immature."

"You did it, too. How could I forget about that? The two of you behind the barn after his dad won a big race, you one under-aged beer too many to have any common sense." Jess barely contained her laughter.

"You were supposed to be the one with the common sense who kept me from doing stupid things!"

"I stayed sober so I could drive your and Vicki's sorry drunk asses home, that's as much responsibility as I'm taking for anything that happened that summer." Jess paused, like she was digging in her memory for more details. "Wasn't his little sister a jockey jumper?"

Caroline gasped, maybe a little too dramatically, happy to shift the topic from Dean. "You're right! I can't remember her name. I wonder if she grew out of it."

"Or moved up, like you did?" Jess elbowed her, then turned back to the computer. "Seriously, what do you think? Like I said, it wouldn't be forever. It might be nice for the summer. Give you something to do until you get money from Bryce."

"I don't know. I'm not sure Dean's forgiven me."

"Come on, Caroline. It was twenty years ago. You're both grown-ups now. I'm sure he's not holding a silly kiss against you."

Probably not. But there were other things he might be. She changed the subject. "What are you doing today?"

Jess glanced at a watch that seemed too big for her small wrist. "I have a lab to TA at ten and then I'll be working on my research project for the rest of the day. You're welcome to stick around. Callum would love the company."

Caroline had no idea what TA meant. Some foreign, academic thing. "Thanks. Though I don't think I have much of a choice."

"That's right, how did I forget?" Jess grinned. "Is it okay if we retrieve your car tonight? Unless you really need to get somewhere now, in which case you can drop me off at the university and do what you have to do."

That seemed like a lot of trouble. Besides, where was she going to go? "I don't have anywhere to be."

When Jess left, Caroline took Callum and wandered to the barn. The Border Collie was attentive, even to her, not straying far before bouncing back to check in. In the back paddock, a foal's head popped up, and he left his mother to come to the fence. The colt was in her face but not nippy, so she let him nuzzle her hair, and tried to ignore the inevitable tug on her heart.

"What am I going to do, Mulder?"

She didn't regret leaving the track, but leaving horses was murkier. Because people had let her down far too often, but Thoroughbreds always came through.

CHAPTER ELEVEN

THE POTHOLES WERE NOT DOING her car any favours. Caroline was tempted to drive as far onto the berm as she could, but putting tire ruts in the grass might not be the best way to impress prospective employers, so the Camry would have to take one for the team. She rolled to a halt when she reached a closed gate blocking her entry to the barns beyond.

What was she doing here?

To her left was a simple two-story red brick farmhouse, the kind that was everywhere in Ontario. It was pretty, with a few small flower beds, and the trim looked as if it had been painted in the not-too-distant past. Caroline backed up and parked next to a black Toyota Corolla showing its age, the paint dull, bumper rusted.

The paddock she now faced was empty, though it appeared to have been used recently enough, the grass sparse and dotted with piles of manure. The fence was weathered, some of the posts chewed. First impression? Northwest Farm didn't look like her idea of where a Plate winner would be born.

It still irked her that Dean Taylor had won a Plate, a race

that had eluded her. But he'd stuck with training when she'd abandoned her career. Left on what was supposed to be a high. And now she was here, feeling like she was starting at the bottom again.

She didn't see anyone. She could just leave. Heaven knew she'd been on the other side enough times when she'd been training. No-show employees were beyond common. Because *this* was a bad idea. If she had to stoop to this level, did it have to be *his* farm?

But then she caught movement in her side mirror — a woman emerging from the back door. She'd missed her chance to bolt. Could she pretend she was lost? Caroline exhaled, climbed out of her car and approached the deck, which appeared to be a newer addition — certainly younger than the hundred-year-old house. The emails she'd exchanged had been with someone named Faye. If it had been Dean, Caroline probably would have lost her nerve.

She sized the woman up. Long, dark hair fell loose around her shoulders. She looked to be in her twenties, put-together, her outfit casual but stylish. The sun caught the glint of a diamond ring and Caroline reflexively touched the bare finger on her left hand. Was Dean married now? The woman was pretty; of course Dean Taylor would have a pretty wife. Behind the screen door, a dog whined.

"Are you here for an interview or a date?"

Caroline stopped, caught off guard, arms stuck to her sides as the woman stepped down from the deck.

"I'm kidding, sorry," the woman said, breaking into a warm smile with her hand outstretched. "I'm Faye Taylor. I assume you're here to see my brother about the job."

The jockey jumper? Caroline's eyebrows twitched, her vision narrowing slightly before she reined in her expression and shook Faye's hand. It was smooth, the nails neatly filed, and

Caroline guessed Faye wasn't hands-on when it came to farm work.

"Nice to meet you." Because she didn't remember being introduced to Faye, or ever seeing her on the backstretch. The front side, yes. Parties, yes. Local bars, yes. Despite all of that, their paths had never directly crossed.

"Dean's in the barn." Faye opened a four-foot gate set in the fenceline separating the parking area from the barnyard, her white Skechers gliding over a well-worn path. Faye wore no socks, her pale blue slim-fit pants skimming her ankles. Her top was a white, long-sleeved boyfriend shirt. Not clothes one wore to the barn.

"Sorry about the smart comment." Faye glanced over as Caroline caught up. "You're just dressed more nicely than I expected for someone coming about a farm job."

Caroline wasn't going to lie — she'd wanted to look her best. It was bad enough she needed this job at all; the least she could do was not look as if her life had fallen apart — even if it had. She told herself she hadn't made a special effort just because it was Dean Taylor, even if it had been on her mind the entire time she'd gone through her wardrobe, all of it packed in the back of her car.

She'd selected dark-wash jeans — belted, thanks to her recent stress weight loss — and a yellow ochre short-sleeved shirt on the dressy side, but in a practical fabric. Something that said she could jump in to lend a hand if needed, though her good Blundstones wouldn't be her first choice for day-to-day chores. Since chopping off her hair, it took little effort to look presentable. Wash and go, that's what she wanted. It was time to simplify her life and start fresh.

"Dean's been so busy," Faye continued. "His assistant at the track quit the same time as our manager. They both say they're just taking a leave for the summer, because, YOLO I guess, right? So be careful, he might try to talk you into doing both jobs."

If he didn't chase her out of the barn with a broom when he saw her.

Had Dean not told Faye they knew each other? Caroline sure hadn't mentioned it in the emails. She clenched her fists, palms damp, pulse jumping a couple of beats. If Dean wasn't expecting her...

Was it too late to run?

"In here," Faye said when they reached the first of two barns.

Caroline sucked in a breath and pulled her shoulders back. Here goes. Jess was probably right. Dean was an easy-going guy, he'd have let that old stuff go. Everything was going to be fine.

The old familiar smell of a well-kept barn gave her heart a nostalgic twist — fresh shavings and hay balancing the sharpness of pine oil and underlying scent of horse. Even though the lights in the barn were on, at first she couldn't see much after coming from the brightness outside, but she heard the clunk of doors shutting and heavy latches being secured before her eyes adjusted enough to make out two forms. A slight woman with a swinging brunette ponytail emerged from a stall with a bucket of feed. Further down, someone who could only be Dean swept the aisle — tall and loose-limbed, intent on his task.

Caroline's gaze locked on him. A trickle of sweat crept down her back. Time had been kinder to Dean Taylor than it had been to her. Why was it men always seemed to get better looking as they got older, while she, at the same age, already felt like a wrinkled crone? It was so unfair.

It was a moment before Dean glanced up, pausing, probably unable to make out her face. He started toward them — then stopped abruptly. No doubt about it, that was recognition on his face. It wasn't an outright scowl — he was much too mild-mannered for that — but his look was wary, possibly with a dose of disappointment, as if he'd been hopeful Faye had brought the solution to his problem, but this was definitely not it.

Faye carried on as if she didn't notice. "Dean, this is Caroline Harrington. And that's our neighbour, Emilie Lachance, who's been helping out."

Dean remained rooted, and Caroline felt stuck.

Emilie glanced at him before turning toward Caroline, speaking into the awkwardness, her smile friendly. "Hi, Caroline."

Caroline thought she saw the young woman's head tilt at Dean as she headed down the aisle, bucket swinging, the coffee can she'd used to measure the rations rattling as she went.

"I'll leave you to it," Faye said. If she was perplexed by her brother's less-than-hospitable behaviour, she didn't show it.

"I'll get out of your way too," Emilie said when she reappeared. "Nice to meet you, Caroline. Wait up, Faye!"

"Thanks again, Em." Dean called after her, toneless, just loudly enough to be heard.

"Two birds, maybe, Dean?" Faye called over her shoulder, and Emilie started laughing as they walked out the end of the barn, leaving Caroline standing there, ten feet from Dean Taylor, feeling she'd been dropped in the middle of an inside joke. If it was any consolation, Dean didn't appear to find it funny.

"Hi Dean," she said, tucking her fingers into her pockets, her confidence leaching away now that she was alone with him. "How've you been?"

The air between them felt thick, Dean taking a beat to respond. "Harrington. Your married name."

Caroline nodded, wishing she had a clever way of breaking

the tension. She should probably leave. Nothing on Dean's face, in his stance, said *bygones*. But she needed a job and a place to live. Dean needed the help. What was most important here? Except, while she could work for Dean Taylor — he was a solid trainer, fair, valued good employees — she'd been foolish to think he might want her working for him.

"Congratulations," he said, as if it were an afterthought.

The word sounded so foreign, it took her a second to absorb it, a reaction delayed by ten years. She nearly waved her bare hand in front of him, but settled on, "It didn't last."

"Sorry." He wasn't convincing.

Dean was a man of few words, but this was ridiculous. She needed to get to the point — and if there was no shot, return to her gin and tears diet. Prolonging the agony was not on her to-do list today. She'd had enough torment to last a lifetime. She was done with it.

"I'm here about the job," she said, mustering assertiveness. "There's an apartment?"

"Is this a joke?"

Every time he spoke, with his minimal syllables, he knocked her down, making her crawl back up. "You know I'm a hard worker. I'm good, and I'm fast. Give me two days to get to know the routine, then you can leave me to it and put your focus back where it should be, on your track horses."

"Whatever possessed you to apply? After... all of it."

Her heart bounded against her chest, words caught in her throat until they came out like a dam had been broken. "I'm in a spot, okay? I left all of it, this life, never dreaming I'd be back. Never thinking the man I married would drop me after tearing me away from my friends and everything I used to love. I might as well be slithering on my belly, that's how low I feel right now." She hadn't planned on spilling her guts to him, but there it was. Did his face soften, if only slightly?

"There are plenty of jobs at the track."

"I don't want to work at the track." He had to have heard the rumours. He had to know about the accident.

"Then why me? There are enough farms around needing help. Why this farm?"

Because you're everything I'm not and want to be, she wanted to scream. *I'm not proud of who I was. I'm not proud of where I am. And because under the ire you have every right to feel, you're kind. You're better than all of them in there. You're better than me.*

"Because I heard you needed someone," she said, her voice barely a whisper. "And I hoped you were as desperate as I am."

Something passed over his face, and for a moment, she was hopeful.

But he said, "Just go, Caroline," and went back to sweeping.

Her face fell, eyes dropping to the floor. Fair enough. He was entitled to feel the way he did, after everything she'd done. She watched him for a moment, a slight hunch to his shoulders as he flicked the broom over the asphalt with fierceness. Her mind raced back to when he'd resurfaced at the track after his father's death, a conflicting combination of eagerness and grief; tall, dark and tragic. The memory filled her with regret.

"If you change your mind, you've got my number. I could start immediately."

She marched out of the barn without looking behind, biting her lip and blinking back the sting in her eyes.

She should have known better. Dean Taylor was like an elephant. Quiet, gentle... and he never forgot.

CHAPTER TWELVE

DEAN STOMPED up the steps to the deck and didn't bother to cushion the screen door as it snapped shut behind him. Faye glanced at him, but he didn't meet her eyes, heading straight for the fridge and extracting a bottle of Will's beer. A hiss escaped as he twisted off the cap.

"Is there a problem?" Faye asked cautiously.

Dean tipped the bottle to his lips. "Caroline Harrington is Caroline Jenkins, and she is a definite problem." The beer wasn't nearly as satisfying as he'd hoped.

"You know her?"

Dean glanced at Faye. There was a quirk to her lips. Was this funny? "Everyone knows everyone at the track."

"You never said anything. Why didn't you tell me?"

Dean hadn't recognized Caroline at first. The short, almost severe haircut had thrown him. Gone was the soft, sweet exterior of the girl he'd first met at eighteen — an exterior he'd learned, before the summer was over, was only a façade. It was as if the real Caroline had finally caught up with the face she showed to the world.

"I didn't know it was her until I saw her. She used her married name on her application."

If he'd recalled it, he would have preempted the interview before Faye set it up. Had Caroline been intentionally trying to fool him? She could have avoided their whole uncomfortable reunion. She must be desperate.

"What happened between you?" Faye asked, her tone still careful, with an added note of curiosity. "You never tell me about your personal life."

Should it embarrass him that there was nothing to tell? Since the car accident, he hadn't been with anyone long enough he'd felt she needed to know. A relationship hadn't seemed right when his sister had been so disrupted by their loss. He'd watched Faye go through it — the men, the partying — and felt a sense of responsibility to be her safe space. She needed someone she could count on, someone who wouldn't judge her, someone who always had her back. And sometimes, when Faye was bouncing between short-term relationships, it had felt as if the two of them might end up growing old in this house together. Now that had all changed. He wasn't sure it had bothered him until recently.

"It wasn't personal," he said.

Faye didn't need to know what had happened that first summer. It had been nothing. One of Caroline's friends had walked hots for Len, so he'd see her around at the end of the morning sometimes. Then she started talking to him. She'd come by his stalls most days when he was doing up horses, and when she didn't, he'd miss her. Some days she'd show up at feed time and help him. A few times she'd even come when his father had told him to go pick up food for the crew on a particularly long day. It was inevitable he'd develop feelings for her, but he never told her. They were friends. Until the stake party at the end of the summer.

Dean would never forget that day. How could he? Catch The Joy had won the Breeders Stakes and with it, the Canadian Triple Crown. What a celebration they'd had at the barn. He didn't remember how, but he'd found himself with her, apart from the others, her hands on his shirt, pulling him down to her. Kissing him. Him kissing her back, figuring it out as he went along. Had there ever been a better day?

But after that, she'd brushed him off. And that was that. Teenagers broke each other's hearts all the time; it was a rite of passage, wasn't it? He'd watched Faye do the same thing, time and again, toying with hearts and discarding them, completely unaware of the hurt she caused. It had taken having her own heart broken to recognize what she'd done. Dean wouldn't judge Caroline for that any more than he had his sister.

Faye frowned, shaking her head before moving on. "I looked her up on Equibase." His sister, who adamantly remained on the fringes of the business of horse racing, save for doing the books, still knew where to find information. "It seems like she was a good trainer."

"She was," Dean said. "Unfortunately, while she didn't exactly break the rules, she knew how to bend them."

"And this affected you, how? Lots of trainers operate like that. Why was she different?"

The memories were as bitter as the beer. "When I took over Dad's horses, Caroline was still around. She'd gotten her trainer's license while I was away — hooked up with a rich guy who set her up with some really nice horses, and had stalls in the same barn. Pretty soon, I was looking over my shoulder, because I couldn't trust her. She had no problem trying to steal my owners or my help. Her grooms would 'borrow' my supplies — consumables like shampoo and liniment she'd never replace. Then she claimed one of my horses, did some underhanded vetwork on him, and after winning a couple of races, sold him to the States. I was never able to find out what happened to him."

It was impossible to keep track of all the horses that left his care, but that one still stung the worst. It was an unspoken rule on the backstretch — you didn't claim a horse from someone in your barn.

"They started winning everything. It was suspicious, but the officials were never able to catch up with them. The next spring, she didn't come back. Quit racing, cold turkey." *Good riddance.*

"Where was I when all this was happening? Why did I not know?" Faye asked.

"You had enough going on back then. I was supposed to be the big brother. I took care of things."

"I would have come and kicked her ass," Faye growled.

Dean laughed. "I know you would have."

"Still... that was all how many years ago now? People can change, Dean. I'm certainly not the same person I was back then. And it's not as if she can do much damage here, anyway, is there? May I also remind you, you're not really in a position to be picky?"

Faye was right. And Caroline was right, too. He was just desperate enough to take a chance on her. He wished he felt satisfaction that she'd gotten her due, but recently he'd felt he was far too close to losing everything himself.

Faye crossed her arms and leaned against the counter. "She's attractive. And well-dressed. I wasn't entirely kidding about the two birds."

"That is out of the question." Caroline Harrington could be the last woman on earth, and he would never consider it.

"She must have her reasons for showing up here. There has to be more to it than just the job. She is ridiculously overqualified."

Dean rolled his eyes. "You're meddlesome, do you know that?"

Faye laughed. "Meddlesome? Who says meddlesome? How old are you, seventy? Maybe I should change the age range of your dating candidates. That's not such a bad idea, you know. Find you some rich old lady. Will's mother was quite taken with you."

"You'd be all right with that, would you?"

"Absolutely not."

"Maybe you should just leave me be and admit some of us are meant to be alone."

"I'm pretty sure that's exactly what Liv said not long before she fell for Nate — at my expense, I might add."

"I like Nate, but even I could see that the two of you weren't exactly a match made in heaven."

"Oh, shut up. Neither of us is sure we like Nate, except that he makes my best friend happy, and he won you your first Plate. We're not allowed to hate him."

Dean had to laugh at that. He dumped the rest of the bottle down the sink, silently apologizing to Will for the beer crime of leaving it unfinished.

He'd sleep on it, and see how he felt in the morning when he was rested and could think more clearly. That would give him time to be sure he wasn't letting his personal feelings skew his thoughts.

Besides, it wasn't forever. At most, it would be three months. At least, he might get a few days to regroup — sort the situation out at the track, get some decent sleep. In the meantime, perhaps a new applicant would appear so undeniably ideal for the role he would never need to speak to Caroline Jenkins — Harrington — again.

CHAPTER THIRTEEN

CAROLINE HADN'T INTENTIONALLY BEEN UP before dawn since... well, since she'd left the track. The email she'd received last night had astonished her because when she'd left Northwest, she'd held it together long enough to drive out the lane before parking on the side of the road and dissolving into a puddle, never expecting to hear anything from them again.

By the time she'd returned to Jess's place, her misery had turned to anger. Who did Dean think he was, anyway? Let him do all the work himself. It wasn't as if he'd find anyone better than her. He should have been honoured she'd applied. It wasn't like she *wanted* to work on a farm. The job was totally beneath her, and she hated the country. She was a city girl, born and raised.

But after she'd read the email — three times to be sure — and recovered from the shock and unexplained gush of tears that followed (relief? Terror?), she'd responded immediately, then let out a whoop. She and Jess had danced around the kitchen, the Border Collie bouncing at their feet.

She'd barely been able to sleep, her mind racing from joy to worry. What had changed Dean's mind? Or had it been Dean at all? The email had suspiciously been unsigned.

Her excitement about working such a menial job surprised her, but she leaned into it. She'd show Dean she could be relied upon, that the person she'd been before had been moulded by the unsavoury influence of Bryce Harrington. She'd make herself indispensable to the Taylors and Northwest.

Jess rose with her and sent her on her way with a travel mug of coffee and some granola bars like she was headed off to school.

"I'll let you know if I'll be back." The job came with an apartment, right? She hadn't even seen it. What if it was creepy?

Doubt crept in further, plaguing her on the drive there. What if it *had* been Faye, and not Dean, who had sent that email? The image of his stormy countenance was like barbed wire wrapped around her heart. Antagonism wasn't in his nature; that emotion came special delivery, for her.

She pulled in next to the Corolla, as if parking beside Dean's truck would be like standing too close to him — and she intended to give him as much space as possible. That was the only way this might work. A light at the back door lit the deck, and a halogen lamp, high on a hydro pole, illuminated the yard. The barn windows were bright yellow squares. She slipped through the small gate and hurried in that direction, her vision shifting to the murky shadows. It was too dark and quiet out here.

The rumble of hungry horses and the sliding of a stall door was a warm hug of a sound, but Caroline hesitated before crossing the line from the inky night to the pool of light tossed from the barn.

"All right, all right." Dean's voice, affectionate, mingled with the animals' chorus.

Deep breath. She stepped forward, turned the latch on the barn door, and slipped in, pulling it tight behind her.

"What are you doing here?"

His tone stopped her in her tracks, all the affection he had for the horses gone. They rumbled their disapproval at the interruption.

Caroline's feet shifted, and she couldn't hold his hard stare. "I got an email last night saying I should come."

Dean shook his head and pulled back the door, nudging the horse out of his way, muttering, "Faye."

She barely heard him, the horses resuming their song. So, he wasn't expecting her. *Great.* But he wasn't chasing her away either. At least, not yet.

His lips pressed into a line. "Well, you're here now. You can help me turn the horses out."

Progress?

Dean finished feeding and put the bucket away, then strode past her, unspeaking. Caroline scrambled to follow.

They reached an older, smaller stable, Dean hooking the door back. Caroline glanced up and tugged the cane bolt at the top and bottom of the other door, and swung it open.

"Only one foal right now. We'll take them first. Seeing as you're here, you can lead the mare. The colt's a jerk." He handed her a rope lead.

She peered past Dean and grinned at the foal, all bright-eyed, fuzzy-eared and old-man whiskers. "How old is he? He's adorable!"

"See if you still feel that way when you have to do this on your own."

Maybe she'd get the chance?

The bay colt strutted right up to her and began nibbling her hoodie. Caroline reached forward and scratched his chest, and the colt grunted with pleasure, his head bobbing. "So cute."

"First tip. Don't do that, or you'll be wearing him before you know it. Grab the mare."

Yes, sir! She turned away, smothering her smile. The mare waited stoically. "Where are we going?"

"It's a bit of a trek. The paddock next to the driveway, across from the house. Keep her behind me."

And so, Caroline got to watch the show. She bit her lip to keep from laughing as Dean contained the colt's leaps and wiggles, though a couple of times her breath caught in her throat when she thought he wasn't going to hold that leggy energy. His patience was admirable.

"How do you do that alone?" she asked once the pair was safely in the paddock. She heard the thrum of the colt's feet as he tore around, and wanted to stay and watch, but Dean was on a mission.

"Jaida is a saint, that's how."

Jaida must be the mother — Caroline could figure that out — but, "That's not very helpful."

Dean shot her a sideways glance, none of the patience he'd had for the colt available for her. "Just hold her lead and she'll follow while you deal with him."

"What's up with the other two mares?" she felt brave enough to ask as they got back to the barn.

"They go out together. One lost her foal in February and is bred back. The other is due in about ten days."

Her mouth opened, then closed. "I don't know anything about foaling."

"We'll worry about that if we get to it."

That statement was less promising.

Except for short exchanges — Dean telling her who to put where — they didn't say much as they turned out the rest of the horses.

"What about that one?" Caroline pointed toward the head

of a big bay, pushed out over the yoke of a gate in the layup barn.

"He's on stall rest. I'll walk him when I get back."

"I can walk him. What's wrong with him?"

"Tendon."

"I know how to rehab a tendon."

"I don't care what you think you know."

It felt like a slap, but she backed off. He was being irrational, but she'd let him hang onto his grudge a while longer.

"Just leave him," Dean insisted.

It sounded like he was saying, *keep your greasy little hands off my horse.* She inched closer to read the index card on the door, the name carefully printed in block letters. RIDE THE WAVE.

That explained it. His Plate horse. The reminder of what Dean had accomplished that she had *not* made her clench her jaw, and she scowled at the horse. The horse looked back like he was ready to laugh at her.

Caroline reset her face and spun on her heels. It was time Dean left, wasn't it? "I'll do the barn. Do I use a wheelbarrow, or...?"

Dean looked as if he still wasn't convinced he trusted her to do even the most basic task.

She persisted. "I may not have done it as often as you because I didn't start when I was in diapers like you did, but I am capable. It's one skill I've always felt I excel at."

His expression didn't change, but his shoulders dropped slightly. "I'll back the spreader in. That is, if you think you can move the tractor forward when you need to. Do you know how to drive a tractor?"

"If you show me, I can learn. How hard can it be? I can drive a stick."

He looked as if he was going to debate that, but instead, started walking. "Go ahead and start dumping buckets."

"Is there a scrub brush somewhere?" she called after him.

"This isn't the track. We don't scrub buckets every day."

She went to the first stall and unhooked the pail, hefting it outside, and wished she'd asked him where she should dump it. With her luck, she'd do it wrong. But he was mad at her anyway, so what did it matter? It killed her not to scrub them. At the track, they cleaned buckets and feed tubs every day. Did he not hold the farm to the same standard? *Slacker*.

Before long she heard the chug of a tractor and she moved faster, wanting to get all the buckets dumped before he returned. Forks, brooms and rakes hung neatly on one wall, and she grabbed a set as the sound of the engine filled the barn, the smell of diesel making her queasy.

"C'mere!" Dean yelled over the steady rumble.

Caroline set the equipment aside and shuffled between the wall and machinery until she was level with Dean. He demonstrated the clutch and the gears, then climbed down, making her clamber up. The seat was covered with an old, folded towel.

"That's the clutch. That's the brake," he said, still raising his voice over the engine. "First, put it into low gear with this shaft here. You'll have to jiggle it a bit to find it. Then on the right, there, put it into first. Try it."

The clutch was higher and stiffer than a car. It took a couple of attempts to find low gear. First was easier. She eased the clutch, and her foot slipped on the steel pedal, the tractor lurching forward. Caroline plunged the clutch to the floor before it stalled.

"Not exactly a Ferrari, is it?" Dean didn't seem to find anything she said funny. "I'm sure I'll manage."

"Turn it off. Kill switch." He gestured. "Key."

Caroline hopped down, grinning. "Didn't die, didn't destroy the place!"

Dean grimaced. "Not yet, anyway."

"Any other instructions? I know you need to be going," she said pointedly.

He still looked unsure. Did he think she was going to burn the barn down? Steal some equipment?

"So we're clear, I haven't said you have the job yet. We'll do a trial period. All right?"

Caroline nodded quickly. She just wanted him to leave her alone.

CHAPTER FOURTEEN

"H𝐞 makes me crazy," Crystal snapped as she put the saddle on Cruze. "I have to tack up by myself, but if a jock's coming, the horse is waiting on the wall for him. You need to talk to him about that. Would it kill him to show me a little respect?"

Dean stared down the shedrow where Squeak propped a bale of straw outside Gastronomy's stall, the colt — yes — all tacked up and waiting for Nate. He could imagine having a word with Squeak — after which Squeak would walk off the shed raging about how you'd think as hard as good grooms were to find around here Dean would know better than to question his ways. On the other hand, Dean could groom horses if he had to, but he couldn't gallop, so he couldn't afford to upset Crystal, either. There was no winning here.

"I'll try," he said. "Thank you for your tolerance, in the meantime."

Crystal gaped at him in disbelief. "Don't give me that crap, Dean. Try, 'sorry, Crystal, I agree he's an asshole and I'll tell him to shape up because you are vital to my operation.'"

Dean cracked a smile. "You are. But I really don't want to be rubbing these horses all by myself, so a little grace?"

She rolled her eyes and groaned. "Fine. What kind of grown man has a name like Squeak, anyway? Hand me the bridle?"

Once he legged Crystal up, he started walking Gastronomy while waiting for Nate to arrive. It would be like a vacation to get away from his crew. The friction had been never-ending since Nikki's departure.

"I'll do your stall, boss," Squeak said. "I'm going to be here till frigging feed time anyway."

Dean sighed and his mind drifted unwittingly to Caroline. As soon as they were done this morning, he'd be checking up on her, making sure she hadn't driven the tractor through a fence. There would be words with Faye later — no way should she have gone behind his back and told Caroline to come.

It was a relief when Nate showed up. Never thought he'd ever say *that*.

"Everything all right?" Nate asked.

"Nothing getting out of this barn won't fix," Dean muttered as he stopped the colt then called, "Head out, Crystal!"

"I told Liv we'd meet them at the gap," Nate said.

Because Liv's horses probably stood nicely enough for that. Crystal didn't quite have the patience to incorporate such things into her routine. Other than that, she was a good exercise rider.

Dean kept the shank on Gastronomy, though the colt walked quietly. He didn't want to be responsible if the two-year-old acted up uncharacteristically and dropped Woodbine's leading rider.

Liv was on the dark bay Dean had seen at the farm, and the filly was so relaxed her hind leg was cocked. Cruze puffed himself up at the sight of the filly and gave a manly nicker.

"Stop it," Crystal growled and popped the colt on the shoulder with her whip. Cruze didn't look the least bit admonished.

Dean shook his head. He'd had to wake Cruze out of a slumber to get him ready, and now the colt thought he was Casanova. If Cruze didn't show some improvement soon, he'd earn himself an appointment with the vet. *Snip, snip.*

"I'll stay to the inside and Nicole can go beside me with Cash," Liv suggested after discreetly moving her filly away from Dean's randy youngster. "He's used to training with Fleur."

"Keep him on the outside then, Crystal," Dean said, relieved that Gastronomy didn't seem to have noticed Liv's filly.

Len was parked at the rail like he'd gotten the memo. Dean didn't think letting a group of two-year-olds breeze their first quarters was noteworthy until he remembered who the Triple Stripe juveniles were. Word must've gotten around. No one batted an eye at Dean's two plain dark bays, even if one was a half-brother to Ride The Wave. Cruze had yet to give anyone reason to make that connection.

"You been keeping a couple of nice babies up your sleeve there, Dean?" Len said. "Fancy company you're keeping."

"We'll see," Dean answered. He pulled out his phone so he could send a video to Andy.

The track wasn't busy, allowing the two-year-olds to go four abreast. Dean followed them as they jogged clockwise along the outside rail and watched as they pulled up and turned in on the backstretch. Cruze sidestepped, impatient, and it wasn't long before they set off galloping, side by side — Liv's filly closest to the rail, then Nicole on Just Jay's full brother, Nate on Gastronomy, and Cruze on the far outside with Crystal.

They quickened around the turn and Liv's filly immediately dropped back. Gastronomy dug in to stay with the chestnut — Nicole had a tight hold on him, moderating the Triple Stripe colt's speed. Cruze looked lost, drifting to the middle of the racetrack, level with the filly. Dean frowned, then remembered to lift his phone. If he could get a decent video — something to show Andy — it might keep the owner happy, smooth over the recent bumps.

He zoomed in, the chestnut and Andy's colt on the rail, neck in neck. Liv's filly dropped further behind, despite Liv's urging, and Cruze was content to stay back with her. Then out of nowhere, Cruze's head shot up and he swooped dramatically inward. Crystal yelled at him and tried to straighten him before he cut off the filly. The filly shortened her stride, falling back even more, and Cruze overreacted to Crystal's correction, swerving abruptly toward the outer rail. The move unbalanced both the colt and Crystal. Cruze tripped, almost falling on his nose, and Crystal tumbled off, Liv's filly leaping awkwardly, barely missing her.

Dean watched dumbstruck as Cruze recovered and ran loose, but Gord and his pony were ready and pounced, catching him before he reached the next turn. Not that Cruze had been travelling quickly — Nate and Nicole were far ahead now, galloping their colts out — but his renewed interest in the filly put Liv in a vulnerable position.

Then Dean remembered — Crystal. She was sitting in the middle of the track, clutching her arm. Dean ducked under the rail, and, checking the track was clear of horses that might run him over, he dashed across and crouched next to her. Her jaw was clenched, teeth slightly bared, her face colourless.

"Should I get an ambulance?" Dean asked, pulling his eyes from her to glance around. Where was it this time of morning? It was always on the backstretch during training and racing.

She shook her head, grimacing. "No. Help me up."

He was careful as he supported her, her good hand

reaching for his arm before snapping back to her maimed wing. She wavered once she was on her feet and threw up. Slowly, Dean guided her off the track. Gord waited at the gap with Cruze. Dean wished he could throw Crystal over the saddle like in some cowboy movie, because how else was he supposed to get them both back to the barn?

"Listen, Crystal. Let's sit you down over here. I'll take Cruze home and come back with my truck, then get you to the hospital."

"How am I supposed to climb into your stupid truck?" she mumbled.

"What would you suggest, then?" He wished she'd agreed to the ambulance.

"Bring my car. I'll be able to get in that."

Feeling like a bad parent, Dean eased her to the ground and left her propped against the pony shack, a small shelter near the gap.

Her car was small — one of those Honda Fits. Dean had to slide the seat back as far as it would go before he could even get in. At least it was automatic — he would have feared for his kneecaps with a standard. It felt like a golf cart and sounded like a toy car. He left Squeak grumbling with both Cruze and Gastronomy to manage, but that was nothing new. Len would give him a hand.

Crystal was right where he'd left her, looking pale and crumpled. "Do you know how many times I had to tell people no, I'm not drunk?"

Dean chuckled. "If you'd just let me call the ambulance, you wouldn't have had that problem. How are you feeling? Still woozy?"

"Better," she said. "But my shoulder hurts like hell."

"Come on. Time to get you back up." He positioned himself on her right side and wrapped an arm around her. The solid safety vest under his fingers might be great for protecting spines and ribs, but did nothing for limbs.

"Whoa. Woozy again," she said.

Dean stopped, worried she was either going to vomit again or pass out. He gauged the distance between where they'd paused and the little car. "Ten more steps."

When she was finally in the Honda, she closed her eyes and leaned back against the headrest. "Home, James."

Definitely in shock. "I really wish you'd let me call an ambulance," he said again.

In the emergency waiting room, he wished it once more, sure it would get her seen faster. He helped get her registered with the triage nurse then sat with her, thinking how he needed to get back and help Squeak, or he'd have big problems tomorrow. Squeak might spontaneously decide he needed a day off after this; the old groom would feel it coming on like a virus.

Dean pulled his phone from his pocket and opened up the video. He wasn't sure it was something he could send Andy. Maybe if he cut it, right *there?* "What spooked him, anyway?"

Crystal's head lolled toward him. "You didn't see the geese? I knew they'd get me one day." She tried to straighten so she could see the screen. "You got video? Send that to me, 'k?"

He'd never understand exercise riders' fascination with their own crashes.

She was pale, and turned so her good shoulder was propped against the back of the chair, resting her head on the wall and closing her eyes.

"I'll check and see how much longer they think it'll be," he said, unable to watch her sit there in pain.

Dean approached the triage nurse hesitantly. Her head was down as she filled something out with a pen, so he cleared his throat. "Excuse me. I'm so sorry to bother you, but —" The nurse looked up, her face pinched. He felt like diving into an apology about how he knew she was probably overworked and underappreciated and patients needed to understand they would be seen as soon as time allowed. "I'm worried about her. And I have a barn full of horses at the track I need to get back to because I'm short-staffed." He didn't know why he added that. His battles were not her problem.

Miraculously, her face softened. "It won't be much longer. If you need to go, I'll keep an eye on her."

"Thank you," he said, and returned to Crystal. "She says it won't be much longer."

"Sure." Crystal didn't even lift her head as she spoke. "What else is she going to say? Go. You'll never hear the end of it if Grumpy McGrumpster has to do up an extra horse or rake the shed. I'll text you when they're ready to let me go."

"All right. But contact me if you need anything, okay?"

"I need a doctor. You've done your best."

As he left, Dean took some solace that she seemed to have retained her sense of humour — except that he was losing his own. Because now, on top of everything, he needed to find someone to gallop his horses.

CHAPTER FIFTEEN

Caroline wiped dust and moisture from her eyes with a corner of her shirt, then finished sweeping. It felt good to sweat again, like her body had been on ice for ten years, waiting to be put to use again. After the water buckets were full, she stared at the feed chart. That would have to wait until Dean got back. Some of the horses got medication, but he kept it all locked away in a cabinet like they did at the track.

"Hey, Caroline, how's it going?"

Her head snapped at the unexpected voice. Since Dean had left, she'd had only the horses and farm sounds to keep her company. The solitude wasn't nearly as bad as it had been before the sun rose. It left plenty of time for soul searching — though it hadn't been a successful quest.

Faye, who she hadn't seen since the day of the interview, waited for her response. Friend or foe? Caroline hadn't decided.

"Pretty well," she responded, then crossed her arms. "I take it you didn't tell Dean you asked me to come?"

Faye smiled sheepishly. "Sometimes he doesn't know

what's best for him. I see he didn't chase you away. Anyway, have you had lunch? If not, I thought you might like to come to the house."

Caroline's stomach grumbled at the mere suggestion of proper food — the granola bar she'd eaten mid-morning hadn't put a dent in the calorie deficit created by farm chores. Should she say yes, or keep her distance until she was sure she was welcome to stay?

"That's very kind of you to offer. I should probably keep going." Even though the barns were done. How was this job supposed to take all day?

"This isn't the racetrack," Faye scoffed. "It's past noon. You get an hour for lunch. Take it, because you won't get it back."

Caroline laughed, her resistance fading. Farm time was a foreign concept to her. She was used to the backstretch where they worked until they were finished, which was typically noon at the latest. "All right."

"Come when you're ready. We'll be on the deck."

We? Was she going to have to sit through an awkward hour with a silent Dean and his chatty sister? She washed up in the barn's restroom, and wished she had a clean shirt.

As Caroline neared the house, she saw two women settling into chairs and — thankfully — no sign of Dean's truck. She climbed the two steps to the deck, a bench along the railing enclosing it, a round glass patio table set for four.

"You remember Emilie," Faye said, gesturing to the younger woman who'd been helping Dean that first day. "And you might already know her sister, Liv?"

Caroline knew who she was, because how could she not? Even though she'd been away for ten years, she'd never completely been able to tear herself from horse racing news. Liv's family farm was just down the road, and she'd trained an incredible horse, recently retired to stud. Despite her status,

Liv was the kind of person Caroline might not have looked twice at had they passed on the street. She was pretty enough, but slight, her long, dark hair pulled into a simple ponytail. Her jeans were faded, her running shoes no longer white, and her loose t-shirt was well-worn, so Caroline stopped feeling conspicuous about her own clothes.

"Hi," Liv said. She smiled carefully, but didn't offer her hand. "I don't think I was around much when you were training, so we likely never met."

Probably not a bad thing. Caroline had heard the little speech Liv gave after her horse won the Breeders' Cup Classic, about racing drug-free. The way Caroline had operated as a trainer hadn't exactly aligned with that lofty initiative.

Faye pushed a tray of paper coffee cups toward her. "Grab a cappuccino. Or I can make you tea or get you something cold, if you prefer."

"Cappuccino's great, thanks," Caroline said, wiggling it free of the pressboard. "Where do you get it around here?"

"Faye runs the Triple Shot Café in town," Emilie said. "It's on the main street, north side, in a strip mall, so you might miss it if you're not looking. Be sure to try the butter tarts when you go." The last bit was added as if visiting was a foregone conclusion.

"This is great cappuccino," Caroline said after taking a sip.

"Wait till you see dessert," Emilie said. "Faye's fiancé is a pastry chef."

"I'm destined to be two hundred pounds." Faye grinned, picking up the salad and passing it to Caroline. "Let's eat. I wouldn't want to be responsible for you being late getting back to work."

Her grin suggested she would be just fine with that and would defend Caroline to Dean if need be. Caroline had no idea what she'd done to earn Faye's allegiance, but she'd take it.

Liv excused herself when her phone vibrated, turning away and typing a message before setting it aside. "That was Dean. I didn't have the chance to tell you." Her eyes flashed to Faye. "We breezed a couple of two-year-olds with his two this morning. Crystal's colt spooked at some Canada Geese and dropped her. Dean's just leaving the hospital now. She still hasn't been seen."

"Oh no!" Faye said.

"Poor Crystal. I hope it's not serious." Emilie frowned.

"Her colt ducked pretty hard," Liv said. "Fleur was so out of it I had a front-row seat."

"Poor Dean," Faye muttered. "He doesn't need to be out an exercise rider, too."

"We'll help him until he finds someone," Liv said.

Caroline kept quiet, trying not to shovel food into her mouth. She hadn't worked this hard in a long time. And she certainly didn't want to contribute to a conversation about track accidents. Just the thought made her skin clammy.

"So," Faye said, turning her attention to Caroline. "Dean mentioned you're married? I can ask you now that you have the job."

Did she actually have the job? Caroline wasn't sure Dean and Faye were on the same page regarding her employment.

"Not anymore," she said and stuffed the sandwich in her mouth, hoping that topic was done. She didn't want to talk about that, either. She should have ignored her stomach and resisted the lunch invite.

"Oh. I'm sorry," Faye said.

Caroline's eyes shifted, and she swallowed. "You're engaged, though?" The only way to avoid more awkward questions was to take control of the conversation. "When's the wedding?"

"End of the summer. Probably. It's not set in stone yet."

"They're getting married," Emilie clarified. "But because Will is a caterer and Faye is, uh, *thrifty*, they're trying to do it on the cheap. Call in favours, that sort of thing."

Caroline had no idea why they were telling her all of this, like she was an old friend they were catching up on all the news since their last get-together. She could use that in her favour, though. It wouldn't hurt to get up to speed. And if everything worked out — namely getting the apartment —it might feel less isolating if lunch invites with Faye and her friends were part of the deal.

"Can you fill me in on what I've missed in the last ten years?" Maybe she'd find out if she did need to be concerned about ever showing her face on the backstretch again.

"As in, who's with whom?" Emilie laughed, sounding as if she was eager to update Caroline on episodes of a reality TV show. "Absolutely. Let's start with Faye, formerly of 'I don't get attached' fame."

Caroline almost spit up the mouthful of water she'd just taken. They were so candid, it was hilarious. Except Liv, who watched with a measured smile.

"Faye finally had a relationship that lasted longer than a month, though it was still with her go-to of Woodbine's hot apprentice rider *du jour*. Have you heard of Nate Miller? Him. Except, unbeknownst to anyone," Emilie paused, rolling her eyes. "Nate was in love with Liv. Faye called him out on it and dumped him. Long, angsty story short, Liv and Nate finally figured it out and got married a year and a half ago. Faye's betrothed, Will, is Nate's best friend from Calgary. He's a musician as well as a pastry chef. They got engaged this past Christmas."

Caroline found herself grinning. This was more fun than she'd had in years. She couldn't wait to tell Jess, even though Jess didn't live for gossip the way Caroline did. The best part was, she had no reason to think any of them knew a thing about her reputation.

"The story gets better," Faye jumped in, shooting a look at Emilie. "Nate has a younger brother. *Obviously,* it was only right that Emilie and the brother would end up together. Even if it wasn't automatic, destiny would not be denied. So, Emilie's next. She's going to marry Tim and be a hockey wife. Yes, that's right, the hot-bug-now-top-Woodbine-rider's brother is a professional hockey player."

"If you stick around, you'll get used to this," Liv interjected.

"I just thought we needed a little welcome to Northwest lunch," Faye said.

"Also known as, tell us everything about yourself we don't already know." Emilie leaned in with an impish expression. "Like, why does Dean hate you?"

Caroline reached for the salad bowl, glancing at Faye. Clearly, his animosity was obvious. Had Dean not told his sister anything? Would Faye be so supportive if he had? She shrugged. "We were rivals. I might have done some things he didn't approve of."

"That story sounds as if it might require wine." Emilie grinned.

Lots of it.

"That could be arranged," Faye quipped. "Not while there's still work to be done, of course. My brother would kill me for getting his new manager drunk before the horses were taken care of."

Emilie snorted, but Caroline couldn't help the worry that seeped in. "You make it sound as if Dean is going to let me stay. You don't even know what happened."

"I am not one to talk about past indiscretions," Faye said. "'Judge not lest you be judged,' right?"

"And now she's quoting bible verses," Liv said dryly.

Faye laughed. "If Liv and I can still be friends after our history, I'm confident you and Dean can overcome your differences. I will be your champion."

"Why?" Caroline was truly mystified.

"Because this farm needs you. Dean needs you."

Caroline couldn't help it. She liked these girls. At first, she'd been intimidated, feeling like a crone among three young roses, but they'd successfully worn down her defences.

"So, I know about Liv and Nate Miller, you and the pastry chef, and Emilie and the hockey player," Caroline asked cautiously. "What about Dean?"

Faye rolled her eyes, pushing a plate of delectable-looking pastries towards her. "Dean? Dean is hopeless."

Squeak was long gone, no surprise.

But hay nets were full, water buckets topped up and feed tubs all in. Squeak wasn't irresponsible, he just had boundaries. Dean couldn't fault him for that.

He took care of the horses — threatening to try to breeze Cruze again tomorrow, because the colt was squealing in his stall instead of sleeping for a change —then picked Crystal up from the hospital, got her prescription for painkillers filled at the pharmacy, and drove her home before returning to the track to swap vehicles. He'd figure out how to get her car back to her another time. It wasn't as if she'd be driving for a while. Diagnosis? Seriously dislocated shoulder. Treatment? Rest and rehabilitation. Three months of it.

His truck was gloriously spacious after Crystal's tin can. Before heading to the farm, he swung by the race office to pick up a worksheet. Only Gastronomy and Liv's chestnut, Just

Cash It, had gone fast enough for their names to appear. Andy would — hopefully — be pleased.

When he rambled up the pot-holed laneway at Northwest, Dean exhaled, seeing Caroline's car still there. As much as he hated to admit it, it was a godsend she'd come today — not that he was ready to thank Faye for overriding him.

He wished he could slink into the house, but he needed to check on her, help bring in horses — and make sure she was coming back tomorrow. Outside the layup barn, colourful dandy brushes were lined up in the grass like so many sunbathers at the beach. Dean stopped short, starting when Caroline burst from the barn swinging a white bucket and started dropping the brushes into it.

"They looked like they hadn't been washed in a while," she explained, her words clipped.

Was she actually calling him out for having dirty brushes? Admittedly, she was used to the track. Grooms disinfected their brushes every day. The farm didn't adhere to the same stringency.

"Thank you," he managed, following slowly as she retreated into the barn's dark aisle.

She'd done a better job of the stalls than he'd been doing. Did he dare mention she didn't need to bed as deep as at the track? He wasn't cheap, but he *was* poor. Shavings cost a fortune.

Even the water buckets looked like they'd been scrubbed, and had she done cobwebs, too? She must really want this job. It still baffled him, both that she wanted to work on a farm, and that she wanted to work for *him*.

Ride The Wave nickered as he approached, and Dean's eyes landed on the front bandages before he dug for a peppermint. The edges of the brown paper covering the poultice peeked out on the injured leg, the clean red nylon wrap spaced with even precision. Day-old bandages didn't look that tidy.

"Faye told me you were held up with your exercise rider, so I took care of him for you. He's walked, hosed and done up." Caroline's voice lilted from the tack room. "How is she, by the way? Is she okay?"

"I told you to leave him." As much as he tried to keep his voice even, it had an edge. He was tired, but he'd still been looking forward to walking his big horse — after something to eat, at least. It was part of his decompression routine, the same way he loved wandering with Gus through the hay fields. Was that the reason it annoyed him so much? Or was it the nagging voice whispering that control was slipping through his fingers? It felt like a competition — and Caroline was determined to beat him. Before long, she'd probably be gunning to take his charges at the track.

"Don't get mad at me for helping." She cut in front of him and lifted The Wave's muzzle in her hands to plant a noisy kiss between his nostrils. "He told me what he likes. We're besties now. I think I might've wrapped that right one too tight, but don't worry, the bandage bow means he'll match now."

This is why hiring someone overqualified was a bad idea. But Dean could hear Faye's words. *You're not really in a position to be picky.* Especially considering Caroline had probably done a better job than he would have in his current state of fatigue. The Wave had been given the time he deserved, when Dean might have short-changed the horse so that he could finally put his feet up after a long, long day.

Caroline stepped back, glancing at him as if she'd just realized how close they stood. "If you're so worried, take them off and reset them."

"I'm sorry. I appreciate it," he said, finding his manners. "And to answer your question, my exercise rider is out for three months. Dislocated shoulder." He reached a hand to The Wave's neck, then looked steadily at Caroline. "*You* gallop." If she was so eager to help him out.

"Not anymore," she said crisply, scooting around him. "I'll bring in those two broodmares while you find something else I've done wrong." She grabbed a pair of rope shanks and strode out of the barn.

Dean tore his eyes from her departing silhouette and turned back to The Wave. "Are you really besties?"

The Wave tossed his head — coincidentally, of course — but Dean laughed.

"Traitor."

CHAPTER SIXTEEN

THE FIRST PERSON Dean saw when he entered the Triple Stripe shed the next morning was Jo St-Laurent, Liv's assistant trainer. A tall, solid man leaned on the wall next to her — Elliot, her fiancé. Another reminder Dean was being left behind. Dean and Jo had gone out exactly once. While they'd not wanted for things to talk about because of the horses, both had agreed at the end of the evening that all they'd felt was mutual respect.

"Hey, Dean," Jo said. "I heard about your exercise rider. Sorry."

"Thanks. I've come to poach yours."

Jo laughed. "Liv should be back from the track soon. We'll figure it out."

The words were barely out of her mouth when Liv came around the corner followed by Nate, both of them on hot, blowing horses, nostrils flared with rapid breaths. Dean stood aside while the workers were tended to.

"What do you need, Dean?" Liv asked once the horses

were untacked and getting baths on the apron in front of the barn.

"I have a few to gallop. And I think I want to send that colt who dropped Crystal again. It wasn't like he made time."

"You could figure out how fast he went," Nate said. "You majored in Physics, didn't you? I'm picturing you in front of a whiteboard with vector diagrams."

Dean was not interested in Miller's smart-ass commentary this morning but stopped himself from responding.

"Ignore him," Liv said, but there was an amused twist to her lips. "What about if we send him with Paz?"

"Our pony is a questionable role model," Nate said drolly.

Liv did ignore him this time, focusing on Dean. "What do you think? I'll get on your colt, Nicole can get on the pony. Paz is due some fun."

"Sorry I have to miss it. Make sure you video again, Dean." Nate kissed Liv and left.

Dean wasn't sorry to see him go.

"We've got one more set," Liv said. "We'll be over after that?"

"Thank you," Dean said, hoping she didn't regret the offer. Liv was a better rider than Crystal, but no one was immune to the antics of an unpredictable two-year-old.

He returned to his barn, ready to light a fire under Squeak because they needed to get three horses ready. At first, he ignored the stranger — a young man, maybe twenty, almost six foot — who looked as if he had turned right when around here everyone turned left. Then Dean remembered — the summer intern from the employment program. That was this morning? It figured. The newcomer rocked on the heels of cowboy boots, hands jammed in his jeans pockets. The shiny boots needed to go. Mucking stalls and bathing horses would rot them in no time.

What was the kid's name? Dean had been so preoccupied lately he'd failed to commit it to memory and was about to check his phone for the email when the kid made eye contact.

"You must be our new recruit," Dean said, offering a hand as he closed the space between them, hoping the greeting would prompt the young man to introduce himself.

The kid returned the gesture confidently. "Nice to meet you, Mr Taylor."

"Dean is fine." No one had even called his father Mr Taylor.

"Thank you, sir."

Dean didn't feel like either a mister or a sir, and couldn't decide if he should appreciate the formality as a sign of respect or disparage it as an indication the kid thought he was old. Considering he couldn't remember the young man's name, the age thing might be justified.

"We've got a busy morning, so don't be offended if you don't get to do a lot right away — or if you're asked to just stand clear. Things can happen quickly with these horses and I don't want you getting hurt."

"Oh, I'm experienced, sir. I'm ready to jump right in."

Dean gave him a patient smile. *It's a different world in here, kid.* Henry? Harley? It would come to him. Now, what could Dean get him to do that wouldn't get him killed on his first day?

"Come with me." Hank?

Dean led the way to the stall of his mare, She Brews, and talked to her kindly as he pushed back the stall gate, snapping it out of the way. He led her to the back wall and tied her up.

"There's a grooming kit on the foot locker across from the stall. That's yours. Use your brushes on your horses only." Not that Squeak would let the kid touch any of his charges. "This is Sheba. Clean her feet and knock her off. You don't need to make a production of it."

The kid looked alarmed. "Knock... her... off?"

"That's track speak for give her a quick brush. Knock the dust off her, so to speak." Dean ducked under the stall guard and tapped the kid on the arm. "You'll learn the language. In a few weeks, it'll be second nature." Dean chose to believe the kid would still be around in a few weeks. Huey?

It had been so long since he'd trained anyone, Dean had forgotten how to go about it. Grooms had always come to him with some degree of experience; it was just a matter of them learning his preferences. Dean watched for a moment as the kid — Harvey? No, it had been something modern — located the hoof pick and entered the stall. He started with the left fore, then shifted to the left hind.

"Do them all from the same side."

The kid looked up. "Really? Why?"

"It's more efficient. They're all used to it. With her, she likes it best if you take the off hind leg back instead of in front of the other hind."

Dean left the kid with a quizzical look on his face. He didn't have time to hover; he needed to get the third horse ready.

He put Liv on Epi, because even though Liv wasn't presently licenced as a jockey she had been in the past, and Andy would like that. Nicole got Fargo, because she was the more experienced of the other two and the old horse could be tough.

"She Brews isn't tacked up yet," Dean said apologetically to Marie. "I have a new groom who just started today. He's as green as they come."

"I can do it," Marie said.

"Watch Marie today," Dean said to the kid. Harold? Harry? "We'll have more time tomorrow so you can try it yourself."

The kid attempted to flirt with Marie as they got She Brews ready. Dean needed to find an ugly old exercise rider to gallop his horses while Crystal was off if this kid had any hope of working out. He found himself wishing — not for the first time — that he could go back in time a month. Back to the status quo. Nikki running the shed. Stacy managing the farm. Crystal and Squeak bickering.

Faye not moving out.

Monique single.

The Wave sound.

A fancy two-year-old at the start of the season, making promises this would be Dean's best yet.

"All set?" he asked when Marie turned She Brews to the door of the stall, bridle on. He nodded at the kid. "Snap a shank on the bit and take him a turn before Marie gets on."

"A what?" the kid asked.

Marie laughed, pointing at the equipment in question, hanging on the stall door. "Lead shank. Don't they teach you anything at school?"

She could get away with saying what Dean couldn't. When the kid walked off leading She Brews, Dean held his breath. If he could make it around, it would be a good start.

"Did he tell you his name?" Dean asked.

Marie, who Dean had never really heard say much, laughed. "You don't know his name?"

Dean shrugged. "I've got it somewhere."

"Hunter."

He had to keep from smacking himself on the forehead. How had he forgotten that?

Hunter successfully made it a turn, and Dean legged Marie up. "Do the stall while we're gone. We'll be back in about twenty minutes."

What were the chances the kid had ever mucked straw? *Don't stab yourself with a pitchfork.*

After the set, Liv stuck around to help, walking Epi while

Dean bathed She Brews, Hunter observing. Squeak had his last horse tacked up for Liv to gallop once she put Epi away, and Dean stayed back to organize Cruze so he'd be ready once she returned.

As long as he told himself not to look at the stalls Hunter had mucked, all was good. Who was Dean to judge, anyway? His own mucking skills weren't up to the likes of Squeak and Nikki... and Caroline. Dean banished her from his mind. She took up unnecessary space.

By the time Nicole showed up with Paz — dressed in his pony tack — Dean felt as if everything might be under control. He tossed Liv up on Cruze and followed them out with a warning to Squeak.

"Take it easy on my new help. Please? No misadventures. No wild goose chases." Racetrackers were notorious pranksters, preying on gullible newcomers like Hunter.

He joined Len at the rail of the training track. Because, of course, Len was there. Especially after yesterday's performance, the old trainer wasn't about to miss this. Cruze had a reputation. For infamy.

"Do over?" Len said, eyes twinkling under the brim of his hat.

Dean nodded. "I'm afraid to watch."

He scanned the ditch for lurking avians. The coast was clear. Besides, Cruze seemed preoccupied with his company. He tried to bite the Triple Stripe pony as they started jogging, and Paz pinned his ears and snarled back. A match made in heaven.

They made it to the backstretch together. Dean could see Cruze's head bobbing when they turned in to stand facing across the infield and he wasn't sure, but it looked like Nicole bopped him in the nose. They set off together, Nicole keeping a tight hold on the colt's head until they reached the head of the stretch. If the pony outworked his colt, Dean would never hear the end of it. He clicked his stopwatch when they reached the red and white pole and hoped for the best.

All Cruze had to do was cover a quarter mile in twenty-six seconds or less — preferably in a straight line.

Cruze made time. Only just, but Dean would take the small victories right now. Things were looking up.

———

Dean returned to the farm to find Caroline leading a mare on either side, Cherry's full belly swinging like a pendulum with each step. He intercepted them before they reached the barn. He'd been counting on Cherry to be honest and stick to her usual predictability, foaling close to her due date, but she was looking like she might have other ideas this year.

"Hold up." He checked Cherry quickly, then took the rope from Caroline. "Keep a close watch on her now. She'll foal soon."

Caroline's brow creased, and it appeared she was biting the inside of her cheek. "What am I looking for?"

"You've never seen a mare foal before?"

She shook her head, leading the grey mare into the barn in front of him.

In the stall, Dean removed Cherry's halter, surprised by the hint of insecurity Caroline showed after all of her earlier attitude. "Trust me, you'll know. Call me if you're the least bit suspicious. I lost a foal this spring, so I'd rather a false alarm than lost time in an emergency." Not that constant monitoring had prevented the tragedy in February.

She hung the rope shank next to his. "Don't you use those milk test strips?"

"They're not going to tell me anything I don't already know."

"How *do* you know?"

Dean raised an eyebrow. Here was something he was actually better at than her. "Come see."

She followed him back into the stall, Cherry too focused on the pile of hay under her feed tub to care about his poking and prodding as he pointed out the indicators.

"It helps I know her. She's a veteran, and she's textbook."

He stood back as Caroline ran her hands over the slack muscles of Cherry's flattened croup, her face studious.

"I think I feel it," she said. Cherry's tail rose lightly as Caroline ran her fingers over the fleshy underside.

"There's a camera." Dean pointed to the corner of the stall.

"Is it one of those webcams? Are you going to give me the URL?"

He had to keep from laughing. The internet here wasn't good enough for that. It was line of sight, and only worked from the apartment over the layup barn. Then it dawned on him. "Shoot. The apartment. Are you okay with staying there? It's unlocked. I'll get you the key later."

Caroline grinned like she'd just won a point in their match. "Thanks."

So, she was moving in. It was that, or bed down in the apartment himself.

"Don't get too comfortable," he grumbled, and she rolled her eyes, hard, as he turned away. "You can bring your car up. There's room to park next to the tractor."

He'd noticed the hatchback packed with her belongings and hadn't asked where she'd been staying. On the one hand, she irked him like fingernails on a chalkboard; on the other, denying her a place to stay — something that had been in black and white on the job posting — was unnecessary.

"Uh, Dean? One more thing?"

He stopped, halfway out the door.

"How am I supposed to call you?"

She held out her phone, open at a new contact she'd created. Dean typed in the digits and handed the phone back. She had an amused look, like getting his number was another point for her.

Faye was in the kitchen, tending a pot of something on the stove, Gus dancing at her feet. He'd had no time for the dog lately. More guilt. But the smell of whatever Faye was cooking made his stomach rumble. Food first, then sleep. If Cherry was this close to foaling, he had to grab it when he could.

"How'd it go today?" Faye asked.

"Good." He grinned. "I got a taste of what having a big outfit must feel like." In just over an hour, Liv and her crew had gotten his horses out — a fraction of the time it took with one exercise rider.

"Liv said she'd help you out as long as you need."

"I can't rely on her forever."

"At least things seem to be going well with Caroline."

Dean snorted. "I guess."

"You're being awfully hard on her. She seems perfectly lovely." Faye arranged a series of meal-size plastic containers on the counter and began portioning her creation into them. "And, she *is* doing you a favour."

He scowled. "She's doing a job. She's being paid. I'm doing *her* a favour."

"How about we agree that I did *you* a favour, overriding your grumpiness?"

He was not a grump. But Caroline was bringing out parts of him he didn't understand.

"In case I need to remind you," Faye continued, turning and leaning against the counter. "I own half this place, so I have a say. Whatever history is between you and this woman, it's just that. History. If she does something truly wrong, like showing up to work drunk, or not showing up at all, then fire her. But as long as the only thing wrong with her is that she bothers you, suck it up."

Dean wandered over, the food calling to him, suppressing a smile. "Yes ma'am."

Faye grinned and nodded. "Glad we got that sorted out."

"By the way, Cherry's getting close, so Caroline will be staying in the apartment tonight."

"It's about time." Faye stashed one of the containers and a little white bag from the café in a red grocery store sack and headed for the door. "Come on, Gus. Let's go take Caroline her dinner."

CHAPTER SEVENTEEN

THE STAIRS to the apartment seemed solid, the railing secure — which was a good thing, because Caroline's legs were not. She was worn out, her body feeling the effects of physical labour after ten years away from it.

She secured the deadbolt behind her. This place was out in the country, with neighbours nowhere in sight, and she didn't imagine there were security cameras around — only the foaling mare got one of those. There wasn't even a lock on the gate to the barnyard. She envisioned intruders trekking across the back fields in the dark, far from the farmhouse where Dean and Faye were oblivious to the danger lurking in the shadows.

The apartment wasn't large — a kitchenette, a sitting room with a television, a bathroom and a small bedroom. What more did she need, though? She'd been lost in Bryce's McMansion — and relieved he hired a cleaner. The wall decor was a far cry from Bryce's collection of huge original abstracts. That was probably another red flag she'd ignored. Not a single horse had decorated his walls. Here, an assortment of old racing posters hung, some in cheap metal frames, others mounted on board. Not a Munnings in sight, but at least there were horses.

Caroline slung her overnight bag onto the bed — all she'd bothered to bring in — and not just because of Dean's comment about not getting comfortable. He'd keep her on. He had to. He had bigger problems with the situation at the track. No, unpacking would have taken more effort than she could muster right now. She'd do it bit by bit — if she became convinced she should stay.

There were a few things left in the fridge and cupboards, and nothing growing, which was a relief. No alcohol anywhere — probably just as well. She grabbed a water bottle from the fridge and sat at the small kitchen table, scarfing down the pasta casserole and salad Faye had brought her, filling the hole in her stomach, if not her heart. She'd save dessert for later. Maybe that would do it.

The silence was eerie. The walls must've been well-insulated because she couldn't hear the horses below. Someone could climb right up those stairs and ambush her. Caroline double-checked the door was locked, then remembered the foaling camera.

A small monitor rested in the kitchen window — that must be it. She located the on switch, the screen brightening to reveal a grainy image of Cherry, quietly munching hay. How was she supposed to deduce anything from that? Moving it was pointless, the signal lost from anywhere but the window sill where she'd found it.

The idea of staying awake all night when she was so exhausted felt impossible. The job posting had said nothing about nightwatching. She should have refused, let Dean do it himself — except it was the only reason he'd finally conceded the apartment. If she failed at this, she'd be kicked out for sure.

She'd better call Jess — who, unlike her, would get to go to bed — and let her know she wouldn't be back tonight.

"Hey, how's it going?" Jess sounded like her mouth was full and picturing her eating at the kitchen island made Caroline feel a little less lonely.

"Dean has finally deigned me worthy of staying in the apartment. Probably just because he says the mare is going to foal soon." With a glance at Cherry's fuzzy shape, Caroline slumped into the couch.

"That's progress."

"I thought yesterday he was going to ask me to gallop for him."

"You could."

"I'm done with galloping. We're too old for that crazy shit."

"You know I'm going to start Mulder if he doesn't sell next year," Jess said.

"Are you now?"

"He'd better sell, that's all I'm saying."

They both laughed.

Caroline knew she should let Jess go, but wasn't ready. "I'm not sure I can do the farm thing, Jess. It's so remote out here. I don't know how you handle it."

"The house isn't that far away, is it?"

"It's far enough that I could bleed out after having my throat slashed."

"Dean would find you in the morning."

"He'd probably think I was a no-show."

"Until the body started to smell."

"He'd be mad at me because of all the blood. It's a bitch to clean up." Caroline dragged herself up to check the monitor. "I'd better go. I don't trust this foaling camera. I'm going down."

"Why do I have a feeling now I'm not going to see you any more than when you were out west?"

"I get a day and a half off every week. We'll get together. I'll be desperate to get off this place."

"We'll go to the Plate!" Jess suggested.

"I don't know about that."

"You can't hide forever, Caroline."

She was sure she could, for the next three months. The farm was one degree of separation too close to the racetrack and her checkered past.

Before leaving the apartment, she glanced once more at the monitor. Her heart stuttered.

Cherry was flat out. In a flash, Caroline raced down the stairs, adrenaline obliterating the ache of her muscles. She skittered to a halt outside the barn and regrouped, trying to be quiet as she entered and sneaked up to the stall.

To be greeted by Cherry, on her sternum, her ears flipping forward as Caroline peeked at her. The mare launched to her feet, shook free the straw sticking to her coat, and began picking at the remaining bits of hay.

False alarm. o

Her pulse recovered as she threw all three mares a flake, checked waters, and paused to give Jaida's colt a scratch — escaping before his grunts of pleasure turned to a nip.

Inside the layup barn, Ride The Wave's head poked out as soon as she flipped on the lights. He already had her trained — she fished a peppermint from her pocket, and he scooped it up, then lipped at her sleeve, looking for more.

"I'm sure I'll see you again before long." She'd need to keep moving to stay awake.

A more thorough search of the kitchen cupboards produced a jar of instant coffee, though it took a knife to loosen the granules. What she wouldn't give for a Starbucks from DoorDash right now. She drank the mixture black — or whatever colour that was — and wished she'd thought to ask Faye for some milk, though the chocolate croissant that had been in the care package made up for it.

The TV remote yielded a more convincing picture than the foaling monitor, but the channels were limited. Hockey. Really? Would it never end? It was June; they should all be playing golf by now.

Outside, the halogen light, high on its pole, barely put a dent in the heavy blanket of darkness closing in now that the sun had disappeared. If she couldn't handle one night, there was no way she'd make it three months. She took her cup to the sink to rinse it out and checked the camera.

It already felt like the longest night of her life.

A text woke her. Damn it, she'd dozed. Caroline squinted at the time, then the message. Four AM; it was Dean, telling her to sleep because he'd be around for a couple of hours. Liv was sending her swing groom over to lend a hand at the track so he wasn't heading in as early as usual, and then Faye would be around. He said Cherry wouldn't foal during the day, but if she made a liar out of him, Caroline could call Liv's farm manager. He left her number.

She fumbled out a thanks and crawled gratefully into bed, fully clothed, and didn't stir until rapping dragged her from a dreamless sleep.

It was Emilie, her smile as bright as the sun that lit a perfect blue sky. She proffered a coffee cup. "Did you sleep?"

"Like the dead," Caroline said, her voice gritty.

"I thought you might appreciate a cappuccino and some help with stalls."

"Wow." She blinked, still groggy. Maybe this was a dream.

At feed time when she brought Cherry in, Caroline peeked

at the mare's udder and it looked just like photos she'd seen in horse care books of waxing, one of the signs of a foal's imminent arrival. What yesterday had been like crystallized honey at the end of each teat today was a creamy ivory. Caroline felt Cherry's croup, and either side of the tail head was even mushier.

"If she doesn't have it tonight, I'll take you to dinner at the nicest restaurant in town after the foal arrives," Dean said after making his own assessment. Then he looked uncomfortable and in a hurry to leave. "Call me. No napping."

He might be telling her stories. She'd read plenty on the internet; people staying awake every night for weeks before a foal arrived. Caroline hoped he was right because the thought of missing another night of sleep pained her — and enduring an awkward dinner with Dean Taylor wasn't on her list of fun things to do, even if it meant him admitting he'd been wrong.

Dean was right. When Cherry was ready to go, Caroline just knew.

She grappled for her phone, hands trembling so badly she nearly dropped it, thumbs thick as she searched for Dean's number in her contacts. There it was.

"'Lo?" His voice was gravelly with sleep.

"She's started!" Caroline breathed.

"On my way," he said, with none of the excitement and terror she felt.

Shoving her phone in the back pocket of her jeans, she bolted down the stairs to the barn. Cherry made a slow circuit of the stall. Her coat had dark patches of sweat, straw sticking to her because she'd been rolling.

Dean sauntered into the barn soon after, hair mussed, wearing a baggy sweatshirt over pyjama bottoms, his lack of urgency frustrating as Caroline tried to hide that she was freaking out. Her already racing heart flip-flopped. Even when he looked a shambles, he was appealing. It was aggravating.

"Grab a tail bandage," he said in a level voice, peering into the stall instead of at her. "There's one ready on the counter in the tack room, a red one. And bring some gloves. The long ones; they're on the counter too."

Caroline nodded and practically skipped there, feeling twelve. She was finally going to see a foal born. *Please let everything go right.* Fumbling, she tucked the bandage under her arm and pulled a pair of the long, translucent surgical sleeves from the box, not knowing how many he would need. Dean accepted the tail bandage wordlessly and slid the stall door open. Caroline hovered.

"You could hold her head for me. Seeing as you're here."

The way he said it reminded her he didn't really *want* her here. He wrapped Cherry's tail with practiced ease, assessing the mare as he did so, and stepped back to the door. Caroline slipped past to watch from behind him.

"Now what?" she asked, voice hushed.

"We wait." He glanced at her. "How have you been in horses this long and never seen a foal born?"

"Farm is a four-letter word, that's how."

To Caroline's surprise, Dean chuckled.

She'd read enough to know horses were different from humans. Labour was much shorter, once the mare decided the time was right. Cherry resumed her circling, as if their interruption had merely pressed a pause button. Her nose grazed the deep straw like she was preparing to lie down. The patches of sweat had grown to darken her whole body.

The mare was in a zone, detached from her surroundings. She rolled once, then got back up, and circled again. A shiny white bubble bulged under her tail and then erupted, sending fluid gushing over her hocks.

"Now we check to make sure the foal's in the right position," Dean said in that same, level tone.

We? Caroline's bravado had left the building.

"Grab a glove," he said.

She held out one of the long sleeves.

He took it then jutted his chin at her. "You should do this. It's really cool."

She looked at him uncertainly, but he had an uncharacteristically encouraging look that gave her flashbacks to the eighteen-year-old she'd met so many years ago.

"What do I do?" she asked.

"Just slide your arm in. You should find the foal's feet first, one in front of the other, then a little further along, the nose."

The walls of the birth canal were slippery, and it was easy to fit her hand in. It amazed her how much space there was, though it had to be wide enough to let a hundred pounds of baby horse through. She felt the first hoof, the other resting alongside the pastern, then the nose, slightly squishy after the firmness of the limbs. A smile crept over her face as she slowly withdrew her arm. When she glanced at Dean he was smiling too.

"Cool, right?"

She laughed. "Aren't you going to check?"

"It's fine. I believe you."

Caroline's eyes locked on his, and it surprised her how much those words meant. Dean pulled his gaze away first, his focus back on the mare.

"Cherry's an old pro, but some of them aren't so bright. Especially maidens, so you have to make sure they lie down in a spot that leaves room or you find yourself trying to deliver a foal into a wall. Fortunately, not too many of them do it standing up."

"I can't imagine a crash landing is a great way to come into the world."

"You catch them as best you can, but it's much better for all concerned when the mare lies down."

Once it started, everything happened quickly. Cherry folded into the straw and flattened. With only a couple of massive, straining contractions, two little feet jutted out, encased in their pearly membrane.

Caroline knelt beside Dean, grasping one leg while he took the other. She shoved aside how near he was and what his calm assuredness was doing to her. She was *not* attracted to that. The physical part she could understand, sure, but the essence of him wasn't something she would sign up for.

"Pull towards the hocks when she pushes," Dean instructed. "Think of the foal diving in an arc over the pelvic rim."

What a perfect visual. Caroline stole a glance at him. His hair fell in his eyes as he did more than his share of the work — while she was feeling things she didn't want to be feeling. She snapped her head back to Cherry and the foal. The head was out now.

Sweat trickled from her brow and down her back. Dean reached over, his arm brushing her hand as he grasped above it and gave a tug on the leg she held. Caroline felt the foal shift and progress a few more inches.

"Almost there," Dean said.

"How the hell do these things survive in the wild?" Caroline gasped for breath. She hadn't expected it to be a workout.

Dean laughed. "I'm not positive Thoroughbreds would."

Just when she was sure it was never coming out, the foal slipped onto the straw like it was on a water slide. Dean peeled the thin membrane away and Caroline watched the foal's first, disoriented movements. It blinked. She blinked.

She hadn't noticed Dean leaving until he tossed her a towel.

"Just rub it all over."

The foal came to life under her touch, its breath short puffs, ribcage heaving like it had just run a race. Only then did she notice tears mingled with the sweat streaming down her face.

Dean crouched next to her, wiping the foal's nostrils with another towel. He stopped, frowning at her. "What's wrong?"

She laughed and swiped the towel over her eyes and cheeks, even though it was soaked with the same rank smell that filled the stall.

"This is both the grossest and most beautiful thing I've ever experienced, that's all." Her knees squished and she would have shuddered had she not been completely taken with the foal's long eyelashes and the huge star that filled its forehead.

She got out of the way and watched Dean move about, disinfecting the umbilical stump and tying the afterbirth out of the way once Cherry clambered to her feet. The mare nickered low to her foal — a filly, Dean announced. The way the baby nickered back melted Caroline's heart.

They left the stall, standing side by side, watching. Fatigue draped Caroline like someone had thrown a heavy cloak over her. She couldn't remember being so tired.

"Now, can we go to bed?" she asked.

Dean slid her a slow gaze, and her face, which surely must have still been flushed from the effort of helping pull the foal, burned.

One side of his mouth twitched. "The night is young, Caroline."

CHAPTER EIGHTEEN

Which meant, making sure the foal stood, making sure the foal nursed, making sure the foal got up and down on its own. Cleaning the stall, putting down fresh straw. Giving Cherry warm water and a hot mash. Inspecting the placenta to check there were no missing pieces. And so on.

Nothing like the innuendo of Caroline's comment. The way her face had found a deeper shade of pink indicated it had been innocent, so why had Dean's mind gone there? Probably a sign that Faye was right. He needed to follow up on that dating app. Because even if the comment hadn't been an allusion and he let go of all the wrong Caroline had done him, he wasn't getting involved with an employee.

"Go get some sleep," he said.

"No, that's okay. It's my job," she insisted, though she looked as if she might pass out on the first horizontal surface she found that wasn't made of asphalt. "You have to go to the track in the morning so you need the rest. Let me know what I have to do."

How did he tell her he needed to do this himself without

hurting her feelings? He'd lost one foal already this year. Everything had gone smoothly so far with Cherry, but he couldn't ignore the possibility of post-foaling complications.

"It's my responsibility," he said. "It wouldn't be fair to put that on you."

"I'll keep you company, then."

He didn't want her company. They might have had a moment as they witnessed that gross and beautiful thing —to use her words — where it felt like their negative history had been smudged away, but the afterglow was gone. "There's no sense both of us being exhausted tomorrow."

"Please?"

Dean didn't know what was behind her earnestness, and it caught him off guard. But he was too tired to argue. "Fine, if that's what you want to do."

They moved a couple of straw bales near the stall and then Dean went to the fridge in the tack room, grabbing two cans.

"Dr Pepper?" she questioned, peering at the logo when he handed her one.

He pulled the tab, a wisp of carbonation escaping. "This was my dad's tradition. We'd always have it after the last foal. The caffeine will help keep us awake."

It wasn't a toast; he didn't wait for her to open her can before taking a sip, the sweetness going right to the part of his brain where those memories were stored. They were good ones, mostly, in this barn. Thankfully, incidents like he'd had in February were rare.

He glanced into the stall where mare and filly made a perfect picture, curled up in their thick bed, then sat on one of the bales, resting his head against the wall. Caroline kept staring at him like they'd shared something profound. But no matter how hard he tried to keep sentimentality at bay, a new foal was always a miracle, and he could tell she'd felt it.

"Do you regret it? All that school?"

Dean slid her a wary look. He'd regret letting her stay if she thought it gave her license to bring up the past. The subject of his education brought with it less popular emotions than the soft drink did. "Yes and no. I always kind of liked school."

"You looked like that kid."

His eyebrows crept up. "What's that supposed to mean?"

"Sorry, you were cute, but a total geek. The kid who played Dungeons and Dragons in high school. Top of the class in math, while people like me were relieved when we graduated and never had to do it again."

"Calculus is fun," he said, putting on a hurt tone.

"How many times have you used *that* training horses? You don't even do the books."

"Bookkeeping and Calculus are worlds apart."

"Whatever you say." She grinned and tried to tuck her hair behind her ear like she used to when they'd first met, but it wasn't long enough anymore. "I was surprised when you left. I thought you wanted to be a trainer. Then I thought, okay. I can see your parents wanting you to get a degree, but I was sure you'd come back after that, not go on to do more school."

"So was I. As it turned out, my father and I didn't see eye to eye on me joining the family business." He didn't know why he'd disclosed that, except that once they'd been friends, and it was easier to lapse than to fight.

"So? Who said you had to work for him?"

"What makes you think I'd have wanted to work for anyone else? He's being inducted into the Canadian Horse Racing Hall of Fame this year. Not everyone wants to lower their standards to get what they want."

"Thanks." Caroline glared at him.

"I didn't mean you." He did.

"Are you sure?" she snapped.

"Are you sure you're not tired?" Because right now, he'd be happy to see her go to bed — alone.

She started twanging the tab on the can with her thumbnail, just to annoy him, he'd bet. "What I really want to know is, if that's how you felt, why didn't you fight for it?"

How could she do that? Come back into his life and pose the question he'd always asked himself? He had to remind himself: they were *not* friends.

She would leave. He would stay. Life would carry on.

"I don't know," he said. "Why did you become the kind of trainer who threw away her horsemanship for shortcuts?"

He expected her to lash out, but her eyes dropped, and she twisted a piece of straw between her fingers. "For the promise of a life I thought I wanted. Nice house, nice things. In case you're wondering, it wasn't worth it. I was horrible, and I know it. If you plan to keep holding it against me, I'll leave. I've done as I was told and not made myself comfortable."

He should want that, for her to go far, far, away and leave him alone. "No."

"Are you sure?" she asked again, meeting his eyes, though this time her voice wavered.

Dean tried to control his exhale. "Yes." He wasn't, not one bit. "You were right. I am desperate." Then he laughed because he couldn't help it.

Caroline's lips crimped into a smile. "So, is it safe to unpack?"

"Make yourself at home."

Cherry clambered to her feet and Dean rose, looking in to see the filly scrambling up on spidery legs and butting her nose under the mare's flank like a pro. He turned back to Caroline. "My turn for a question."

"Sure."

"Are you positive you won't come gallop for me?" He was even more desperate for that.

She looked away, tossing back what was left of the soft drink. "Completely."

"Will you tell me why? I don't believe it's just because you're afraid of the reception you'll receive in there." Anyone who might know her would get over it, though if she was only galloping, who would she be bothering anyway?

"That's part of it," she said.

"What's the other part?" he prodded, crossing his arms and leaning against the stall door.

"You don't remember?" It sounded like an accusation, then all that condemnation turned inward, pain lining her face. "Someone died because of me."

Dean raked his mind, trying to think of the rider fatalities that had happened since he'd returned to take over his father's horses. They were infrequent enough he should be able to recall. The season before she'd disappeared, they hadn't shared a barn anymore. She'd moved up, her stalls in one of the newer buildings.

"I'm sorry, Caroline, I don't remember."

She frowned like she didn't believe him. "I was working a horse on the main track and my left stirrup leather broke. Came off like a lead balloon. My horse freaked out and veered right into a galloper. The horse was okay, but the exercise rider was killed."

It came back to him, but only vaguely. He hadn't known the exercise rider who had died, and the rest of the details had never reached him. What stuck with him most was how crazy brave the people who rode his horses were — and how happy he was to stay on the ground. So how could he judge Caroline for doing the same?

"I didn't know you were involved," he said. "I appreciate you telling me."

She nodded and lapsed into silence, *quid pro quo* over.

By the time Dean was satisfied Cherry and the foal were all right and it was safe to get some sleep, both he and Caroline were struggling to stay conscious. Not enough hours later, he accepted the travel mug Faye passed him on his way out the door. He might have to borrow Len's cot for a nap at the end of morning before he drove home.

Caroline looked as haggard as he did when he checked on the mare and foal before leaving. Coffee and thoughts of her kept him awake on the trip in. *Farm is a four-letter word.* She was such a racetracker — a racetracker who didn't want to be at the racetrack.

As haunted as she was by the accident, it wouldn't be fair to try to change her mind; she'd have to come to the decision herself. And if she did, Dean might admit that the person he'd thought he'd never trust might become someone he could rely on — at least until the end of the summer.

CHAPTER NINETEEN

The filly was too precious for words. All morning, as she dragged herself through chores, Caroline couldn't stop checking on Cherry and the baby, and had to keep herself from texting poorly exposed photos to Dean.

Last night had been surreal. She'd been entirely out of her element — foaling was his arena, not hers, and watching him calmly take charge had been strangely comforting. It had been so nice just to feel close to somebody again, even if it was all her imagination. Then she'd gone and almost ruined everything. The subject of his father was obviously a sore spot with him, but he'd thrown it back in her face, evening the score — then gone one up by dredging up her memory of the accident.

The bottom line was, he was letting her stay, and he texted her early afternoon to say he'd be late getting back; could she take care of The Wave?

Ha. You do trust me.

Caroline smirked and tucked her phone away. No time like the present. She picked up the shank outside The Wave's stall. "Walk with me, handsome."

Her body didn't know what had hit it with this zero-to-sixty fitness program. The Wave strode with purpose, forcing her to pick up her tired feet as they circled the barns. A fence enclosed the yard so if something did happen, a loose horse wasn't getting far. She transferred the leather lead to her left hand, running her right over the muscles of the horse's neck. What would he be like to ride?

Where had that come from? She hadn't been on a horse since the accident. But she wanted to throw the tack on this one; to be on him rather than alongside. She felt safe with The Wave, like he would take care of everything. And here, there was no one else to worry about. If she came off, she was the only one who'd get hurt; The Wave was too sensible to do anything but drop his head and start nibbling the grass along the edges of the drive. He'd probably be the horse who came over and nudged her till she got back to her feet and climbed aboard again.

It was a logical next step in The Wave's recovery. Riding on this firm ground was perfect for tendon rehab. And she wanted to feel that big walk carrying her, to remember the sensation of a powerful horse beneath her.

They were almost finished their allotted time when Dean's truck rumbled up the driveway. She paused. Before last night, Caroline wouldn't have sought Dean out unless she had to — that seemed to work best for both of them — but today it seemed rude not to acknowledge his arrival. So she wheeled The Wave around, cutting the last circuit short, and took him to a spot behind the house that hadn't yet been grazed down. If Dean chose to ignore her, fine, but she would not outright avoid him.

Still, it surprised her when, instead of going directly to the house, he came through the small gate next to the vehicle entrance, sauntering over in that almost lazy, loose-limbed way he had — not that Dean was anything close to lazy. He reminded her of The Wave. They covered ground in a similar fashion.

"How's he doing?" Dean tucked his hands in the pockets of his faded jeans.

He wasn't standing that close, but her breath caught. Nerdy teenager had grown into... this. Caroline flashed a quick smile and returned to the horse, something she could allow herself to fully admire. "Great! Check it out. You can hardly tell it's there."

She pulled The Wave from the patch of grass onto the stonedust, squaring up his front feet. Dean ran his fingers over the tendon before lifting the hoof, shifting his body so he was angled as he palpated it, his torso twisted, too-long hair falling from his forehead. His t-shirt was too loose to really get a clear picture, but Caroline couldn't help noticing the broadness of his back and the muscles of his shoulders, no longer those of a still-growing boy. The Wave bumped her with his nose then wiggled his upper lip against her thigh, showing no discomfort as Dean prodded — pulling Caroline's eyes back to safety.

The Wave *was* ready for the next step. More walking, then adding in some trot work. With a rider. She was just about to open her mouth when Dean set the foot down and gave The Wave a pat.

"You're right. I'll give Liv a call. He's going over to Triple Stripe to breed a couple of test mares. I'll let you know when it's set up." He didn't quite meet her eyes as he added, "Good work. Thanks."

Caroline's glare burned into that strong, broad back as he walked away. *Good work. Thanks.* Like she was his peon. Which she was. Then he stopped and turned halfway toward her — catching her staring. She dropped her eyes to The Wave.

"Let's put him in a small paddock for a bit so they can have him on turnout over there. Give him a bit of ace to take the edge off."

If she hadn't been holding a horse, she'd have propped her hands on her hips. "Are you going to get it for me? Seeing as you keep everything locked away."

"The key is under the cabinet in the tack room. I can probably trust you with ace. I'm sure you're well familiar with it."

Zing.

She'd thought they'd made progress last night in moving past this animosity. Seems she was wrong.

"Come on, handsome," she said, not watching Dean leave, The Wave falling into step next to her as she resumed her march.

She hadn't considered The Wave's future. It wasn't as if he was some big American champion breeding farms in Kentucky would be clamouring over. There was no major syndicate in the works for this horse, she was sure of that. Nothing against The Wave or Dean, but that was reality. She supposed The Wave deserved a chance as much as any of the stallions in Ontario, so it was fine, if Dean had the money to support him. Did he, though?

The weeds along the fencelines needed to be trimmed; fair enough, Dean had been too busy to worry about that. It was probably the manager's job, which meant it was her job, now. Once The Wave was at Triple Stripe, she'd have extra time, so she'd get it done. The broken fence rails, too. The place was run down. A bit neglected. It would give her a sense of purpose to spruce it up.

There wasn't much in Dean's medication cabinet. A bottle of the injectable sedative, acepromazine, and a bottle of Banamine for mild colics and eye ailments. Some oral meds: bute, sulfas. His jibe aside, Caroline wasn't good with needles.

Only vets could inject horses at the track. If a trainer was found with needles or syringes, it was big trouble.

She'd been good friends with her vet.

Ace could be given orally. That's what she'd done, back in the day, when she'd had a horse in the morning who needed a bit to keep them chill; it just meant more of a wait before it took effect. She spent the time knocking down cobwebs, even if it felt like as soon as she did it, she had to do it again. She shuddered thinking how many spiders made their homes in these old barns.

"You mellow?" Caroline leaned on her broom as she peered into the stall. The Wave's lower lip drooped, his eyes heavy-lidded. She grinned. "I'll say."

A flake of hay waited in the small paddock just outside the barn — a space not big enough for a horse to work up speed if he decided to run — but it was a complete non-event. The Wave wandered over to the flake and nibbled: the perfect dose of sensible. Caroline glanced over her shoulder at the sound of footsteps. Dean. No surprise; he trusted her, but he didn't.

"This is exciting," he said, leaning on the fence.

"Better than TV," she agreed.

It took a moment for The Wave to notice Dean, but when he did, he ambled over, tail swishing like an afterthought. Dean dug a peppermint from his pocket.

"Remind me to put a bag of those in his care package," Caroline said.

Dean laughed. "I think they're well-versed in the peppermint protocol at Triple Stripe. He's going tomorrow, by the way."

"So who will they breed him to?" she asked.

"Cherry, for one. And they have a Belgian nurse mare they have to breed."

"How come?"

"That's part of the deal. Nurse mares are sent back in foal."

Yet another thing she did not know about the breeding side of the business. "I'd love to see that baby."

"Sport horse people scoop them up. Emilie could probably tell you more."

The Wave came to Caroline next, lifting his nose above the top rail, his droopy brown eyes full of expectation.

"Fine," she said, pulling at The Wave's lip before giving him what he wanted. She fought the way he tugged at her heart. He was leaving her, too, to be a dad. She should probably stick to geldings.

CHAPTER TWENTY

The Wave sauntered into the barn with his usual, casual walk, Caroline holding the shank loose. Dean didn't miss the fondness in her eyes; the big bay horse had grown on her like he grew on everyone. He wondered if The Wave's foray to the breeding shed would change his attitude, bring out some aggression. Sure, the horse had his grown-up moments, but in general, he was a puppy dog.

Caroline walked the horse into his stall. "Do you want bandages on him?"

"It's five minutes away and I've got the trailer set up for a box. Just brush him off. I'll go hook up and pull around."

He stopped at the house to grab a couple of bottles of water and some granola bars and threw them on the front seat. The bratty foal, always wondering what he was missing out on, came to the fence on the other side of the driveway as he opened the gate to the yard. He reached through the rails and tried to give the colt a scratch but was met with bitey baby teeth instead, so he just laughed and went back to the truck, leaving the youngster with his head stuck through the fence, full of whiskery disappointment. They'd all be happier when Cherry's foal was old enough to play with him.

Caroline waited, leaning on the barn's doorframe as Dean hopped out of the cab. She pushed herself up to help him open the side ramp.

"Haynet's already in there," he said. "Go ahead and grab him, please."

The Wave emerged into the sunshine sporting shipping bandages, Caroline with a self-satisfied twist of her lips. Dean laughed, then the sight lit him with pride. His Plate winner, by his dad's Plate winner. Just as quickly, doubt extinguished it. Was he doing the right thing? He wished The Wave had a more commercial pedigree to attract breeders. Dean couldn't afford to be sentimental. In his head, his father laughed at him.

"What's wrong?" Caroline asked as she walked past him and up the ramp.

Dean shook it off, securing the partition once she slipped out of the box. "Nothing. Let's go."

She helped with the ramp, her eyebrows arched, and took a beat to answer. "I'm coming?"

"Do you want to? Triple Stripe is a farm worth seeing, if you haven't before."

"Sure. I'm all caught up here."

Her face was still lined with suspicion as she set the water and granola bars on the console before climbing in.

"Help yourself," he said, the engine rumbling to life.

"Thanks." She snapped in the seatbelt and cracked open a bottle.

"Don't get too comfy."

Caroline scowled. "Are we doing this again? Is that why you wanted me to come, to fire me? I thought we were past that."

Dean suppressed a smile. Still so prickly. He steered the rig around the corner, sweeping wide to make the opening for the driveway. "I thought I might be able to impose on you to close the gate after I pull through."

Her scowl dissolved into a rueful half-grin. She released the seat belt as he rolled to a stop. "Sorry."

He watched her in the sideview mirrors once she hopped out, grinning when she stopped to greet the curious colt before wrapping the chain around the two parts of the closed gate and hurrying back.

"Thank you." Dean shifted into low gear and took his time along the pot-holed driveway. His gratitude was met with another wary look. "I was taught to always say thanks."

"You're welcome, then," she said, her tone still suggesting she had something to be defensive about. She retrieved her water and looked out the passenger-side window. "Have you lived around here all your life?"

Dean nodded. "Raised on the farm."

"I guess you've seen a lot of changes in the area over the years."

"You make me sound old."

"You are old." She laughed. "And I'm just as old, so we'll move on before you remind me."

He glimpsed her in his peripheral vision as he checked for traffic before pulling out onto the sideroad. Even in the short time she'd worked for him, her hair had grown. The subtle change softened her appearance. The cut had seemed so spartan, as short as it had been when she'd come for the interview.

The truck wasn't even up to speed before he put the turn signal on and slowed, approaching the Triple Stripe driveway on the right. Caroline gazed at the wrought-iron gates while he powered down the window and punched the sequence into the keypad.

"Fancy," she said, peering out. "And you have the code.

Aren't *you* important." Her vision travelled past him, to the house with its gardens, and then the training track, as they drove down the long lane. "Nice place."

The admiration with which she said it made Dean wonder how shabby she must think his farm was. He'd never envied Liv, and she'd never made him feel less-than, but sometimes he'd sensed it from Caroline. And hadn't she kissed him at that stake party and then acted as if she regretted it — then landed herself a rich man? But she'd told Dean it hadn't been worth it. He wasn't sure what that meant, exactly.

Two horses came into view when they reached the stallion barn, each with a generous paddock. A big dark bay lifted his head and stared back coolly before returning to his grazing, while the other used their arrival as an excuse to cavort before he froze — head high, mane and tail drifting in the breeze — and trumpeted. Welcome or warning? The Wave whinnied in response.

Caroline hopped out before Dean put the truck into park. He grinned when Kerrie, Triple Stripe's farm manager, appeared from the barn.

"Hey, Dean," she called as he swung his door shut and circled the hood.

"This is Caroline," he said, gesturing toward her. "She's filling in for Stacy for the summer."

"I heard about Stacy and Nikki's grand adventure," Kerrie said as she offered her hand to Caroline. "I'm —"

"Kerrie-Lynn Evans." Caroline gaped, wrapping her fingers around Kerrie's. "No way."

Dean stared at her, feeling a little embarrassed. It had taken him months to figure out who Kerrie was after she'd started as manager for Liv early last year. Caroline had recognized her instantly — the goalie for Canada's gold medal-winning

Olympic women's hockey team a few years back; a national hero.

"Where do you want him?" Dean asked.

"Across from Just Lucky, please," Kerrie said.

The stall was like a suite after the Northwest layup barn. Ride The Wave would think he'd won the lottery. He promptly dropped to his knees, flopped down, and rolled in the deep bed of fresh shavings, grunting with pleasure.

Dean crossed his arms with a half-hearted smile. "Here I'm feeling like I'm dropping my kid off at camp for the first time in his life, and he's not going to miss me at all."

"Sorry, Dad," Caroline quipped. "I don't think he'll mind this camp one bit."

———

Caroline watched, star-struck, as Kerrie-Lynn-freaking-Evans led the country's top stallions into the barn. She almost pinched herself.

"How about a quick drive-around tour before we leave?" Dean asked.

"Yes, please," she replied quickly.

"I didn't know you were a hockey fan," Dean said as they drove around a wooded area.

"I'm not," she snapped before she could stop herself. Bryce barged back into her mind when she'd been happily enjoying this outing — with Dean. "Why is everyone so obsessed with hockey in this country? Do you even know what our national sport is?"

"Lacrosse," Dean said mildly.

Of course, he knew. He probably had endless trivia holed up in that oversized brain of his. "It should be curling," she decided. "Have you ever watched the Winter Olympics and seen our team kick butt at curling?"

"Yes. But we have a pretty good women's hockey team, too."

He had her there. She pushed out a long breath. "I'm sorry. The hockey comment was triggering. My ex loved hockey. But it doesn't mean I can't appreciate an athlete like Kerri-Lynn Evans."

The truck emerged into another, larger, clearing. Double fence lines created an alleyway between pastures dotted with mares and foals, and a long barn stood to the right.

"It's nice you and Liv are such good friends."

Dean's eyes shifted to her briefly. "If you're suggesting there was ever anything between us, there wasn't. Except a little wishful thinking on my part."

His lips curved into a soft smile. Such a rare, candid offering. Caroline hadn't known, only suspected. "It makes sense. Like in the old days, when relationships were decided to forge powerful families."

"Like Triple Stripe and Northwest are racing dynasties?"

"Sure."

"I told her it would make a great story."

"Did you really?"

He shrugged. "It was too late by then."

Too late. What was that song about being late for the love of your life? She wondered if she'd missed out on her own, twenty years ago.

"I saw nothing so noble in Bryce. I wanted the money and the lifestyle because my family didn't have much growing up. I was the kid who always worked for riding lessons, and let's face it, there's no money in riding horses, so when I learned about the track, well, that was perfect. There was money. Lots of it."

"Did you miss the day when they taught you there's no money in racing?" Dean said dryly.

"That's only if you *own* horses. When you stick to training the right horses for the right clients, it's there."

"Ah. That's where I went wrong."

"That's true love, though, right? In it for the horses, not the money."

"Works well in theory. In practice, you have to make enough to keep everyone fed."

She kept her eyes on his face a bit too long, unsure if the hint of worry she'd heard was only her imagination or if she'd been right about his money problems.

"Will Cherry come over here too?" she asked.

"We'll breed her off the trailer. You know, ship her here, cover her, take her home. She doesn't need to stay."

"And The Wave will come home?"

He nodded. "He'll just be gone a couple of weeks. The season closes in the middle of July, and no one really wants to keep their breeding sheds open that late. All we're trying to do is see if he's fertile. If he is, I'll know I have something to market, and I'll hopefully come to an agreement with Liv for next season. In the meantime, it's cheaper to keep him on my own farm."

"And if he's not?" The thought upset her. It hit too close to home. Would Dean not want The Wave if he couldn't repro-duce — just like Bryce had chosen his high school sweetheart because she'd had his child, when Caroline couldn't?

Dean shrugged. "I'll figure that out once I know."

She worked up her nerve. The Wave needed her — and she might need him just as much. "Can I ride him when he comes back?"

Dean glanced at her quickly before returning his eyes to the lane. "I thought you didn't ride anymore."

"I don't *gallop* anymore," she clarified. "Riding is to galloping as bookkeeping is to Calculus."

Dean chuckled. "To be clear, though, I could do the books if I needed to. Faye likes to keep a hand in things."

"Because she has nothing better to do, like run her own business, or work on her new house?"

"If Faye didn't like to keep a hand in things, *you* would not be here."

"Fine. But to be clear..." Caroline drawled, pausing for effect. "I could gallop if I wanted to. But I don't."

He grinned. "Okay."

"Okay, I can ride him, or okay, that makes sense? Or not?"

"Both, I suppose. If you want to ride him, be my guest. He was never tough. And I think he'd enjoy it."

Caroline turned her gaze toward the window — mostly because it hid her smile.

CHAPTER TWENTY-ONE

FARGO PULLED Dean along the narrow strip of grass outside the barn in a vain search for better pickings. The older gelding's season was going according to script: two good races — a win and a second — then yesterday, he'd finished dead last, twelve lengths behind the winner.

Dean's other horses weren't much more inspiring. She Brews had picked up a shoeing nail, and while it hadn't affected any vital structures in her foot, the mare was three-legged lame with an abscess brewing. Normally, he would have sent her to the farm for a few weeks, but the money the employment program gave him subsidized Hunter's wages, and Sheba was a nice, quiet horse for the kid to learn on, so she stayed.

Cruze was still Cruze, though it felt like he was finally headed in the right direction. One day soon, he'd breeze with Gastronomy again — and hopefully this time, it would go better. Now Dean just needed to find races where Andy's older horses could pick up cheques. That might give him a break from the owner's incessant pressure when it came to the two-year-old.

A red Honda Civic pulled up next to his truck, and Dean's mood immediately lifted.

Emilie climbed out. "Hey, Dean. How's Fargo doing?"

"Yesterday wasn't his day. But he's fine."

"I was talking to the board at New Chapter about him," Emilie said, leaning against the barn, her eyes on Fargo's busy lips. "They have a spot for him at their farm, if you're considering retiring him. I know you don't need another pasture ornament right now."

Dean caught her expression and tone — careful, half pleading. "That's very kind, Em." He dropped his gaze to the gelding's face, a baseball-sized patch of white half-hidden by the sweep of his black forelock. "I'm going to give him one more race, and if he doesn't finish in the money, I'll likely take you up on it."

He'd played out this movie often enough. Other years, Dean had given the gelding a break once his form dropped off — sent him home for the summer, brought him back in the fall for a couple more starts — but now they were into diminishing returns. This year, he didn't have the reserves to feed an idle horse, and Fargo was sound enough to have a second career. Emilie and the people who ran the retirement group would find the perfect home for him.

Dean glanced up, Emilie still watching Fargo's futile search for good grazing. She was hiding her disappointment, he could tell, and he pushed aside the guilt. "I know he didn't look great out there today, Em, but if I thought he was in jeopardy of injuring himself, I'd hand you the shank right now."

"I know. You're one of the good guys." She smiled at him and, with a little wave, returned to her car.

Dean watched her drive out, wondering if he was.

"All right, old man." He dragged Fargo from the patchy grass. "Time to go. I've got a date."

Life was settling into the new normal. With Ride The Wave at Triple Stripe, Cherry's foal on the ground, and enough trust in Caroline to relax about the farm, Dean had finally — with only a little prodding from Faye — returned to the dating profile she'd set up. The way the matches had filled the inbox in his absence intimidated him. While he was trying to keep his business afloat, people were meeting and falling in love. It was an alternate universe.

Throwing caution to the wind, he'd started with the one he'd messaged the day Faye and Will had found their house. After some back and forth, he'd arranged to meet her. He hoped changing clothes was enough to get rid of the worst of the horse smell and that the pleasant aromas of the café would take care of the rest. Not the best he could do, but if a faint whiff of horse turned her off, it wouldn't work anyway. Best to find that out straight off.

"Wish me luck," he said to Fargo as he snapped the stall screen shut and hung the stuffed haynet. Fargo gave him the side-eye and dove into his nest of timothy and alfalfa.

———————

Refusing to be like the other solitary patrons glued to their phones, Dean rifled through the daily papers and magazines in a rack by the door and selected something to peruse. A magazine article grabbed his interest, and the noises around him — the barista crafting the most recent order, the exchanges between employees, the sweep of the door as it opened with an assault of warmth on the air-conditioned cool of the café — all of it faded into the background.

"Dean?"

He pulled his gaze from the glossy pages, something familiar about the voice. Then his eyes fell on the woman standing near the table, her face slightly flushed, her wavy, auburn hair falling to her shoulders. Dean pushed himself up slowly, at a loss for words.

"Krissy! Hi!" He found his voice. "What are you doing here? It's been a while." He hugged her awkwardly and glanced at his watch, wondering if his date would be put off if she arrived and found him talking to another attractive woman. "I'm meeting someone, but we should catch up sometime."

Krissy pushed the hair back from one side of her face with a sheepish curve of her lips. "You're meeting me, actually."

"I'm sorry?"

"I have a confession to make. I saw your profile. I knew it was you. And how could I resist a dashing horse trainer?"

Dean was confused but recovered enough to say, "Have a seat, then. What would you like? I'll go order."

He waited for the cashier to ring up his purchase, resisting the temptation to glance over his shoulder toward the table. Of all the cafés in the world, what were the chances of his university girlfriend finding him? Maybe this was the serendipity he'd hoped for, the dating app he'd resisted the vector. He juggled two cups and a plate, setting everything on the table and sliding Krissy her latte.

"Cheesecake?" she said, her hands curling around her mug as she inclined her chin at the slice he'd placed between them.

"It seemed appropriate." They'd often shared a piece during study marathons, papers and textbooks sprawled across the table of the coffee shop they'd frequented. He lifted his espresso to his lips. "So why the subterfuge?" The photo on her profile could have been her, but the name she'd used hadn't been one he recognized. Twice in one year, he'd been blindsided by unfamiliar names for people he knew well.

"You're new to this, aren't you?"

"Online dating?" He laughed. "Yes. Does everyone use fake names?"

"Not everyone, but you can't be too careful. When I broke up with my ex, it was messy. Anonymity makes me feel safer."

The more stories he heard, the more he questioned why people kept going back for more. What was he doing? Liv's words from two years ago came back to him. *You and I were always the ones who wondered why everyone else put themselves through the hell of relationships* — when she'd found herself in that very position, like he was better off the way he was.

"You were married?" Her profile mentioned a daughter, but he hadn't assumed.

"Very briefly. To, ah, my advisor."

"What?" he sputtered, laughing. "O'Reilly? Really?"

"It was after you left. We had a thing, I got pregnant, his wife left him, he married me."

Dean pushed the cheesecake toward her, letting her decide if she wanted to provide any more detail, because he was dumbstruck.

Krissy sighed, dropping her eyes and picking up her fork. "Then he had a fling with another of his grad students."

"I'm sorry," Dean said.

"I should have known better. But that's easier said than done."

"How old is your daughter?"

Krissy lifted her head, and Dean thought from the uncertainty in her eyes that this was probably the point dates bailed on her. Not many thirty-something men wanted to jump right into family status, no matter how much they said they were ready to settle down.

"Eight." She smiled as she said it. "You never got married, then?"

"No."

"How are you still single? You're a catch. Do you know how many girls in our department gushed about you?"

He snorted, heat prickling the skin of his neck. "I doubt that."

"Oh yes. I was the envy of them all."

Her soft laugh made him wonder if this was a date rather than just Krissy wanting to catch up. And why not? He was here for second chances, if that's what this was. And if it wasn't? He could use the practice if he continued with Faye's plot. "I had my hands full, running the farm and training the horses at the track — and worrying about my younger sister. A personal relationship never seemed a priority."

"And now?"

"I guess I finally had to admit my sister doesn't need me anymore. She has her own business, and she's engaged. She and her fiancé just bought a house."

"What you did was pretty incredible. You weren't very old yourself. That was a lot of responsibility to take on."

He'd never thought about it that way; he'd just done it. And hadn't it been the perfect excuse to drop the grad school fiasco and return to the horses? "We needed each other. I'm proud of what she's done with her life. She had a really hard time after the accident. She was supposed to go with our parents on that trip and somehow thought the crash was her fault."

"Oh no, that's terrible! Poor thing."

"All I could think was how much worse it would have been if she'd been with them."

He likely would have sold the farm and gone back to school, finished his masters, worked a job in the regular world. If it had only been him, he'd never have mustered the gumption to try his hand at training. It would have been too much, him against it all. Faye had given him a reason to keep the farm.

Wanting to offer her a tiny piece of stability when her world was inside-out meant he didn't have time to think; he just had to make it happen. And when she was older and managing better, she'd pulled her weight. The two of them had kept it afloat. Somehow, being alone had become a habit — because he'd never felt alone.

"You said you work around here?" Dean asked. He didn't want to talk about himself. "What do you do?"

"Product development." She sipped her latte. "I work with nutraceuticals, mostly."

"Very on-trend," he said. He lifted his fork and cut into the cheesecake. Whatever this was, it felt comfortable, like old times.

"Not as exciting as training racehorses," she said, forking a bite for herself.

"Think of the money I would have saved my parents if I'd convinced them to let me skip the completely unrelated schooling."

"So, you're a well-educated horse trainer. Does that help?"

"Not at all."

"Why's that?"

"Let's just say tradition ranks over science in the racing world." He sounded like Liv, but he was hardly making the waves she was. Just... riding them.

"It must be so much more satisfying than working in a lab."

He didn't know how to respond, because right now he lacked conviction. Later this summer he'd stand up at the Canadian Horse Racing Hall of Fame induction ceremony on behalf of his late father — as he struggled to keep the legacy his parents had created from slipping away.

So he changed the subject. Again. "Does your daughter like horses?"

"An eight-year-old horse crazy girl? Who's ever heard of

that?" Krissy laughed. "She adores them. I don't know where she got it from. I'm hoping her father comes through so we can send her to camp this summer."

"You should bring her out to the farm sometime," he suggested. Because again, why not? Even if nothing was happening here, he was happy to be the man who gave his old flame's kid an encounter with her favourite animal.

"She would love that."

"I don't have a pony we can put her on, but I've got two foals," he said.

"That would be amazing." Krissy took another forkful of cheesecake and pushed the plate back to him, leaving him the last bite. "Speaking of my daughter, I have to go rescue my mom. It was so nice to see you again."

Dean walked her to her car, the lights of a silver Audi flashing as the locks released with a clunk. Krissy rested her fingers on the door handle, opening it slightly, and turned to face him.

"I really didn't mean this as a date," she said. "Vaguely suggestive comments aside. I'm sorry if I ambushed you. I was trying to be cute. I'm not expecting us to pick up where we left off, don't worry."

Clenching and releasing his truck keys, Dean was all too aware of how bad he was at this. He could only be honest. "It wasn't the worst ambush. I'll call you about coming out to the farm. We'll see where it goes."

She smiled, stepping forward and stretching up, quickly kissing him on the cheek before slipping into the car.

Dean waited until she drove off to head to his truck. The engine roared to life, and he tried to decide what he felt. Nothing, really. Which wasn't such a bad thing, because whenever he'd felt something for someone — those sparks everyone chased — the feelings had never been mutual. What if just being comfortable was enough?

CHAPTER TWENTY-TWO

"Aren't we almost done?" Caroline gasped, gulping for air.

"Hardly!" Jess cackled.

"Why did I agree to this again?"

"To get fit for riding! Trust me, when you climb on that horse, you'll be glad."

She couldn't complain about being almost forty, because Jess was the same age. She couldn't complain about being tired from barn work, because Jess had her own barn. It'd made sense when Caroline told Jess she needed to get fit because Dean agreed to let her ride The Wave, but this was overkill. All she wanted to do was take The Wave around the hay fields at a walk, maybe a bit of trot once he was ready. It wasn't like she was going back to galloping.

Jess eased to a halt, her bike askew as she planted one foot, leaving the other resting on a pedal. She pulled her water bottle from the holder and eyed Caroline. "You okay?"

"Barely." Her supporting leg trembled as she fumbled for her own water. She took tiny sips, her throat raw, not sure which burned more, her lungs or her quads, then threw her head back and drizzled water over her face like she'd seen hockey players do on TV. "Don't you dare say 'no pain, no gain.'"

The lofty canopy of green overhead filtered the light, blocking the sun's full intensity. It was a gorgeous day. Why was she doing *this* on her day off, when she could be relaxing? This was patio weather, not die on a trail in some random conservation area weather.

"How's The Wave doing, anyway?"

"I haven't heard." Caroline wiped her eyes with the hem of her t-shirt. "Dean is pining."

"How *is* Dean?" There was a teasing curl to Jess's lips.

Caroline scowled and slipped her water bottle back into its cage. "How much farther? I need to keep moving or I won't be able to get started again and you'll have to carry me back to the car."

They coasted down a small hill, Caroline sucking in air and blowing it out again, trying to even out her breathing so when they hit the hill on the other side, she didn't pass out. Jess glanced over her shoulder, grinning, before she stood in the pedals and tackled the incline, making Caroline go harder.

The conservation area's gravel parking lot and Jess's rusted Toyota Tacoma were such a welcome sight that Caroline almost kissed the ground. Except, of course, she'd never be able to make it back to her feet. How was she ever going to manage the stairs of the apartment so she could collapse on the couch when she got back? Would Dean know if she threw a horse blanket over some bales of straw and crashed in the barn?

Jess hoisted her bike into the bed of the truck and Caroline stared. There was no way she was going to be able to do that. She had no idea riding a bike would be so hard on her arms, too.

"Want me to do it for you?" Jess asked, like she'd read Caroline's mind.

"Yes. Please." She clutched the truck's siderail when Jess took the bike away, then shuffled, stooped like she was a hundred years old. Even her fingers ached. "Aren't you even a little bit tired?"

"Of course I am," Jess said, swinging open the driver's side and reaching behind the seat. "But my muscles are more accustomed to it than yours. Next ride will be better."

"Next ride?" The passenger door felt made of lead, and Caroline eyeballed the seat. It wasn't as high as Dean's truck, but would still take an effort with her jelly legs and noodle arms.

"You said you want to get fit. You have to keep going! One night this week, maybe? Somewhere close to your farm."

Her farm? Forget going for another ride so soon, her brain got stuck on that thought — until a flash of flesh distracted her. "What are you doing?"

"You brought a change of clothes, didn't you? Wet bike shorts are too gross to sit in all the way home. You'll get chilled."

"You're half naked in the middle of a parking lot!"

"There's no one else here," Jess scoffed

Caroline looked into the trees while Jess whipped her shirt off. Jess had officially turned into one of those mountain biking freaks. "I don't have as far to go as you. I'll be fine." It was uncomfortable, but she'd deal.

Jess hopped behind the wheel and started the truck. "Fine. Ready?"

Psyching herself up, Caroline reached for the handle with one hand and the back of the seat with the other and dragged herself in, then snapped the seatbelt in place so she didn't fall out as she leaned to pull the door shut. She closed her eyes and moaned, sinking against the headrest.

"Protein bar?"

Caroline cranked one eye open and reached for it. Just as Jess predicted, her warm muscles were cooling, and she shivered. "Thanks."

A hoodie landed in her lap, then Jess rattled on about the importance of consuming something post-exercise — but Caroline wasn't listening. She was dreaming about sleep, and trying not to think about how she would manage work tomorrow. So far, this summer seemed to be one assault on her muscles after another.

"You never answered my question."

She rolled her head in Jess's direction but didn't open her eyes. "Hmm?"

"How's Dean?"

Caroline straightened her neck, grumbling, "Infuriating."

Jess laughed. "Why?"

"Because he runs so hot and cold. One minute, I think great, we're getting along. Like the night the mare foaled. Then he makes some passive-aggressive comment that makes it obvious he doesn't trust me."

"This isn't about him not trusting you. What is it you want?"

"I want the last twenty years of my life back."

"Sorry, I can't help you out there."

"You're doing the wrong kind of science, then. You should be working on time travel."

"Like quantum physics?"

Maybe Dean could help her. He'd done Physics, hadn't he?

Caroline sighed, her heart aching as much as her body. She wanted all of it to go away; she was too old to be a slave to these emotions. "He's just so... good. As much as he's been grumpy with me, it's not like I don't deserve it. And when he forgets about it, he's just so nice. How many guys our age — single guys

— are that nice? He doesn't even know how to be properly combative. It's so... nice," she said again. What a useless, overused word, but what else could she call it? He'd even ruined her vocabulary. "I'm starving." Could she blame it on that instead?

Jess laughed. "I told you. Next time, bring a change of clothes, and we'll stop somewhere after."

The trees on either side of the dirt sideroad leading to Northwest Farm were lush and full, and it didn't seem quite so much like the middle of nowhere anymore. As they passed the white rails and stone gate at Triple Stripe, Caroline wondered about The Wave. She hadn't felt confident enough to ask if she could visit, telling herself he wouldn't be away long. This was for him — the physical pain, if not the angst. Her emotions confused everything. Because it didn't matter if her feelings for the horse felt safer than feelings for Dean — she'd be leaving them both behind at the end of the summer.

"Just pull up to the gate. I can walk the rest of the way," Caroline said when Jess turned into the potholed driveway.

"You sure?"

"I'll need the walk to loosen my muscles so I can do those stairs."

"I'll grab the bike for you."

"You're giving it to me?"

"Might as well. You might want to ride around here before I see you again."

She might. For The Wave. "Thanks, Jess. Text me when you get home."

Jess grinned. "Two to one you'll be asleep by then."

Caroline waved before Jess turned her truck around, then rolled the bike to the gate, her helmet hanging off the handlebars. She debated whether to hop on and ride back to her apartment. Walking might be best, given how unsteady her legs felt.

But she decided to ride it and began to pedal, slowly, eyes fixed at her front wheel.

Which is why she didn't notice Dean coming out of the layup barn when she rounded the corner. She hit the brakes, skidding on the gravel, and with every last ounce of self-preservation, managed not to wipe out.

"This thing will be the death of me," she muttered, her whole body trembling as she climbed off.

"Maybe we should get you a bell," Dean said.

Caroline pressed her lips together, trying to be mad, but she started to laugh. "Sorry."

"Have a good ride?"

"I made it back in one piece. Though I still have a little ways to go, so that could change."

"Great day for it. See, the farm's not so bad. You actually get a day off to go see your friends."

"What a concept."

"If you ever want to go for a ride after work one day, let me know."

"You have a bike?"

He nodded. "I haven't managed it much this year with the way things have been, but normally I try to get out at least once a week."

Was he serious? She and Dean, riding bikes on trails like she'd just done with Jess? She'd barely been able to keep up today. But it was a nice gesture — or was it? He'd probably kick her butt.

"I'm trying to picture you in spandex," she deflected, glad for the oversized t-shirt that fell to mid-thigh when she noticed his gaze drop.

He shook his head, rolling his eyes. "I'll leave you with that vision, then."

As he walked away, she couldn't get it out of her mind.

CHAPTER TWENTY-THREE

DEAN PLACED a set of tack on the truck's back seat and headed home. He'd tried to play it cool when Caroline asked if she could ride The Wave, even though he hoped, despite her accident, it would lead to her galloping for him. Was that selfish, when she was obviously traumatized by the memory? Probably, but it wouldn't stop him from gently enabling it in any way he could.

He stopped at the café and picked up drinks and some butter tarts, and it wasn't until he was driving away he realized that tiny twist in his chest on seeing Monique was gone. Instead of wanting to linger after she served him, he took his purchases, thanked her, and left, looking forward to getting back to the farm.

It hadn't looked this good in a long time. Stacy had kept up with the lawn mowing and weed eating, but Caroline seemed to take special pride in it. She'd even made planters for the front of the barns, and they overflowed with red and white flowers. When he'd pulled cash from his pocket to reimburse her, she'd refused.

She was in the stall, playing with the filly. If anything would win Caroline over to the farm, it was that foal. The pretty bay was a sweetheart, that big softball-sized star on her forehead reminding Dean of Fargo.

"Chad's on his way," she said when he handed her a cappuccino.

All the vet was doing was checking Cherry for ovulation. Yesterday's there-and-back-again breeding trip to Triple Stripe had been seamless. Dean had almost left the filly behind — many of the big breeding sheds didn't want the distraction of a foal — but Caroline wouldn't hear of it. She stayed on the trailer to keep an eye on the baby while Cherry and Ride The Wave had their rendez-vous.

The vet's visit was short. "Yep," Chad said moments after beginning the scan. He withdrew his arm and discarded the soiled examination sleeve on the floor. "We'll check to see if she's in foal in two weeks."

And a long two weeks they would be. There was so much waiting in the breeding game.

Dean stooped to pick up the sleeve and tossed it into the feed bag that served as a garbage receptacle as Chad hefted the ultrasound machine into his SUV. Dr Thomas, the older vet Chad worked for, likely wouldn't have bothered with the technology, performing a manual exam instead. It had surprised Dean when Chad explained ultrasound was the only way he'd been taught in vet school, and he was just now learning the old ways.

"Thanks, Chad. Have a good day." Dean handed him a cup and a small paper bag from Faye's bakery. Chad's tired eyes lit up when he peeked at the butter tart. It was non-stop for reproductive vets from the arrival of the first foals in January until the sheds closed in July.

Caroline waited in the shade of the barn. Now that the

heat of summer was upon them, the other two mares and the bratty colt were on night turnout, so they were all in.

"We can bring The Wave home tomorrow," he said.

A smile took over her face. He didn't want to ruin it by letting her know he wasn't hopeful about The Wave's prospects as a stallion.

With nothing to be done until later in the day, Dean sauntered out of the barn, trying to ignore how natural it felt that Caroline fell into step beside him. "I'll come back out at four and help you move horses around," he said. "Unless —"

Caroline stopped at the base of the stairs to the apartment. "What?"

"Do you want to maybe, I don't know, join me for a bike ride?" The words came out like he was fourteen, asking her for a date. And why *would* she want to spend her free time with him?

But her eyes brightened. "Really? I'd love that. Today, a bike; tomorrow, The Wave!"

Dean grinned. "How soon can you be ready?"

In twenty minutes, she rolled her bike through the gate, a backpack slung over one shoulder. An oversized t-shirt covered her hips, and her legs were white-white below tight black bike shorts. Her quads were pretty impressive; the rides with her friend and those apartment stairs were doing a nice job. When he realized he'd been staring, he pulled his eyes back to her face. Her lips formed a line with a wry uptick at one end.

"All set?" he asked, and lifted her bike into the bed of the pickup next to his before she could do it herself. She didn't protest. It shocked him, just a little.

Caroline hopped in the cab. She seemed twitchy, too quiet, like she was nervous. Was she regretting it? She could have complained it was too hot, or that she was too tired, but she'd said yes.

Despite the soaring temperature, the weather was incredible. Dean parked in the shade of the dirt lot at the agreement forest. Caroline let the tailgate down and was hoisting her bike out before he'd swapped his running shoes for clip-ins.

"These helmets seem so unsubstantial after riding helmets," she said as she snapped hers in place. "Would they really help if I crashed ass-over-tea kettle into some rocks?"

"Let's not find out. It's not a technical trail." Dean tucked his water bottle into the cage and threw a leg over, clipping one foot into the pedal. "It would not be in my best interests to get you injured."

She eyed his shoes. "You're physically attaching yourself to the bike? Isn't that a recipe for disaster?"

"If I launch myself, they pop out." Dean grinned before pushing off with his free foot, starting slowly, waiting for her to follow. He needed to lead because he knew the way — but also because her in front of him would be a distraction. He probably would crash.

The trail was as easy as he promised, and he was tempted to hit it hard, to clear the cobwebs and leave behind everything that mired his thoughts. His lack of horses. The Wave's future. Faye leaving to set up house with Will. It was peaceful, with just the whirr of the bike wheels and the whoosh of air rushing past his ears. He was so used to riding alone, for a while he forgot Caroline was behind him. When he glanced behind, she was keeping up and didn't look like she was struggling, so he kicked it up a notch, revelling in the cooling breeze on his face, fingers curled around the handlebars, swooping under the awning of leafy branches overhead. It felt good to feel good, his heart pounding, shirt soaked through, his spirits soaring to the trees and eking up to the sky above. This is why he did this.

Slowing for a breather, he pulled out his water and tipped

his head back, squirting some into his mouth. He twisted a foot free and planted it on the ground.

"All right?" he asked.

Caroline braked alongside him, straddling her bike and reaching for her bottle. "Perfect." She gave him a twisty smile, her face flushed, holding his eyes a beat before taking in the spot. "It's pretty in here."

"It's great," he agreed, looking up through the trees and breathing in. "I love it. I figured we'd just do the short loop today."

"Works for me." Caroline tucked her bottle away. "Does this take us right back to the parking lot?"

"It does."

And before he was clipped in, she was racing down the path. He took off after her, catching up. The trail was wide enough he could have gone past, but he'd never been that competitive. Maybe that was his problem — why Caroline had gone for Bryce instead of him, why Liv had gone for Nate, why Monique had gone for Rory.

Why his dad had insisted on grad school.

He didn't fight hard enough.

But here was Caroline, in front of him. Metaphorically, and literally. He dropped his eyes to the dirt in front of his tire, needing to get rid of inappropriate thoughts about his barn manager — and... cycling buddy? Also, he'd invited Krissy and her daughter to the farm this weekend. His previously simple life was feeling a tiny bit complicated.

The parking lot appeared both too soon and not soon enough. They lifted the bikes into the truck.

"That was just right," she said, tossing her helmet onto the back seat and pulling a towel from her bag. If she noticed the set of tack still there — and how could she not — she didn't say anything.

Caroline rubbed her sweat-darkened hair, then finger-combed it — and didn't skip a beat as she peeled off her t-shirt, swiftly replacing it with a dry tank top. Not so quick that he didn't get an unexpected eyeful of skin, or that she didn't catch him watching.

"I'm sure you've seen a sports bra before." She didn't exactly look away as he swapped his drenched tech shirt for a clean T. *All's fair.*

Dean grabbed the compact cooler stashed behind the seat and spread a tartan throw over the tailgate. "We're not in a rush, are we? Want something to eat?"

"Did Faye pack you a lunch?" she teased.

"Made it all by myself. Just some salad and half a sandwich." He set out a couple of Tupperware containers and a few utensils, and pulled himself up.

She followed suit and reached for one of the containers, cracking the lid. "Looks healthy. I had no idea you were a cook."

"I can feed myself. My mother always said it would get me a wife. Didn't work though." He grinned before scooping a mouthful.

"Would have worked on me." Caroline grabbed a fork. "Bryce never cooked."

"Maybe I should have told you I knew my way around a kitchen twenty years ago."

Her chewing slowed, then stopped, and Dean couldn't look away, wishing he hadn't said it.

"I was so dumb back then," she muttered, the way she ducked his gaze making it clear she wasn't joking. "I'm sorry, Dean."

He wasn't expecting that — or that he wanted to kiss her, here, now, under these trees. But she was still his employee, and for all he knew, still married. Just because she'd left Harrington and didn't wear a ring didn't mean she was free.

"Have you heard from Bryce since you left?"

She shook her head. Frowned. Picked the salad back up. "This is good."

He took the hint — she didn't want to talk about it. Just as well. Employee, remember?

But just until the end of the summer.

Whose voice was that? Not his father's. Probably Faye's. At this rate, he'd need psychotherapy.

"Faye spoils me," he admitted. "I haven't had to do much since those early days when I first came back after the accident, but I guess I'll have to start again."

Something like sympathy creased Caroline's features. "You're going to miss her, aren't you?"

"I am." Dean handed her a brownie. "I did not make these."

Caroline reached for it without hesitation. "Mmm." She moaned after taking a bite. "I have a feeling Faye won't let you starve."

CHAPTER TWENTY-FOUR

THE SET of tack Dean had brought from the track two days ago taunted. What had seemed a good idea when Caroline had asked him about riding The Wave felt like utter foolishness now that the horse was back from his brief foray in the breeding shed.

"I'll stick around and give you a leg up," Dean said.

She shook her head with enough force her hair, which was starting to grow out, bounced. "I'll be fine."

"Are you sure?"

"Yes, I'm sure!" she said, snapping off each word.

Dean took a step back. "Okay. Well, keep your phone with you and call me if you need anything."

"Go relax on your deck with a beer and once I'm up, we'll come around and say hello. How's that?" She didn't need him hovering like an anxious broodmare. It was making her even more nervous.

He nodded. "I'll leave you to it, then."

Caroline held her breath, waiting until he was gone, then

released it in a huff. *Okay.* There was no backing out now. She was doing this. Without an audience.

First, she checked every inch of the equipment, testing the pliability, and inspecting every stitch. No excuses there; it had been well cared for. She set the grooming kit next to The Wave's stall and then dragged a muck bucket outside, overturning it in front of the barn. The Wave would stand, Caroline knew he would, even if most Thoroughbreds straight off the track would not.

Her boots and helmet were in the car. They'd been buried, but she'd dug them out so they'd be ready for this day. Why she hadn't sold or gotten rid of it all, she didn't know. She'd never intended to get on a horse again. If this became a regular thing, she'd have to buy a new helmet, at least; the one she'd galloped in over ten years ago was well past its "use by" date, if there was such a thing. It wasn't as if it was stamped somewhere like on a bag of milk. Her bike helmet was newer, but it wouldn't be ideal protection should she topple from the back of a nearly seventeen-hand horse.

She was fine. She wasn't coming off.

She tore off the bright purple cover and goggles, tossing them on the car seat. They were unnecessary.

"All right, handsome," she said, retrieving The Wave from his paddock. He bumped her with his nose and, well-trained human that she was, she produced a peppermint.

All the stalls in the layup barn had tie rings, so she snapped the old rubber bungee to his halter and set to work grooming him, something she'd done every day, save for at the beginning when Dean had told her not to touch him. There was no rush. She had all the time in the world.

To build her nerve, solidify her resolve.

Though, if she didn't show up in a reasonable amount of

time, Dean would come looking, and that would be embarrassing. The thread of embarrassment was a great motivator.

The Wave leaned into the curry comb, and Caroline threw her weight behind it, losing herself in the simple act. It wasn't as if he was dirty — Kerrie had probably groomed him every day at Triple Stripe, if the lustre of his coat was any indication — but she needed the ritual. The preparation was part of the ride, or it should be. One of the things she'd gotten away from when she'd been training. Letting others get her horses ready — which was a groom's job, to be fair — removed a step in the connection she'd missed.

The Wave didn't bat an eye as she slid the martingale over his head and set the saddle on top of the pads. She slipped the girth through the loop that secured the martingale between his legs and buckled the girth, snugging it up. Even after ten years away, it was second nature.

All that was left was the bridle and her helmet. Horses were supposed to tune into a human's emotional state, but The Wave dozed, resting one hind leg, tail flicking at the odd fly like a track pony waiting for his next assignment — unaffected by her anxiety like it was the most natural thing in the world to return from two weeks on a fancy farm where he'd met a couple of mares, to be tacked up for a casual ride by someone who'd lost all her confidence in her ability to ride such an animal.

That day ten years ago, she'd failed in the most basic of rider tenets: *keep a leg on either side*. Then she'd failed at the next one: *always get back on when you fall off*. She hadn't rectified it later that morning. Or the next day. Or the next week.

Did ten years later count?

The helmet, dried out from disuse, fit snugly over her kerchief like an old friend, quietly encouraging. She tugged the zipper of the impact vest to the top and grabbed the bridle. The

Wave made it easy, dropping his head, reaching for the bit. *You want this for me, too.*

Helmet, vest, phone. If she was going to be unsafe — hopping aboard a recently off-the-track Thoroughbred stallion without the safety net a second set of hands would provide — at least she'd be a little *less* unsafe. If things went sideways, she could call Dean. If she was conscious, anyway.

She didn't bother with a shank, walking The Wave outside to the overturned muck bucket, a hand on the thick leather of the track bridle's near-side line, tapping into his calm. Caroline popped the stirrup leather a couple of times so The Wave felt a tug, but he merely flicked an ear. It's not as if he'd never felt weight in the irons. She flipped a stray piece of his mane to the right side. She knotted the thick lines. The Wave sighed. Caroline mimicked him.

Deep breath — it was just like diving into a cold lake. Put a foot in the stirrup and throw a leg over.

So she did.

The instant her jeans connected with the worn seat of the old exercise saddle, it came back in a rush. Something giving way, her left leg collapsing beneath her, the impact with the hard synthetic track surface, the blackness. Regaining consciousness to the horror of the scene before her.

The rest of it piled on. Clandestine vet visits, near misses. Suspicious officials, the feeling of always ducking into dark, narrow alleyways to hide from them. The looks from other trainers. Trainers like Dean, judging, judging, judging. And rightly so.

The accident had been her catalyst, like the universe was telling her *enough*. She'd walked away — from the scene, from training, from the backstretch. From the province. The sad reality was, she'd escaped nothing. She'd taken her infamy with her, carrying it as a constant companion while Bryce seemed to live the ruse so well. The big house, the nice car, two provinces away from the past. *Her* past. Until Bryce's past had waltzed in and sent her to face her own.

The Wave absorbed it all. He curled his neck around to touch his nose to her toe, as if to tell her, *time to move on now.* Tucking her toes into each iron, she wiped her eyes and straightened, shoulders back, and picked up the knot, giving him a nudge.

They'd just go around the yard, the same place she'd hand-walked him. If she came off, it wouldn't be a soft landing, but it would hurt no matter what. While her hands and reflexes might go through the motions as easily as they had a decade ago, her body wouldn't be as forgiving. But The Wave would be safe in the enclosed space. He'd probably even get Dean, like Lassie, bringing help.

The rock of the big horse's stride lulled her, each of her fears slowly replaced with a joy she hadn't felt in so, so long. Jess was right; the bike riding helped, her seat secure. No doubt she'd still ache tomorrow because no one could tell her cycling could replicate riding — for one, a bike was a lot narrower than a horse, especially a big one like The Wave. But she trusted this horse. This horse would take care of her.

"Let's go see Dean." Because she'd promised — but would he be there?

She'd chosen the long way, though it wasn't really long enough. He'd see her face, which must be red and blotchy. But he wouldn't ask why. Dean wasn't like that. He was like The Wave. He'd just absorb.

And he *was* there. When she was close enough, she thought she caught the hint of a smile, a tall glass in one hand, moisture condensing on the outside. Whatever it was, it made her aware of how dry her mouth was, her nerves depleting all her saliva and sending a profusion of fluid directly to her sweat glands.

Dean unfolded from the chair and set the glass on the table in his slow, easy way, then descended the steps, meeting them at the fence separating the house's backyard from the barnyard. The thick track lines slipped through her fingers, and The Wave dipped his muzzle to Dean's open hand. It wasn't a bad view, up here on top of the world.

What was Dean thinking? Did it make him happy to see his big horse hacked about, or did it just remind him The Wave, his Plate horse — his big horse — wasn't a racehorse anymore? To racetrackers, riding horses were a lower class. How could an animal once worth six figures now be stripped of his value? Maybe off-track Thoroughbreds didn't trade hands for a dollar like they used to, but transactions after their racing careers were finished lacked a set of zeros, sometimes more.

Dean's eyes slid up to hers, just the hint of a curve to his lips. "You always did look good on a horse."

Caroline blinked, and swallowed. He'd dropped his gaze already, so she let herself stare. *I'm sorry, was that a compliment, or innuendo?* Or just her imagination that he'd said it at all? She didn't feel cheeky enough to retort, not today, allowing him the satisfaction of leaving her without speech.

He ran a hand along The Wave's neck, meeting her eyes again. "You good?"

That could mean so many things, but she took it in its most literal sense. "Yeah, I'm good."

CHAPTER TWENTY-FIVE

THIS WAS ENOUGH. Just walking through the fields, the sun tanning her arms, a warm breeze carrying her horse's mane. She didn't need the speed and danger of the racetrack, just a leg on each side, her hips and seat feeling the reach of the horse's hind legs, her body remembering how to move with him.

How had she let fear take this from her? She could see now it was more than Bryce reducing her to a shadow of her former self. Riding The Wave — she had to grin every time she thought it — she was finding her way back.

Next to her, Emilie rode her gelding, Curtis, on the buckle, the horses' heads bobbing in time. The Wave didn't need the company, but Caroline appreciated it. She liked Em. She stared up at the fluffy cumulus clouds tumbling across the glorious blue sky, inhaling the smell of leather and wildflowers. It was picture-book, and for once she was part of the story.

"So why don't you want to gallop anymore?"

Caroline's eyes flicked to Emilie, then back to The Wave's ears. "Did Dean put you up to this?" She'd thought he'd heard her and understood.

Emilie's brow furrowed. "What?"

So, not Dean, then. She could give a pat — though very believable — answer. *I'm too old for that.* When it came to riding racehorses, the fifteen years she probably had on Emilie was a lot. But the younger woman's open face invited honesty, so Caroline told her the whole story.

Emilie shuddered, and it was a moment before she found her voice. "I'm so sorry."

"I'll never be able to forgive myself for that day."

"What makes you think it was your fault? It was terrible, I'm sure, but that's horses. Sometimes terrible things happen."

"It *was* my fault, though. I got bad about checking my tack once I started training, and worse about cleaning it. I'd leave it to one of the grooms, who resented it because that's not part of their job description. The stitching was rotted. It never would have happened if I'd noticed." At the track, a world of traffic and speed, it was unforgivable.

"Don't you ever miss it?"

"No. I've had my fill of adrenaline." Why did it sound as if she were convincing herself?

"My sister was in an accident like that. She and her horse were badly hurt, but they're both okay now."

"How long did it take her to get back on?"

Emilie snorted. "Four weeks? I can't remember exactly. Way before she should have. Just the pony, but still."

"Jockeys are crazy that way." And no one had died.

"Nate was in a bad spill too, in a race, where another rider died."

Had Emilie been reading her mind? "I didn't know that either," Caroline said quietly.

"Liv said he almost gave it up then. She convinced him not to."

Was that the difference, then? Bryce hadn't cared one way

or another. Despite all the horses he'd owned, he wasn't a horse person. He didn't get it. But the point she probably should be taking — rather than feeling sorry for herself — was that other people went through horrific things too, and somehow moved past.

"How are things with Dean?" Emilie asked, mercifully letting the subject drop.

"What do you mean?" Caroline asked too quickly.

"Are you ever going to let us know what happened between you two?" An impish grin lifted Emilie's lips. "Please tell me it's juicy. Dean is such a closed book, none of us know a thing."

"Sorry to disappoint you. Our differences were professional." She'd leave out the part about that end-of-summer kiss. She'd had her shot, and hadn't followed through. "I did stuff I'm not proud of, but sometimes you can't afford to be idealistic when you're a woman in a man's world."

"Like my sister?" Emilie's eyebrows peaked, a tilt to her head.

"That's not fair. I'm not sure your sister is even real."

Emilie laughed. "I've had doubts myself. Back to Dean. What about now? Do you like him? That would be perfect. Then we'd get to keep you!"

"It's kind of soon to get your hopes up," Caroline said, pursing her lips at the reminder this was a temporary situation. She'd given up on denying her feelings.

"So you do!"

"We've barely started tolerating each other." She sighed. "I'm not sure he'll ever see past who I was. I don't deserve a guy like him. Karma is paying me for the life I've lived."

Emilie groaned. "You're one of those Karma people? Just when I was starting to like you." She flashed a grin, then sobered. Her expressions were like the weather in spring, always changing. "You shouldn't say stuff like that. It doesn't matter if you've got baggage. It's up to you whether you carry it or leave it behind."

This kid. She was too wise for her years. "I thought you were a physiotherapist, not a psychotherapist?"

Emilie grinned. "You're just my newest patient."

The farm came into view and Caroline felt a pang in her chest. The ride was ending too soon. They could joke about Emilie being a psychotherapist, but this had been restorative, not to mention free.

"Who's that with Dean?" Caroline asked, squinting as they fell into single file down the alleyway between paddocks.

Emilie shrugged. "No idea. Never seen her before."

That feeling of Karma crept up the back of Caroline's neck. A young girl, eight or nine years old, stood under the unfamiliar red-headed woman's arm.

"Hey, Dean," Emilie said once they were close. They halted the horses in front of the small group.

"Hi Em." Dean smiled and ran a hand over The Wave's neck, peering up at Caroline. "He looks happy."

"He's enjoying his retirement," she said mildly.

"This is my friend Krissy, and her daughter." Dean turned toward the woman and child. "That's our neighbour, Emilie, and her horse Curtis, and this is my farm manager, Caroline, and my horse, Ride The Wave. Want to say hi, Carlie?"

The girl smiled and nodded. Caroline let The Wave drop his head, trusting Dean to intercede if necessary. The big horse pressed his muzzle into Carlie's outstretched palm.

"Here, you'll need one of these." Dean passed the child a peppermint. "You know to keep your hand flat, right? He'll do the rest."

The bit in The Wave's mouth didn't impede his ability to hoover up the candy. After he'd crunched it, smacking his lips, he gently snuffled the girl up and down, looking for more, and Carlie giggled.

Caroline scratched The Wave's withers. *You are a saint.*

Emilie looked at Carlie gravely. "Curtis says it would be rude not to give him a peppermint, too."

Carlie glanced at Dean. Caroline pressed her mouth into a tight-lipped smile as he gave the girl another peppermint from his apparently bottomless pockets. The child presented it to Emilie's gelding. Curtis lipped it up politely.

"Want to come up?" Emilie said.

The little girl's eyes grew wide. This time she looked at her mother. "Can I?"

Krissy, in turn, looked at Dean. "Is it safe?"

"What about a helmet?" Dean glanced at Emilie.

"I've got this." Caroline hopped off, pulling the reins over The Wave's head and handing them to Emilie. She removed her helmet, then paused. It was sweaty and too big, but there might be a solution.

"Is it okay if I take off your hat for a second?" she asked, and the girl nodded.

Caroline removed Carlie's ballcap carefully so as not to disrupt the girl's ponytail, then put the hat on backward. Once she set the helmet over it and snapped the harness in place, she checked the fit, Carlie grinning.

"Not bad. You've got a big head." Caroline grinned back. "Ready?"

Carlie beamed. "Yes!"

Caroline took The Wave's reins, emotions battling as she watched Dean lift the kid into position in front of Emilie. It was awkward — Emilie had to shift toward the saddle's cantle to make room — but the girl didn't care. Her mother bit her lower lip, phone out, videoing.

"Want to walk a few steps?" Emilie asked, and when the

answer was another enthusiastic nod, she caught Dean's eye. "Lead us a bit?"

Emilie kept her arms around the girl as Dean did a little out and back, Carlie's smile constant. Caroline's eyes flitted to the redhead, grateful the woman was absorbed in her videography so Caroline could study her. She supposed Krissy was pretty, soft without being plump. She wore makeup and her nails were done; her outfit was tasteful, the colours complimenting her skin and hair. Caroline wouldn't have thought that was what Dean liked, but what did she know?

"We should probably apologize," Caroline said, giving Krissy a rueful smile, trying to be grown-up about this. "I think we've recruited a new horse girl."

Dean reached up and lifted Carlie from the saddle, Caroline's heart twisting as he rested the girl on his hip while deftly removing the helmet with his free hand, handing it back to Caroline. "Thanks."

Emilie dismounted. "I guess we'd better go take care of these two. Nice to meet you, Krissy. Nice to meet you, Carlie."

Caroline echoed weakly as they led the horses away, but she couldn't help glancing over her shoulder, seeing Dean and his guests walk towards the house.

"Krissy and Carlie? Really?" she hissed.

"I know, totally pretentious." But Emilie was laughing.

"Just when I was starting to like you, Em."

Emilie laughed harder. "You think he's *gorgeous*. You want to *kiss* him," she crooned.

Caroline scowled. "Aren't you too young to know *Miss Congeniality*?" Then she sighed, defeated. "See, though? That's what Dean needs. The pretty redhead with the cute kid he can buy a pony for. Good for him."

Emilie got back on Curtis to hack home, Caroline sulking as she took care of The Wave, resisting the temptation to peek around the end of the barn and see if she could spot Dean with Krissy and the girl. This needed to stop. She wasn't a teenager. She'd get over these ridiculous feelings. Only six more weeks and she'd be on her way to whatever was next for her life. It was time she focused on that. She tossed The Wave a flake of hay and jumped when a figure loomed at the end of the barn just as she was grabbing a shank to start bringing in.

"Dean!' She gasped, pressing a hand to the closest stall door, her heart rate tripping. "I thought you'd be busy with your guests." It took effort to keep her tone upbeat, free of the snark she'd let seep into her discussion with Emilie.

"They've gone," he said, his face giving nothing away. He carried a white bucket. "I wanted to bring this down here. I'll help you with the horses."

"What is it?"

"Krissy works for Nutritex. They primarily produce human nutraceuticals but have some pet and equine products. This is a 'wellness supplement.'"

Whatever that meant. It explained the logo on Carlie's hat, but Caroline couldn't recall why it was familiar.

Dean continued past on his way to the feed room. "I think my owner mentioned this product. I'll have to tell him I've got some. Not sure why I brought it down here."

They didn't talk as they worked. Dean was probably all happy about his new relationship, while Caroline stewed. At least his help meant she'd get to eat her dinner on time after the hack had put her behind schedule. She was ready to escape to the apartment so she could mope properly.

"Thank you," he said when they were finished, hanging his lead next to hers. "Carlie probably hasn't stopped talking Krissy's ear off yet."

"It was Emilie's idea," Caroline deflected. She was finding it harder to keep the grouchiness out of her voice.

"You were good with her," Dean said, his tone soft. "You and Harrington never had kids."

It was a statement, not a question. A safe assumption.

"Nope." She dared him to say the wrong thing. *There's still time. You'd make a good mother.*

Instead, he turned to The Wave and ran a hand under the black mane, letting the horse bite at his flat palm. "Horses are just like oversized toddlers, aren't they?" He grinned at The Wave and headed for the end of the barn. "Have a nice evening, Caroline."

She watched his back, his easy stride, hating the stupid sense of longing she felt. Then something burned in her chest. It took a moment to identify, it had been dormant so long. She'd been competitive, before Bryce had stripped that from her, too. Why should she let this Krissy waltz in here with her cute daughter and nutraceuticals that promised to make champion racehorses out of duds?

Dean was out of sight now. Caroline closed her eyes, breathing in through her nose and out through her mouth. Behind her, The Wave snorted. It felt like encouragement. She broke into a run.

"Dean! Hang on."

Dust swirled around his feet and settled as he turned, eyebrows raised.

"I'll do it," she said. "I'll gallop for you."

He grinned, as if he'd known all along.

CHAPTER TWENTY-SIX

THE LIGHTS WERE on and Caroline was halfway through feeding when Dean walked into the barn. He checked his watch, like he must have the time wrong.

"Good morning," she chirped.

"You're surprisingly bright." For four AM. Manic, maybe? He wasn't sure he'd expected her to follow through on agreeing to gallop after such an abrupt change of heart. Dean had pictured her shutting off the alarm and rolling over, knowing he would feed and turn out before he left, allowing her an extra hour of sleep before she tackled the daily farm chores.

"I'm surprising even myself how much I'm looking forward to this. I should be dreading it, but I'm not. Maybe it's because you'll give me credibility. You're such a good guy, if I were really that terrible, you'd have nothing to do with me." She started laughing.

"Why is that funny?"

"Because six weeks ago, you *didn't* want anything to do with me. Look at us now."

"Don't make me regret this, Caroline." She didn't need to know he'd secretly hoped this was how things would go.

They turned out in silence, the spring in Caroline's step still puzzling him. If she was seeing the humour in this, maybe he should too. Because she was right. Six weeks ago, he *had* wondered if it'd been a mistake. Now, he wondered if she was the answer — to so many things.

Her gear was just inside the door — helmet, boots, safety vest — and when he hung his shank next to hers once the barns were empty, he glanced at her. "Do you want me to carry anything?"

"Yes," she said. She dashed to the tack room and emerged with the exercise saddle and bridle she'd been using on The Wave.

Dean gathered it from her arms, stopping himself from stating the obvious. *I have tack at the track, you know.* Because the way she met his eyes suggested there was a reason for this, like this set of tack would give her confidence. He wouldn't question it. Racetrackers were superstitious. His job wasn't to give her a hard time; his job was to facilitate so that he had an exercise rider again. If she needed that exact set of tack, she got it. If she needed him to find her a Boston Cream doughnut from Tim's, he was doing it.

He hesitated. "Do you want to ride in with me?"

A cheeky light reignited in her eyes as she collected her gear. "Will you help me muck stalls this afternoon?"

"Of course. I don't expect you to work all morning then do them yourself while I have a nap."

"You look like you're going to need a nap, though."

He shook his head and switched the lights off. "I'm happy to have you come with me. Or drive yourself, whichever you prefer."

"Can you say that again? The part you're happy about."

Without responding, he left her to keep pace, hiding his smile. Because he was happy, for the first time in what felt like a long time.

"It's unlocked," he said as they neared the truck.

"Aren't you afraid it'll get stolen, leaving it open like that overnight?"

"You lived in the city too long."

She opened the passenger door. "And you're too trusting. Except when it comes to me, of course."

Her grin made him chuckle. He needed to trust her. And he already had, with so much, hadn't he?

As the truck bumped out the driveway, Caroline reached for the radio, changing it from his jazz station to classic rock. The look on her face as she leaned back into the seat dared him to challenge her. At least she didn't help herself to his coffee.

In hindsight, he should have brought her one, but he could fix that. He picked up his phone and punched in a text, expecting Caroline to admonish him for doing so while driving, but she ignored him, humming along to the radio. When he pulled up in front of the café, Faye was waiting. She passed a tall paper cup through the window. The aromatic scent of espresso and steamed milk filled the cab.

"You're the best," Dean said.

"I know." Faye gave him a wry smile. "Have a good day, kids."

Dean transferred the cup to a wide-eyed Caroline.

"Thank you," she said, then settled back into the seat, eyes closed and lips in a soft upward curve. She breathed in the steam rising from the lid. "I love your sister."

Dean smiled as he turned the truck around. "Me too."

The pre-dawn traffic on the highway to the big city amazed him each day, all the little ants marching off to work. Sometimes it didn't seem that long ago he'd driven this same route with his father. Back then, there were fewer cars on the road in the wee hours. These days, he was used to making this trip alone, because even before Faye had the café and Will, she'd rarely come in the mornings.

But Caroline was silent, removing the need for conversation. What was she thinking? Part of him wanted to ask, while another part was afraid it would dredge up the past again, when he was starting to like her. For everything she'd done wrong as a trainer, galloping horses was one thing she'd done very, very right. Dean couldn't remember her ever having a seriously injured horse. That was what baffled him about the way she'd gone. She was good; did she just not believe it? Or was the allure of the money too much of a temptation? They were all tempted at some point. What made one person justify the risk — to their career and the horses — but not another?

They were halfway there when he realized the flaw in today's plan. "You're not licensed. I can't let you get on any horses."

Caroline snorted. "You're such a straight arrow. It's the year of living dangerously, Dean."

"I thought you were reformed."

"Where would be the fun in that? Relax. People will see me and I won't look out of place because I'm familiar. They'll be too busy trying to figure out why they know me. And if they do, well, who cares? You're the only one who might have hated me enough back then to report me to the authorities. Just, maybe, you know, distract Gord the outrider if he's at the training track? Because I'm not going to the main, all right?"

"I knew this was a bad idea," he mumbled, clenching the steering wheel and staring at the road.

She became quiet again, and he realized she'd fallen asleep, her head tipped to the window, mouth slightly open. Whatever had made her so chipper first thing had worn off, like a kid crashing after the excitement of a big day. Not even exiting the highway roused her. When he reached the East Gate security booth, Dean held out his badge to be scanned.

"What about that one?" the guard said, thrusting his chin toward Dean's comatose passenger.

"Are you going to make me sign her in? Really?"

"Pull over." The guard waved him off.

Dean snatched back his pass and crept under the striped barrier once it rose, directing the truck into a spot just past the security trailer. "Caroline. Wake up."

She started, pushing her face off the window. "Are we here? Why'd you let me fall asleep?"

"Because it shut you up."

Her mouth fell open, face full of indignation. "I'm doing you a favour."

"Not so sure about that anymore. Get out."

She finally realized where they were. "Wait — no."

"Come on. So much for your anonymity."

"If you'd woken me up I could have hidden."

Dean swung the driver's side door closed, wondering why this was feeling like an undercover operation. He wasn't a rule-breaker, but he *would* have smuggled her in. That had been his intent, hadn't it? Well, it wasn't as if security was going to broadcast it over the backstretch, if that's what she was worried about.

The guard in the trailer showed no signs of recognizing her. Dean signed her in as a guest, and a photo plus some paperwork later, they were on their way again.

Caroline frowned as he parked in front of the dark shedrow. "Don't you have grooms?"

"The new kid hitches a ride with a friend and can't get here until five-thirty. When you said you were coming, I gave my other groom the day off. He's been around a long time and still believes women don't belong in the backstretch." Plus, there was a chance Squeak might know her. Dean could save her the grief, for the first day, at least.

"Women and wheelbarrows?" she quipped.

"How about dumping waters and cleaning some buckets and feed tubs?" he said, leading the way to the shed. "Remember how to do that?"

She nodded. "Yes, sir!"

Len squinted when Dean ran into him on the way to the tack room. "Who's that? She looks familiar."

"That's my temporary farm manager." Caroline was far enough away that the dim light on the shedrow prevented identification. The trademark blonde ponytail she'd worn back in the day that would have tipped Len off was gone.

Len scrunched his nose. "It'll come to me." Then he grabbed Dean's arm, chuckling. "Caroline Jenkins. I'll be damned. How did that happen?"

Dean shrugged. "She answered my ad." He pulled away. There'd be plenty of time for Len to drag the rest of the story out of him later.

He remembered the set of tack in the truck and retrieved it, setting it on the rail. The buckets hung on the posts in front of the stalls, refilled; the feed tubs were snapped to the doors. Did she operate at warp speed?

"You can get on Fargo first," he suggested. "Take him on a walkabout. Give him an easy day."

Caroline turned slowly from where she'd been tickling Cruze between his nostrils with a piece of hay, her brow furrowed, lips pursed.

"A walkabout? Why don't you have security announce it?" she hissed. "'Caroline Jenkins-slash-Harrington is back! Give her a wide berth in case of tack malfunctions and unethical behaviour!' You should probably grab me an orange vest to be sure no one misses me."

Her eyes were so wide and body so tight, Dean thought she was going to bolt, like she'd suddenly decided this was a big mistake. Cruze tried to reach for her, frustrated the game had come to such an abrupt end. Dean set his hands on her shoulders. She was trembling, vibrating at a critical frequency and seemed to need help keeping her feet on the shed. Caroline tipped her face up, meeting his gaze, and blinked.

"It's okay," he said. "I thought it would be nice for both of you to go on a little tour, but you're right. Maybe not a great idea. Take him straight to the training track and jog him a bit. Or if you've changed your mind and don't want to do this, that's fine."

Her shoulders rose and fell with a long exhale, then her eyes darted to his hands.

Right. Dean stepped away, his neck suddenly feeling too hot. "Sorry."

Caroline ducked past him and grabbed her helmet. "Where is this horse? Let's get this show on the road."

CHAPTER TWENTY-SEVEN

THE GLOVES WERE hard to pull on because her palms were so sweaty — which was exactly why she'd brought them. The last thing Caroline needed was the lines slipping. Just because Dean said this horse was old and creaky didn't mean he couldn't run off with her. Another difference between a bike and a racehorse: a bike didn't pull.

The young groom brought the horse around, stopping in front of her. Dean hovered, but Caroline's eyes remained fixed on the saddle. She closed them, trying to convince her pulse to settle. *This is no different from getting on The Wave at the farm.* Except it was totally different. But what was she going to do? Go hide in the tack room?

Check the tack. That wasn't stalling; that was necessary. She snugged the girth a hole and straightened the martingale loop. Pulled the rings up to the throatlatch to ensure it was the proper length — long enough it wouldn't restrict the horse if his head went up, short enough there was no risk of a leg getting caught. Made sure the bit was even in his mouth, the throatlatch a perfect fist from Fargo's jaw. Scooted around the groom to run hands and eyes over the other side to be sure everything was right. A pilot doing her pre-flight check.

Finally, she gathered the reins and placed a hand on the cantle, eyes flitting to Dean.

"Ready?" he asked.

She nodded. "I'm going to need your help. I suck at this. And I'm no featherweight."

"You were never that bad."

"I was a lot lighter then."

"I've got you, Caroline."

She met his gaze, steady and reassuring — and so close her heart skipped a beat. She was probably safer up on the horse than on the ground, next to him. He practically lifted her into the tack; the man knew how to give a leg up. From there, it was all surprisingly automatic — tying her knot, tightening the girth, shortening her irons, the left one lower than the right like how the jockeys rode. She didn't crank them high like she would have done if she was in shape. She'd let herself ease into it.

Fargo certainly knew the way to the training track. Caroline barely realized Dean walked beside them until he asked, "Good?"

It felt familiar, and right. Dipping her chin she replied, "Good."

If anyone noticed her, she didn't notice them noticing. Knuckles firm at Fargo's withers, eyes between the gelding's pricked ears, she left Dean at the on-gap, posting to the gelding's trot.

He felt a little stiff but was well-behaved, as Dean had promised. They were among the first on the dirt oval, the sun merely a suggestion on the horizon as they jogged. When she pulled him up just past the off-gap and let him stand, facing the infield, Fargo dropped his head and snorted, and Caroline reached down and stroked his neck before sending him counter-clockwise at a little hobby-horse gallop. All she wanted to do was test her legs, see if she could still stand up so if Dean put her on something he needed to gallop, she wouldn't look like a hack.

Fargo humoured her. Galloping used a different set of muscles and a lot more core strength than the putzing around she'd been doing on the farm with The Wave. She silently thanked Jess and Dean for the bike rides, because she felt more secure than she would have without them. So much for that old belief that nothing but riding got you riding-fit. *Cross-training for the win.*

Still, by the time she made it once around, her muscles were quivering. She hadn't looked at Dean as she'd gone past. She probably would have fallen off in embarrassment. Both she and Fargo were in no hurry to return to the barn, so she let him amble along, keeping her eyes down to avoid anyone who might recognize her, until she realized the only familiar face she saw was Dean's. Was the worry on his face for her, or his horse?

"Everything all right?" he asked.

"He's fine." She let the lines slip between her fingers, Fargo stretching down to nibble the sparse grass near the rail. "You said give him an easy day. That was an easy day. He feels a little stiff, that's all."

Dean nodded, seeming to accept her response. "How'd you feel?"

"Great, actually." And she meant it. Muscles that had trembled were now nicely warmed. And she hadn't thought for a millisecond about the accident.

She watched Dean instead of their surroundings as they walked back. So far, no one had called out, but it was busier now, and she just wanted to get back under cover of the shedrow. This couldn't last forever. Someone would say hi to Dean. They would know his regular exercise rider was out and that Liv and her troops had been helping him. They'd look more closely.

The groom and hotwalker took over as soon as she pulled off the saddle. She cradled the tack like she didn't want to let it go.

"Game for another?" Dean asked.

"Sure." She needed to keep the momentum going.

"Liv's coming, so you can take the two-year-olds out as a set. Cruze and Gastronomy."

"Which is the one that broke your exercise rider?"

Dean chuckled. "Cruze. Liv's been getting on him, so you can get on Gastronomy."

Cruze was one of the few horses she could identify — process of elimination; he was the only one without a plate displaying a registered name, his halter a hand-me-down. She set the tack in front of his stall. "I'm not afraid of a spooky two-year-old. Cruze is yours, right? You should probably let the famous rider take the client's horse."

"It's not as if he's here, and it's not as if you're breezing."

"I want to ride him, okay?" Because if she was doing this, she couldn't pick and choose. Besides, from what Dean had said about his colt, he wasn't tough, just easily distracted.

"All right. You'll want to ride long with him. And keep your eyes open for geese."

Caroline snorted. The Canada Geese on the backstretch were no joke. Some things never changed.

Liv said an understated hello when she arrived, but didn't try to make small talk on the way out, other than sharing her insight on Cruze — "He's lazy, and he's looky, but once he knows you won't let him off the hook he's all right" — and Caroline was happy to stay in her own head.

It was as if Cruze started searching for geese as soon as they walked on the track. Caroline kept him moving forward, trying not to look for them herself. He had a cute little jog, and his ears started flicking back toward her as she bumped him with her heels every stride to keep him going. No doubt about it, she was going to be tired by the end of the day. It took as much energy to keep a slow horse going as it did to hold a tough one. An older horse carried you; you had to carry a baby.

He was more forward when she turned him to gallop. After his big brother, Ride The Wave, Cruze's stride was shorter, less assertive, but he had a lot of growing up to do yet. It helped that Liv had discretely maneuvered Gastronomy to the outside so that Cruze had little opportunity to be silly.

"You and I are going to be friends," she vowed, scratching his neck when they pulled up and turned in before leaving the track. "We're going to make Dean some money."

Liv didn't mock her for her pronouncement.

Every muscle in her body chattered at her as she dragged off the saddle and bridle, stumbling a little as she trudged through the straw. She hoisted the tack onto the rail as if it weighed fifty pounds instead of ten, zipped off the vest and pulled her sweat-drenched t-shirt away from her skin, trying not to think of the stalls still to do back at the farm. If Dean bailed on her, she'd kill him.

She needed to keep moving before rigor set in. The wind dried her shirt and hair, and Dean was quick with the sponge as he bathed Cruze, the way his big hands squeezed the soapy water over the colt seeming to take merely three swipes per side. He rinsed and scraped just as fast, then took the shank from her.

"Time for you to get licensed. Try to look like you haven't been wearing a helmet all morning." He grinned, reaching out and mussing her hair.

She ran her palm slowly over her head, not quite believing

he'd just done that. It felt... affectionate. Why was he being affectionate?

Don't read anything into it. He's just happy he might have an exercise rider again.

As she waited her turn at the licensing office, avoiding eye contact, she stared at the photo on her old badge. She didn't know why she'd kept it. The blonde in the picture looked so young and ready to take on the world. An image, not a reflection.

"Caroline! You're back!"

Her head snapped up, and she mustered a smile. "I am," she said, stepping forward and pushing the legal-sized form across the counter.

"Exercise rider? For Dean." The woman's eyebrows twitched as she glanced at the paper. Caroline imagined the talk once she left. Soon, the whole backstretch would know. "Do you want a new photo?"

"Absolutely," Caroline responded.

New photo, new leaf.

———

They stopped for fast food on the way home, and Caroline was hit with a wave of nostalgia for that first summer. She didn't bring it up, even if she wondered if Dean felt it, too. She wanted that summer back. She wanted to do it better this time.

"You still eat stuff like this?" she asked as they waited in line at the drive-thru.

"With a sister and future brother-in-law who are food snobs and friends whose livelihoods depend on restrictive diets, sometimes I have to."

Caroline snorted. "Is this your dirty little secret? Junk food? Where do you hide the wrappers?"

"The barn garbage, of course. Faye would never look there."

She started laughing, and soon Dean was laughing with her, the two of them snickering like a couple of fools as Dean pulled up to the payment window. The poor kid there stared at them with his mouth agape, likely wishing these weird old people would be quiet so he could announce what was owed and take the money. Dean handed him a couple of bills and drove to the pickup window, not waiting for his change.

"How much did you give him?" Caroline choked out, gulping for air. As if her core muscles weren't already sore, her sides ached with laughter.

"Couldn't have been that much," Dean said, wiping the corners of his eyes as he braked. "I didn't have a lot to begin with."

He was grinning, but it reminded Caroline how tough things were for him right now. She said it again, but only to herself, picturing Cruze's active ears tuning into her voice: *We're going to make Dean some money.*

Dean caught her napping — again — waking her up once he parked at the farmhouse. Even the potholes hadn't roused her. The work and greasy food knocked her right out. It gave her a much-needed boost, and she threw herself into doing stalls — mind over matter when her body wanted her to give in to the encroaching soreness from her reintroduction to galloping.

Dean, on the other hand, dragged.

"Why don't you go lie down somewhere?" she said. "You're not much help anyway."

Dean paused, shavings spilling from his fork as he caught her eye. He looked as if he was either considering it or going to snap at her. "Are you popping caffeine pills or something? You're making me tired just watching you."

"That's just it, you're not supposed to be watching, you're supposed to be working." She grinned.

"We're almost done," he said. "I'm not going anywhere."

"Hurry up with that stall so I can move the tractor forward."

He did feeds as she swept up. Dean glanced at his watch once they had everything put away. "Despite my holding you back, we made good time. It's too early to bring the horses in. Come up to the house. I've got a better selection of beverages there. Plus, as much as I love the barn, it's nicer sitting on the deck than here."

Caroline gawked, not hiding her shock. "You're inviting me to the house?"

Dean shrugged. "Don't come, then. I need something cold to drink."

He didn't wait for her, leaving her standing with her feet stuck to the asphalt aisle.

Dean was just being nice. He was a nice guy. But the invitation made her heart swell, so she wasn't about to turn it down. She caught up to him, and they walked side by side to the red-brick century home.

"Have a seat," he said, pausing with his hand on the door. "What do you want?"

"There's a choice?"

"There's always a choice." He paused, like he was putting too much thought into that concept, before listing the options. "Water, probably iced tea, beer..."

"I'll have whatever you're having," she said, sitting on the bench and leaning back against the railing. She didn't know what to do with her hands. She'd spent the whole day with him and suddenly she felt awkward.

When Dean opened the door, the Taylor's big Golden Retriever bounded over with a face-splitting grin and tried to climb into her lap, obliterating her self-consciousness. She had no choice but to wrap her arms around the huge bundle of soft yellow fur and give him a hug.

Dean returned with an open beer bottle in each hand. "Gus, could you at least try to act like you're not a complete hooligan?"

Caroline's laugh came out as an *oof* as Gus pushed off her to bounce over to Dean, leaving her covered in long, silky hairs. He circled Dean once before racing down the steps to the massive maple that partially shaded the deck.

Dean handed her the beer. "Sorry about that. He's not very friendly, as you can see."

"That's all right. It's been a long time since someone gave me a proper hug. It was nice."

She thought that would get a laugh, but there was no amusement in the look he gave her. He probably thought she sounded pathetic.

"I hope beer is okay." He settled into one of the patio chairs.

Caroline peered at the label. "I should have known you grew up to be the guy who drank fancy craft beer."

"I don't, normally. These are Will's."

"What's your poison, then?"

"Nothing in particular. I'm more of a social drinker."

"So we're social drinking, then?" she said, taking a careful sip, meeting his gaze.

"Is that inappropriate?"

What was he suggesting? Her eyes went to the mares and foals in the front paddock — it was nice enough today they'd been able to put everyone out early — because it was safer than looking at Dean. She was tired, that was all. She could *not* trust her emotions when she was this worn out.

She didn't mind the silence, even if it surprised her how

comfortable it was. She was definitely falling a little bit in love with this place. Which was bad, because it was a temporary thing. In the fall, she'd return to... what? There was nothing to go back to, only finding a way to move forward after this lovely stopover on her journey to an unknown future.

"This has been the best day I've had in a long, long time," she said, her tone soft.

Dean looked at her sideways. "You like having your fingers worked to the bone?"

She rolled her eyes with a shake of her head, then sobered. "I used to love this game. Then I got mixed up with Bryce. I bought into everything he fed me." She stared down at the beer bottle. "I want it back. I want it to be fun again. Today was fun."

Dean cranked his eyebrows. "So you're just using me?"

Caroline laughed. "Do you have a problem with that?"

She couldn't read his expression, and decided not to try.

CHAPTER TWENTY-EIGHT

A FOURTEEN-DAY SCAN in the middle of July seemed like a longshot, but Dean kept his eyes on the monitor as the vet moved the transducer inside Cherry, both of them hoping for the black dot of an embryo. Caroline held the mare's head with one hand and distracted Cherry's filly with the other to keep the foal from trying to sneak out into the aisle.

It was taking too long. It was never a good sign when it took too long.

Chad removed his arm and peeled off the long examination glove. "We can check her in a couple more days. Sometimes this early you can't find them for one reason or another."

Which Dean knew. But he also knew the nurse mare at Triple Stripe who had been bred a couple of days before Cherry couldn't be confirmed in foal, either. That didn't bode well for The Wave's future as a stallion. It wasn't a complete surprise — he'd seen the sample they'd taken when The Wave had covered Cherry. There wasn't a lot of activity in those swimmers, but he'd hoped anyway — because he always hoped.

When Dean returned from walking Chad to his truck, Caroline was leaning on the wall outside the stall, hands tucked behind her back, her face crinkled with worry. He stood in front of her, tempted to set his hands on her shoulders again, to smooth away the tightness, but he forced himself to cross his arms instead.

"Welcome to the breeding business," he said. "It's not that different from racing. You win some, you lose some."

"But what will happen to The Wave?"

Was that what she was concerned about? His temporary farm manager had fallen for the big horse. No one could blame her for that, but it caught him off guard. He could tell she was fond of The Wave, but she'd always been affectionate with her horses as a trainer. It had never kept her from being ruthless with them.

Dean shrugged. "I'll find a way to keep him. He's my Plate horse. He's not going anywhere."

Her shoulders dropped as the tension left them, and she was trying to keep from smiling, her lips tight, creased at the corners. She turned toward the bratty colt's stall, peering between the bars. "Are we leaving these guys in again till later?"

Dean nodded. "It's still pretty hot. We'll kick them out once it cools off and get the stalls done after that."

"How long are you going to keep helping me?" She looked over her shoulder with a cheeky twist to her lips.

"As long as you keep helping me at the track."

She'd slipped into a role that was so much more than getting on horses. With her experience, even Squeak respected her. Somehow her no-nonsense demeanor gave her a natural authority. If he had more horses — and the role wasn't a complete insult given her background — he'd ask her to be his assistant. Except for the small problem of Nikki coming back. Would the two of them clash?

"Which reminds me," he said. "Do you feel ready to breeze something?"

There was a beat of hesitation, a slight tightening of her jaw, before she answered. "Sure. Who?"

"Cruze. You get along with him well." Liv had continued to work the colt, but Caroline galloped him daily. Dean didn't want to assume she was prepared for it psychologically.

"I just have one request," she said.

"What's that?"

"Please don't make me breeze a horse with Nate Miller?"

"Why?"

"Because it's my first time in over ten years. My first time since the accident. What if I suck? What if Cruze decides that's the day he's going to drop me and I fall off?" The light-heartedness in her words faded. "Worse, what if when I come off, Cruze crashes into him and I'm at fault for injuring Woodbine's leading rider?"

Dean had to smother a laugh. That was quite the diegesis she'd conjured up. But when she didn't break into another smile, real fear behind her stare, he kept himself from being flip.

"Have you ever talked to someone about all that, Caroline?"

A pink flush crept into her cheeks, and she looked away. "I saw a therapist for a while before I left Bryce. But not about that."

"Nate Miller might be exactly the person who could help."

She glanced at him. "So I've heard."

"Would you feel better breezing him alone? Training track, later in the morning. Just you and Cruze and the geese."

Finally, she cracked a smile. "Maybe we could get permission for my friend Jess to come with her Border Collie to manage them."

"I wonder who I'd have to talk to for that?" he said. "The stewards? Maintenance? Security?"

Caroline laughed, and it seemed to loosen all her anxiety. "Probably all of them."

***

The door creaked as Caroline closed it, shoulders slumped. The apartment was so empty, so impersonal. Someone else's space, part of her temporary life. It felt like a letdown every time she entered... alone. The disappointment of learning Cherry wasn't in foal was just another layer of despondence. At least it sounded like Dean would do right by The Wave.

Sparsely populated cupboards stared back at her as she opened and closed each one. She wished she had the ingredients to cook something, not just bare essentials. Then she could have invited Dean for dinner. Too forward? He might be sick of her, spending so much time together. But she felt like every day they took a few tentative steps ahead.

She had no business thinking the way she was when her divorce wasn't even final. Until recently, she hadn't cared that Bryce hadn't contacted her. But now, she wanted that door closed, the key tossed into Lake Ontario. She was ready to let the past go, an oversized balloon — no, a whole bundle of them — drifting through the atmosphere.

Except Emilie would berate her for adversely affecting the environment — killing birds or something equally tragic. *Fine.* She'd stab every last one with a big, fat needle instead, and dispose of them responsibly.

Her phone rang, and she snatched it from where she'd left it on the counter, her other hand still wrapped around a snack-size yogurt — which was looking pretty sad. The sight of Jess's name pulled her spirits from the pit they'd tumbled into.

"Jess! I'm so happy you called." Caroline collapsed onto the couch, sinking into the worn cushions.

It took a beat for Jess to answer. "Really? Why?"

"No reason, especially. Sorry. Why'd you call?"

"I remembered what I'd heard about Nutritex and their equine products."

Caroline sat up. She'd looked at the bucket Krissy had brought Dean — after Dean was gone, of course — and taken photos of the label, sending it to Jess. Something had nagged Caroline about the company, something she'd forgotten. Jess had gone back to school for biochemistry; she knew how all these supplements worked.

"Tell me!"

"There was someone a while back privately compounding supplements." Jess said the word like she was making air quotes. "He'd come around the track and sell them on the sly to trainers."

It hit Caroline like a brick had been dropped on her skull. "How did I forget that?" Because she'd been one of those trainers. She could picture him. He was attractive: blond hair neatly cut, casually but stylishly dressed. He'd flirted with her — harmlessly. It had just been about making the sale. "What was his name? It'll come to me. But it wasn't Krissy."

"Maybe she's helping him. Or maybe she's taken over. I'm pretty sure it's a thyroid supplement of some kind," Jess said.

That was it. Was it the same product Caroline had used? It had been effective — but risky. Some horses reacted to it.

"Things have changed since you were training," Jess

continued. "Almost everything is illegal on race day, and if there isn't a withdrawal time on that label —"

Which there wasn't. "Dean could innocently find himself with a positive test," Caroline finished. Part of the game was knowing when you had to stop using something so that it wouldn't show up in a post-race sample.

"Best case," Jess said.

"What's the worst case?"

"He could find himself with a dead horse. There were a couple of suspicious sudden deaths last season, and the rumour is it's connected to that company. They don't have concrete evidence of a correlation between thyroxine and sudden deaths but —"

"Speak English to me, Jess."

"You know what I'm saying."

The reaction to the product Caroline remembered had been scary, but transient. She didn't recall hearing about any horses dying.

"Could you test it?" Caroline asked quickly. "You have access to all that fancy equipment."

Jess snorted. "Do you know nothing about university department funding?"

Caroline laughed. "No, why would I?"

"Let's just say we don't have the most sophisticated tools here. You'd have to send it to an independent lab."

"Okay. How do I do that?"

"Are you serious? Why are you doing this?"

Caroline sighed, sinking back into the cushions. "Dean is such a good guy, Jess. I don't want to see him get in trouble for something he would never intentionally do. And losing a horse would kill him." Professionally *and* emotionally.

"You really care about him, don't you?" Jess said, her voice soft.

Caroline draped her forearm over her face. "I don't know. That doesn't matter. But if I can't go back and change the past, the least I can do is help keep him from ending up in a bad spot."

How might her life have been different if she'd been mature enough to see how she would have been better off with a guy like Dean than flash-in-the-pan Bryce? Ed Taylor had liked her; she could have helped the older man see that Dean's place was with him, at the track. She could have been the mediator.

Then she would have been there for Dean after the accident. They'd have made a great training team. Dean's sensibility would have balanced her ambition, and her drive would've lit a spark under him. Or maybe there never would have been an accident at all. The two of them could have gone out on their own. Forget Ed Taylor.

If only.

After remembering to ask Jess how things were going, Caroline disconnected, always sorry for their chats to end. She checked the weather app — the temperature would drop in a few hours, so there was nothing to do until then. Heat engulfed her when she left the air-conditioned apartment and stole down the stairs. She wondered what Dean was doing.

Horses rumbled in their stalls, but she ignored them. She'd stashed the bucket, hoping Dean would forget about it. There it was, right where she'd left it. Sure enough, Jess was right. No company name or logo, no contact information, just an inauspicious title, an ingredient line, and a production stamp — one of those coded ones only the manufacturer could interpret.

As much as she wanted to dislike Krissy, could the woman really be that much of an ogre? If Krissy liked Dean and Dean made his living from horses, she wouldn't want to see them hurt, would she? Caroline still had to tell him. Or she could just get rid of it. Dump it in the spreader next time she was mucking out on her own.

No. She would tell him. Because if he didn't believe her, she'd know they hadn't come as far as she so desperately hoped. Better to find out now, before she invested any more of herself in him.

CHAPTER TWENTY-NINE

"Take the rings off him." Caroline snatched the bridle from Dean and unbuckled the lines, letting the martingale attachment slide off. "Maybe if you start treating him like a racehorse, he'll act like one."

She handed him the leather triangle, leaving him dangling it from the brass snap as she ducked into the stall. She was bristly this morning.

"You're the one getting on him," Dean muttered. Though the rings hadn't prevented Cruze from spooking at the geese, he doubted the colt would run off with Caroline. He kind of wished Cruze would — they might find out if he had some ability. So far, his times had been mediocre at best.

She appeared at the doorway and Dean handed her a shank. Cruze took the opportunity to rub his head against her, just like The Wave liked to do. Caroline pushed him away gently.

"Time to work, mister. If you go good, maybe I'll let you do that after."

Her irons were the shortest Dean had seen since re-entry,

but she'd kept to the black vest and coverless helmet. The lack of colour made her seem homeless — detached, non-committal — when once that purple silk had been her trademark. Under the black vest was a splash of deep red, long sleeves coming to her wrists, like one of those black and white photos where a drop of hue had been added. He wanted to think it was a nod to his colours, like maybe she was letting herself feel part of his life. Such thoughts kept sneaking in, unbidden, but was there any point in fighting it?

Len waited at the rail by the clocker's stand in his usual spot as if it had been pre-arranged. Some days, it was annoying that Len seemed to always be looking over his shoulder. Others, it was a strange comfort, because he could imagine his father there with him, like when Dean had been a teenager — before everything had changed.

"How is *that* going?" Len said by way of greeting.

Dean didn't think Len meant the horse. He leaned his forearms on the rail, keeping his eyes on the pair as they jogged off. Cruze's head was too high — looking for geese, no doubt. He should have insisted she keep the rings on. The polos he'd put on the two-year-old's front legs — Dean didn't quite trust Hunter to do that yet — stood out against the colt's dark coat, accentuating the energy in his stride. Cruze was even starting to tuck up a bit. Maybe there was hope he'd get to the races this year.

"Ask me again in ten minutes." Dean meant the horse.

"Good on you for giving her a chance," Len said, not letting him off the hook. "She's a good girl. Harrington led her astray."

"Harrington didn't deserve her."

Len grinned and patted him on the back, and Dean hid behind his binoculars. He had to stop letting those things enter his mind, let alone come out of his mouth.

Caroline and Cruze stood at the quarter pole, Cruze waiting, as reliable as an old pony horse. A month ago, he never would have done that because Crystal didn't have the patience to insist on it. Caroline treated the colt like she expected great things of him.

They galloped around the turn and into the stretch, Cruze striding out with ears like antennae, searching for trouble. *No geese in sight, buddy. Keep focused on the task.* Caroline reached forward to stroke his neck, and Cruze dropped his head, ears swivelling.

Cruze almost looked like a racehorse as he travelled along the backstretch. Caroline picked him up approaching the pole. The colt's ears twitched ahead, then back to her. His stride lengthened as he glided to the rail. At the pole, he flew.

As they dashed down the lane, Dean prayed the Canada Geese were entertaining themselves elsewhere, not lurking in the ditch where he couldn't see them, planning a stealth attack. Folded over the colt, her hands giving with every stride, Caroline rode him through the wire, not standing up to ease him until she neared the turn.

"She hasn't lost it," Len said. "That's the best that colt has ever gone."

Dean didn't need Len to tell him that, as surprised as he was it was true. He smiled. "Let's hope he doesn't get shins after that."

Len stepped back from the rail. "Just a couple more weeks until the induction ceremony, eh?"

His smile fell away. He'd conveniently forgotten about that. They received two tickets for free, but he'd have Faye get a table. He wanted all their friends there: Will, Liv and Nate, Emilie and Tim. There would be one empty seat.

"You want to come?" he asked. Who better than his father's best friend and mentor to occupy it?

"You mean like your date?" Len said wryly. "It would keep

me up past my bedtime. Besides, it's not me you should be asking." He ambled off.

Dean stared after him before slowly turning to find Caroline. It wasn't hard to figure out what Len was suggesting, but felt like it would be crossing a line he kept saying he wouldn't go over.

They came toward him, her nondescript helmet bobbed as Cruze bounced. The colt's nostrils flared, a new light in his eyes, veins dancing across his neck, black with sweat. Caroline beamed.

"Apparently he's been waiting for you all his life," Dean said.

"Oh, please," she scoffed, but the grin didn't recede. "It's because all the planets are in alignment."

Cruze settled into a walk next to Dean. Happy energy wafted from horse and rider, and he soaked it in.

"Everything clicked for him today," Caroline went on. "All the proper brain cells lit up."

"The right neurons fired, activating those fast-twitch muscles." Dean grinned.

"It was a mind-body connection," Caroline deadpanned. "Truly a mystical experience. For both of us."

She cracked a smile, cheeks flushed, looking completely alive for the first time since she'd walked into the layup barn at the farm weeks ago. How shrouded she'd been. He was happy she was happy — and Cruze was happy. Though the way this year had been going, the colt probably *would* buck his shins now that he'd figured out what speed was.

"Come on, Dean. With all those long, slow miles this colt has done — of his own accord — he's probably got great bone density. He won't buck his shins."

Dean glanced up at her quickly. He hadn't realized he'd said that out loud, probably so used to walking back alone, talking to himself. He grinned and quipped, "I thought you might've started feeding him that supplement on the sly."

There was no zippy comeback, and she blanched, the smile gone. Had she?

"He doesn't need that stuff." Her tone was insistent. "He did that out there because you took the time. You should probably take your friend Liv a big box of Faye's pastries, too, because he was primed. He barely even thought about the geese." The smile made a subtle comeback, playing at one corner of her lips.

"I keep forgetting to bring it in, anyway," Dean said. "I could use it for Gastronomy. Andy keeps pestering me; it might get him off my back."

Because if the owner was paying attention, he was *not* going to be happy about Cruze working better than Gastronomy had to date, especially when Cruze's previous efforts had been lacklustre. If Andy didn't see for himself, one of his cronies would certainly tell him a two-year-old in Dean Taylor's barn had worked well this morning — and Andy would know it wasn't his.

Once all the horses were trained, Dean headed to his office, leaving the shed humming. Not quite like a well-oiled machine — more like an old car with some new parts, working out the kinks. It had character. He didn't hate it.

He left the door open and made his notes on the training chart. Fargo was the only one running this weekend. Dean would bring in the van and take him home to the farm afterward. He had to remember to check in with Emilie. She'd be ecstatic to hear he'd decided to retire the old campaigner.

Caroline walked past with an armful of tack. A few moments later, she appeared in the doorway, running a hand through her sweat-darkened hair, smoothing it away from her forehead.

"Do you think you could breeze Cruze in company next time?" Dean asked, tapping his pen on the desk.

"With who?"

He'd caught her off guard, like her mind had been elsewhere. "I'm sure I can arrange for whomever you want. My friends are very accommodating."

"You have incredible friends."

"I do."

She nodded, and he thought she was going to leave, but she stepped into the room and shut the door behind her. Dean's forehead tightened and he shifted in his seat, straightening as she sat on the overturned bucket parked in the corner. The room felt small.

Caroline leaned forward, her brow furrowed, fists bunched at her knees. "You can't feed that supplement, Dean. I keep hiding it hoping you'll forget about it. I asked my friend Jess if she knew anything about it. She's majoring in Biochemistry, so she pays attention to rumours about these things. She says it's not safe."

Dean listened to her explain what her friend had told her. It wasn't all news. He'd heard about a few mysterious cases, deaths during training hours where horses were sent for post-mortems, and no one ever heard the conclusions. Horses' hearts were a wildcard all by themselves; it wasn't ever hard to believe the findings were inconclusive. He hadn't noticed the label though. He'd trusted what Krissy told him about the product, and it aligned with everything he'd heard on the backstretch. The good things, anyway.

"It wouldn't do them any good if they were flogging something harmful, would it?" he said.

"Why not label it, though? All I'm saying is, when Jess sees a red flag, it's best to pay attention. If I'd listened to what she thought of my ex, I wouldn't be waiting on my divorce." She might have been trying for a wry smile but looked miserable instead.

"You probably wouldn't be sitting here, either," he said.

"Don't use that as justification. Throw the stuff out or give it back. Trust me, you don't want to go down that road. Even if it isn't dangerous, you might win more races, but you'll end up not liking yourself very much."

Caroline slipped out with less aplomb than when she'd arrived. She was probably right. It wasn't worth the risk, even if Andy would especially like that it was free. But he didn't believe Krissy would mislead him or put an animal in danger. Someone must have misinformed her, or tainted product got out, despite all the checks and balances. Humans made mistakes. He even, without completely buying into conspiracy theories about Big Pharma, believed everything wasn't always on the up and up. Nothing ever was, when there was money at play.

CHAPTER THIRTY

So MANY BRIDLES. Dean had more bridles than horses, a different bit on each one. It's how they operated at the track. Want to try a different bit on a horse? Just pick up the bridle. Nosebands were separate, for easy customization. Not all horses went in one, or a horse might be fine with a plain cavesson while another benefited from a figure-eight. Caroline had never tried Cruze in a shadow roll — though he hadn't been spooky with her.

She worked conditioner into the parts everyone neglected — where the reins and headstall connected to the bit. The leather was reinforced there, so it was naturally stiffer than the other parts, but how often did anyone take bridles apart to be sure the leather was healthy? She gently scraped the ridge of the lined browband to remove all traces of soap residue and used the tongue on each buckle to poke out the sludge collected in the holes. Stainless steel hardware was buffed and bits washed. Dean's tack had never been this clean, Caroline was sure of it.

She was officially obsessed.

With only six horses, they didn't use much tack on the daily, so Caroline took her time and cleaned it meticulously. It hadn't been terrible when she'd started two weeks ago, but there were places where dried soap had collected like plaque on teeth which carried the same risk of rotting. Now, she was working her way through every last bit of dried old leather she could find. There were crown pieces, chin straps, miscellaneous other bridle parts, stirrup leathers ... some of it had to be from when Ed Taylor had been training.

"What's taking you so long?" Dean squeezed into the small room and brushed past her, diving into a tote in the corner. "We're all done up. I'm ready to feed lunch."

Caroline rubbed the spot on her elbow where he'd touched it, distracted by the buzz it sent up her arm. "Almost done," she said, watching his long arms rifle through the bin. "I got a little carried away."

When Dean's head emerged from the tote with a spare halter, he looked around. "Did you clean every piece of tack in here?"

"I'm trying to give the boss a good impression," she said. It sounded better than admitting she might be developing a neurosis. Was a compulsive disorder really a bad thing when it was for safety's sake? She *had* graduated from only using the set Dean had brought to the farm for The Wave. That meant she didn't have a complex, right?

Dean laughed, patting her on the shoulder as he passed her again. "Great work. I'll be back in ten and we can get out of here."

Caroline stared after him as he left. He'd touched her. Again. So he wasn't mad at her for what she'd told him about the supplement? Or did Cruze breezing well override everything? Probably that.

Only the saddles were left, two of them waiting on the

rickety old sawhorse — something else that had surely been around since Ed. Dipping the sponge cautiously into the water — murky now, with a film of sludge on top — she tried to find something to think about besides Dean.

"Caro-line..."

With a snap her head came up, something familiar in the sing-song of the man's voice. Spiders of recognition crept up her neck, and she froze. Jack Faron.

Caroline recovered, reaching for the bar of glycerine soap, her jaw tight. "What do you want?"

"I heard you were back."

He sauntered closer and wrapped an arm around one of the posts that supported the overhang. Faron looked like he hadn't touched a horse all morning, with his clean dark-wash jeans, tidy polo shirt, and dark hair. He must colour it. There wasn't a single strand of grey, and he had to be in his late forties now. Caroline caught a glimpse of Dean on the shedrow — faded t-shirt, his too-long hair windblown — knowing there were callouses on his hands. Two men, both trainers, total opposites.

She pulled a stirrup down and tugged the buckle out so she could soap the leather, refusing to look at Faron. "What's it to you?"

"Oh, Caroline. Why so hostile? Can't an old friend stop by and say hello?"

"You weren't my friend. You were Bryce's friend." Did Bryce know she was here? Not that it was a secret anymore. Word travelled at lightspeed in this community. Faron must've known within days, if not hours, of her return. Why was he here now?

"What are you doing, working for Dean Taylor, of all people? I would have given you a job. Come to think of it, I could probably get you some horses. You didn't come back just to gallop."

Yes, actually, she had. "Thank you, but I'm not interested."

A sly grin split his lips. "I see."

Caroline flushed. *No, you don't.* When her eyes drifted to the shed again, she found Dean watching, one of those damned unreadable expressions on his face. She ducked her head to the saddle and scrubbed like the seat was spattered in mud instead of merely dusty.

"Is there something else I can help you with?" she asked with all the friendliness of a honey badger.

Faron still had that infuriating grin on his face. "There might be, actually. I saw you on that decent older horse of his. Longago Faraway. What's he like? Is he sound?"

She tossed the sponge into the tack bucket, her hands in fists on her hips. "You need to go. Don't make me get my whip." Why had she chosen that? Faron was probably just the kind of creep who liked that sort of thing.

He laughed, letting go of the post and taking a couple of steps backward. "Good seeing you again, Caroline. If you change your mind, you know how to find me."

She'd panhandle at Union Station before that happened.

Dean had disappeared again — into a stall? Talking to Len? No, setting feeds. He moved down the shed, grasping a feed tub in each hand. Squeak took one from him and hooked it to the door. They were almost finished. Caroline scrambled to put away the saddles and locked the tack room behind her.

"Get caught up with your old pal?" Dean asked, stopping in front of Cruze's stall to snap the tub in place.

"He's not my pal," she snapped, crossing her arms.

"I was kidding," Dean said.

Was he, though? "Are you almost ready to go?"

Dean laughed. "You in a hurry to be somewhere?"

"What if I am?"

"I swear you two are like an old married couple," Squeak muttered, hanging up a stray rake.

Dean mirrored her frown as they stared at each other. Then he slung an arm over her shoulders and steered her toward the truck.

"Come on, honey, time to go home."

She gulped, afraid her heart would explode, the way it raced. *Home.* Maybe he was just being funny, but something warm and soothing filled her chest.

CHAPTER THIRTY-ONE

JULY WAS ALMOST OVER, the summer racing past. Life was so much easier when the mares and foals spent more time outside. It was unbelievable the chaos of straw and manure they created. The heat wave had finally moved on, so they only came in to eat these days. Caroline paused from breezing through stalls to set a reminder on her phone to watch Fargo's race, then tried to chase away the thoughts that romped in.

Dean. Dean and the supplement. Dean and this job.

Dean and her heart, going off script.

When she finished sweeping up, she brought The Wave in and gave him a few minutes with some alfalfa while she got the tack out. Fargo's stall was ready with fresh shavings, a clean water bucket, and a flake of hay under the feed tub.

They hacked around the hay fields, Caroline adding jog sets to the routine. She longed to gallop him, but with his uncertain future, his tendon needed to be rehabbed properly. Done right, he could have another career. Probably as a gelding.

After their ride, she took him outside to the hose, the mist cooling her face as she sprayed him off. She scraped away the dripping water and then sponged his face and legs. When she put him back in his paddock, he rolled, and she laughed. Horse therapy had done its magic; she felt light again.

She was so engrossed — in this horse, this perfect day, this quaint farm and the feeling that, in this instant, everything was right in her world — that the sound of car tires on gravel didn't register at first. It was too early for Dean to be back. Caroline didn't recognize the vehicle. What was it doing, coming back here? That was the bonus of the gate — she didn't get randos coming in off the road. No one showed up unless they were supposed to be here— vet, feed delivery, Emilie. Someone would have to be pretty bold to come uninvited.

Cars weren't her thing, so she couldn't identify the make and model, but it looked new under the film of dust diminishing the lustre of the paint job, tinted windows preventing a view of the driver. Caroline was too aware she was alone — just when she'd thought she was getting over her feelings of isolation, living out here. Where was her phone? She should take a photo of the licence plate. Then she remembered — she'd left it in the barn.

Boldly, she took a step toward the vehicle as it rolled to a stop, ready to confront the stranger, still holding the rope lead — not much of a weapon. A leather shank wielded a sting; a chain would have been better yet. The Wave didn't need that, so this length of woven cotton was her only defence. Even if The Wave had been on the end of it, he didn't have an ounce of aggression in his body. Not that kind of hero.

But the man emerging from the car was no stranger, and he siphoned off all the joy this day had given her.

"How did you find me?" The words stuttered out like they'd been passed through a cheese grater.

Bryce swung the car door shut. Just because he'd ruined her

life didn't mean he wasn't still handsome. Not the same way Dean was, because Bryce was shorter, his body that of a man who spent more time behind a desk than at the gym or working a farm. Why was she comparing him to Dean at all? She rubbed her chest just below her collarbone as if she could smooth away the pain that twinged behind her ribcage, even if now, it was like an itchy, healing scab instead of a gaping laceration. *Don't let him tear off the scab.*

"I like the hair."

She touched the ends as if she'd forgotten she had hair at all, then caught herself, returning her fists to her hips, superwoman pose, and waited for him to explain himself.

"You weren't easy to find."

"That was the point." Then she remembered. "Faron." Had that slime really needed to talk to her, though? He could have passed the information along without his *friendly* visit. "Why are you here?"

At times in the last few weeks, she'd let herself believe that part of her life had never happened, but here it was, standing in front of her. Bryce looked as natty as ever — charcoal grey brushed twill pants, a navy dress shirt that made her think his tie wasn't far away, his hair impeccably cut and coiffed. Despite his always-perfect appearance, he hadn't stood out on the backstretch, because she'd seen all kinds there, from those one step away from homelessness, to celebrities and rich owners dressed to the nines who sailed in on big race days to see their equine investments. Here, on this farm, the four-letter word that had become her refuge, he did not fit.

"It was important to see you."

Important for you. It might have felt good to lash out at him, but at the moment, it just felt like a waste of energy.

"I need to say it in person. I'm sorry, Caroline."

Did she have to acknowledge his apology? Soothe his guilt? Was he expecting forgiveness?

If she forgave him, could she forgive herself, too?

"I want you to have this."

The white business envelope he held out made her suspicious, but she reached for it. It wasn't sealed, and she had to control her expression when she glanced at the number on the cheque inside.

"You shouldn't have to work while you're waiting for things to be finalized. I'm sorry you had to resort to this."

Caroline glanced up at him. She would take his cheque. And she'd let him feel that way because of what he'd done, but this place was the best thing that had ever happened to her.

———

Hunter had Fargo looking better than the claiming tag he was running for — maybe too good — but this was where the old gelding belonged. It was an unavoidable part of horse racing. Not every horse could compete in stakes and allowance company. Almost every time Fargo had gone to the post in his career, there had been a price on his head.

Dean waved them into the saddling stall. The kid was getting the hang of this job — just in time for his placement to be over in a few weeks.

Which should make Dean happy. It meant Stacy and Nikki would return. And while Hunter had proven reliable and reasonably competent, Dean still missed Nikki. It was his other temporary employee who would leave a hole when she left.

The rider appeared at Dean's elbow in the Northwest silks: red and white checks, red and white-striped sleeves. Ed Taylor hadn't been the most imaginative when it came to design. Now and again, Faye made an appeal for a fresh look, but changing them felt disloyal. Dean considered them classic. He hadn't been alive when Secretariat raced, but who didn't know the iconic Meadow Stables' white and royal blue?

At the riders up call, he lifted the feather-light apprentice into the saddle and watched them file out with the rest of the field. Fargo didn't need experience on his back, so Dean had opted for the ten-pound weight allowance of a triple bug.

"There's a claim, eh?" one of the other trainers said as they funnelled out of the saddling enclosure.

"Is there?" Dean held the door to the escalator open, letting the other man go first. His heart bounced for a beat, then settled. No one was taking Fargo. The favourite was a four-year-old dropping more drastically than Dean's horse. That was the logical claim in this group, not an eight-year-old with three times as many starts.

A scattering of people occupied seats around him as he settled into his usual place on the second-floor tier. The empty spots on either side of him felt especially vacant today. Why? He was used to watching races alone.

It was Caroline, of course. She should be here. The race was early enough, he should have told her he'd help with stalls. It made a long day even longer, but that was okay. She was working hard, doing both jobs. The least he could do was pitch in. They made a good team.

The admission jolted him. All the reasons he had to keep it at bay were gone. If he let himself, he could picture it. Her next to him, helping. In it for the long haul. But in another month, it would be over. What would that mean for Caroline? He tried to tell himself that wasn't his problem, but it didn't stick.

The horses gathered behind the starting gate for the six-furlong race, the gate crew slotting each one in. The runners were all professionals, not one of them balking at the routine.

On a good day, Fargo could beat this field. He'd had his share of those. Maybe he had one more in him.

Dean's heart didn't usually pound like this before the start, hands white-knuckling the binoculars. The horses leapt from their stalls like the charge of the Musical Ride and Fargo jumped clear to capture the rail. When they reached the first quarter mile, Dean glanced at the time. It wasn't fast, but it didn't need to be. If the apprentice could sit tight, Fargo might hold on, gallop away on the front end like he'd done before — and retire on a winning note. The truck and trailer waited at the barn, ready to take him back to the farm as soon as he was cooled out.

Fargo was still there — on top — as the field rounded the turn. Were the other jockeys asleep? *Rock-a-bye baby*, he started singing, then stopped when he remembered the words. *Don't fall over, Fargo.*

Dean jumped to his feet as they swept around the turn, bellowing as loud as he had when Ride The Wave won the Plate. He abandoned his binoculars on the seat, pumping a fist. "Come on, Fargo. You can do this. Hang on!"

Instead, the late-running favourite, flanked by two other closers, swallowed Fargo up, a quartet of horses sweeping under the wire. Fargo was the fourth.

Dean kicked the seat in front of him, then felt guilty about it. He should have gone for experience instead of the weight allowance. Nate would have conserved Fargo's speed, nursed the lead, squeaked out the win.

His soles felt leaden as he trudged down the stairs. It was all right. In a few hours, Fargo would be on the farm, nibbling grass, tail swishing at the lazy late-summer flies. They'd be back by feed time.

The apprentice slid off the saddle, giving Fargo a short pat on the neck before heading to the scales to weigh in.

"Thanks, Kiaan." Dean dredged up a smile. There was nothing more to say to the jockey. He'd done what he could. It had been a savvy ride for someone so young.

Hunter was staring at something in his hand when he should have been getting Fargo moving, the horse's nostrils flaring from his exertion. Then he held the item up, eyes shining.

Dean's gaze dropped from his face to the strip of paper, the stack of letters spelling out the word CLAIM.

Caroline made sure Bryce closed the gate behind him. There was no way to process all the feelings battling for air time in her mind, so she'd leave it all there for later and get back to work.

It wasn't until she stopped focusing on the sound of the departing engine that she heard the music, and remembered. Fargo! She sprinted into the barn, following the alarm tune, and snatched up her phone.

No! It was too late, she'd missed the race. She'd have to wait for the replay to be posted — so she called Jess instead, wandering back out into the sunshine and telling her friend about her visitor.

"I should probably take back what I said about him being generous." With her free hand, she picked deadheads from the flowers outside the layup barn.

"I think not," Jess snapped in her ear. "He should have come up with it sooner."

"He didn't know where I was."

"*Please.* He could have asked me if he was serious. I'm still friends with him on Facebook."

Caroline gasped. "Traitor!"

"I thought it might be useful. Aren't you curious?"

"Not in the least." One day she might be. It was too soon.

The Wave's head lifted from his grazing, stealing Caroline's attention. He'd noticed it before she had — the slow rumble of a truck, accompanied by jangling and knocking. She peered around the corner.

"I've got to go, Jess. Dean's back with the horse." That was quick. It felt too soon for Fargo to be cooled out and here already.

The rig crept up the lane. The Wave whinnied a greeting, but Fargo didn't call back. Caroline watched Dean climb out of the cab and open the gate. She grabbed a shank and waited for him to pull around.

What was taking him so long? She went to see, and found him unhitching the trailer. He hopped from the truck bed.

"What are you doing?" she asked. "Where's Fargo? Is he okay?"

Dean didn't meet her eyes, his face murky, and suddenly the beautiful afternoon felt chilly.

"He was claimed."

Caroline gaped. "Who —?" She stopped herself before she said the rest that came to mind. *Who in their right mind would take that old horse?*

The look he slid her was dark, clouds spiked with thunderbolts. "Faron."

"What?"

The trailer creaked as he cranked, lifting it off the ball. When he finished, he climbed wordlessly into the truck and drove it to the house.

Caroline couldn't move. What was Jack doing, claiming a horse like Fargo? He couldn't possibly think he could improve the veteran gelding's form — any idiot could see Fargo was on his way out. It was too early in the season to be scooping up horses to take south for the winter and Fargo was levels below what Faron would ever want. None of it made sense.

The slam of the truck's tailgate made her jump even from a distance. A part of her wanted to go to Dean when every detail of his body language told her to steer clear. Before she could take action, he disappeared into the house. Her shoulders fell. The mares and foals stood at the gate of the paddock across from the house, staring in that direction too, like they thought they should get an early dinner.

But then Dean reappeared, Gus bounding ahead of him. The Golden detoured to visit Caroline — but Dean stormed right on by. Gus took off after him. *Damn it.* If she knew what was good for her, she'd let him be. Apparently, she didn't. She raced after him, too. She was two strides behind him when he turned on her.

"Is that why Faron came around the other day? Were you talking about my horse?"

Caroline stopped in her tracks and took a step back. "No! I would never!"

When he looked at her and laughed, it left her cold.

"You have to believe me." The pleading in her voice reverberated in her throat.

His shoulders sagged and he sighed, his whole body deflating. "I believe you."

He drifted away, reaching the edge of the pond and folding to the ground, sitting cross-legged and staring across the water. Gus scuttled down the bank and stood, front paws in the water. Caroline eased down next to Dean, two feet separating them. She wanted to hug him, but that was a crazy idea.

"I should have listened to Emilie," he said.

What could she say? She had zero credibility here. She'd done almost exactly the same thing to him when she'd trained. Just because Bryce had played a huge part in who she'd been back then didn't excuse her. Just that once, could she not have stood up for what was right?

Maybe she should hug him. What was he going to do, throw her in the pond?

Well... he might.

He picked up a rock and tossed it into the water, and Gus launched after it, swimming, then diving. Crazy Golden.

"What was the name of that horse I took from you?" She spoke cautiously; acknowledging it felt like poking needles into her skin.

Dean looked shocked that she'd broached the subject. His gaze narrowed, simmering, before he returned it to his dog's antics. "Etched In Iron. We called her FeFe. Get it?"

Caroline frowned, baffled. "No, sorry."

"Fe is the symbol for iron on the periodic table."

She smacked her forehead with the heel of her hand. "Of course!" She rolled her eyes. "Like I ever even knew that. I thought maybe you were a Fefe Dobson fan."

"Who?"

She tried to sing the first part of the chorus of "Bye Bye Boyfriend." It made her want to jump to her feet and belt it out with an air mic, sending every word to Bryce.

Dean shook his head. "Nope."

"What is wrong with you?" She gave him an exaggerated sigh then dropped her eyes, lacing her fingers together in her lap. "I'm so sorry I did that."

"You didn't break any rules." But he didn't look at her as he said it.

"It was still a shitty thing to do. We were friends."

He scanned her face, his gaze scrutinizing. Eyes that should be warm, like milk chocolate, were piercing, unfamiliar. "Were we really then, anymore?"

Her response was little more than a whisper, laden with

years of shame. "Do you think it's too late for us to be friends again?"

Dean shrugged. "I think it's kind of already happened. All sly-like." He gave her the smallest of smiles.

Now could she hug him?

"Get out of there, Gus. Give it up," Dean called to the determined Golden. With one last circle, Gus swam back and bounded out of the pond, water gushing from his long coat. "Oh. Sorry."

"Why?" Caroline shifted her eyes to Dean. His had a glint, his lips twisting. Then Gus barged up, pausing to let loose a shake that splattered them both in droplets of pond water before he flopped in her lap. "Ugh, Gus!"

But a wet, smelly dog was a welcome distraction from the events of the day. The visit from Bryce, Fargo getting claimed, this strange moment with Dean. Was he really accepting this truce between them that easily, or was he just being nice? Or diplomatic, because he needed her now? He was stoic, and well capable of keeping his true feelings to himself.

Why couldn't she accept that they were getting along, for real? But she wasn't done making it up to him. She wasn't done making it right.

CHAPTER THIRTY-TWO

CAROLINE RAN her eyes over the saddle and checked Cruze's girth. She didn't have to touch a thing. "He looks good, Hunter. I'll see if we're ready to go."

She saw Dean down the shed in front of Gastronomy's stall, locked on his phone, thumbs responding to some text or another, his lips settled into a grim line. The phone pinged before it was even back in his pocket. He keyed in something short and tucked it away.

"What's up?" she asked.

"Change of plans. You're still on Cruze, but Nate will get on Andy's colt. Andy's coming to watch."

It was Caroline's turn to frown. Liv was supposed to work Gastronomy.

"You're okay working with Nate?" he asked.

She shrugged. She'd regained enough confidence for it now. "Sure. He's just another jock. Once upon a time, he might have been working for me, right?"

Dean's look was appraising, like he was deciding if Nate would have ridden for a trainer like her. "Right."

Whatever. She used to breeze horses with riders all the time, so the *who* wasn't the real issue — it was the *where* she was still coming to terms with. They were going to the main track. Caroline hoped she'd built enough trust in Cruze to overcome her worry. He was growing up, her little summer project. The bigger concern should be that Gastronomy might not live up to his owner's expectations — with said owner in attendance. If Nate Miller was all that, he'd make up for the colt's lack, wouldn't he?

Caroline hadn't met Nate yet. She'd seen him around — she recognized him from some of the win photos in Dean's office — but always in passing, on a horse. They'd exchanged nods and good mornings. Other than seeming friendly, polite, she didn't know him. What kind of man would attract the affection of someone as inward as Liv Lachance? Caroline was curious.

She spotted him as soon as he walked on the shed — he stopped to chat with Squeak in front of Gastronomy's stall. He was taller than most local jockeys, his lean frame more typical of the riders overseas.

"Hey Nate." Dean's voice came from behind her. "Get the bridles on and let's go," he instructed the grooms. Then he disappeared.

Andy must be here, though Caroline had seen no sign. She didn't care about meeting *him*, happy to be an anonymous exercise rider, but should she go over and say hello to Nate? She wasn't Dean's assistant — trainer mode was not required — so walking up and introducing herself felt presumptuous.

Nate solved her dilemma by approaching and Caroline quickly wiped what was surely a bewildered look from her face. She'd been staring at him, and while she was sure it wasn't uncommon for women to stare at Nate Miller, her gawking had been more like he was a problem that needed sorting.

"Hi, Caroline. I don't think we've actually met." There was something behind his expression. Not exactly humour. Possibly curiosity, like her own. What had he heard about her? From Liv, from Emilie. From Dean? Did she rate enough in their estimation to garner interest?

She shook his hand and took a moment to steal a good look. It wasn't hard to admit he was attractive, with an unassuming smile and blue eyes few women would be able to keep themselves from swimming in. But it would take more than good looks to hold the attention of someone like Liv. And while he was tall for a rider, he was shorter than Caroline. Dean was more her type. *Why had that popped into her head?*

"So, you're who Dean fired Liv for." He grinned.

"Only to make you look better." It was a relief when the comeback came easily. She couldn't allow herself to be intimidated by this guy.

Caroline expected him to shoot something right back — *I don't need anyone to make me look good* — but he just laughed, and checked the time.

Squeak brought Gastronomy around and Caroline threw Nate up. Once she was on Cruze, the two-year-olds headed for the track.

"Have you met Andy?" Caroline asked, scanning their surroundings — not that she would be able to identify the man.

"He was at the Plate when The Wave won," Nate said. "I'm sure we shook hands, but he was more concerned with entertaining his entourage than the horse or the help."

She cracked a grin. "You're counting yourself among the help?"

"Sure." He grinned back. "Especially with a guy like that."

According to Dean, Andy rarely came to the races to watch his horses, let alone visit them in the morning. Sounded like the perfect owner to Caroline. *Stay away and let me do my job.* So why was Andy here now? Why this morning?

There was still no sign of Dean and the owner as they emerged from the tunnel to the track. She'd bet they'd driven to the grandstand — Andy didn't sound like the type to watch with the common people on the rail. She could relax, for a little while.

But she didn't. Nerves she'd thought were behind her surfaced, creepy little moths in her stomach reminding her of that day ten years ago when someone had died out here because of her. She glanced at Nate as they nudged the colts into a jog. Cruze cantered a stride before she brought him back.

"What's the matter?" he asked.

"How did you get over it?" she blurted.

Nate slid her a long look. "What, exactly?"

"The accident."

He snorted. "Which one?"

What was she doing, asking him about this? He wouldn't want to think about it — couldn't afford to, for that matter — but she barrelled on. "The one where someone died."

He grimaced, focusing between his mount's ears. "You just cut right for the jugular, don't you, Caroline?"

She frowned. So much for hitting it off with Nate. She had no choice but to explain. "It happened to me. Before your time. Not in a race, of course, but... here, in the morning."

He was silent, pulling Gastronomy up at the wire. "Then what you're doing now is what you do to get over it. You get back on and go back out."

"It's taken ten years."

"It takes as long as it takes. You ready?"

She stared across the infield. *Deep breaths.* She'd brought Cruze out here to gallop before, later in the morning so there was little traffic, and no one had died. No one would die today, either. She nodded, and steered her horse to the right, the colt stepping off eagerly.

Cruze leaned on her hands as the two-year-olds galloped in the middle of the track. Caroline realized Nate was singing, softly.

"That's original," she muttered. She'd had "Sweet Caroline" crooned at her in jest more times than she could count.

"*Dun, dun, dun,*" he warbled in response.

"I take it Liv's not with you for your sense of humour," she called over, trying to keep from smiling.

"It's for my voice, obviously," he said.

She laughed. He got points for breaking through her anxiety. She'd even forgotten to search the apron and grandstand for Dean and Andy.

Now, she focused on Cruze, feeling the evenness of his gait, watching his swivelling ears, sensing the spark of attitude that had surfaced since that good breeze. She and Nate had their orders. The plan wasn't complicated. They'd stay together, and then in the final jumps, Nate would let Gastronomy pull ahead so the owner would be happy. Keeping owners happy was what this business was all about, even when, sometimes, keeping horses happy got shoved to the side — but today's exercise wouldn't cause any harm. All Caroline had to do was play her part.

Entering the backstretch, she realized Cruze had missed the memo.

He was strong, while next to him, Gastronomy galloped along like they were on a Sunday outing, Nate standing easily in the irons. Caroline needed her bodyweight to keep Cruze next to his stablemate.

"You okay over there?" Nate called, the wind that lifted the colts' manes snatching at his words.

"Fine," she yelled through gritted teeth. It didn't matter

that he probably couldn't hear her. Cruze was taking all her concentration.

Since when did Cruze know where the pole was? *So you've been paying attention after all.* He sought the rail and she let him drop to it, but couldn't relax her muscles. He needed a pilot, not a passenger today. When she'd breezed him before, she'd just let him go, happy that he could make time without her needing to encourage him. Somewhere, a switch had flipped. He was ready, looking for it. He shot ahead of Gastronomy.

"Easy, mister," she grumbled, trying to temper his speed so Nate could get Gastronomy back up beside him. *Hang out with your buddy. Think "team sport," all right?*

The turn backed him off enough for Caroline to regain control. Cruze felt incredible. It made her heart soar — like maybe he would be a racehorse after all. Andy's colt kept pace now, thank goodness. The red and white quarter pole flashed by, and Cruze decided it was game on, battling Caroline for his head.

She was out of practice, her muscles not remembering how to keep this kind of power under wraps. *Not today, horse, please?* Inside the eighth pole, Cruze nosed ahead. *This is not the plan! Stick to the plan.*

"Come on, you sack! I thought you were a rider!" she yelled at Nate, but that only fired Cruze up more.

It was pointless, of course. Nate was trying to light a fire under Gastronomy without appearing as if he was doing it. If they both didn't know the owner was watching, he probably would have given his colt a smack with the stick, but that would only make it more obvious that Dean's colt was stealing the show. *Why today, Cruze?*

"Okay, you can stop now!" she yodelled at the colt's ears —

ears that were flipped ahead, ignoring her. Was she going to need the outrider to help her pull him up?

"They galloped out good," Nate quipped when they eased, Cruze relenting at last, the two-year-olds coasting into the backstretch. "You sure that's the same colt that broke Crystal?"

Caroline still gasped for breath, so she couldn't have responded if she wanted to. Her heart pounded against her ribcage. Her arms shook so badly she wasn't sure she could bring the horse to a walk. Nate looked like he might reach over and give her a hand. *Thanks so much for embarrassing me, horse.*

He reached forward and rubbed Gastronomy's neck once they were finally stopped, backs to the outside rail, looking over to the grandstand. "It wasn't that fast."

"I hope you're right," she said, still sucking in air.

"Of course I'm right." He tapped his helmet with a finger.

Caroline's clock was rusty, so she'd have to trust Nate's — at least until they got official word from the clocker. It might be good, though, if it had been fast, because Gastronomy had only been a neck behind, so on paper, they'd have the same time. Which would have been fine... if Andy hadn't witnessed it.

CHAPTER THIRTY-THREE

Dean climbed out of Andy's Cadillac SUV, more comfortable breathing the tang of the backstretch's bins, full of soiled bedding, than the new-car smell of the owner's vehicle. Andy didn't ever *not* have a car with new-car smell; he always leased, so he had a current model every two years. Dean had been tempted to play with the gadgets. The gas-guzzling beast even had a refrigerated compartment in the console. That could be handy for long hauls with the horse trailer, but there was no new truck on Dean's horizon. His Chevy had to last forever.

"Call me once they've cooled out," Andy said.

Dean rested his hands on the frame, bending to see Andy twisted toward him, wedged in the driver's seat with one arm on the wheel. "Sure thing." He tapped the top of the vehicle and swung the door closed, shutting Andy into his window-tinted cavern. The owner's uncharacteristic attendance made him uneasy.

Squeak wrapped the lead shank around Gastronomy's

halter, the colt's nostrils flaring from the work. Nate was already gone.

"I'll take him a couple of turns, boss," the groom said.

Dean found Hunter fumbling with the halter as Caroline dismounted. She glanced at Dean as she unbuckled the girth.

"They both looked good," he said, keeping expression from his face.

"Was Andy happy?" she asked.

"Andy is never happy." But he'd seemed surprisingly okay with seeing Dean's colt dust his. It was concerning.

Caroline took the bridle from Hunter, walking past Dean to where Cruze's water bucket hung outside the stall. She dunked the bit and set the saddle on the rail. "You'd be better off without him."

Dean snorted. Andy owned two of the five horses in the barn — and half of another. Exactly fifty percent of Dean's business right now.

She tipped off her helmet, ruffling her hair. Her face was flushed from the effort of holding Cruze out on the track — Dean hadn't missed how tough the colt had been, borderline getting away on her. "It's true."

"Are you going to find me new owners?" He wouldn't put it past her. She had connections, and just enough of the gift of the gab to chat prospects up.

Caroline grinned. "I could be your agent."

"You're hired."

"Funny, I don't think you ever said that to me."

"That's because Faye gave you the job."

"Aren't you glad your sister has such good sense?"

Dean laughed. "More than you know."

Caroline's eyes shifted and her lips had a funny little twist. He was stuck for a beat, studying her discomfort, until Hunter hollered, "Coming out!" Dean and Caroline scattered, because Cruze was on a mission, pumped and looking for a drink.

"Right," Dean said, ducking Caroline's eyes, which seemed to scrutinize him the same way he'd just been watching her. "I'll hold Gastronomy for his bath."

Brenda, the hotwalker, was off. She'd been asking for days more frequently, claiming it was summer and she wanted to spend time with her grandkids. Dean had a feeling she was — what did they call it these days? — Quiet quitting. Because Brenda wasn't oblivious. She knew there weren't enough horses to justify her salary, but Dean didn't have the heart to fire her. Caroline didn't complain about walking, like many exercise riders might — Crystal being one of them — so he should man up and lay Brenda off until things turned around.

Once the workers were cooled out and nibbling at the sparse grass on the strip of lawn outside the barn, Dean went looking for Len. He found the older man in a stall kneeling at a horse's front end, steadfastly rubbing liniment into the leg, its strong scent dominating the air.

"Missed you out at the track," Dean said. Len was a fixture. Dean hadn't seen him at the rail this morning, so he wanted to check in.

Len sat back on his heels, twisting stiffly toward the door like his neck didn't move that way anymore. "My son's coming to take me to a doctor's appointment. Have to get these horses done up."

"Everything okay?"

"Oh, sure. Just a checkup."

"Do you want us to feed for you?"

"That's all right. I should be back by then."

"Give me a call if you get held up. You know how doctors like to make you wait." And wait.

Len reached for a thick cotton to his left. "Your two-year-olds work good?"

Dean rubbed the back of his neck, leaning against the doorframe. "My colt worked a little too good."

Len chuckled. "How is that bad?"

"Andy was here to watch."

"Ah. Owners." Like that said it all — because it did. Len understood, even if he owned all the horses he trained now. All three of them. "Are you worried?"

"About Andy? I don't know. We have a lot of history. But he seems restless."

Len finished the bandage and, with a grunt, pulled himself to his feet, using the horse as support. Dean worried he wouldn't make it up one of these times. The horse turned his head toward Len when Len unsnapped him from the wall, pressing gently into the old man's chest to let him slip the halter off.

"I've got a few minutes before my son gets here," Len said, giving the halter a quick swipe with a sponge. "Come sit in the office."

The concrete box Len led Dean to wasn't much different from his own, except for the rusty old tabby cat curled on a cot that took up the room's width. Len's desk, smaller than Dean's, was littered with the usual ephemera: condition books, a pile of *Racing Forms*, a scattering of pens. Win photos decorated the walls — both framed and unframed — like every other trainer's office on the grounds. Some of the images were older than Dean.

He could almost hear Len's knees creak as the older man lowered himself into the desk chair. Dean settled next to the cat, the tabby twitching an eyebrow as the cot gave beneath his weight. He stroked the soft, tawny fur automatically, the feline's warm body vibrating.

The old man's eyes scanned the walls. "I miss your father," he said.

Dean wanted to say he missed him too, but it wasn't that simple.

"Are you ready for tonight?" Len asked.

The induction ceremony. It was on the doorstep like an unwelcome relative. Dean had words prepared, but ready? Even though he'd known for months, he didn't feel any more prepared than he had before delivering Ed Taylor's eulogy. Tonight, he'd be recycling both the speech and the emotions.

"It's going to happen whether I am or not," he said.

"Your father would be proud of you."

It was a nice sentiment, but he wouldn't be, not really. He might be proud of the move to drop Fargo into that claiming race, but not of the guilt that continued to assault Dean. "There's still a spot at the table for you, you know."

"I already told you it's past my bedtime," Len said, lacing his fingers over his abdomen and rocking back in the chair. "Things working out with Caroline?"

Dean's eyebrows twitched at the timing of that question. "I might actually miss her when she's gone." He grinned even though it was true.

"If you let her leave, you're not as smart as I thought."

"How can I afford to keep her?" Nikki, Stacy, Crystal — all three of them were expecting their jobs back. The understanding with Caroline had always been that the arrangement was temporary.

"This isn't about money," Len said.

Everything felt like it was about money right now. "What are you saying?" Dean didn't like the irritation that crept into his voice.

A tap on the open door interrupted them. Len and Dean both rose as Len's son waited outside. Dean shook the son's hand and slipped past. "Let me know if you need anything, Len."

"Good luck," Len called.

The shedrow was neat, the flowers watered. One afternoon when Dean had returned to feed, shortly after Caroline had started coming in — a day when they had driven in separate vehicles — he'd been greeted with hanging baskets of red and white flowers, suspended along the rail in front of his stalls. It would have made his mother happy. She'd never spent much time on the backstretch, but had always ensured there were flowers. Caroline had even enlisted Hunter to help her repaint the foot lockers and wall boxes, and kept on him to wipe off the stall plaques every morning. It looked like a first-class operation, thanks to her — even if it wasn't.

She waited, sitting on a squat white bucket in front of the tack room, mindlessly scrolling on her phone. He thought about Len, and what the old man hadn't said. There wouldn't be any harm, really, in inviting her tonight, would there? It didn't have to mean anything. It would be his way of thanking her, just like he'd invited Liv and Nate and Emilie and Tim.

"What's that?" he asked, nodding at the bucket. It looked new, not something she'd dragged out to sit on. He didn't remember ordering anything.

Her face tipped up, corners of her lips curved downward. "It looks suspiciously like the bucket Krissy gave you at the farm."

"Huh. That's strange. Did she drop it off?" He didn't think Krissy had other connections on the backstretch, but it was possible — though he would've thought she'd let him know if she was coming.

Caroline stood and nudged it away with her toe like it was a dead rodent. "No. I didn't recognize the person who brought it, but they assured me it was for you."

It reminded him he'd forgotten to call Andy. Dean picked the bucket up and stashed it in the office before locking the door. "Ready to go?"

She nodded curtly and began walking to the truck. As he followed her, his phone pinged a text notification. Andy.

Sent you a bucket of that supplement I've been talking about. Start my horses on it.

Dean frowned at the message. He looked up, finding Caroline watching him, her expression as judgemental as Len's old cat. When he hit the locks on his key fob, she turned away, opening the door and climbing in. He sent a quick response. *Colt cooled out fine.*

"Andy," he said when he joined her. "He sent that supplement. Agreeing to feed it might be the only way to placate him."

A fresh glaze of disappointment enclosed her face. But what was he supposed to do? If feeding Krissy's experimental formula would keep Andy paying the bills, did he have a choice?

"You do what you have to do," Caroline said, rearranging her features into feigned disinterest. "But I can't be around for that. I'm supposed to be keeping my nose clean."

"It's a nutraceutical, not cocaine," he said before he could stop himself.

"How do you know? It's not as if *that* hasn't been tried on racehorses." Her gaze was fixed out the passenger window as he started the engine. "When do Nikki and Stacy get back?"

"After Labour Day."

"I'll find someone to gallop for you, and I'll stay at the farm. I won't leave you high and dry there, but someone else can get on your horses."

Dean stared at her. That had escalated. So, he had to choose between her and the owner who, at the moment, was paying all their salaries? Not that Dean could afford to pay himself these days.

But Caroline did more than get on his horses; she'd started to feel like the glue that held his life together. He couldn't convince himself Andy's demands were more important than she'd become, especially when she was thinking about the horses and Andy only cared about money.

But did he dare call Andy's bluff? Because, what if he wasn't bluffing?

CHAPTER THIRTY-FOUR

THE VOLUME POUNDING her eardrums probably wasn't healthy, but Caroline was so tired of Dean's jazz station, she needed some thumping bass. She was glad he'd gone back to the track to feed. Without his help, she'd finished the stalls in good time. He slowed her down.

Donning sunglasses, sunscreen on her arms and legs, and a ball cap to protect her head, she climbed on the riding mower, her wrath simmering to a steady burn. Dean didn't care if she came or went. It had been convenient of her to appear, to take this job, to step up and save his sorry ass at the track, but now that the end was in sight, he had no problem saying, *sayonara, baby*.

She zoomed around in front of the old farmhouse, pondering how the landscapers people hired to maintain their properties achieved those perfect patterns. It reminded her of fancy checkers on a horse dolled up for race day, like grooms did at places like Triple Stripe. She made a mental note to find a YouTube video on lawn cutting in case there was a special way she should be doing it, just because it would make the task more interesting. Cutting the lawn bored her silly, whereas stalls were enjoyable — she could zone out and let her mind wander, coming up with answers to all of the world's problems, if not her own.

Why had she thought Dean would pick her over his long-time owner? He *was* better off without Andy Dupont, but that was easy for her to say. Her wages appeared in her bank account twice a month without fail, the number nearly double now that she galloped for Dean.

If he did tell Andy and they lost those horses at the track — *they*, like there was a *we* — would he be able to keep her on at the farm? It was a conundrum. What a Dean word. She had to find him new owners — better owners. Maybe get him some yearlings and start them for him. She could give him a reason to keep her around.

It was official: she was crazy.

Because his regular farm manager was coming back. Labour Day. Less than four weeks. After that, she'd be kicked to the curb. That was the deal.

The lawn never took long. There wasn't much to cut because the farm had been designed for horses, not to be a ritzy country estate. Paddock space was maximized — Dean would probably have horses grazing on the front lawn if Faye let him. A fancy car she didn't recognize pulled into the driveway and travelled cautiously, trying to avoid the potholes. Caroline slowed the mower, squinting with suspicion. A tall redhead with bouncy waves stepped from behind the wheel, looking like she'd come straight from the salon. It was Krissy. Caroline's skin prickled.

It was too soon for Dean to be home from feeding, so if Krissy was accompanying Dean to the Hall of Fame banquet, she was far too early. It irked her that Krissy seemed to have charmed Dean when Caroline could see through the façade to the slick drug rep beneath.

She drove to the house and climbed off the tractor. Krissy stood at the back door, appearing as if she'd just knocked, Gus the Golden whining on the other side. She wondered if Krissy would even remember her. Meeting the temporary farm manager probably didn't have the same impact as Caroline encountering a girlfriend she was sure didn't have Dean's best interests at heart.

"May I help you?" she called.

Krissy pivoted from the door, and the surprise on her face morphed smoothly into a smile. "Caroline, isn't it?"

Of course. Krissy was a good salesperson; remembering names was important. "Hi Krissy."

"Is Dean around?"

"He went to the track to feed. He's probably leaving to head back right about now."

"I should have texted." Krissy pulled out her phone.

"He probably wouldn't get it anyway. He's a by-the-rules kind of guy. Don't text and drive," Caroline said dryly, then felt stupid. Krissy probably knew that Dean did, in fact, text and drive. "Would you like me to give him a message for you?"

Krissy remained on the deck, poised at the top of the steps. It was a power move, and Caroline hated that the woman towered. She propped her hands on her hips. Just because she was dressed in a sweaty shirt and shorts and not a silk blouse and tight skirt like Krissy didn't mean she couldn't call this woman out.

"I know what you're doing. You're just using him for your own agenda. It's bad enough you'd do that to him, but it's harming horses, too. When he realizes that, he's not going to be happy."

"And just how would he find out?" Krissy tilted her head,

her lips curving into a too-sweet smile. "I know who you are, too, Caroline. And no matter how reformed you think you are, with your good girl act, you can never truly leave a past like that behind. So don't stand there thinking you're better than me. And when it comes down to it, who do you think he'll believe? Dean and I go way back."

They did? So did Dean and Caroline — but not in a good way.

Krissy stepped carefully down to Caroline's level so they were eye to eye for a moment then breezed by. "I'll catch up with him later."

Caroline didn't bother to watch her go, climbing aboard the mower, setting her earbuds in place and turning the volume back high enough to drown out the roar of the engine, the drone of the blades, the voices in her head. There were more important things to do than worry about Krissy. What Krissy said was probably true — she couldn't leave the past behind, so why would Dean ever listen to her? Still, she hoped he'd seen enough in these last two months to do exactly that.

Once she finished up the lawn and put the mower away, she tacked up The Wave in the cool of the barn. They headed out to the hay fields so she wouldn't have to face Dean when he got home. She didn't want to talk to him right now.

This is what she would miss, more than anything. Darn this horse for burrowing his way into her heart. Maybe she should buy him. What else was she going to do with her money besides spend it on rent and groceries?

Should she swallow her pride and back down on her stance? Or, what if she dumped out those buckets and filled them with something harmless, like sugar? For the amount that was in a scoop, it wouldn't hurt the horses. Dean's charges probably consumed that much sugar a day in peppermints. Then he could think he was doing what Andy wanted without any danger to the animals — when he should be saying, *there's no magic pill, dumbass.* But Dean was too nice to say that. Blunt was not in his wheelhouse.

Her heart did weird things when she noticed him getting out of his truck. Caroline's head didn't want to see him, but apparently that crazy organ pounding in her chest had different ideas. She'd take another lap and hope he disappeared into the house. He likely didn't want to see her, either. But when she and The Wave rounded the corner to the barn, he was there. Why couldn't he just leave her to wallow and go off to his fancy event?

"How's the big horse?" he asked, rubbing The Wave's face. His touch activated the horse's peppermint sensors, The Wave bumping his nose to Dean's hip.

Caroline didn't dismount. She liked having the height advantage. "He's good."

"And how are you?"

She met his eyes and questioned again if holding her ground was worth it. She had no concrete proof that the supplement was dangerous or illegal. It might be harmless. But it was the principle. So she didn't answer, waiting him out.

"I'll talk to Andy and tell him I'm not going to feed the supplement."

Caroline bit the inside of her cheek to keep from smiling, giving him a nod and hopping off. "It's the right thing to do."

Dean didn't move, one of his hands on the inside rein, the other on The Wave's nose as she loosened the girth and ran up the stirrup. She ducked around to run up the other iron, stealing a glance. Something about the way he looked at her wiped away the insecurity she'd felt around Krissy. He began walking The Wave into the barn, and she kept the horse between them because she didn't trust herself not to do something silly.

He stopped beside the stall, holding The Wave as she removed the saddle and put it in the tack room. Dean had replaced the bridle with a halter by the time she got back, and he stood there, grasping the reins and crown piece, features uncharacteristically open, searching her face. It felt like he was giving her a glimpse of everything he carried inside.

"I don't expect it to go over well, so please don't leave."

She had to keep herself from reaching for him. She'd wrap her arms around him, then only let him go to put her hands on either side of his face, staring him down until she kissed him, murmuring *I won't, I won't, I won't* against his lips.

Caroline blinked away the sensation, reaching for The Wave, settling on kissing the horse instead, a sisterly peck on the cheek. "I won't."

Now, or ever? Now was enough, for the moment.

Dean's feet shifted, his gaze dropping. It was a beat too long before he handed her the bridle and said, "Well. I'll leave you to it. I have to get ready for that Hall of Fame thing." He made a face like he was about to visit the dentist for a tooth extraction, not to accept his father's induction.

"Have fun," she muttered in his wake.

CHAPTER THIRTY-FIVE

Pausing at the entrance to the convention centre, Dean tugged at the collar of his shirt. There weren't many things he was convinced required a suit and tie, but this was one of them — his father's induction into the Canadian Horse Racing Hall of Fame.

He sauntered through the room where the silent auction was set up, token drink in his hand, and it felt like wandering into a world created by the man he was here to honour. Every so often, he was interrupted by congratulatory remarks, and those old enough to have known Ed Taylor volunteered kind words. Dean smiled and thanked them dutifully, trying not to let accolades for a man who was larger than life make him feel small.

Unlike previous occasions when he'd been merely an attendee, this year there would be no remaining in the shadows, clapping politely for those celebrated, escaping promptly — sometimes even before the end of the ceremony. He needed to stand up in front of all these people — colleagues and the upper echelon of Thoroughbred and Standardbred racing in Canada — and maintain his composure. Faye would be at his side, though he couldn't trust her not to be emotional. In a way, it felt like the funeral all over again, though he'd decided he didn't need to say as much as he had that day. It wasn't his induction. That wasn't in the stars.

He bid on a couple of items he was sure he wouldn't win: a hot air balloon ride, tickets to an NBA basketball game. Things he could imagine himself enjoying but the expense of which he could never justify. Sometimes he got free tickets to a hockey game now that Emilie's boyfriend, Tim, played for Toronto, so it wasn't as if he was deprived of fun. Big days like the Plate made him feel part of something larger and more meaningful — a sphere that Dean believed Ed Taylor had always intended to keep him away from.

A touch jarred him, and he almost spilled his drink as an arm linked through his. Looking down, he met the gaze and veneers of an auburn-haired woman, the emerald-coloured dress giving the illusion her hazel eyes were green — either that or she wore special contact lenses. Dean grappled for her name. She was the wife or daughter of an owner — he remembered that much.

"Such an exciting evening for you, Dean," she said like they were old friends. "You must be so proud."

"Thank you, yes," he stammered. Was proud the word? It suggested he'd been responsible for his father's success when he'd never been allowed to play more than a bit part.

"There you are!"

Faye's voice smoothed away the tension in his shoulders. What impeccable timing. She looped her arm through his other elbow and he almost spilled his drink again. At this rate, an innocent bystander was going to wear it.

"I was so sorry to hear about your husband, Maisie," Faye said, leaning around him. "And I apologize for stealing my brother away. I'm sure you'll have time to catch up later."

Not likely. Dean shifted the glass to his other hand as soon as he was free of the woman and let Faye sweep him off.

He leaned down, murmuring, "Have I told you lately you're the best?"

She grinned. "Everyone's already at our table."

They were the people whose presence mattered, and not one had ever met Ed Taylor, as far as Dean knew, here for no other reason than to support him and Faye. Will, Emilie and Tim, Liv and even Nate; seeing them all filled him up, until his eyes landed on the empty extra chair.

He'd chickened out. There was no other way to say it, no pride to protect. Caroline had stood with his Plate horse, assuring him she wouldn't leave, and he couldn't express what he'd wanted. Because if he'd asked her at that moment, it would have meant something. Maybe not to her, but to him.

"Found him," Faye announced, releasing his arm and slipping into the seat next to Will. "I had to drag him from the widow he was trying to pick up."

"Rescue him, more like," Nate quipped. "You know what they're like, eh Tim?"

Tim flushed. "Fierce."

Dean laughed. He hadn't stayed long at last year's Plate Ball — the whole thing with Liv the year before had soured his association with the event — but he'd seen the onslaught of older women who had converged on Nate's painfully shy younger brother once they realized he knew how to dance. According to Faye, they'd kept him on his feet all night.

"She certainly didn't look as if she was grieving," Faye said.

Dean settled into the chair next to her and finally released his grip on the tumbler. In less than a month, she'd be married.

His little sister — though he hadn't thought of her that way in a long time. Faye had left behind that tormented kid, while on a night like tonight, Dean wondered if he'd made any progress at all.

"That two-year-old of yours should be just about ready to run, shouldn't he?" Nate said.

And at that moment, Dean liked the guy. It was a relief to talk horses instead of history. He'd been worried there would be a lot of sentiment flying around the table. He should have known better, with this group.

"Wonders never cease," Dean said wryly. A few months ago, he would have voted Cruze the horse least likely to make it to the races this season. "He just needs his gate card. There's a race the day after Plate Day that would suit him."

Liv and Nate exchanged a glance. "Probably the same race I'm looking at for our colt," Liv said.

"I guess I won't be asking if you can ride him, then," Dean said to Nate. "But maybe one of you can work him from the gate for me?"

"Sure," Liv said. "We'll figure it out. Your colt and Cash can go together. How about your other two-year-old?"

Dean ran a hand through his hair, thinking of Andy. Would it give Andy a false sense of expectation if Gastronomy got his gate card too? Once he told the owner that his colt didn't need a supplement, he needed two months on the farm, it might not matter anymore. Dean imagined the words lighting a fuse, picturing himself waiting for Andy to explode.

"No," he said. "He's not ready."

When the ceremony began, Dean's unease returned. He was too distracted to pay full attention to the other honourees, reciting the words he planned to say in his head in hopes he wouldn't trip over his tongue once he spoke. Clapping interrupted him, his cue to join in. Then they were next. Faye wrapped her hand around his and they wove their way through the tables to the front of the hall.

He cleared his throat. "My father was fifty-four when he died, and I have no doubt he would have gone on to accomplish much more. Maybe he would have won the Prince of Wales with Ride The Wave and had a second Triple Crown winner." A ripple of laughter. "All I do know is that I wish he were here to accept this tremendous honour himself, with my mother beside him and Shawn standing here with Faye and me. Thank you."

Short, if not sweet. There was applause, and he squeezed Faye and directed her back to the table as she dabbed her eyes with a tissue. Now, if only he could leave.

When the end of the evening came, none of them lingered. Dean sat in his truck, loosening his tie and watching them go — Liv with Nate in the Porsche, Emilie and Tim in the vintage Mustang Tim had inherited from his brother last summer, Will with Faye in the old black Corolla. One of these days that old Toyota was going to die, the body disintegrating into a pile of oxidized metal. The engine would last forever.

Traffic droned in front of him on Derry Road, the jazz station providing background music. Laughter drew him and he noticed the woman who'd spoken to him earlier teetering on her heels with a couple of female friends. If he'd been bolder, he'd have picked up what she was putting down. But no. He did what he always did. Sat and watched and waited.

Finally, he started the truck and headed home. There was no other way this night could have ended for him. He had to get back to Gus. Faye wasn't staying at the house tonight, and the thought of asking Caroline to let his dog out while he was with someone else didn't sit right, even if he wasn't ready to admit why.

The first thing he noticed when he reached the house

was the barn lights were on. It was long past night check time. That couldn't mean anything good. Why hadn't Caroline called him? Dean left the truck pointed at the gate and ran.

When he burst through the door, Caroline jumped up, her phone clattering to the ground next to the bale of hay she'd been seated on as she grabbed for a pitchfork, eyes wide and legs braced. Dean stopped in his tracks and almost put his hands in the air.

Caroline's shoulders relaxed, though her face remained white. "You scared me half to death!"

"What's wrong?" His heart thumped and he scanned the stalls for signs of a horse in distress, but The Wave was the only one in the barn. He nickered and pawed, eyes alight with expectation. Dean automatically patted his pockets for peppermints but came up empty.

"Nothing," she said.

"Why are you sitting in the barn at eleven o'clock at night?"

"It's lonely in that apartment. Knowing I was by myself on the farm made me nervous."

The way her confession landed, she might as well have stabbed him. He should have just asked her to come instead of overthinking the whole thing.

"Can you put the pitchfork down now?" he asked.

She gave him a sheepish grin and set the implement aside, parking herself back on the bale. The Wave nibbled on her hair. "How was the dinner?"

Dean shrugged and sat on a foot locker opposite her, leaning against the wall. "It was all right."

Her eyebrows peaked. "Your father was inducted into the Canadian Horse Racing Hall of Fame, and it was just all right?"

"It's an incredible honour. But it wasn't mine, was it? It's not easy going to something like that where everyone knows you're just an inferior stand-in."

"That's ridiculous. You've barely started your career when it comes to this game. How old was your dad when he died?"

"Fifty-four."

"When did he train his first Plate winner?"

"It was that summer." The summer he'd met Caroline. "I was eighteen. So he was... forty-eight."

"And how old were you when The Wave won his Plate?"

"Thirty-six."

"I rest my case."

She was the last person he'd expected a pep talk from tonight. He'd hid his sense of unworthiness from the others at dinner because the event wasn't about him. They'd sat around the table joking about who'd be next — both Liv and Nate were on career paths headed in that direction, the way the last three years had gone for both of them. Dean, not so much.

"Was tonight hard?" she asked.

There was no humour in his laugh. "In about a dozen different ways." She wouldn't understand some of them — the social situation, the public speaking — but he didn't think that's what she meant.

He stared at the ceiling, "I can't help wondering, if he'd let me stay, things might have been different."

"The accident, you mean."

Dean nodded. Was that logical? That changing that variable on the space-time continuum would have set their lives on a different course? He'd never know, because he could never go back.

"Have you ever considered getting away when you did was the best thing that could have happened to you? You became your own man, not just your father's shadow."

He thought of Krissy's comment when they'd reconnected in the café. "Yeah, I'm a catch."

"Shut up. You are. You're kind, and generous, and fair. To horses, and to people. And you give a hell of a leg up." She cracked a grin, but then she wasn't smiling anymore. "You may just be the best man I know."

The softness of her words and eyes unsettled him — but being kind, generous, and fair didn't get you owners in this business.

Caroline pulled a long piece of hay from the bale. She wasn't looking at him anymore. "Did you take your girlfriend tonight?"

His eyebrows furrowed. "What are you talking about?"

"The woman who came with her daughter. Krissy."

Dean didn't miss her mocking tone. "She's not my girlfriend."

"She was here this afternoon looking for you."

"Was she?" That was strange. He hadn't seen Krissy since the day she and Carlie had come to the farm.

"I chased her away with a pitchfork."

Dean laughed when he probably shouldn't have. Caroline was clearly convinced Krissy's intentions with the supplement were less than honourable.

It was nice not to be alone, and if Gus hadn't been at the house, crossing his legs, it would have been nice to stay. Dean pushed himself up. "If everything's all right, I should go. You okay?"

The way she looked at him made him wonder if she wasn't. But Caroline stood, brushing hay from her jeans. "Yeah. See you in the morning."

He wandered closer and stopped himself from picking a leafy branch of alfalfa from her hair. The Wave dozed in the corner. "Call me if the boogie man comes."

The night sky was clear, filled with flickering stars and steady planets. He never would've thought Caroline was exactly who he'd needed tonight, but she'd been there, making sense, and he'd shared thoughts he'd never told anyone else, blurring the line he'd set between them.

Gus waited at the house. Dean almost walked the dog back to the barn to see if Caroline was still there, but it was disappointingly dark.

CHAPTER THIRTY-SIX

THERE WAS something disconcerting about Andy coming to watch Gastronomy breeze twice in a row — just like it was not quite right that the owner hadn't detonated when Dean told him a scoop of powder wasn't the answer to the colt's lack of progress.

He considered asking Liv to work Cruze, thinking she might get his colt to relax better, but he didn't dare do anything to ruffle Caroline's feathers right now. It was like walking a tightrope, balancing owner and exercise rider. Dean needed them both.

The breeze went according to script this time, Gastronomy reaching the wire a nose up on Cruze, but Andy wasn't a fool. Even he couldn't miss the stranglehold Caroline had on Cruze to keep him beside his workmate. That should have worked in Dean's favour — couldn't Andy see with his own eyes that the two colts were at different maturity levels? A supplement or shot couldn't make up for that.

The air conditioning blasted in Andy's SUV as they

returned to the barn. Dean wished he could roll down the window. He didn't trust the almost-smile on his owner's face.

"Tell me what you think about my colt. What you really think," Andy said.

A pop song jumped into Dean's head. *Tell me what you want, what you really really want...* He couldn't remember who sang that — Caroline would know. Either way, it felt like a setup. But he'd be forthright, for the sake of the colt.

"I think he'd benefit from some time off. He hasn't progressed as well as I'd like this summer. A month or two on the farm would do him good. We could bring him back in the fall, and he still might make it to the races by the end of the season."

Andy nodded sagely, as if considering Dean's words. "Why haven't you offered me an interest in your colt?"

Dean couldn't control the way his eyebrows rose. He wasn't ready for *that.* "To be honest, I didn't think he was much until recently."

"I didn't know he was a half-brother to Ride The Wave. I like what I've seen. I want in."

Dean kept his knee from bouncing as his mind raced. It would give him some breathing room. The sales were coming up, and Jacob, the client he'd sold that nice two-year-old for at the beginning of the season, was interested in buying a couple of yearlings. Maybe Caroline would find a new owner or two. And if Cruze did make some money, Dean would still get half. But he hesitated when it made absolutely no sense not to agree.

He cracked the door open before Andy had brought the vehicle to a complete stop at the end of his barn. "Leave it with me. I've got to help cool out these horses. I'll call you later."

Why had he not said, "Sure, Andy," and come up with a fair figure, like he'd done many times before? Instead, he launched out of the SUV like he was making an escape. *Call him back, right now.*

He cooled Gastronomy out himself so he could be sure he wasn't making things up, but all the signs were there. It took longer than he liked for Gastronomy's respiration to return to normal. He drank too much water. If only the colt would come up with something non-negotiable, like sore shins or stress fractures. What a terrible thing to think. Caroline was probably right. He was better off without Andy, because if Andy didn't trust his judgement anymore, what was the point?

At the end of the morning, he retreated to his office and shut the door, but he couldn't make the call. He burst back out. Caroline ran a sponge over a bridle hanging from the hook in front of the tack room.

Her eyebrows peaked. "Is there a fire in there?"

Dean ran a hand through his hair. She'd talk sense into him. "Andy wants a piece of Cruze."

Her hands stopped moving, eyes widening under the fringe of hair falling across her forehead. "Tell him no!"

Her words were so unexpected it took Dean aback. "I'm sorry?"

"Why would you even think about doing that?"

"It's what we do," he said carefully.

"It's what you *did*. You don't have to do it again."

"Come on, Caroline. You know how this works. If someone offers you money for a two-year-old — in this case, an *unstarted* two-year-old — you take it and run." That's what she was supposed to be telling him. The world felt upside down. "Saying no is never the right decision. And in this case, Cruze stays in my barn so I make training fees on him."

"But the guy is a jerk."

Dean laughed. "Says the woman who trained for — and married — Bryce Harrington?"

Her jaw tightened and her face went an angry red. "I'm not with him anymore though, am I?" she snapped.

Her point wormed in. Staying with a bad owner wasn't all that unlike remaining in a toxic relationship. But Dean wasn't going to fire Andy for offering to buy a piece of a horse. So what if Andy had been ready to throw The Wave under a bus?

That still irked him.

He ran a hand over his face and stared at the shedrow, finding Cruze pulling timothy from his haynet, ears pointed in Dean's direction, listening like a kid who had plotted with his mom about something both knew Dad would not want to buy into.

Dean sighed and turned back to Caroline, poking a finger at her. "If he colics tonight, you're walking him."

Her lips were still pressed together, but she was fighting a smile. "Deal."

"If he hurts himself, you're rehabbing him."

"Not a problem."

Dean stopped there. Best not to tempt fate.

The shiny new halter stood out in the bundle of repairs. Caroline slipped into Cruze's stall, giving him a swat when he tried to bite her thigh. She took advantage of his stunned moment of stillness to snag his nose and buckle the crown piece behind his ears. It was about time the colt, who now resided in the box once occupied by his successful big brother, had a proper halter.

Cruze shoved his head over the yoke when she left him and Caroline snapped a photo, making sure to capture the plate. She might have to start an Instagram page for her new life.

When Dean announced there was a race for Cruze in the

next condition book, she'd finally learned the colt's registered name. *Subatomic*. It was a disappointment, if not entirely a surprise.

"I thought because he's Ride The Wave's half-brother," she'd complained, "he'd have a cool name like that. Something that makes you think of beaches and surfing in the Pacific Ocean. You should have called him *Teahupo'o*."

"I'm sorry?" Dean had looked puzzled.

"It's where they had the Olympic surfing."

"They did? More importantly, they have surfing in the Olympics?"

"You really do live under a rock, don't you?"

Dean had ignored her jibe. "Ride The Wave isn't about surfing. It's physics."

Was he having her on? "I missed that day, professor. How?"

"Wave theory explains the way light travels."

"Um. Okay, Einstein."

"It's not that complicated. You must've taken it in school at some point."

"Sure." If she had, she'd purged it from her brain.

"He hasn't raced yet, so if you fork out the cash, we could still call him that. What was it again? Ta-ah-something?"

"No! Changing his name would be bad luck." But she'd grinned so hard her face hurt because he'd said *we*.

She'd forgotten how great it felt to be part of the journey, taking a young horse — who only a few months ago had seemed destined to be some kid's riding pony — and turning him into an athlete inspiring all of the hopes and dreams this game was about. Everything finally felt like it was going right. Cruze was training like a racehorse, and Dean was probably setting Andy straight right now. She knew he still had his doubts, but Cruze would prove her right. Purses were insane right now, so when he won first time out, he'd make enough to take the pressure off and help Dean get his confidence back. He'd been so morose the other night. But when he'd said Krissy wasn't his girlfriend, Caroline's determination to help him get through this redoubled. They'd put all their pieces back together. Dean had to feel it, this *kinship*...

She laughed. That was such a Dean word.

A truck pulled up at the end of the barn, its driver hopping out and opening the back. Caroline eyed the blacksmith, bulging arms under a cut-off t-shirt, hoisting his caddy out. He hiked down the shed. He was a burly one. *Fleshy*, she and Jess would have said when they were younger and cattier. She slipped a hand to her mouth to cover her smile. Nope, not grown up yet.

"You must be the new exercise girl," he said, setting down his box.

"Caroline," she responded, reaching for the shank on Cruze's door instead of offering her hand.

"Nice to meet you. I'm Clay. You holding the horse?"

Did she really need to answer that? Instead, she ducked into the colt's stall to pull Cruze out, setting him up in the middle of the sandy aisle.

Her phone pinged, and she pulled it from her back pocket. Cruze reached for it, all lips and teeth, and she stretched her arm to keep it away from him, apologizing to Clay for the way the colt leaned on him.

"Stand up," she hissed, thumbing a one-handed reply to Jess's text.

"Hey, Clay."

Caroline stopped herself from turning, Dean's voice making her skin tingle. He came up behind her, standing close enough she felt a pull, like a magnet, and had to stop herself from leaning into it, his rangy form a complete one-eighty from the blacksmith's heft.

Clay twisted, keeping Cruze's left front between his knees. "Hey, Dean. How's it going? I finally got to meet your girl Carrie here."

Caroline swung the end of the length of leather in a tight circle and clenched her jaw. "Caroline."

"What's the matter, you don't like Carrie?"

"You heard her, Clay. Car-o-line. That's three syllables. Can you manage that?" Dean said.

Caroline's brows stretched to her hairline. She didn't know whether to laugh or tell Dean not to piss the shoer off.

"Care-oh-line," Clay mimicked, drawing out the last beat. Then he chuckled and went back to work.

She scrutinized every nip and rasp, every nail, but there was no faulting Clay's work. Dean saw him out to his truck as she put Cruze away.

"He's a good blacksmith," Dean said when he returned, crossing his arms. He sounded like he was defending the guy.

"I didn't think you used him for his sparkling personality. I know not everyone can be as charming as you." Caroline scooped up the hoof clippings and raked away the footprints in the dirt.

The look on his face was one of consternation — that was a Dean word, too. He must be wondering: was she joking? Was she serious?

"Nice halter," he noted with a nod at the well-crafted combination of glossy leather and gleaming brass, hung on the door nail by its square fittings. "Thanks for getting that. Let me know what I owe you."

"It's my gift to the big horse."

He pressed his lips together in a frown, and she thought he might protest. Triple-stitched track halters weren't cheap — but he tickled Cruze's nose instead. "You've found your fairy godmother, buddy."

Caroline leaned against the stall door, the metal cool against her back. "Did you talk to Andy? How'd he take it?"

The way Dean clenched his jaw and wouldn't look at her made her bristle. If he hadn't done it and Andy now owned a piece of this horse — Andy could pay for the damn halter.

Dean turned, meeting her eyes. "Not great. He's taking his horses away."

CHAPTER THIRTY-SEVEN

"How can you be so calm?"

Dean stared through the windshield, arm resting across the wheel as he drove. Calm? He wasn't calm. He felt he'd been run over by a semi and left to die. Speaking took energy he didn't have.

"I'm going to have to lay Hunter off," he said. At least, with just a couple of weeks left in the summer, the kid might not mind so much. "Squeak too."

"You don't have to pay me," she said quickly.

"I can't let you work for free, Caroline."

"I had a little windfall."

"There's a big difference between buying a new halter and refusing income."

"Bryce gave me some money."

Dean slid her a glance. He wanted to ask what that meant. Would she finish the summer, then leave? That was the agreement, all she'd committed to. "You should save that money."

"Then think of all that shit I stole from you back in the day. I owe you."

He laughed. "You were terrible."

"You can pay me back when Cruze wins first time out."

That used to be him, the guy his friends made fun of for always being high on his horses. "Now who's trying to jinx us?"

He stopped to pick up the mail when they got back to the farm, not bothering to look through the bundle of newsprint. Normally, the sight of Faye's rusted Toyota when he pulled into Northwest's lane would have cheered him, but not today. He didn't want to tell her. So close to her wedding, Faye deserved to be happy, unfettered by his business failings. But he couldn't keep it from her, no matter the timing.

Caroline hopped out of the truck and pointed a finger at him. "Two weeks till Cruze runs. Don't do anything drastic. Promise?"

"That's not fair."

"Two weeks."

He sighed and removed his keys from the ignition. "All right."

What was he going to do, anyway?

Faye was in the kitchen, bustling around. Gus rushed over with his big grin and ploofy tail, oblivious to Dean's dark mood. As usual, something smelled incredible. Could he close the door behind him and stay in here forever?

She pushed a white bakery box toward him. "Cinnamon rolls for my cinnamon roll." Faye smiled like she'd said something clever.

Dean didn't understand. He'd been in graduate school, but she'd always been the smart one. The rolls were still warm — and the sugar might give his brain fuel to figure things out.

"Sit down," Faye said, handing him a plate for the roll he'd been about to bite into and nudging him to the table. She produced a to-go cup, the Triple Shot logo stamped on the side.

"How did you —"

"Sixth sense," she said. "Or maybe just luck."

"Glad one of us has some of that," Dean said, pulling out a chair. He flipped through the mail as if something in the grocery store flyers held the answer to his problems, pausing to pull off chunks of the bun. This time, he recognized the white envelope from the Realtor. They were persistent, always scrounging for listings.

Faye gave him a few moments of munching in silence before she asked, "Tell me."

So Dean did. About Andy's dissatisfaction —not news. About his offer. About his reaction when Dean told him *no*.

It took a beat for Faye to respond, rearranging her expression from shock to indignation. "That was really a deal-breaker? After all these years?"

"I think it's been building. Loyalty can only last so long. He did stick around longer than anyone else."

"You've always gone partners with him on horses. What was different?"

His gaze flicked to hers before he took a sip of the espresso. It wasn't scalding hot the way he liked it — no matter how often Faye chastised him that *burnt* was not how good coffee should be.

"Caroline talked me out of it."

Faye's eyebrows lifted, her lips twitching. Dean expected her to call him out, but she said, "Well, you must trust her judgement. And maybe she's not wrong. The time has come to believe in yourself instead of Dad's legacy. Leave what's behind, behind."

The broken record in his head spun on. "Or maybe it's time to admit I'll never be the trainer he was and let it go."

"You're different, not worse. The business isn't the same anymore, either, and it needs trainers like you."

"Owners don't want trainers like me." He picked the envelope from the pile and tossed it in front of her. "Open it."

With a skeptical glance, she did. Her eyes scanned the page, then levelled on his. "This can go right in the recycle bin."

"We should think about it. The market is on fire right now."

Faye would know what this place was worth. The closing on the vacant home she and Will had purchased had come fast and furious, with it the stress of a mortgage and the challenge of renovations. Every time he saw her these days — which wasn't very often — she went on about both.

"You're serious," she said.

"Wouldn't it be smarter to sell when we want to, rather than because we have to? It would take some of the pressure off you with your house. You could start saving for your kids' education. By the time they're old enough, you'll probably need a second mortgage to send them through university."

Faye smirked. "They're going to be working from the time they're old enough to carry a tray or work a mixer. They can pay their own way through school."

He had to smile. He could picture Mean Mom Faye. No free ride. They'd need Uncle Dean for the fun stuff.

"Where would you go?" she asked.

He shrugged. "Lots of trainers live in condos near the track."

Faye snorted. "You? In a condo?"

"Why not?"

"What about the horses?"

The two younger broodmares were solid breed-to-race mares; he could sell them. Cherry's best reproductive years were behind her, so it only made sense to pension her — selling the farm might give him enough cushion to pay for pasture board somewhere. Emilie would find a home for The Wave, once he was gelded.

Dean could be one of those guys who trained a couple of his own, then went off to his day job where he made enough to keep doing what he loved on the side — as a hobby, not a career. He'd tried being a trainer. He'd had some success. But his optimism had worn out, taking his tenacity with it.

"Have you talked to Gus about this?" Faye asked.

"We haven't talked about Gus."

They'd both been avoiding that subject. For a moment, Faye looked like the fifteen-year-old girl he'd returned to after the accident — *I don't want to talk about it* — because she loved the Golden Retriever as much as he did.

"That dog would pine away in a condo," she said. "And if you moved to the city, when would I ever see you?"

"You seemed to manage to see Will just fine when he lived in the city."

Her lips lifted into a wry twist. "That's because he had the motivation to come see me."

"If you had Gus, I'd be motivated."

She sighed. "I can't take Gus from you."

Faye didn't say it, but Dean could feel it. *Because you don't have anyone else.*

"He'll adapt to living in a condo," he said.

"But will you?"

"Think of how much time I'd have. No commute. I could ride my bike more. Visit as much as you'd have me. I could do things in the city. I might actually meet someone because I'd have the time to use that dating app you insisted on setting up for me. Do you honestly think I'm going to meet anyone the way my life is right now?"

Faye rolled her eyes, muttering, "You are so dense sometimes."

What was that supposed to mean? "Come on, Faye. You know as well as I do something has to change."

"You're having a bad year. Things will turn around. You know how this business works."

"It's never been this bad and it's not fair to you, is it? To hang on, just because?" Because he was trying to prove he could do what their father had done, when it was obvious he could not.

"None of it would still be here if it wasn't for you. You remember that don't you?"

She was being generous. All he'd done was buy them some time, and it felt like time had run out.

Faye stood, Gus scrambling to his feet next to her. "I've got to get back to the shop. You are coming to the Plate this weekend, right?"

He hadn't planned on it. With no horse running on the card, the prospect of sitting at home with Gus and watching it on TV seemed far more appealing than battling crowds at Woodbine. But Krissy had called and gone on about how much Carlie wanted to go, and he hadn't been able to say no. If he could provide a spark of joy in a kid's life, that was one small, good, thing in the middle of the turmoil.

"Krissy's meeting me there with her daughter."

"Is there something going on with her I should know about?"

Dean almost laughed because she always seemed to know before he did what wasn't happening with his love life. "No, we're just friends. It feels good doing something nice for the kid."

"Good," Faye said, finding her shoes by the door. "Catch you later."

She slipped out, leaving the dog staring at the door, tail

drifting side to side. Good? Good for doing something nice for Carlie, or good Krissy was just a friend?

"We'll go for our walk in a bit, buddy," Dean said, putting the plate into the dishwasher. Then he found the real estate agent's letter and punched the ten digits into his phone. She picked up too promptly for him to change his mind.

Dean inhaled. "Hi, yes. You left a card in my mailbox a while back. Are you still looking for country properties?"

CHAPTER THIRTY-EIGHT

Hooves clattered on asphalt, profanities and shouts of warning snapping Dean's eyes to the ruckus. A flash of seal brown flew directly at him and he leapt out of the way, sliding into the ditch.

There was something familiar about the muscled hindquarters of the departing horse, reins flapping and irons flying, black tail flagged over the flash of aluminum shoes.

"He misses you, Dean."

Dean glanced back toward the tunnel, Nate Miller trying to settle a dancing horse agitated by the commotion. Dean's eyes found Caroline's. She and She Brews were frozen, Sheba wide-eyed, on edge, while Caroline murmured, "*Easy, mare.*"

"Fargo," she said, frowning. "What the hell have they done to him?"

Dean climbed back onto the path. That frenzied animal had been Fargo? His step faltered, body instinctively turning to go after his horse. But Fargo wasn't his horse anymore.

He and Caroline were silent while others asked the ejected exercise rider if he was okay, getting a joking response peppered with more obscenities. The flow of traffic resumed, and Dean escorted Sheba through the tunnel. Fargo had not once refused to train in the years Dean had him. How had they screwed him up in a month?

The horses galloping on the main oval were a blur. When Caroline came off the track, Dean asked how the mare went because he hadn't noticed. He couldn't get the images out of his head. Fargo nearly mowing him down. Fargo running away.

He wished he could unsee it. Before that, he'd accepted the claim. It wasn't the first time Faron had taken a horse from him. But such an overt display of unhappiness would keep him up at night.

The shed was alive with chatter when they returned, Squeak recounting some story as he followed Caroline and She Brews into the mare's box. "He came barrelling in here like a barn-sour trail horse. Ducked right into his old stall and stood there like he was waiting for lunch." Squeak chuckled.

"Fargo?" Caroline asked as she slid the saddle off She Brews.

Squeak nodded. "I took him back to Faron's barn."

Caroline and Dean exchanged glances but not words. It was a good thing Dean hadn't been here. He probably would have confiscated the tack, painted a blaze on Fargo's face and tried to hide him until he could take him to the farm. Not his farm, where Fargo's rightful owners would look first. Was there still a paddock standing at Faye's new-old house? Faye would send him for a psychiatric assessment — unless he landed himself in jail for theft. At least he wouldn't have to worry about the cost of living. Could he finish his masters there?

"They're having all sorts of problems with him," Squeak prattled on, handing Caroline the bridle. "Old Fargo, stirring things up. Whoever woulda thunk, eh?"

Dean grimaced. He needed to move on. "Did you have the chance to tack up Sunny in the kerfuffle?"

Caroline recovered enough from the groom's tale to snort, no doubt at his word choice.

"Hunter got him ready for me," Squeak said. "I didn't have the heart to make the kid take Fargo back. He's pretty upset about it."

Dean couldn't blame him. "Let me know when Nate gets here. I'll be in the office." He didn't want his staff to see him moping like a twelve-year-old whose first pony had been sold.

When he got to the office, he couldn't sit, so he paced. Fargo deserved better. If only he'd listened to Emilie. But he had bigger problems than Fargo right now, didn't he? Like two more empty stalls now that Gastronomy and Epi were gone. He'd supervised their departure yesterday, with no idea who their new trainer was. Graciously — *haha* — Andy had allowed Dean to buy out his share of Sun and Stars. Dean had taken it in trade for the training fees Andy owed him. *Poof!* There went August's income.

"Hey, Dean. Dean?"

Dean's head snapped up. Nate stood in the doorway, expression somewhere between concern and laughter.

"You're early," Dean said.

"Is that a problem?"

"Riders are supposed to keep everyone waiting."

"Sorry, I'll try to do better. You look upset."

Dean sighed. "Fargo. It's Fargo."

"I told you he misses you." There was no humour on Nate's face now.

"What do you know?" Dean asked.

"They haven't been able to get him to the track this week."

"That's not like Fargo. The reason he's still running is because he loves to train."

"I don't know what happened, but he's not a happy camper over there."

"He's still in jail, so I guess they're waiting to run him back for bottoms." That was the claiming rule — if his new trainer wanted Fargo to compete at a lower level than what he'd been claimed for, they had to wait thirty days.

"Or they'll take him to the Fort."

"He hates Fort Erie."

"Him and me both," Nate quipped. "But if they can't even get him to the track, he's not gonna run."

But what if they took him to the Fort, and had no better luck? Faron wasn't exactly a straight arrow. Fargo could disappear to an obscure farm in the Niagara region and drop completely off Dean's radar.

Forget about it. The horse was not his responsibility anymore. His father was wrong. His heart was not too big for this sport.

"Can I have the keys to the truck? I want to make a kitchen run. I need my purse."

Dean reached into his pocket but pulled out a wad of cash. "Well, here, let me give you some money. Get me some chips."

Caroline waved him off. "My treat."

His brow furrowed, but he relinquished the keys. *Can't a girl buy her boss and co-workers a snack without raising suspicion?*

Dean glanced at her feet when she returned the fob. "Aren't you going to take off your boots?"

She smiled and shook her head. No, she wanted to be wearing her boots for this. She took Squeak's and Hunter's orders and marched off, hoping Dean didn't notice she went in the wrong direction.

By the time Caroline reached her destination, it felt like steam was building in her eardrums. She barged into Jack Faron's barn, scanning the shedrow.

"Where's your boss?" she said to the first groom she encountered. For a split second, she felt sorry for him. She knew how Faron paid his help — poorly, and illegally.

The groom stopped, mid-sweep. "I think he's around the other side."

Caroline nodded. "Thanks." Why would he know, really? Faron was barely here. He wasn't the most hands-on of employers.

Faron had the maximum number of stalls with branded wall plaques garnishing each door. The shedrow was tidy, Faron's assistants running the operation like little drill sergeants. What the staff didn't earn from their weekly wages, they made up in stake bonuses because the barn won a lot of races. That's why his employees put up with the rest of it.

She spotted the swine in question just the other side of the gap in the middle of the long shedrow, where horses could cut through the centre of the barn. He was talking to a taller man — a jock's agent, Caroline guessed, but not someone she knew. Faces had changed in the last ten years. The way the agent's gaze slid down her body made her want to kick him in the shins. Just another sleazeball. He fit right in around here.

Faron brightened when he noticed her. "Well, hello, Caroline. Nice of you to stop by."

With momentum behind her, she rammed her palms into Faron's soft chest, sending him staggering. He braced a hand on the wall to regain his balance, laughing. *Laughing!*

He straightened, brushing the front of his polo shirt like her hands had left grime behind. "Caroline, have you met Marcus

Jordan, Tony Perry's agent? Marcus, this is my friend Caroline Harrington. Do you still go by Harrington?"

Caroline glowered at Faron, not sure which grated worse, the way he said "friend" or the sound of Bryce's last name. Marcus Jordan's palm was damp in her grasp. The agent took a step backward once his hand slithered away, eyes shifting.

"I'll catch up with you later," he said. "Uh, nice to meet you, Caroline."

She ignored him and zeroed back in on Faron. "Somewhere more private, perhaps?"

Faron nodded, his smarmy smile not hiding the hint of fear behind his eyes. This is why she'd left her boots on. They made her taller than him, and he looked just a tiny bit intimidated. She followed him to his office, stepping up into the space — and questioning her decision for the first time. She didn't close the door behind her.

Faron settled behind a large, modern desk. "Have a seat."

Caroline didn't.

He clasped his hands together and rested them on the blotter. "Are you here about my offer?"

She scowled. "Hardly. Why did you claim Dean's horse? You know he's never going to win another race."

"Oh, he'll win somewhere." Faron seemed to have regained his confidence now that they were inside his hovel.

Which was pretty posh, actually. Much larger than Dean's cubby of an office. Faron didn't have a Plate win photo, though. His father hadn't trained a Canadian Triple Crown champion. Faron's dad owned a few car dealerships, if Caroline remembered correctly. Sounded about right, anyway.

"He didn't look like he wanted to be anywhere near a racetrack this morning. And he's not exactly your type, is he? A ten thousand dollar claimer is beneath you."

"One of my grooms wanted a horse. Something sound to

play around with, take somewhere this winter. Taylor's horse fit the bill. The horse doesn't have to like it or last long. The kid just wants to have some fun."

"A dozen horses back here would have filled those criteria. Younger horses."

"That horse may be old, but he's durable. Taylor doesn't mess with his stock much. Which is why it's such a puzzle that you're with him. Are you sure I can't give you a job? If you don't want to train your own, you could run my operation for me. Work with nice horses. Name your price, I'll make it happen."

"I don't need your money," Caroline snapped.

"Bryce must've cut you a nice cheque."

She didn't take the bait. Time to do what she came for. "Friday is a month, right?" Caroline approached the desk, pulling a folded slip of paper from her back pocket. She smoothed it out on the glossy mahogany surface and selected a pen from Faron's desk. "I'll post-date it for then. Fifteen should be plenty to cover it."

Faron laughed. "What makes you think I'd sell him to you?"

She scribbled her signature on the line and stared at it a moment — still Harrington, but she'd officially change it back to Jenkins as soon as the divorce was final — any day now, right?

Caroline tossed it in front of him. "Because I know all your dirty secrets, Jack. If you want them to stay in the closet, you'll take this like a good boy and find your groom another horse. Now where is he? I want to see him." She tucked the pen in her back pocket.

Faron picked up the cheque, then leaned back in his well-padded chair. "He's on his way to Fort Erie."

"What?"

Faron shrugged. "After his performance this morning, we thought he might like it better down there."

Caroline clenched her jaw. "Fine. I'll arrange transport."

"It's a good thing Taylor has you. He's gonna need a shoulder. Or at least your money. He's on his way out, by the looks of things."

She spun on her heel and headed for the door.

"Pleasure doing business with you," Faron called after her.

Caroline waited until she was out of the barn before she extracted her phone and pulled up Jess's number. "What are you doing Sunday?"

Jess responded slowly. "The usual, I guess. Nothing special."

"Are you up for a road trip?"

"Uh... what did you have in mind?"

"I need to go to the Fort. To get a horse."

"You do?"

"I do."

"What horse?"

"Dean's horse. The one that was claimed from him."

"I see."

"Your trailer is still roadworthy, right?"

"Well... barely, but yeah. Why don't you borrow Dean's?"

"Because that would ruin it."

"He doesn't know? What are you doing, Caroline?"

"I'm getting the horse safe. Then his story can carry on as it was supposed to before Jack Faron screwed it up. You'll do it, right?"

Jess laughed. "Of course I will. How could I say no to a rescue mission? I can pick you up for the Plate on Saturday, then you can stay over at my place and we'll go from there Sunday morning."

Perfect. Step one taken care of. Emilie next. Though that

probably should have been her first move — making sure New Chapter still had a spot for Fargo. They'd take him to North-west first, though. Caroline couldn't wait to see Dean's face when he saw his old horse on the farm — the way Fargo should have been a month ago.

She hoped Dean didn't hate her.

It wasn't lost on her that the sum she'd paid to ensure the gelding's safety was absurd. Fargo would never run a race again. The horse wasn't worth a quarter of the figure she'd signed away. It had been a little bit crazy.

She liked it.

From here on he'd chase horse show ribbons worth a couple of bucks. Some kid would shower him with treats and buy him too many saddle pads. Every colour of the rainbow, because they all looked good on a dark bay.

She was so wound up, she almost forgot she was supposed to be going to the kitchen. Zipping in and out without making eye contact with anyone, she hummed all the way back to Dean's barn.

CHAPTER THIRTY-NINE

Ruby red dress, with a big, matching hat. Caroline paused in front of the narrow mirror in her bedroom and turned sideways — no one was going to miss her.

"How do I look?" she asked. "Fit for the — ahem — *King's* Plate? I leave and they go and change the name on me and run it at the wrong time." It would take some getting used to. It had always been the Queen's Plate, and it was supposed to happen at the beginning of summer, not the end.

"You look great," Jess assured. "Let's go."

She followed Jess through the living room to the door. "What are my chances of getting down the stairs in these heels?"

"Do you get workers' comp with this job?" Jess asked.

"I do, but I'm not sure this would count. And I would feel bad if Dean had no help again." She removed the spiky shoes, dangling them from the straps. "Who's driving?"

"I think the obvious answer is me," Jess said.

"What are you saying?"

"I'm going with precedent."

Caroline grinned. There had been many memorable Plate parties in the past — and a few she'd forgotten.

"While on the one hand, I'm glad you're still responsible, doesn't it get boring?" Caroline said as she carefully navigated the steps in her bare feet, the wood damp beneath her soles from a morning rainfall.

"So funny."

She slipped the shoes back on when she reached the bottom, using the railing for support. The heels made her even taller than Jess in her flats.

"Are you sure you don't want me to bring my truck up here so you don't have to walk?" Jess asked.

"It'll be good practice. Also, if I'm crippled by the time we get to your truck, I'll still have the option of choosing something more sensible."

"Wouldn't it make more sense to take something more sensible with you anyway?"

Caroline laughed. "Good point. See? You've always been the smart one. Wait here."

Leaving the shoes with Jess, she dashed up the stairs, praying she didn't pick up a splinter. The runners Caroline grabbed were comfy, if not fashion-forward.

"I would need a walker to make my way around in those. My feet hurt just looking at them," Jess said as she handed back the heels and they resumed the hike to the truck.

"So how come Lab Guy didn't want to come?" That's what she'd decided to call Jess's boyfriend.

Jess snorted. "Picture one of the guys from *The Big Bang Theory* at the Plate."

"How can I? You won't let me meet him. I should get to judge for myself."

"Don't hold your breath."

"Why?"

"I don't know. Too many worlds colliding, something like that. I really never expected him to be around this long. See, that's what happens when I get bored."

"You date inappropriate men?"

"He's harmless. Just... even more boring than me." Jess grinned.

"Point taken." But Caroline wasn't sure a quiet, low-key man was a bad thing. Dean popped into her head. He might be on the nerdy side, but he was definitely good-looking. And in a suit, like he had been for the Hall of Fame induction? She fanned herself with her clutch at the memory.

"Do you want me to put the air on?" Jess asked.

Caroline laughed. "I'm fine." Was she, though?

Jess's quirky music played through the stereo, a few lofty clouds zipping by in the blue sky. A perfect day for the Plate. Caroline couldn't figure out why she was nervous. She'd been to the race a dozen times. Everyone knew she was back now. The Plate was always a good time. They'd eat some food, complain about the visitors, coo over the horses dressed up for the big day, scream them home as they ran.

By the time they arrived, it was late enough that they had a hard time finding a parking spot. Caroline opted for the heels just the same. Her feet and pain were not strangers.

Tents and food trucks and backdrops for branded photo ops jammed the area around the walking ring, a huge boom with a camera looming to capture the action in the paddock. The announcer's voice echoed with a race call, the tinny sound muffled by the jovial crowd.

"Where do we start?" Jess asked once they made it through the gates and walked into the fray of bodies.

"Look, Caesars!" Caroline waved at one of the tents, patrons emerging carrying frosted Mason jars rimmed with celery salt and decorated with a slice of lime, a leafy celery stalk contributing a sprig of green. "There."

Once they had their own, Caroline held hers aloft. "Cheers. Here's to overcoming bad decisions."

They clinked, and squeezed lime into the flame-red beverage, using the celery as a stir-stick.

Jess scanned the vendors and wandered toward the food trucks. "We should eat something. Let's go see."

Gourmet macaroni and cheese, Pad Thai poutine... this was a good idea.

"Cheesecake!" Jess squealed.

"Does that make a complete meal, with the Caesar?" Caroline mused. "Want to split a macaroni and cheese?" They stopped in front of the bright yellow truck.

"Then cheesecake?" Jess suggested. Suddenly, her eyes lit up and she pointed. "Look, horses!"

Caroline pivoted. The runners for the next race strutted up the path, eyes bright, ears forward, rippling muscles and streaming tails. Did they never outgrow that sight? She thought she had, but Jess's announcement made her smile.

"We need a program," Jess said. "I'll go find one if you grab the food. We'll meet at the walking ring?"

Caroline nodded, and Jess scurried off. After ordering, she found a bench and watched the paddock proceedings, the scene a microcosm of memories — trainers talking to their jocks, grooms circling polished charges around the willows, owners chatting excitedly. She hadn't thought she missed it, but she'd been lying to herself.

She didn't wait for Jess to dig into the steaming food, her gaze roaming the diorama. When Jess appeared, Caroline snatched the program from her and handed her a fork.

"Eat. It's delicious." She scanned the names. "Hey, Liv's got one in this race."

She located the horse by its green number five saddle cloth. Liv, dressed in black dress pants and a white sleeveless blouse, talked to Nate in the red, white and navy Triple Stripe colours. Emilie and a taller man Caroline guessed was Tim, stood with them. She took a moment to study him. Em had done well for herself there.

"It's on the turf. Want to go around and watch it?" Jess said.

Caroline nodded. "We'd better finish this up."

She speared a clump of macaroni, shoving it into her mouth in a very unladylike fashion, and Jess followed suit. Once the riders were up, splashes of colours on the backs of primed athletes, Caroline and Jess waited as they filed past, and then they were in motion, weaving through the bodies, dropping the empty pressed cardboard in the trash on the way past.

"Caroline!"

She stopped in her tracks and searched the faces. "It's Faye!"

Their hats made for an awkward hug. Jess gave a small wave when Caroline introduced them. It was easy to forget that, just two and a half months ago, Faye had been the object of their not-so-kind gossip. Now, she'd become one of Caroline's favourite people.

"Liv's invited us up to the box. I'm sure she'd want you to join us. It's just her and Em and Tim."

"Oh, amazing, thank you," said Caroline. "Where's Will?"

Faye swept them toward the escalator. "He had a catering gig today so he's not coming."

Liv was merely polite before ignoring them all and focusing on the horse as they settled into seats. Having a box wasn't exactly special for Caroline — it was one of the perks she'd enjoyed with Bryce. Faye and Emilie chatted — Emilie had a way of keeping one eye on what was happening on the track and one on the conversation. Tim didn't seem to care they weren't paying any attention to him. He sat behind Liv, watching almost as intently except for the binoculars, like he was trying to learn by osmosis.

"Is that Dean?" Emilie said.

Caroline's ears perked, she couldn't help it. She tried to follow Emilie's gaze, searching the heads below on the apron. She hadn't known he was coming. Hadn't asked, to be fair. Because he'd said she could have the afternoon off, she'd assumed he was sticking around the farm. Wrongly.

It didn't take her long to spot him, as if her eyes were trained just for that. There was a kid on his shoulders, pointing at the horses as they went by for the post parade. Caroline's heart sank when she recognized the girl. It was Krissy's daughter, Carlie, in a pretty flowered dress and matching fascinator. Sure enough, there was Krissy next to Dean, a white hat with a wide brim shading her face from the sun, a jade green outfit skimming her curves.

"Where?" Jess whispered in her ear. Caroline pointed him out.

Even Liv dropped her binoculars. "Who's that with him?"

"Krissy," Faye said. "He says they're just friends. But I'm not buying it."

Caroline felt the look Emilie slid her way but refused to meet it.

"I know her!" Jess said, and everyone turned because, after the hellos, she hadn't spoken to anyone but Caroline. "I've seen her around campus with one of the department heads. A number of times."

"She works for a pharmaceutical company," Faye said. "Collaborating on some research, maybe?"

"They never look like they're talking about science, just saying," Jess said dryly.

"He needs to know," Faye said.

"I can't tell him," Caroline muttered.

"I will."

Everyone stared at Liv.

She shrugged. "He'll believe me." Because what would Liv have to gain by lying about that? She returned to the horses on the track.

Liv's horse ran a good second, then she was gone with a stream of breezy farewells, off to the backstretch to check on him. Emilie and Tim left with her, and Faye said she was going to find Dean. Caroline didn't suggest she and Jess go along.

"I need another one of those Caesars." She didn't want to spoil the day for Jess, or she'd have asked if they could go home.

"How about cheesecake?" Jess suggested.

"I bet you could eat a whole piece by yourself. I need alcohol. Then maybe there's a nice unsuspecting city boy I can hook up with." Forget Bryce. Forget Dean. Time for a new pond. She ignored the combination of worry and irritation on Jess's face.

She talked them into one of the trackside events requiring a special ticket and dragged Jess, looking like a sullen teenager, along. Couldn't Jess loosen up just once in her life? It was Plate Day. They hadn't done Plate Day in over a decade. Partying was in. Dean Taylor was out.

They rejoined the others to watch the big race, a current zapping through the sea of bodies. It made Caroline nostalgic, tears welling, much to her shock. She brushed them away with the back of her hand, leaning forward next to Jess, straining to see the gate far down the track, even though the big screen in the infield followed the horses as they approached the starting point.

Anticipation swelled. Zero minutes to post. The doors flew open to the deafening roar of the crowd, drowning out the announcer. The field flew down the stretch and thundered by the grandstand.

Caroline cheered for no horse in particular, having no stake in the outcome, not caring who won or where she was a year from now.

The clamour swept her away. She bounced on the balls of her feet like her heart wasn't misplaced and the result mattered when the field came around again, driving for the wire, the riders asking for every ounce of heart, their mounts' ears pinned, gutting it out. Caroline had no idea who the winner was as they galloped out in a rush of colour.

She could take Bryce's money and move to Europe, or New Zealand. It was tough to emigrate to New Zealand, she'd heard, but they had horses there. Emilie's riding coach had spent time there. Maybe she had connections or knew of a rich horse owner who needed a trophy wife.

"Where's the party this year, Em?" Caroline asked as the Governor-General's Horse guards arrived to whisk the King's representative away.

"Off the track. Security's finally cracking down so there's nothing on the backstretch this year. I'll send you the address. See you there?"

"We're in! It'll be just like old times, right Jess?"

Jess frowned. "That's what I'm afraid of."

CHAPTER FORTY

SOMETHING wet and gross tickled her ear, and Caroline batted it away. "Stop it," she mumbled into the pillow her throbbing head was pinned to. Whoever this creep was she'd had the bad judgement to go home with last night, he needed to get his tongue out of her ear and let her go back to sleep.

He snuffled around her hair. She cracked an eye open. "Callum, you dork, get off me."

Reluctantly, she pushed herself up, limbs tangled in the quilt she'd been under, but it was a relief to see the red and white Border Collie's grinning face instead of a man, even if it felt like déjà vu, as if all of it had been a dream. Working for Dean. Going back to the track. Cruze.

The hat she'd worn to yesterday's Plate rested on the coffee table. Definitely not a dream. She was never drinking that much ever again.

Three months later, she'd made zero progress. No, worse. She'd regressed to making a fool of herself in front of the very community she thought she'd escaped. The only saving grace

299

was Dean, as much a party pooper as ever, hadn't been there to witness it.

She couldn't even remember getting to Jess's, but that had been the plan. It was slowly coming back to her.

Fargo. This morning, they were supposed to be picking him up in Fort Erie. The image of Dean with Krissy's kid on his shoulders flared in her mind, making her squint as if she'd been assaulted with bright sunlight even though the blinds in Jess's living room were still drawn.

She folded the quilt and padded to the bathroom, once again sending thanks to Jess, wherever she was, for having ibuprofen in the cupboard, and for the washcloth her friend had left next to the basin. Caroline scrubbed her face clear of crusted makeup, but there was no erasing the regret.

A door creaked open, and Callum flashed past.

"She's alive," Jess said. She sounded pissed off.

"Have you done the horses already?" Caroline followed Jess into the living room. "You should have got me up, I would have come out."

"I'm used to managing on my own. You needed sleep more than I needed help." Jess's lips still formed a hard line. "There's coffee."

Snappish. But Caroline deserved it. She shuffled to the kitchen and poured herself a cup, then stood at the window, staring out at Jess's little farm remembering how last time she'd been here, she'd wondered how Jess didn't go crazy, living out here by herself. Now she knew.

She missed Northwest. She was used to waking up there, used to seeing Dean before dawn. Used to wordlessly bringing horses in or turning horses out — together. Used to the long drive into the track, discussing the day's training in snippets. What she wasn't used to was this unwanted longing, or the pang she'd felt when she'd recognized him yesterday at the races; the surge of overprotective anger when Jess told them about knowing Krissy.

The feeling of helplessness that Dean had to make his own choices.

"When do you want to leave?" Jess asked, slipping into one of the chairs at the counter.

"What time is it now?" Caroline answered her own question with a glance at the wall clock next to the sink. Eight. "How long does it take from here?"

"About an hour and a half."

"If we get there after training, that should be good." Caroline figured backwards in her head. "Nine-thirty? Or we can leave now and I can buy you breakfast somewhere." She'd owe Jess so much more than that for helping out.

"Parking a truck and trailer in a restaurant lot is awkward."

That was true, not just Jess being prickly. Caroline finished her coffee and rinsed out the cup. "I'll make you breakfast, then."

That finally earned her a grin. "I've always wanted to hear those words."

Caroline laughed and began checking the cupboards, something she should have done before making the offer. "You really need a better man." Even Bryce had made Caroline breakfast. Only once, but still.

After pancakes with maple syrup and another cup of coffee, they departed, leaving a forlorn Callum staring at the back door.

"He'll be on the couch before we're out the driveway," Jess said. "Don't feel too bad for him."

Caroline let Jess navigate the backroads in silence, the landscape green and rolling, deep dips and slow climbs that made the truck's tired engine work. Finally, she glanced sheepishly at Jess.

"How badly did I embarrass myself last night?"

Jess smirked. "You've been worse. All you really did was flirt, but then you devolved into pining about Dean like some heartbroken teenager and anyone who'd been interested left you alone."

Caroline sank her head into her hands. "Ugh." She wasn't sure if her shame was because now her feelings were public knowledge or because those feelings were such a lost cause. "Why am I even doing this?" Like bringing Fargo home would somehow convey her feelings for the man.

"You have to do it for the horse. Dean will appreciate and respect that."

Thinking of all of the times she'd blatantly ignored Jess's advice, it was time to embrace it. Because Dean's respect was important to her. She'd lost it, long ago. If that was the only thing he gave her, it would be enough.

That might be a lie. She wanted more.

"But Caroline... what have you got to lose by just telling him how you feel?"

Everything. Because if this connection she was sure she felt was all in her head and she had to move on, she'd lose all the things that had become meaningful to her.

The boring highway to the border track gave her time to brood, staring out the window at the way development had built up in her absence, Ontario's Golden Horseshoe creeping further around Lake Ontario. It made her miss Saskatchewan just a little, big sky and endless farmland, still dotted with old grain elevators. A place people liked to say was so flat you could watch your dog run away for days. Here, the crowded industry and housing ruined the view of the Niagara Escarpment slicing up to the clouds on her right, and she had to look across Jess to see the glittering surface of Lake Ontario on the left, which was awkward. So Caroline stared at the grey of the multiple lanes before them, over the towering Skyway bridge, leaving Hamilton behind, the endless buildings finally thinning out the further they travelled.

They stopped for gas, and Caroline gave Jess cash for Starbucks and treats as she filled up the tank, paying with Bryce's card. He hadn't cut her off yet, and she wasn't going to remind him. She would let him pay for as much as she could get away with for as long as possible — and not feel the least bit guilty for it.

She imagined many passengers on this route were headed for wineries or the outlet mall or Niagara Falls. But Jess drove past all those tourist hotspots, finally reaching the outskirts of Fort Erie.

Jess pulled up to the security booth, told the guard they were here to pick up a horse, and the guard waved her through without interrogating them. Yep, gotta love Fort Erie's laid-back atmosphere. Truck and trailer crept through the backside to the loading area. Jess shut off the engine, and they both hopped out.

The sight of the sign for Faron's stable gave Caroline a chill, and it struck her all of a sudden that Faron could double-cross her. She'd been too unsuspecting, believing her threats about exposing the things she knew about him would truly deter him. Because he knew things about her, too, didn't he?

She had her bill of sale ready, folded and tucked in her back pocket, but Faron's assistant didn't ask for proof. He even handed over the horse's papers, then showed her to the stall.

"He's fat," the assistant said. "Couldn't get him to the track here, either, so all he's been doing is eating."

She barely hid her smug smile. Fargo did look tubbier than when she'd seen him last. When he nickered at her, all doubt melted away. She'd do this for every horse slipping through the ranks if she could. He pressed his head to her chest and she had to swallow hard.

"Hi Fargo. I'm going to bust you out of this place." She put his old halter on and attached the shank. "Let's blow this pop stand."

As she led him out, she tossed a "Thanks" the assistant's way and marched out of the barn. Jess scrambled ahead of her and dropped the ramp. Fargo practically jumped on, and both Caroline and Jess laughed as they secured him in the sturdy steel bumper pull.

"Can't say I blame you, buddy!" Jess said as she latched the ramp.

"Let's get you home." Caroline rubbed his face with her palm before slipping out the side door.

Once she climbed into the cab and snapped the seat belt in place, she sent Emilie a text. *Sprung!*

Caroline watched the trailer in the sideview mirror, praying Jess's old truck didn't break down on the Skyway. Her heart was in her throat until Jess pulled into the rutted Northwest laneway, slowly bumping down it with the mares and foals following along the fence, stretching over and through the rails as truck and trailer rolled to a halt in front of the gate. Fargo yelled and Jaida trilled back, her bratty colt letting out a high-pitched echo.

When Jess pulled up next to the layup barn, The Wave sauntered to the fence, ears pricked, quietly assessing the unfamiliar vehicle.

"I'm going to put him right out," Caroline said, as she hooked Fargo up, Jess waiting for the okay to drop the ramp. "I'm trusting you to be sensible without tranq, okay old man?"

She wanted that picture, the one Dean had planned the day Fargo had instead been claimed: the veteran grazing adjacent to his big horse, safe and sound and ready for the next stage of his life.

Fargo didn't move, as if he didn't believe he was free. His nostrils flared, taking in the smells, ears flickering. The Wave craned his neck over the top rail of the enclosure next door, a double fence line separating them. Finally, Fargo dropped his head, crumpling to his knees and rolling in a poof of dust. He clambered up only to drop on his other side. Rising with a satisfied snort, he shook off a cloud and sashayed away in search of the best spot to nibble, nose trailing the grass.

"Mission accomplished," Jess said, grinning. "I'd better get back to my own crew."

"Thank you." Caroline grabbed her and pulled her into a hug. "For this, and for saving me from going home with a random guy last night."

"You can age out of that any time, you know."

"I thought I had!"

She was still watching Fargo when Dean showed up. Caroline had warned Faye so his sister wouldn't tip him off. She glanced over her shoulder as he approached, Gus trotting next to him. Dean slowed when he noticed her, his brow wrinkled. Caroline's nerve endings lit up as he drew closer, and the look on his face deepened, eyes flicking to hers. Fargo wandered over.

"Hey, buddy," he said quietly, then to Caroline, "What did you do? I can't afford this right now."

She'd had this insane idea he'd be happy, but it had been a silly, sentimental thought. "You don't have to. He's mine, not yours — at least until I sign him over to New Chapter. Unless I have to sign him over to you first, so that you can sign him over to them, so you get the tax receipt for the donation."

His eyebrows disappeared beneath the persistent lock of hair falling across his forehead. "You've got this all figured out."

"I'll pay you board while he's here."

"You don't have to do that."

"I already sent it to Faye."

"You paid up front?"

"He's a riding horse now. That's how riding horse people pay."

Dean laughed. She wasn't expecting the arm he put around her shoulders, or the gentle squeeze.

"Thank you," he said. Then he walked away, calling Gus.

Caroline wondered where he went in his head when he wandered.

The truth was, Dean didn't need sentimental gestures. She wished she could buy him a couple of really nice horses, but she didn't have that kind of money, so she'd have to find someone who did.

Faye's appearance was a pleasant surprise. She swung a bag from the café in one hand as she joined Caroline at the fence.

"That can only mean good things." Caroline grinned, peeking into the sack.

"How'd it go?" Faye asked.

Caroline shrugged, breaking off a piece of chocolate croissant. "The rescue mission went great. The reception fell a little flat."

"He's got a lot on his mind. He'll come around."

"You got my e-transfer for Fargo's board?"

Faye nodded. "I have something else for you."

Caroline accepted the envelope Faye passed her and stared at the card inside, reading the words printed on the off-white stock. "You're inviting me to your wedding?"

Faye pushed herself back from the fence. "Bring someone, if you like. Choose wisely."

CHAPTER FORTY-ONE

"Wakey wakey, kiddo. Time to rise and shine!"

Caroline's sing-song did nothing to rouse Cruze from his flat-out midafternoon slumber. Conserving his energy, Dean hoped. The colt had no idea what was coming, so Dean could hardly blame him for his uninspiring lack of enthusiasm.

Cruze righted himself with a grunt as she entered the stall and reluctantly launched to his feet. He stretched up, chin tucked, then extended one hind leg, pointing the toe. A shuddering shake loosed the straw that clung to him, leaving its imprint on his skin — though there was still half a bale woven through his tail. Good thing Caroline had started early. That tail was going to take some time to sort out.

"Can you get me a bucket and sponge?" she called, tying Cruze to the back wall. "He used a pile of manure as a pillow."

At least the colt wasn't grey.

The soft brush and rag she ran over the two-year-old's deep espresso coat brought up his dapples so they looked like little cups of crema from Faye's café. Muscles that had been soft and undefined in the spring now bore distinct creases. Even his hooves had a lustre from the oil Caroline had applied that morning. Cruze *looked* incredible, at least.

With only three horses in the barn, it was just Dean and Caroline now. His mind flashed back to the spring, when he'd stood here with another first-time starter. The expectation he'd felt that day with Fox was absent. It wasn't fair to count on Cruze to pull his career from this bog, a last gasp to save his livelihood. Dean wasn't even sure Cruze belonged in this maiden allowance field instead of a claiming race, but he couldn't bear the thought of losing another horse. Fargo had reminded him that no one was safe, and Caroline wouldn't have as easy a time freeing a two-year-old from the clutches of the likes of Jack Faron.

Dean had been equal parts exasperated and touched when he'd seen the old gelding in that paddock on the farm next to The Wave. Caroline had all the bases covered, though, so his anger hadn't lasted.

He made the walk over to the front side with Cruze and Caroline because it would've seemed pretentious to drive. This part wasn't new to Cruze — Caroline had both ridden him over in the mornings and schooled him in hand between races in the afternoon. That didn't keep Cruze from fishtailing, gawking at the sights as they reached the frontside. The colt pulled them along, puffed up like a rooster, all the way into the saddling enclosure. Dean could only laugh. *May you be all that and more, little man.*

He kept snatching glances at Cruze as he and the valet put the tack on. The colt stood alert but relaxed, and when Dean caught Caroline's eyes, she shrugged in a *we'll take it* gesture. She slipped off the halter and Dean put the blinkers on. The colt's sudden good behaviour was so unexpected Dean almost forgot to remove the polos until Caroline reminded him.

"I think he can run a bit," he told the same apprentice

who'd ridden Fargo, the kid more experienced now, if not lighting the jockey standings on fire. "He doesn't like Canada Geese, so hopefully you won't see any out there this afternoon."

The kid laughed like he thought Dean was joking.

After he tossed the apprentice up and Caroline led them away, he let himself take a good look at Liv's colt. Just Cash It definitely belonged here, a handsome, good-looking chestnut like his older brother Just Jay, the horse who had taken Liv from Dubai to Royal Ascot to the Breeders' Cup at Del Mar. Despite being better on paper than Dean's colt — both his pedigree and recorded works — he was just as much an unknown at this stage as Cruze. The Triple Stripe colt was the favourite, though. That pedigree carried a lot of weight.

"Cruze looks great," Liv said as they met up on the way to the escalator.

"So does Cash."

"Good luck."

"Same to you."

They exchanged wry smiles before splitting off to sit apart. Emilie joined Liv, waving at him. Dean found his usual spot and levelled his binoculars on the gap where the horses entered the track.

"May I sit here?"

Crystal, his old exercise rider, hovered over the chair next to him. "Of course! How are you doing?"

"Not bad. I wasn't going to miss this. I can't believe you got him to the races. You deserve a trophy for that."

Dean laughed, then spotted Caroline coming up the stairs from the apron, shank looped in one hand, her nylon number pinny bunched in the other. She eyed Crystal with suspicion.

"Caroline gets at least half the credit," he said by way of introduction. "Probably more."

Crystal grinned. "Are you the brave soul who's been

galloping him? That definitely gets you a bigger trophy than Dean."

Caroline's features eased into a smile. "You must be Crystal."

"I hope you paid the gate crew to have some geese behind the gate. He'll win for sure just to get away from them," Crystal cracked.

"Hey, there's Hunter," Caroline said, waving him over. She'd helped find him a job with another trainer for the rest of the summer.

"The gang's all here." Dean would bet Squeak was watching in the kitchen. Just having them around him bolstered Dean's optimism. This was horse racing. *Don't ever forget that.* Cruze could be anything.

"He's behaving," Caroline said.

Dean bounced his knee, focused as the colt went through his warmup. His heart thudded, steady but hard against his chest. A good race wouldn't change his life, but it would sure change his outlook.

He switched to toe-tapping as the field loaded into the gate because his quadricep threatened to spasm. The assistant starters wrestled with leaping juveniles while Cruze stood in his slot like a star, thanks to all those times Crystal had schooled him, taking advantage of the colt's sluggish personality to introduce him to the contraption. Getting his card had been a formality — which Caroline had insisted on doing herself, reminding Dean she'd accepted responsibility for his decision to keep Cruze.

She seemed to be accepting responsibility for a lot.

He held his breath once they were all in. *Safe trip, buddy.*

The doors sprang open.

The apprentice did a good job of settling Cruze, keeping him clear in the second flight with Cash trailing behind him, like Just Jay used to do. They shot across the backstretch, the first quarter ticking off smartly. Dean didn't need the announcer's droning call to tell him where his horse was — and where Cash was.

Cruze held his position on the turn. He looked strong, better than Dean could have imagined. Cash started working his way up the inside. Dean crept to the edge of his seat. The fast pace would benefit both colts.

Cash kept sneaking up the rail. Cruze gained on the outside. If the fading front-runner closed the gaping hole on the inside, Nate would be in trouble with Cash — while Cruze and the apprentice were all clear, steadily eating up ground as they rounded the long bend.

Dean didn't dare think it, but he did anyway. Cruze could do this. Cruze could win. All they needed was a little luck, for things to go Cruze's way and not Cash's. The two-year-olds careened into the homestretch like a group of kids being let out of school for the holidays — here, there and everywhere.

It was chaotic.

The pacesetter veered into Cruze's path. His rider checked him and Cruze lurched right, avoiding his rival's heels — but then ducked back in sharply, suddenly looking every bit the green youngster he was. Next to Dean, Caroline gasped, jumping up as the apprentice tipped sideways, hanging off the side of Cruze's neck. Cruze faltered, the awkward weight distribution setting him off stride — then Dean swore he saw the colt drop his head, sending his rider tumbling to the track.

He threw his hands in the air and slumped back into his seat. Thank goodness Cruze was in the middle of the racetrack, clear of the other runners. Behind the colt, a familiar scene played out, the apprentice slowly climbing to his feet.

Cash stole the lead, zipping neatly up the rail, pulling away from the others with an eighth of a mile to go. Cruze, reins flapping around his ears, took up the chase. Nate's head snapped to the side as he caught sight of the loose horse, ten feet to Cash's side. Caroline's fingernails dug into Dean's shoulder. The outrider's pony danced in anticipation beyond the wire.

Cruze charged, flat out. He pulled even, ears pinned, and whipped right on by, gleefully galloping out until the outrider swept in and snagged him. He and Gord's pony must be on a first-name basis by now.

Caroline's head sagged against Dean's shoulder

"Well," Dean said, placing his hands on his knees. Caroline straightened. "I think it's fair to say he *can* run a bit."

Too bad he had to keep his rider to get the winner's purse.

Cruze's notoriety preceded him. On the walk back to the barn, Caroline grinned and waved at the barrage of jokes like she was accepting accolades. Dean kept his hands in his pockets, head down.

It was fine. The colt was safe and the jockey unhurt. There would be other races.

"He did run fast enough to beat the winner," she said, as if to justify the thickness of the poultice she smoothed over Cruze's forelegs from knee to fetlock once he was cooled out.

Dean admired how she managed to get all the mud on the horse and none on herself. An impressive skill. He always managed to wear it. He scratched the colt's face and fed him a piece of day-old croissant. "I think you'll have to get your jockey's license and ride him next time."

Caroline snorted. "My left leg couldn't make weight." She dipped the brown paper in the bucket and let the water drip off. "I was terrified he was going to take out Liv's horse," she said.

She was right. It could have been much, much worse. Dean rubbed his shoulder. Good thing he didn't have a girlfriend. He was sure Caroline's fingernails had left a mark.

Cruze's fan club gathered outside the stall — Crystal, Hunter, even Squeak, who, in a rare display of generosity, provided beer from the backstretch bootlegger. The atmosphere was jovial, considering the horse hadn't made any of them a cent. No bets cashed. Cruze hadn't even earned the $500 he would've received for officially finishing the race. The colt seemed proud of his effort, pulling at his haynet while giving Dean the side-eye in hopes he had more flaky pastry. *Look what I can do, but it doesn't count!*

Horses. Always finding new ways to surprise him.

If Cruze had won, Dean would've taken the whole gang out somewhere to eat. Instead, he and Caroline hit the drive-thru on the way home. Caroline absently sipped her strawberry milkshake while staring out the window. They were both exhausted — race days were long, and felt even longer when the result was disappointing — but she looked contemplative.

He couldn't help pondering his own future. He'd given her two weeks, as promised; now it was time to be reasonable. The ballpark figure the real estate agent had thrown out wasn't pocket change. If Dean convinced Faye to sell, it wasn't as if he'd have to move immediately. A long closing would allow him to finish out this season. It would give him time to figure out what to do with the yearlings and the two foals, soon to be weaned. The Wave needed an appointment at the clinic, because his infertile big horse had to be gelded.

None of it would be easy, but he had to look on the bright side. He wasn't destitute. He had choices.

He could choose to stay.

That was when he realized Caroline was eyeing him.

"Why'd you talk to a real estate agent the other day?"

Dean's vision darted from the road. He felt like a kid who'd been exposed, thinking about something he shouldn't. "How do you know about that?"

"They aren't hard to spot. They have a way about them. You aren't actually considering selling the farm, are you?"

"I don't know what I'm going to do."

"Yes, you do. You said you wished you'd fought harder when your father sent you away to school, so you're going to fight now. Because what used to be your father's legacy is now yours and Faye's. You'll keep it going, like you always have. You'll find a way."

"How can you be so sure?"

"Because now I'm here to help you."

There was no cheeky smile, only a cross between an earnest plea and loyal assurance. What was he supposed to do with that? He couldn't ask her to keep working for him until he found a way to bring some money in.

"That horse was supposed to win to cover your wages," he said dryly.

"So I got it wrong. That's on me. He'll win next time. Did you see the final time for that race? He's a nice colt, Dean. Instead of putting a for sale sign on the front lawn, you should be looking at a condition book and picking his next race."

She said it with such confidence, it was impossible to deny. He'd been stuck on the letdown, when they'd accomplished something significant: they'd gotten a two-year-old to the races. Cruze had demonstrated he had some ability. Once more, Caroline was right.

They'd find Cruze another race. Because everyone deserved a second chance. She was a case in point, wasn't she?

Every time he drove up the pot-holed laneway at Northwest he remembered he still needed to order that load of screenings. This time, he took it all in more carefully. The fencing was weathered but not falling down. The house was charming, if not modern. The barns were functional, if not fancy. And regardless of the number the real estate agent had given him, all of it was more valuable to him than it would ever be to anyone else. How could he even think of giving it up?

"I'll do night check." Caroline stretched before pushing open the truck door. "See you in the morning."

"Good night, Caroline."

There was a note from Faye that she'd taken Gus for his romp before going for some wedding-related errand or another, and that the crew from Triple Stripe had taken care of the stalls as promised, so Dean didn't apologize for setting the butter tart she'd brought him on a plate and retiring to the living room. He didn't apologize for letting Gus hop on the couch next to him, the Golden resting his head on Dean's thigh and staring up at him hopefully as he bit into the tart. He drew the line at sharing his pastry, though.

He dragged himself up the stairs for a shower and then climbed into bed, sure he'd be asleep before his head hit the pillow. Instead, he lay awake, staring at the ceiling. Crickets chirped like they were right outside his window. They probably did it every night, but he'd barely noticed before. He didn't have trouble sleeping, so what was this? Life didn't get to him, he just let things roll off his back, believing everything would work out.

But everything wasn't as it had been, and at the centre of it all was Caroline. He thought of himself alone here, and Caroline alone there, and for the first time wondered if it was meant to be that way.

CHAPTER FORTY-TWO

Jess had said yes to coming to the wedding, though she'd moaned about getting dressed up twice in a matter of weeks. Because that's what Faye had meant by "bring someone," of course — a non-male friend. As if Caroline had a list of men to choose from.

The reception would be at Triple Stripe — she could walk back to Dean's farm if she ended up wallowing in self-pity. She had to prepare for the possibility of seeing Dean with Krissy again. Caroline didn't talk with Liv every day, and it wasn't as if they were texting buddies, so she didn't know if Liv had told Dean about Krissy and the professor. *Krissy and the Professor.* It sounded like a lewd book or movie.

No, she would not drink her woes away. It was time she had more self-respect than that.

The country church was picture-perfect, with the limestone a warm grey in the late-August afternoon light and a central bell tower over the entrance. Gardens flanked the steps with late-summer blooms. Inside was just as beautiful, coloured light dappling the pews as the sun shone through intricate stained-glass windows. Faye had gone traditional, ushers escorting them to their seats. Caroline grinned at Tim, and he nodded politely. She didn't recognize the man who'd taken Jess's arm, but he was cute and trying to chat her up so Caroline would find out later if he was single — because Jess needed to lose Lab Guy. Caroline could dole out relationship advice too, when it was that obvious.

Everything was just so — she'd expected nothing less from Faye. There was a pang deep in her chest. Caroline had always wanted a wedding like this, but she and Bryce had eloped. She wasn't sure Jess had forgiven her for it yet.

The wood of the benches was smooth from a century of visitors sliding into their places — for services, for funerals, for weddings just like this one. Caroline scanned the faces filling the small sanctuary but there were no racetrackers among them. She wasn't sure she recognized any of the guests, though she guessed at Will's parents across the aisle splitting the rows, a younger woman next to the man she'd put money on being his father. And that might be Liv's parents a few rows up, if memory served her right. They owned racehorses, after all. It was hard to be sure from only the occasional glimpse of a profile.

There was even an organ playing, softly in the background, though Caroline couldn't see it. She never would have pegged Faye as the type to have a wedding like this. When the music stopped, the murmurs took over. The minister appeared at the altar, the men filing in to his left.

Will looked a little pale and Caroline almost laughed. Nate and Tim stood next to him, and as the third guy joined them, hands clasped solemnly in front of him, Caroline elbowed Jess. Jess blushed. Caroline grinned. There might be something to work with there.

The processional music began, heads turning and bodies

shifting toward the back of the church. Monique appeared first, tall and gorgeous in her strapless smoky blue dress, blond hair styled in a down do that made Caroline run her fingers through her own — growing out, but still a long way from those wavy tresses. Emilie's dress matched in colour but not style, a pleated front with a halter neckline, the full skirt flowing to the floor, her smile only barely restrained. Liv followed, trying to appear as if this were not the last place she wanted to be, but she looked fabulous in a sleeveless shift the same dusky blue as the others. She might have mastered the demure smile, but no one was going to mess with her, with those arms, the definition of her deltoids accentuated by the way she gripped the bouquet of pretty blue cornflowers and cheerful daisies. *Don't let the dress fool you.*

The organ fell silent, and the lull was long enough whispers weaved through the guests. Caroline had a sinking feeling she'd read Faye all wrong, picturing her tearing off the white dress, kicking off her heels and running away with the bug boy who'd ridden Cruze — even if she wished she'd done exactly that at her own wedding. Except if she had, maybe she wouldn't be here. Not that she knew what here was, exactly.

Over the hush, Caroline swore she heard tapping as someone counted out a snappy beat. *One-two-three-four...* And with verve, the organ launched into the opening bars of a jaunty tune that made her grin. She tried to place it. Definitely not "The Wedding March." When the singing started, it hit her.

Jess snorted. "Brown-Eyed Girl?"

And here she came.

Of course, Faye was stunning. Caroline had heard all about the dress. It was hard to believe it had been Faye's mother's from the 80s, redesigned by one of her church lady friends. So fabulous that Caroline felt guilty because she couldn't keep her eyes from straying to Dean. It was Jess's turn to elbow her. She gulped a lungful of air, as if she'd needed the nudge to remember to breathe.

"Well, he cleans up nice," Jess whispered in her ear.

Faye didn't dance, but Emilie did. The men sang, and Jess and Caroline clapped in time along with the rest of the guests. This was officially the most fun Caroline had experienced at a wedding.

Dean gave Faye a hug and a kiss on the cheek before he left her at the altar with Will. Then he retreated to the front pew. All by himself.

"I can't believe I'm about to do this," Caroline muttered.

She needed to be quick, while the guests were still taking their seats, murmuring about the unusual processional. Grabbing Jess's wrist, she dragged her friend into the aisle.

"What are you doing?" Jess hissed, resisting, but Caroline tugged harder.

"We're sitting with Dean."

He looked surprised, then amused. Before she could stop herself, she patted him on the leg. "You did great." Because even with — or more so because of — the complicated relationship he'd had with his father, it had to be hard to step into those shoes on a day like today.

She refused to cry during the ceremony, but when she did, Dean passed her his smoky blue pocket square. What came out of her throat was an embarrassing cross between a sob and a laugh, because the gesture made her melt. Faye would kill him for messing up his outfit before the photos. Caroline hoped he had a spare.

Liv flopped into a seat next to Caroline, fingers curled around a champagne flute. "She's safely married, my job is done, right?" She leaned forward and crossed her legs, dangling a kitten heel from her toes.

Nate settled beside her. "I believe you're responsible for a toast."

"I was trying to forget that."

"Think of it as practice for the next time you have to say a few words for television."

Liv glowered at him and recrossed her legs so she angled toward Caroline and Jess.

For the number of times Caroline and Liv had ridden out and back from the track in the last few months, they'd exchanged little more than passing remarks. She didn't see Liv as aloof so much as... internal. Perhaps a bit of bubbly loosened her edges, lowered her wall — or else it was the fact the reception was at Triple Stripe, her home.

A tent graced the lawn, but the weather was too beautiful to remain beneath it before the meal began. Tall maples bordered the field on two sides, the green of their leaves a more stately terra verte than the viridian of July when Caroline had first visited. Even the light was different. She brushed away thoughts that this was summer's end, not letting herself wonder what was next. Maybe then she'd never have to leave.

Three months ago, she wouldn't have imagined these people would become her friends. She sipped a mocktail, as bubbly and golden in colour as what Liv clutched, the King's Plate misadventure too recent in her memory. Will and Faye chatted with the parents. Emilie and Tim stood with Monique and her boyfriend. Caroline didn't see the unnamed cute groomsman, so Jess was off the hook for now.

"You rode for a while, didn't you?" Caroline asked Liv. Something she knew already, but she needed a conversation starter. Not that topics wouldn't be endless, with the subject of horses to delve into.

"Yes," Liv said. "I quit school to ride, and did that for almost three years, badly —"

"Not badly," Nate interrupted.

"Not with much success," Liv countered, shooting Nate a glare, warning him not to disagree. "Then I got hurt and got my trainer's license —"

"And trained a Plate winner," Nate interjected.

Liv ignored him this time. "I went back to riding, until our trainer's wife became ill and he took some time off. I assumed the position, under duress."

"And trained a Dubai World Cup and Breeders' Cup Classic winner," Nate said decisively.

"So it hasn't been the worst job." Liv grinned. "But I still want to go back to riding. I need to *ride* a Plate winner."

"Greedy," Nate quipped.

Liv laughed, elbowing him.

"I like a woman who knows what she wants," Caroline said.

"You get it," Liv said with a small gesture of her glass. "I need to find the right person to take over. I keep hoping Jo, our assistant, will change her mind, or Roger will decide he has a few bucket list items to check off. He hasn't had a Derby horse, right? I'm sure Claire's going to give us a Derby horse."

"Because it would be such a hardship if you had to train a Derby horse and let me ride it," Nate said.

"You get all the fun, Miller. It's just not fair."

Caroline's eyes slid from one to the other. It was like observing a good-natured but competitive ping-pong match.

"Do you think you'll go back to training?" Liv asked.

Caroline hadn't even considered it. Would she? "Right now I'm enjoying the relative lack of responsibility."

"See? I get that too. It's a huge responsibility."

Did Liv know how badly Caroline had shirked that responsibility? If Liv was looking for a trainer, Caroline wasn't the one. That didn't stop the wheels from starting to turn.

Dinner was via food stations set up beneath the expansive canopy. Faye had seated Caroline and Jess with Will's parents — mom, dad, and step-mom — Liv's parents, and Dean. From Day One, Faye had been on Caroline's team. The wedding invite had come with an understood mission. Her social skills might be rusty, but it was time to polish them off and put them to work.

At first, Caroline observed, after polite introductions all around. She recognized the carefully cloaked animosity between Will's mother and father — who sat with his much younger new wife. It reminded her of her own parents. One of the good things about eloping — she hadn't given them a reason to be in the same room.

Liv's parents were just as demure as Liv was. So what had happened with Emilie? Had she not shared such a strong family resemblance, Caroline might have wondered if she'd been adopted. Maybe it was a second child thing.

Caroline homed in on Will's mother, Julia. "Have you ever thought about owning a racehorse?"

Julia was elegant, with a stylish bob, her hair the same colour as the warm grey limestone of the church. While she'd insisted her formal title not be used — she was a doctor — Caroline had a feeling the woman secretly wished everyone would, like her position made her just a little bit better than the rest of them. Caroline had dealt with enough people like Julia as a trainer — and as Bryce's wife — to not be put off.

"I can't say it's something that's ever entered my sphere of thought," Julia said with a ladylike chuckle.

Caroline leaned into Dean as she engaged the woman's

eyes. "We could have so much fun. The yearling sales are coming up. I could pick something out. Dean could train it."

His eyes cut to hers, with a *What are you doing?* expression. If he had to ask that, he wasn't as smart as Caroline thought.

Julia lit up, like that made it the best idea. She clearly had a crush on him. Dean looked just uncomfortable enough sitting next to her that the feeling didn't appear mutual.

"Dean's an excellent trainer," Liv's father, Claude, interjected. "You'd be in good hands."

It was going better than if Caroline had scripted the scene. And not a word about Dean's father, the Hall of Famer, to qualify the endorsement.

"Tim's interested too," Caroline said.

"Nate's brother? The hockey player?" Julia's eyes sparkled.

"How long are you here for, Julia? We should do lunch."

CHAPTER FORTY-THREE

DARKNESS WAS FALLING, the western horizon glowing orange against the indigo sky, tiny white lights adding to the tent's festive atmosphere, a contrast to Dean's mood. The end of August meant warm days and cool nights — and a state of denial about what would come as the seasons changed. He didn't hate winter, though. This year, it felt like December's end to the racing season couldn't come fast enough.

Under the marquee, music began to play. Dean would have loved nothing more than to sneak away, wander around the farm, hang out with some horses — but he couldn't ghost his sister's big party. Faye wanted all the traditions, and that meant dancing. He sighed and went back in, the strains calling him like a mother summoning a child for dinner when it was too nice to come inside. Duty called.

Caroline still chatted with Julia, who was by now a few glasses of wine in. At this rate, Will's mom would agree to a string of horses. Was having your brother-in-law's mother as an owner a good idea? If Caroline was around to intercede, it might be okay. She could be his racing manager. Might as well give her a title in this fantasy venture she was plotting.

She'd shifted to his vacated chair, so he settled next to her. Sitting between the two women earlier had not been comfortable. Caroline flashed him a grin, her face alive. She was in her element.

Faye swept up behind him, the skirt of her dress rustling, leaning next to his ear. "I know you don't want to hear it, but we're starting soon. After the First Dance, you'll dance with me. Then after the wedding party starts theirs, you'll dance with Will's mom?"

It was posed like a question, but Dean nodded obediently. Faye had warned him, and this was Faye's day.

He didn't know if Faye and Will had taken some lessons, but they looked pretty good to Dean. He probably should have done the same, but in her happiness, Faye didn't seem to notice how starchy he was, and alcohol had dissolved Julia from no-nonsense physician to shameless flirt. Over her shoulder, he saw Caroline laughing at him both delicately holding Julia up and keeping her at arm's length until the song ended.

Of all the people in the world, he did not expect Nate to rescue him. Dean watched distractedly as Nate assumed control of Julia. Nate wasn't that big a guy — would he be okay? Dean's concern was fleeting, replaced by the fact that Liv stood before him.

"I owe you a dance."

"How about a drink instead?" he tried, fighting back against the memory of the awkward Plate Ball two years ago.

"No. We can do this."

Dean grinned then, surprising himself. "If you say so."

She was different — felt different — than she had then. And not physically, because he wasn't letting himself think about that. She'd grown up. Liv had been through a lot since that night — coal makes diamonds. Not his diamond, but he appreciated the transformation nonetheless.

"What's with this Krissy woman?"

He gaped before catching himself. Trust Liv not to beat around the bush. "We're old friends. We were together for a while when I was at school, but it ended when I left. Then she found me on that ridiculous dating app Faye signed me up for. We're just catching up. The kid is sweet." A bullet-point explanation.

"Word on the street is she's using you."

"The street being Caroline?"

Liv's lips twisted. "No. I met her friend Jess at the Plate. She's doing a master's at your school. She recognized Krissy. Said she sees her all the time with one of the department heads and that they're very... friendly."

Dean felt a twinge in his gut but ignored it. "She used to be married to him. Carlie is his daughter."

"The way Jess talked, it would appear they're still together."

"I'm sure she misinterpreted what she saw."

"It wasn't a one-time thing," Liv said. "But, it's more than that. This thing with the supplement."

The emphasis she put on the word suggested she didn't believe that's all it was, either.

"I didn't use it."

"The company you keep, though."

Dean leaned back slightly at the implication, not judgement so much as a careful warning. "A few months ago, that would have been Caroline."

"The only Caroline I've ever known is smart, and honest, and hard-working. And quite devoted to you."

It felt as if she'd whacked him across the side of his head with a pool noodle, the subtle impact just enough to shake loose all the things he'd pushed aside in his mind — but he'd known somehow, hadn't he?

He realized they'd stopped moving, suddenly wondering if they'd ever started — or just been standing here through the entire conversation. "She works for me." It was a feeble protest.

Liv choked back a laugh. "Like that's ever stopped anyone on the backstretch."

"May I cut in?"

Dean dragged his eyes from Liv's. Tim? He'd expected Nate, but either way — rescued, again.

"By all means," Dean said, stepping back with a nod.

"No. I mean on Liv. Go away."

Liv laughed as Tim stepped between her and Dean, grabbing his wrist and then putting Dean's hand on his shoulder. Dean wordlessly allowed Tim to manipulate him.

"Relax," Tim said, once he seemed satisfied with Dean's stance. "I'm not going to kiss you or anything. You need some pointers."

Dean was aware that the music had shifted from DJ to live band. Faye had promised there would be several old songs — to appease the church ladies she'd befriended at a dance last Christmas where they'd played such tunes — but this was going way back. Nate sat at a keyboard singing "You Light Up My Life."

"*One* two-three," Tim said.

"Even I know how to waltz, Tim."

"Not very well. You move like you're wearing lead shoes. You play hockey; I know you can do better."

"What's going on?" Dean was beginning to feel like he was in a play where no one had given him his lines.

"We're trying to help you."

"So this is some kind of intervention?" The play was a comedy. "For what?"

"Lighter. Balls of your feet."

"A dancing intervention?"

Tim scowled. "Listen to me. Caroline likes you."

Hearing it said out loud, so directly, all Dean could do was deflect. "It's like I'm back in high school, except the music isn't quite right."

"This is no time to joke. You need to step up. Words are hard. I know about these things. But I believe in you." Then Tim broke into a rare, dazzling smile before he stepped back in a low bow and strode away.

In Tim's place stood Caroline, smiling. "My turn."

For, one, two, thudding heartbeats, Dean felt like that uncertain teenager from high school, gazing down at her smile. The song had changed — now Nate was crooning, "I Only Have Eyes For You," and Dean didn't know whether to be annoyed with his friends for being so obvious or grateful that they were invested enough to be forthright.

Caroline's blond hair still wasn't as long as before. The pale green of her dress, patterned with large, warm white flowers, made her eyes appear to reflect the hue, when Dean was sure they were blue — or that he'd never properly noticed the colour before. But more than her physicality, he saw someone who was everything Liv had noted — smart, honest, hard-working. Devoted? What had he ever done to earn that?

With her heels, she was a couple of inches taller than he was accustomed to, her eyes just below his. And neither was he used to her being as near as she was when she tucked into his arms, so neatly it was as if she'd been there all along.

"Were you in on the setup?" he asked, reminding himself to breathe, to step, to be light.

Caroline tilted her head. "Setup? I just got tired of watching you dance with everyone else."

"I'm warning you, I'm not much of a dancer."

"I'm not so sure about that." Her words were tender, then she blinked away the softness of her expression. "This song is even older than we are."

"I Only Have Eyes For You" was still playing, and when Caroline nestled closer, resting her head against his shoulder, Dean didn't push her away. He could get used to this. It was an unexpected thought, but he didn't dismiss it, letting it rest there in his mind. He was sorry when the song came to an end, the church ladies warbling to the final refrain.

She looked up at him with a flush of embarrassment. "Sorry."

"Don't be." He wasn't ready to let her go, but the tempo changed with the next song, breaking the spell.

Caroline threw her head back and groaned, then narrowed her gaze at the band as they started up "Sweet Caroline." She shrugged at Dean and grabbed his hand. He was her prop as she swung his arms and ducked under his elbow, twirling and yelling *bah-bah-bah* and *So good! So good!* with everyone on cue, laughing and breathless when the song ended.

She popped up and kissed him on the cheek. "I should go check on Jess."

Caroline skipped to their table and guzzled a glass of water before disappearing into the crowd, leaving the lyrics still playing in Dean's head and a stark vacancy in the space she'd occupied.

He drifted over to where Liv's parents were seated with Will's mom, chatting. Dean reached for his glass and sipped, trying to keep himself from searching for Caroline. He could be bold. He could ask her to dance again.

A hand touched his shoulder. It was her. His smile came easily.

"I'm going to head out," she said, speaking over the hum of voices. "I should check on the horses."

Dean's face fell before he could stop it. "Is Jess driving you back?"

"No, she had to leave. Her barn helper had an emergency, so she's gone to do late feed for her horses. It's such a nice night, I'll walk."

"Are you sure?" Dean dropped his eyes to her feet, but the heels she'd worn earlier had been replaced by running shoes. "Wise. But aren't you the woman who's afraid of the dark?"

Caroline laughed. "I'm conquering my fears. If I can breeze horses again, I should not be afraid of being alone in rural Ontario after nightfall."

"I'll walk with you." The thought was spoken before Dean could stop it. He could conquer his fears, too.

Her eyes widened. "Shouldn't you stay?"

"I can come back."

Caroline smiled. "Well then, I'd like that."

"You're not offended by the suggestion?"

One corner of her mouth crimped. "No. I'm not saying yes because I need to be protected. I'm saying yes because I like your company."

The main laneway to Triple Stripe was paved but unlit, and the rising moon gave just enough light to create subtle shadows. Dean almost reached for Caroline's hand, but stopped himself — though the gesture might have said what he hadn't put into words. As well as the comfortable shoes, she'd thought ahead and brought a cardigan, so there would be no chivalrous offering of his jacket, but he ducked behind her to shift to her right when they reached the road so she was to the inside. Caroline glanced at him with that smile again, the moonlight painting her features in a soft blue.

"Are you okay?" she asked.

"Sure. Why?"

"You and Faye have had each other's back for a long time. It must be hard."

"I'm happy for her. And I've had a long time to get used to the idea of being on my own."

All his friends had paired off. Faye and Will, Liv and Nate, Emilie and Tim, and yes, Monique and Rory. Even Chad, the vet, and Sylvie, daughter of Triple Stripe's former trainer, Roger Cloutier. Two, by two, by two, by two, by two. By one — but did it have to be that way?

"I need to tell you something," he said.

Worry drew lines on her face, and Dean wished he was better at this. *Words are hard, Tim.* He was thirty-eight. Did that never change?

"There really is nothing going on with Krissy, but I'll talk to her. As much as I agree with you about the supplement, I don't have anything concrete to go on, so maybe it's just as well I come at it from the personal angle. I feel bad for her daughter. Carlie's a nice kid."

"You're so good with her," Caroline said. "I was jealous at the Plate."

He laughed. "You saw us?"

"Busted. I'm sounding like a stalker."

"I don't think I've ever had a stalker." He grinned.

She frowned, when he'd been expecting a laugh. "I can't have kids."

His jaw slackened, the air suddenly thick and uneasy between them. "I'm sorry," he said at last, because would she have told him if that wasn't something she wanted?

Caroline shook her head quickly, her face angled away from him. "No, I am. I don't know why I said that. Too much information."

"Not really."

There was appreciation in the glance that flitted his way.

"It's why we broke up. Me and Bryce. Well — indirectly, I suppose. It wasn't as if Bryce was hurting for money, so we tried everything. I was just starting to think about adoption. Then his high school sweetheart showed up with a kid in tow, telling him he was a father."

"How old was the kid?" High school had been a while ago for Bryce. He was older than Dean.

"That's just it. Five. I'm sure you can do the math, being a genius and all. DNA confirmed it. It wasn't long before they were back together again, and I was out. I guess I deserved it."

"No. He was never good enough for you."

She gave him a wistful look. "I would've thought you of all people would agree."

"You don't think I'm mad at you for what happened after Catch The Joy's stake party twenty years ago, do you?"

"I wouldn't blame you if you were."

"We were eighteen. It was a kiss."

The moonlight caught the upward flick of her lashes. "I can look at a yearling and see the future racehorse. I would give anything for a do-over to see the man in that eighteen-year-old boy."

Her words hit him like she'd slammed the heel of her hand into his solar plexus. Caroline shot ahead, stopping and turning when she realized he was no longer next to her. She held out her hand. Dean took it.

He walked with her all the way to the base of the apartment stairs, and when she faced him, she was so near it felt like a dare. Dean didn't back away, stretching and bunching his fingers at his sides. He felt his pulse at his wrists, at his throat, the rushing of blood in his ears like the roar of the ocean.

She tipped her head back, mouth stained pink with what remained of her lipstick. His chest tightened with the restraint of not gulping in the scarce oxygen between them.

"Don't make me fire you, Caroline," he said, the words like gravel over his vocal cords.

Her lips curved into a slow smile. "You can't fire me," she whispered. "I quit."

It was all the permission he needed, hands reaching for her neck, meeting her lips. Forgetting he was out of practice. Forgetting everything as her hands touched his chest, his heart thumping into her palms.

"I've always wanted to say that," she murmured, and he could taste her grin.

His hands slipped to her elbows, forehead resting against hers as his pulse tried valiantly to return to normal.

"I'm going to go," he said evenly. "And let my dog out. Then maybe on the walk back to the reception I can figure out where I'm going to find a new exercise rider." He grinned, and forced himself to back slowly away, still stuck on her eyes.

CHAPTER FORTY-FOUR

Dean dreamt Caroline lined up enough new owners to fill twenty stalls. When his alarm woke him, he knew that wasn't true. He'd get to the track and there would be just three horses waiting. But Caroline had been no dream.

He dressed for work like every other morning, made bad coffee, let Gus out, ate enough to tide him over until later when he'd grab something from the food truck. What was different was Caroline kissing him when he reached the barn, her arms draped around his neck.

"Caroline —"

"I quit, remember? You haven't paid me in three weeks. I'm just a friend helping out."

He didn't object, and he didn't remove his hands from her hips. "We still need to talk."

"We will. Later. I don't know about you, but I'm not awake yet. I can't handle those late nights like I used to." She grinned. "Let's get these horses out."

Nothing was special about the morning on the backstretch

or how the horses trained. Caroline did up the last horse while Dean retreated to his office to make notes and consult the condition book. He circled the next seven-furlong maiden race for two-year-old colts and geldings — Cruze's second chance — and fought his drooping eyelids before giving up to rest his head on his folded arms. It made him think of grade school. Did they still do that to kids when the class was being bad?

He was tempted to ignore the tap on the door, but this wasn't kindergarten. Sighing, he pushed himself up. "Enter," he said, leaning back in the chair and swivelling to face the visitor.

"Napping or hiding?" Nate asked. He looked as if he wasn't sure he should step inside, then did anyway.

"Good question. To what do I owe the honour?"

Dean hoped that would preempt any talk about the previous evening, but Nate was all business. Despite the low-grade resentment Dean felt for the man who had swept in from another province to win the girl next door, he always appreciated that, most of the time, Nate came himself to discuss Dean's horses. Most riders of his stature left the task to their agents.

Nate sat on the overturned bucket parked in the corner. "I think you should run Cruze in the Bull Page Stakes."

Dean laughed. "Did Caroline put you up to this?"

"Cash is out. Liv decided to put him away for the season, which means I could ride your horse. If you want. I think if I can stay on," Nate paused, grinning, "he has a shot in there."

"He's still a maiden, so I thought I'd try and break that first. I'm sure you've heard of conditions?"

"You sound like Liv. We want the old Dean back. The old Dean would be on board."

"You're serious."

"Why not? You'd run him back at seven furlongs, right?"

"He's never seen the turf."

"He grew up on the turf," Nate scoffed. "He'll be fine."

Dean sighed. Nate was right. The old Dean would have jumped on this. Why fight it? "You'll have to work him over the course."

"Sure. If Caroline will let me." Nate stood, cracking another grin as he reached for the door handle. *"Bah-bah-bah."*

"Get out of here."

Nate ducked the condition book Dean flung at him and slipped out as quickly as he'd come. Dean picked up the booklet, tossing it onto his desk, and left the room to check on Caroline. Why was he not surprised to find her nearby, cleaning tack?

He crossed his arms and leaned against a post, watching her lather a martingale. "The Bull Page?"

Caroline shrugged and said the same thing Nate had. "Why not? Ontario-sired, costs you nothing to nominate. What have you got to lose?"

Nothing. Things could go just as wrong running in another maiden race as in a stake, and fear of embarrassment was not a viable excuse.

"Just the two people I want to see." Len shuffled into the bay, tugging on the brim of his tattered old hat. He looked stiffer each time Dean saw him.

Caroline smiled warmly. "Hi Len."

"How was the wedding?" Len asked.

She ducked her head like she was focusing on the tack, but Dean saw her lips twitch, her eyes crinkling as she left him to reply.

"Good," Dean answered. He'd danced with a man. He'd kissed his temporary farm manager. *Unusual* would have been a more accurate response.

"Glad to hear," Len said. "A big day, little Faye getting

married." Len still thought of Faye as the pre-teen who'd skulked around Ed Taylor's barn twenty years ago.

"What can we do for you, Len?" Dean wished he had a comfy seat to offer the older man, fearing if Len lowered to an overturned bucket, they'd never get him on his feet again.

Len pressed his lips together and pulled on his cap once more. "I'm going to retire. My health isn't the greatest, so it's time. I don't want you to find me keeled over in a stall one day."

So, his son had finally talked him into it? Dean's sadness was laced with relief, because he didn't want that either.

"I'm hoping you'll take my horses. I know they're not much, but I have enough money set aside to carry them to the end of the season. We can reassess then. Maybe we can ask your friend Emilie to find homes for them."

"Sure, Len," Dean said quietly. "Of course. But only if you promise to visit."

Len chuckled. "I don't think I could go cold turkey." He turned to leave, then paused. "We should buy a yearling together."

Dean glanced at Caroline, who grinned again. "Have you looked at the book?" he asked Len, lost for anything else to say.

"There are a couple in there I like. I'll send you the hip numbers. Maybe the two of you can go see them."

Once Len was out of sight, Caroline raised her palm. "I had nothing to do with that." She checked the time on her phone. "We have to get out of here. I'm meeting Julia for lunch. And don't make any plans for tomorrow after training, because the list of yearlings we need to check out isn't getting any shorter."

Len's three would give them six and the day rate from them would help. Yearlings were an investment in the future with no guarantees, but it felt as if things were finally moving in the right direction, a current stirring stagnant waters. Blonde, about five-seven, and currently putting away his tack.

Caroline changed the radio station before snapping in the seat belt after Dean started the truck. They had a deal now: his music driving in, her music driving home. She picked up a sales catalogue from the floor, paging through. His was on the back seat, tabbed at the hip numbers that had caught his eye. It felt like window shopping, because who was he buying for? Certainly not himself, unless he did go in with Len. He had two homebreds at the farm, so regardless of his financial situation, he had no plans to purchase another yearling. Jacob, who had owned Fox, the two-year-old he'd sold to the US, hadn't gotten back to him yet, and Dean worried he'd heard Andy had moved his horses. His oldest owner deserting him didn't exactly instill confidence. But Caroline was finding him new owners — for a new era.

"Question," she said as the truck rolled out of the backside. "Could I rent some stalls from you? There are empty ones in the layup barn."

As if he wasn't reminded of that every single day. Dean shrugged. "Sure. What for? Raising chickens?"

She snorted. "Yearlings. If we're buying a few, I might as well start them."

His gaze lingered on her. If he let her, she'd build his business back up, and then some. At this point, he wasn't sure he could stop her; she was a runaway train and he was along for the ride. The amazing thing was, he had no desire to resist.

"Dean!"

He snapped his head back to the road in time to hit the brakes, stopping short of the red tail lights in front of them. A horn blared, restarting his heart with a jolt. He needed to quit staring at her to check she was real.

Caroline's hands eased from where she'd braced them on the dashboard. "What did you want to talk about? Before you kill us both."

He collected himself, hands tightening on the wheel. "What's next."

"What's next? For... what?" Her words came out carefully placed, making him wonder if she was as overwhelmed by what was happening between them as he was.

"For us."

Her mouth opened and closed, a minnow searching for oxygen. She shut the catalogue, sitting up and squaring her shoulders. "Okay."

"Nikki and Stacy are coming back. I didn't exactly promise their jobs would still be here, but, we need a plan."

Even though he kept his vision on the road, he caught the way her eyes flicked in his direction. *We.*

She found her tongue — it never stalled on her for long. "Well, I quit, and with Len's horses, you'll need help. So if Nikki still wants to work for you, take her back." Her lips slanted in an impish tilt. "If you hire me as a freelancer to gallop, does that break the rules?"

He laughed. "That sounds like a loophole."

"I'll be busy with the yearlings, so you should probably take your manager back, too. But I'll have to move out."

He could feel her gaze on him. The realization siphoned joy from his veins — while she might not be out of his life when Nikki and Stacy returned, she'd be leaving the farm, just when he'd figured out she belonged.

"Feel free to stay in the apartment till then," he offered weakly.

"It's fine. I'll stay with Jess. Nothing much will change except — this."

"I like this." It might be because of work, but it wasn't work, and the only time they spent together that qualified as such.

Dean stole a glance. Caroline's eyes dropped to her lap and she opened the catalogue again. What was the alternative? He wanted her near, but this thing between them — if he was admitting there was a thing — was still very new.

"It's probably for the best," she said.

"We should take things slow."

"We can do that." Caroline grinned. "As long as we have fast horses."

"That's pretty hokey," Dean said, but he grinned back.

CHAPTER FORTY-FIVE

ENERGETIC CRIES PUNCTUATED the auctioneer's steady chant, the background hum of spectators' voices completing the symphony. Caroline smiled and breathed it all in: the horses, the mulch beneath their feet, the hint of oil that kept the dust down — and the waft of too much cologne somewhere nearby.

A rotund man wearing a sports coat and open-necked shirt sidled over to give her room at the rail. He had the kind of face she'd forget unless he gave her a good reason not to. Was that mean? It was probably mean.

"Thank you," she said, opening the sales catalogue to the first of several dog-eared pages before she was inevitably drawn to the yearlings parading in the walking area before her. Some were quiet, some were nervous; some executed airs above the ground as the bid spotters yipped and waved.

"You buying?" the man asked.

Caroline didn't know if he was being friendly or flirting, but everyone here could be a potential client, so she played nice. "I might be."

She was dressed like a country horsewoman in the expensive Dubarry boots Bryce had given her one Christmas — which had never seen a barn until today. Her slim-fit khakis could pass for loose tan breeches, a brown tweed jacket covering her white open-necked shirt, and a silk scarf with running horses draped around her neck. The look was straight out of *Horse and Hound*. If there was one positive thing in the taste of autumn these last days of August were giving them, it was the excuse to wear a great outfit.

Numbers flashed on a screen, updating in both American and Canadian dollars as the caller announced each bid. Caroline caught sight of Dean on the other side of the walking ring, half a head taller than most of the crowd. He'd gone back to take another look at one of the later hip numbers. She gave him a little wave. Why was he frowning? Glancing at her phone, she saw he'd texted a few minutes ago, asking where she was. In the din, she hadn't heard the notification.

Working, she texted back, adding a winky emoji. Dean never used emojis — hated them — so Caroline took special pleasure in using as many as possible. *Stay over there. I'll come find you in a minute.* She met his eyes again. He still frowned.

Caroline turned to her neighbour. "How about you?"

"Might be," he answered. "If my trainer can get something in my budget. Everything he's told me to consider has gone way over."

"If you're successful finding a horse and looking for a place to break it that won't rip you off, give me a call. I start a select number of yearlings." She handed him one of her new business cards. Earlier, she'd left flyers in the pavilion's lobby and tacked one to the corkboard next to the door. They were classy, if she did say so herself. *Canva for the win.*

"Here's mine," he said. "So if I call, you'll know who you're talking to. I might be in the market for a new trainer, too. Do you know anyone honest?"

"I might." Caroline took the card without looking at it, tucking it into her jacket pocket. "Sorry, I hate to dash, but I just noticed one of my clients. Nice to meet you..." She was rusty at this. She should have noted his name.

"Andy," he said.

She caught her expression before her eyes rounded. "Nice to meet you, Andy. I'm, uh, Carrie. Call me if I can help." Then she rushed off, weaving through the packed bodies.

"What were you doing talking to Andy?" Dean hissed in her ear, pulling her to a spot that wasn't directly across from his former owner — who, they'd learned, had sent his horses to Jack Faron, of all people.

"I didn't know it was him till the end! I think he's eating crow, though, if that makes you feel any better. You can bet Faron will try to swindle him on a yearling, but I don't think your old friend is a dummy. Except for leaving you."

Caroline thought Dean was going to kiss her, sure he was considering it. PDAs at the sales? That would make the rounds on the backstretch. She settled for his smile instead and huddled next to him, their arms touching, even if it looked less intimate than it felt.

The filly Caroline hoped to buy for Julia would be coming into the walking area soon. She'd set up credit with the office, and Dean had brought the truck and trailer. The yearling sales always made her think of a Dorothy Parker quote. *"Let's have a drink and then let's you and I go out and get a horsie, Freddie — just a little one, darling, just a little one."* In the old days, she would have been drinking, a plastic glass propped to hold her book open to the current page. Dean didn't drink much. It was not a bad thing. The new her could embrace that.

Caroline recognized the filly when she arrived and caught a head-on view, her crooked blaze distinctive. Her legs didn't deviate from straightness as she walked, her short baby tail swishing with a sultry rhythm each time one of her hind legs reached under her. She had good feet, a nice eye, and a sensible way about her. And she was pretty, though Caroline wasn't sure Julia would know the difference.

The filly circled the podium where the spotters worked, ears flickering as she registered the hum of the hive without jumping out of her skin at their exclamations. When it was her turn in the ring, Caroline almost went into the pavilion to bid from the seats, but staying in the back provided a modicum of anonymity — at least until the results were updated.

The bidding started slowly, and Caroline stayed out of it. If it was going to be sluggish, she might have a chance. Finally, she caught the spotter's eye and jumped in. Every time her nod was countered, he came back to her. She couldn't see who the other party was. They volleyed back and forth, but Caroline was reaching her limit. *Yes* to another five hundred, a baby step. Her opponent agreed to the same increment. She hesitated when the spotter returned to her for another five, playing along, then acquiesced, holding her breath as the auctioneer pleaded and cajoled with the other bidder.

"*Going once...*"

She scanned the faces along the perimeter of the ring, her search obscured by yearlings, strutting, bouncing, skittering.

"*Going twice...*"

Her fingers worried the edge of the book's cover.

"*Sold, in the back.*"

With a whoosh, she let out a long breath.

"Congratulations," Dean said. "That was a good buy."

Caroline grinned up at him. "I've forgotten how much fun this is."

A young woman arrived with a clipboard and before Caroline signed the sales slip, she paused, because writing the last name — Bryce's name — made her want to hurl. She stabbed the pen into the paper with her scrawl and handed the clip-board back to the runner. That official divorce document couldn't come soon enough.

"Come on, Freddie." She grabbed Dean's hand and pulled him from the rail, laughing at the puzzled look on his face. "Let's go say hi to our horse."

He followed closely as she led the way through the pack — one part serious buyers, one part tire-kickers, one part socializ-ers. Now that she'd purchased something, the close quarters made her claustrophobic, the thrill of it wearing off. She craved the quiet of the barns and was so intent on that, she ran head-long into someone.

"Oh, hey, Nate," she gasped, relieved it was someone familiar.

"What are you doing here?" Dean said.

Caroline had stopped so suddenly he'd run right into her, clutching her shoulders from behind, wedging her in an awkward sandwich. She extricated herself, glancing from one to the other.

"Nice to see you too, Dean," Nate said wryly. "I was looking for you."

"Why?"

"Have you seen the nominations for the Bull Page?"

"No. Completely forgot, to be honest."

"Uh-huh," Nate said, grinning now. "Here." He handed Dean a sheet.

Dean's eyes ran over it, then locked on, the tendons on the backs of his hands tight.

"What?" Caroline nudged him. "Let me see."

She plucked it from his fingers. "Silent Fox? Who's that? I'm so out of touch. I really need to get caught up."

Dean pressed his lips together, his jaw set. "That's the colt I sold earlier this year. Looks like he might be coming to visit."

CHAPTER FORTY-SIX

THE BLEACHERS GAVE a broad view of the expansive racetrack, courses within courses, landscaping surrounding the infield ponds. Dean liked it best up here, away from the chatter at the rail, his own private viewing box, the sweeping turf course practically in their laps. He could hear Caroline's foot bouncing, imagine her knee jittering. Cruze looked lost, a diminutive form amid the grandness of his surroundings, neck on the vertical, ears forward, eyes alight as he galloped next to his old friend Paz.

Liv had volunteered to accompany the colt with her pony. Protecting her interests, no doubt, given Cruze's reputation. This experience was new for the two-year-old. *Don't make Nate regret this, horse.*

What had made Dean think he could leave this? He needed Cruze to give him a reason to stay. A few extra yearlings in the layup barn at home was not enough.

Liv released Cruze at the pole but didn't pull the older gelding up immediately, letting Paz roll along just behind him. It turbo-charged Cruze, catapulting him into the long, downhill turn. Dean forgot to start his watch, binoculars trained on his colt, zooming along the rail. He could wait to hear the official time.

The apron next to the long, long stretch of green was empty. On race day, it would be a different story, bodies filling that space that might yell and throw things, though a race like the Bull Page wouldn't be anything like the frenzy of the Plate. Sometimes busy could be better. Horses saw things humans couldn't: imaginary ghosts and goblins lurking in what appeared an innocent space. But Cruze remained focused.

The colt finished well, no mishaps — though Dean held his breath until he picked the pair up, galloping out after the tote board no longer obscured his vision. He waited until Liv had collected Nate and the two-year-old before nudging Caroline to get moving.

"He looked good," she said, skipping down the steps in front of him. They power-walked along the horse path toward the tunnel. A gaggle of Canada Geese loitered in the ditch.

"Thank you for your cooperation," Dean said to them.

Caroline snorted.

A week and a half until the race. That solid breeze on the turf eased some of his doubt, but did Cruze belong in there? The other prospects were all winners — some stakes winners already — and Fox's presence would scare many of them off. What was he doing considering sending out a colt whose greatest claim to fame was dropping his rider in his only race and running off? The jokes still hadn't stopped. *He don't need no rider, Dean! Maybe the stewards would give you permission to run without one.*

It was a nomination, not an entry. Just because the colt's name was on that sheet didn't mean he had to run. He'd enter Cruze in the maiden race the day before as insurance in case the stake came up too tough. Or Dean lost his nerve.

He saw Liv and Paz before Cruze, the colt on her other side. She smiled as Dean and Caroline caught up.

"That was all right," she said. "A minute flat."

"That track with you, Timex?" Dean asked, catching Nate's eye.

"Yeah. Pretty much." Nate laughed, but he was completely serious when he said, "He felt great, Dean. Don't you dare chicken out."

Was he that transparent?

Back at his barn, Dean watched Caroline halter Cruze and hand Nate the bridle. Nate brushed past him to dunk the bit in the colt's water bucket before depositing the tack on the rail.

"Thanks, Dean."

He knew that's what riders said — thanking the trainer for their business, essentially — but Dean couldn't stop wondering how he would ever repay his friends for all they'd done to support him this year.

Cruze's nostrils flared, a flutter of tissue with each exchange of air as Caroline wound the brass chain around the noseband. Delicate veins laced the colt's neck. Dean threw a cooler on, buckling the front.

He reached for the shank, fingers brushing Caroline's, her eyes flickering to his. "I'll walk him."

Caroline stepped aside. "I'll get his bath ready."

He met her outside after taking the colt a couple of turns. Cruze's incessant play occupied Dean as Caroline splashed hot sudsy water over the colt's dark coat, teeth biting at the shank while Dean tried to evade his attempts. The colt's respiration had already dropped, recovering quickly from the effort. He'd be fit enough for that race. If he and Nate could make it to the finish line as a unit, the colt might pick up a cheque.

The old Dean would have said, *We could win this.* How sweet would it be to beat Fox — the one he'd sold for six figures

— with his backward little homebred? The new Dean needed to learn to dream again.

Walking was meditative. Dean and Cruze toured the shed, passing other trainers' grooms ducking in and out of stalls as they catered to their charges. Every now and then, someone threw a comment Dean's way, but for the most part, he was left to his thoughts. Life was not terrible today. He had a talented, if unproven, two-year-old, and an unofficial partner in crime, something he was still trying to wrap his head around.

When the colt was cooled out, he sat across from the stall and watched Caroline smear cooling mud from fetlock joint to knee in a thin layer, moulding together the thick gobs all the way back down, like Cruze was their Plate horse. He wasn't, not yet. But winning the Bull Page would justify looking at another race, another step. They'd hop from one stone to the next, navigating the current that always sought to send them off course, and hope by next summer, they made it to the other side.

Emilie showed up as Caroline hung Cruze's halter. Dean gave her a squeeze, then Emilie hugged Caroline. His friends had adopted her without reservation.

"Tim is so excited about going partners on your yearling," Emilie said, grinning. "He's got a note on his phone of name suggestions."

Orchestrated by Caroline, of course, Dean had sold Tim a third-interest in one of his homebred yearlings — a half-brother to Cruze and The Wave. Dean had registered enough horses that as long as Tim's ideas weren't too bizarre and the moniker met the Jockey Club's requirements, he'd let the kid pick it.

"These are Len's three up here." Caroline led the way. "We'll run the three-year-old again, but the other two, Len's agreed to retire. He doesn't need to be paying day rates on them if they're just standing around filling stalls."

She and Emilie discussed getting video and making social media posts to help rehome the horses, then the three of them wandered back to Cruze's stall.

"I hear he liked the turf," Emilie said. "Was that the first time Nate's been on him?"

"I guess it was," Dean said.

"Silent Fox's new trainer asked Nate to ride him, did you know?"

Dean did not. Nate could've taken the mount on the horse who would be favourite, but instead chose Cruze, a wildcard of a prospect. Because he believed in the colt. Because he believed in Dean. That faith was humbling.

"Have you seen the photos of Fox on Facebook?" Emilie said. "They're shipping him from Saratoga on Wednesday."

"Where'd you see that?" Dean asked.

"On the internet," Caroline said drolly. "It's amazing, you should check it out."

Dean smirked. "The internet brought me Krissy, so I'm not sold on that."

Emilie and Caroline laughed, and Cruze tossed his head like a movie horse. Dean half expected him to whinny, laughing with them. The whole Krissy thing still stung. All the more reason to be grateful for real friends.

Emilie left as quickly as she'd arrived, always in motion, while Dean felt as if he'd spent most of this morning watching and not working. He turned to Caroline. "What's left to do?"

"Just the tack. I'll start it if you feed lunch."

He grained their six charges and then tossed a chunk of barley grass onto the mat at the front of each stall. When he removed the tubs to set afternoon feeds, each one was licked clean, not a morsel remaining. Cruze grabbed the barley between his teeth and shook it, a piece flying into the shed as it tore apart.

Dean retrieved it and tossed it back onto the mat. "I'll bring you some day-old croissants tomorrow." As long as the authorities didn't decide butter and gluten were performance-enhancing. "And if you win the Bull Page, I promise you'll get fresh ones."

———

Dean responded to the tinny voice from the speaker at the drive-thru with his order, and Caroline chimed in with hers.

"Let me pay," she insisted as he pulled forward. "You always buy."

She leaned across him to shove bills out the truck's window. Could she not have just given them to him? His skin seared where she touched him, and he glanced down, expecting to see burns. The worst part was she was grinning. Smugly.

He'd told her they should take it slow. That was logical. They weren't teenagers. Part of him wished they were, that he could avoid all this over-thinking and just let things happen. Instead, he was trying to figure out what going slow meant. Should he ask her out on a date? Dinner and a movie? Dean was sure Liv and Nate had never done dinner and a movie. They weren't the worst example. Maybe if he and Caroline tried to ignore each other for a few years, they'd finally spontaneously combust into true love. Except he couldn't see Caroline going along with that, and he knew what happened when he kept putting things off.

Her eyebrows arched when he pulled into a parking spot in the cramped lot.

"Let's eat while it's hot," he said.

Wordlessly, she set the large fries between them, then turned up the radio to fill the silence as he bit into his burger. She picked at her own, her eyes constantly shifting to him. One day, he would erase what was left of her insecurity instead of feeling like he was leading her on, feeding her crumbs when he wanted the whole cake. He crushed his empty wrapper into a ball and stole a sip of her shake. She never finished them, anyway.

"Stacy and Nikki have postponed their return by two weeks. I thought I'd better check with you rather than assume you'd stay at the farm."

Her features relaxed, and she took the shake from his grasp, eying him as she drew the pink liquid through the straw.

"I'll consider it," she said, controlling lips that threatened to twitch into a grin.

He hadn't thought she'd refuse, but didn't realize how badly he wanted her to say yes. "You do that. Just don't ask for a raise." He hesitated. "After that..."

Her eyebrows lifted, lips still on the straw.

"I don't want you to leave." There. He'd said it.

"What do you suggest, that I squat in the feed room? This was the deal. Three months. I understood that from the beginning."

"You could move in."

"I'm not living with you."

"I wasn't suggesting — we haven't even —"

"Oh my gosh." She laughed. "You're blushing."

"You'd have your own room. A bathroom, even." It had worked fine when Monique had stayed there last winter.

"You and I both know what would happen."

He looked out the driver's side, wishing it was cold enough that rolling down the window would do something about the temperature inside the cab.

Caroline laughed again. "I'm sorry, I didn't mean to make you uncomfortable. But if you want to take things slowly — and that's smart, really it is — me moving in would ruin any chance of that ever happening, and this is too good to screw up."

He might not be the best at reading women, but he had a pretty good feeling that if they were somewhere private, she'd be climbing over the console and into his lap. Instead, she settled for kneeling on her bucket seat and leaning across, grabbing the front of his t-shirt and dragging his face to hers.

"Besides," she said, her lips a tantalizing sigh from his, "If I don't move away, how will I know if you'd miss me if I were gone?"

He inhaled, already tasting the strawberry on her breath. "I don't think that will be an issue."

CHAPTER FORTY-SEVEN

It was a script for a bad horse movie, the kind that made real equine professionals throw popcorn at the screen. *Underdog horse pulls off upset victory to win The Big Race and save the farm.* Cruze would be easy to cast. There was no shortage of plain, dark bay Thoroughbreds in the world.

Except this was a small, Ontario-sired stakes race, not the Derby or Breeders' Cup. And if Cruze won, it wouldn't guarantee all would be well in Dean's world, even if it would be a very welcome drop in a too-empty bucket, an indication of possible good things to come.

In real life, Cruze could hurt himself. He could die suddenly, like Liv's colt two summers ago. Or put in another disappointing performance, suggesting he'd be better suited as one of Caroline and Emilie's riding horse projects. With ten minutes to post for the Bull Page, it was anyone's guess.

Dean hadn't been able to stop himself from following the buzz surrounding Silent Fox's arrival. He and Len had stood elbow to elbow at the rail like old times, watching the colt gallop — except the two-year-old they assessed was no longer Dean's trainee.

It was no surprise Fox was favoured to win. He looked incredible, and he'd won three races since the transfer, undefeated in his short career. Instead of contesting tougher competition in New York, he was up here to grab some devalued Canadian dollars, an easy paycheque. His connections spoke of keeping next year's King's Plate in their sights. Maybe they'd come in person for that one, instead of sending an assistant trainer and groom and enlisting a local conditioner to saddle him.

Cruze was 50–1. The DNF — did not finish — in his only start wasn't attracting many bettors and his inside post position didn't help. Dean didn't exactly like the draw himself.

Someone bumped his arm, knocking him out of his thoughts.

"May I sit with you?"

Seeing Liv split his face into a smile, making him aware just how tight he'd been clenching his jaw. "Sure. You're on our team today." It wasn't lost on him she'd played a significant role in Cruze's development, taking over after Crystal had been hurt.

"He looks good," she said, dropping to the seat next to him.

"Can't you find anything more original to say?"

"You've become a crusty one."

Dean laughed. "Sorry. Hopefully I'll be happier after the race."

Caroline charged up the steps and parked on his other side, draping the shank across her lap. She twisted toward him and fingered his lapel. His father would be proud that he'd given in to her suggestion to wear a jacket and tie, but it had been all for Caroline. He found her hard to say no to.

"I didn't think it was appropriate to say in the paddock, but you look sharp," she said. "Ready for TV."

"What?"

She patted him on the leg. "Nothing. Where's Em, Liv?"

"She's around. I'm sure she'll join us soon."

The outrider jogged at the front of the procession, six two-year-olds strung out behind him, Cruze the first of them. Dean focused his binoculars on the colt, Cruze in his usual wide-eyed goose-watch state, next to his pony. Two pairs down, wearing the blue number three cloth, was Fox, alert, but chill.

A commotion distracted Dean, and he reflexively glanced over his shoulder. Another tension-relieving grin as Faye waved at him, Will behind her, Emilie picking up the rear.

"We made it!" Faye took the seat next to Liv and rolled her eyes. "Will had to bet and I was afraid he'd get lost without me."

"I still don't have the hang of this place," Will admitted sheepishly.

"You bet on my horse?" Dean said. "You'll jinx him."

Will looked worried, but Faye reached across Liv and slapped Dean's arm. "Stop it. You're the least superstitious person I know."

"That was before this year."

"The horse is fifty to one; he's worth a couple of bucks," Faye said.

Truth be told, Dean had put fifty across on the colt. He didn't always bet his horses, but at those odds, it was worth the gamble.

"You're not nervous, are you Dean?" Emilie said, poised on the chair next to Caroline.

"Of course he's nervous," Caroline said, flashing Dean a smile. "It's a stake race."

"In which my horse may or may not belong."

"And he could either make you look like a genius, or a fool," she quipped.

"Exactly. But if I look like a fool, I'm blaming Nate." Dean looked around, his sister, brother-in-law, friends, all by his side. Come what may, they were here for it.

With the purse distributed between the first five finishers, Cruze just had to keep his rider and beat one horse to pick up a cheque. *Don't aim too high there.* Liv was right. What had happened to him? He'd always been teased about being high on his horses — back when he had horses worth getting high on.

The gate was opposite them, high on the outer turf course, a clear view as the two-year-olds filed in. Cruze stood quietly in the one hole. *Don't go to sleep in there, buddy.* Dean barely heard the announcer's voice when the last horse went in. Within seconds, they were off.

Cruze shot out, and Liv laughed. "Looked kind of like Chique there."

"I hope Nate doesn't think he's on Chique," Dean muttered as the rider hustled the colt, getting first call. "Now, now. Take it easy."

Soon the field swallowed Cruze up, two horses surging past. The one on the inside dropped to the rail once clear, his neighbour tight beside him. Fox ran alongside Cruze like they were old buddies. It left Cruze tucked in a neat little pocket with no way out.

It's early. It's all right.

The first quarter mile zoomed past as they entered the sloping turn. Five furlongs left. Good thing, because Cruze still had nowhere to go. Dean inched to the edge of his seat. The two trailers crept up. Cruze looked like he was being mobbed.

They're on the turf. They'll break up in the stretch.

They had to.

There's time. Lots of time. That straight is very, very long.

A hole opened up between the two leaders and Fox slipped easily through, taking off with an electric burst, leaving the others flat-footed. Nate worked on Cruze, inspiring the chase, and aimed for the same hole. Good thing Cruze wasn't big because the space was closing.

Dean's heart leapt into his throat, watching the five horse bear out, jostling Cruze like a bully on the school playground, causing a domino effect as Cruze bumped the neighbour to his right. But the scrimmage loosened everything up and, miraculously, gave Cruze the room he needed. Nate threw himself into catching Fox.

"Come on Cruze!'" Caroline jumped to her feet just as Dean did, slapping her leg and hollering in his ear. Faye and Emilie screamed. Even Liv yelled, Will's voice joining the chorus.

Come on, Cruze. Dean glanced at Fox on the lead, gauging the distance to the wire. It was coming too fast. *He's going to be second. He's not catching Fox.*

Caroline gripped his arm, bouncing. "He's digging in. He's going to do it! Get up there, Cruze!"

"Come on Cruze!" Dean dropped the binoculars, the colt gaining, gaining, wearing down his former stablemate. Fox's jockey glanced over. Nate drove on. It was going to be close, so close. The colts flashed past the wire, mirror images, and Dean had no idea who'd won.

"Let's go!" Caroline gave him a shove, saying it like it was theirs.

Dean stared at the tote board as they jogged down the stairs, willing the result to be posted.

Caroline's screech pierced his eardrum, and she threw her arms in the air. Dean gaped at the number one on top of the results board. He spun to Caroline and grabbed her, pulling her in tight.

"What did I tell you?" Caroline beamed.

He lost himself in that face for a moment, then, right there in the middle of the mayhem, he kissed her.

"Dean," she murmured, pulling back, palm flat over his pounding heart. "I have to go catch the horse."

"The outrider's got him."

"Congratulations." She grinned up at him and pushed away.

They crossed the main track to the infield winner's circle, the track photographer shouting orders Dean barely heard as Faye and Will kept their distance while Caroline positioned Cruze. Dean stood next to her, resting a hand lightly on her back, and waved Faye and Will closer.

The photographer took his shots, then Nate hopped down, slid off his saddle, and weighed in. Caroline wheeled Cruze away and Dean followed.

"Get back there!" Caroline said. "Interviews! See you at the test barn when you're done."

Then Dean saw the camera, and the microphone, and the resident reporter motioning Dean and Nate to join him.

Someone had given Nate a white Ontario Sires Stakes ball cap and Nate moulded the peak before running a hand through his damp hair and setting it on his head. Dean's palms sweated while he listened to Nate talk about his trip.

"I had all the confidence in the world in this colt. Dean and his team have done a great job with him."

Dean was just a small-time trainer, but look at the team behind him. Stacy had helped foal and raise the colt, Clay took care of his feet, Chad and Ben handled the vet work on the farm, Jake took care of that on the backstretch. Nikki had groomed him, then Hunter. Crystal had been the first to gallop him on the track. He'd been started at Triple Stripe. And Caroline, Caroline...

"What about you, Dean? Were you confident today? Fifty to one!"

"I'm not going to lie. I had my doubts about running here after that first start, but Nate thought it was worth a shot. Turns out he was right. That's why he makes the big bucks."

"Was it satisfying to beat Silent Fox?"

"It's a little bittersweet. I love that horse, and I'm happy his new connections have done so well with him. But I didn't mind beating him today. It's been a tough year."

He thanked Nate and then thanked that team in what became a speech worthy of the Academy Awards. Turned out he had a thing or two to say.

"And what's next for this colt, Dean? Is it safe to say you're thinking about the Cup and Saucer?" Nate tipped his bottle toward Dean like it was a microphone.

Dean draped an arm over Nate's shoulders. "Well, Nate, we'll see how he comes out of the race, but that's a logical consideration. I think this colt will stretch out and get a mile and a sixteenth, and he obviously loves the turf."

"I am *so* driving home tonight," Caroline muttered.

"Appears so," Liv agreed, grinning. "Good thing tomorrow's a dark day."

Will had bought the beer, showing up with it by the time Caroline returned from the test barn with Cruze. Dean deserved to let loose, blow off a little steam; he'd been so tense lately, with good reason. Cruze was nose-deep in his dinner, the way he rattled his tub making Caroline think he'd come out of this race just fine. Faye brought a fresh croissant for his dessert.

No one stayed long. They were all too tired and just

sensible enough not to prolong the party. Caroline checked on the horses and fed Cruze his croissant before wrangling Dean.

"Come on, Trainer of the Year. Let's get you home."

"I like the sound of that," he said, slinging an arm around her neck.

So did she. "Where are your keys?"

Dean dropped them in her waiting palm without argument. She waited while he got in the passenger side to be sure he could manage. He wasn't falling over, but sober he was not.

"This is weird," he said as she climbed behind the wheel. "I've never sat on this side. So much legroom. It's nice."

Caroline had to adjust the seat significantly to be close enough to reach the pedals. How was he so drunk? He'd had what, two beers? What a lightweight.

Though she'd been in this truck countless times in the last two months, it was a different story to drive it. The thing was a beast compared to her small car. She kept to the speed limit, both hands on the wheel. Cruze hadn't made enough money today to pay for a new vehicle.

She probably didn't need to walk him to the house, but Dean was sleepy — though sober enough now to unlock the door. She'd never been inside and glanced around the quaint country kitchen as Gus circled their legs.

Dean turned to her, hands going loosely to her hips. "Are you sure you don't want to take that room?"

She tipped her face to his. "We agreed, remember?"

"No, no I don't. What did we agree, exactly?"

"I wouldn't want to take advantage of you in your current state."

"You have my consent."

"I think you should go lie down. I'll take Gus for a walk. For a tall guy, you sure can't hold your liquor."

He bent and kissed her gently. "Sorry about that."

Beer breath. She tried not to make a face. "Just don't make a habit of it."

Gus was happy to come with her when she called. Someone had put in the time training him, because he listened to her. He kept her company, and though it wasn't the same as Dean, the dog helped her feel safe. She was so much better than she had been, more used to the sounds of the night. The horses were all well and where they were supposed to be. Caroline said hello to each one — the new yearlings she was getting to know and her old friends. She paused to give The Wave a peppermint and extra attention.

"Your little brother did good today," she said, letting him nuzzle her neck. "Maybe he'll follow in your footsteps and be a Plate horse for your dad next year."

Would she be part of it?

She was packed, back to living out of a suitcase. Because she *had* made herself at home, gradually spreading her belongings out despite her best attempts to prevent it. It had always felt like borrowed space, never truly hers. If she only knew exactly what was next, she'd feel better.

She did not need to jump right into a new relationship. The last thing she wanted was to wreck this. She should savour the steady building of something new. Consider carefully, instead of cannonballing in. Once she moved in with Jess, she'd still be here almost every day, working with the yearlings. She'd still see Dean both here and at the track. Time would tell if that was or wasn't enough.

He was sound asleep on the couch by the time she returned with Gus. Caroline brushed his hair from his forehead and kissed it, the skin there smoothed of all the summer's tension.

"See you later, Gus. Take care of him for me."

CHAPTER FORTY-EIGHT

Six weeks *later*

Once upon a time, these elevators had attendants, but Dean couldn't remember if that memory was his or if he'd adopted those of his father, or Len. The space he stepped into was empty, and his finger hovered over the number five as the doors thunked closed. He poked the button, and the box lurched upward before travelling smoothly to the fifth floor. Dean undid his heavy coat, then rubbed his palms on his thighs and straightened his tie as the doors opened again, licking his lips before stepping out.

The Turf Club was now the Woodbine Club, and the decor had changed from those early recollections. In his youth, he'd stall as he returned from the restrooms, studying the oil paintings of past Plate winners gracing the walls, some yellowed with age. It lost its elegance without those paintings, but that was the way of things now. The ideals Dean had grown up with were gone.

He strode to the dining area, seeing Liv right away, sure this meeting was about more than a friendly drink. A server appeared and took his order once he removed his coat and folded into the seat opposite her.

"Cruze is starting to look like he could be something special," Liv said, sipping water.

Her glass of wine remained untouched, like she'd only asked for it to justify her presence in the coterie. Her father maintained a membership; Dean had let the Taylor's go soon after his parents' death. Now he only came if he had a horse in a stake race or received an invite. This was a combination of the two.

He reached for the other water glass to give his restless hands something to do. "Is this where you try to buy him?"

Liv laughed. "That's actually not what this is."

The server interrupted, placing a pint of dark beer in front of him. Dean glanced up. "Thanks."

Cruze's Cup and Saucer win today probably should have incited more of a celebration — it wasn't any less thrilling than his first victory — but so much had changed in the six weeks since the Bull Page. It was November, and Will and Faye were already busy with catering jobs for the holidays. The hockey season was in full swing, and Emilie was watching Tim play. The colder weather and shorter daylight hours made hanging out at the barn less inviting. All any of them wanted to do was get home at the end of a long day, though the farm felt less like home since Caroline had moved out. She'd become part of the fabric of the place, of him.

Stacy and Nikki were back. Dean had a nice two-year-old. He had all the things he'd wanted before it had gone sideways back in May, but none of it felt right without Caroline at the centre.

He still saw her every day. She still got on his horses, but there wasn't as much to do with Nikki back. Caroline left earlier to work with the yearlings at the farm, and when she gave them a day off, sometimes they had lunch — was that dating? — but that had ended with October. He missed her and had to do something about it.

"So," he prodded. "What is this, then?"

Liv set her glass down and cradled it between her hands. "It's about a job."

Dean's brow wrinkled. "A job?" What did that have to do with him?

"It's no secret I want to ride again," she began, and she was right. Among her friends, at least, it wasn't. "What would you think of training for Triple Stripe?"

Dean turned his head slightly, inclining an ear toward her, sure he'd lost his hearing. "I'm sorry, what?"

Liv's face brightened, and there was rare excitement in her voice. "I don't know why I never thought of it before. Probably because I never thought you'd be interested until everything that happened this year. Let's just say, Andy's loss could be my gain."

His jaw slackened. "You're serious."

"Why wouldn't I be?"

"Because, I don't know." Because he'd almost lost all of it this year? His owners, his livelihood, his confidence? Why would an operation like Triple Stripe consider someone like him? *Dean's an excellent trainer,* Liv's father had said at Faye and Will's reception. While his self-assurance had evaporated like water on a hot day, everyone else was capturing it, returning it to liquid, rehydrating him. The *why* was because of them.

Liv leaned forward. "So, is that crazy? Something you'd think about?"

"Well — yes." Probably crazy, but, did he really need to think about it at all? "Would I get a few stalls for my own horses?"

"Of course."

"Do I have to go to Florida?"

"I think we could work around that if you don't want to, even if I question your sanity. No one says you have to be sane to be a horse trainer. Being a little unstable is probably a prerequisite."

"I'm honoured," he sputtered.

"Does that mean you'll do it?"

He should say he needed some time — training for Liv's family felt like a huge step — but, "I can't come up with a reason to say no."

Liv raised her wine glass. "That's worth drinking to."

Dean met it with his beer. "You're going to be one of those owners, aren't you?"

"Afraid so." Liv grinned. "Though I won't officially be an owner."

"So, the Northwest and Triple Stripe dynasties will be united after all," he said.

"I'm sorry?" Liv laughed.

"Just something Caroline said to me once, when she asked about me and you."

"She's become an institution."

It was Dean's turn to laugh. "That's a good way of putting it. I'm not sure I can imagine it all without her now."

The look Liv gave him was like she was thinking, *see, it happened to you, too.* "I'm happy for you." She set her glass back down. "You should tell her to join us. Nate'll be done soon."

"What's happened to you?" Dean teased. "That sounded sociable."

"See? I need this. I need to get back to riding so I can be myself again."

"I didn't say it was bad."

They watched the last race from their warm spot behind panes of glass. This high in the grandstand, the view was panoramic. When it was light, Lake Ontario was visible, but right now after sunset, the track was illuminated, the horses and jockeys tiny stars of the show as they burst from the starting gate and flew along the backstretch. Nate didn't win this one. Dean and Liv watched from their parapet as he rode back to the front of the stands, the horse's breath frosty plumes.

"I don't know how they do it," Dean said. The riders stripped off saddles with gloved hands, faces covered, but otherwise wearing little protection from the bitter wind.

"With much complaining and counting of days till the end," Liv said wryly.

"And you want to go back to that?"

"Maybe I'll ride in California."

"Then you and Nate can be stars of a reality TV series."

She snorted. "That sounds like a surefire way to end up divorced."

Caroline appeared still bundled in her winter jacket like the ride up in the elevator hadn't been long enough to lessen the chill of an afternoon working outdoors. Nikki had offered to run Cruze, but Caroline had insisted. She smiled when Dean helped her out of the coat and hung it on the back of her chair, unwinding her scarf to lay it on top. She still wore the black jeans she'd brought Cruze over in, which were somehow not covered in dried white poultice, but she'd exchanged the heavy sweater for a white blouse under a lavender jacket that gave her chameleon eyes a purplish tint. A silver chain caught the light. Maybe she'd like jewellery for Christmas. Dean would have to enlist Faye's help for that.

Nate was the last to arrive. He looked exhausted and waved off the server when asked what he wanted to drink, instead taking a sip of Liv's wine.

"So?" he asked, eyeing Dean. "Are you on board?"

"He hasn't officially said yes," Liv said.

Caroline grinned. "Someone fill me in."

Dean glanced at her. She wasn't fooling him. That wasn't an innocent face.

"It was you, wasn't it?"

The nasty northwest wind whipped across the parking lot as they walked to their vehicles. Caroline huddled against Dean, hood pulled tight, her face buried against him. She barely made out his words.

She shrugged. "I heard her talking about needing a trainer so she could go back to riding. I may have put a bug in her ear."

"It might take a while to sink in."

"When do you start?"

"Next season."

"And Florida?"

"I don't want to spend winters in Florida."

"What?" The thought that anyone would *not* want to spend the coldest months of the year down south was unfathomable. "How can you say that?"

"I know you're afraid of the dark, but I didn't think you were afraid of the cold. You've been living in Saskatchewan for the last ten winters." He stopped next to her car, arms wrapping around her. "Is this a deal-breaker?"

She sighed, throwing her head back dramatically. "I will require Irish coffees and copious quantities of delectable pastries with a roaring fire to endure." She kissed his twisted lips, quite proud of her mouthful of a response.

One of his eyebrows quirked. "Does that mean you're finally moving in?"

Caroline wanted nothing more than to be curled up with him in that cosy old farmhouse; shivering in this arctic blast was not the place to discuss this. *Sure, we can take it slow.* But she was tired of slow. Fast horses were *not* enough.

The paperwork for the divorce had finally come through. For the first time in far, far too long, Caroline felt free — free to get it right. No shortcuts. No half-assed gestures. If hindsight was twenty-twenty, what was the point in wasting time? She got along with Nikki at the track. She got along with Stacy at the farm. But she missed feeling special, being the one Dean relied on for everything.

Caroline levelled him with her gaze. "You're going to have to do better than that."

"Better? What do you mean?"

"I told you, I'm not moving in with you."

"What are you suggesting?" His tone was cautious.

"You know."

"You don't want..." Dean stammered. The way his forehead creased under that stray lock of dark hair was adorable. "But — we agreed — slow?"

"Dean. We've known each other for twenty years."

"Sure, but —"

She gripped the lapels of his wool coat. "Tell me you don't think we're good together. Tell me you don't love me. Tell me you don't want to marry me." Maybe the cold was making her manic, her words fierce, a challenge. Her hands closed into fists against his chest, eyes shining, her voice faltering to a whisper. "Tell me I've made it up to you. Tell me you'll let me spend the rest of my life convincing you I've changed. Tell me you forgive me."

His eyes searched her face, and he reached a hand up, brushing fingers against her cheek. "Of course I love you. Of course I want to marry you. We're great together. There's nothing left to forgive. Nothing to make up for."

She sucked back a sob as he gently kissed away a tear. "I never gave you back your handkerchief from the wedding," she said, her voice still quavering. "I could use it right now."

Dean laughed. "You mean you don't keep it next to your heart, always?"

Caroline swatted him. But she *had* thought about it. Said organ thump, thump, thumped against her chest, steady, like him.

The initial shock was gone from his eyes. "I always thought if I ever proposed to someone, I would do it right."

She felt a ridiculous stab of jealousy. "You've thought about it?"

"In general terms, I guess."

"You can still do that. I'm here for the grand proposal."

"But it won't be a surprise."

"Pro tip: most proposals aren't a complete surprise, especially at our age. You want to be sure the other person will say yes, don't you?"

"That would help."

"I promise to be surprised. Just don't wait too long."

Reluctantly, she turned to unlock her door. It was too cold to stand out here any longer. She paused with a foot on the floorboard. "You'll have to go to Florida to check on the horses from time to time, right?"

"I suppose."

"I hear Liv and Nate have a lovely condo on the beach."

Dean nodded, a wry twist to his lips. "It's nice."

"I could tag along."

"You could." He pulled her into him again and kissed her.

Caroline groaned when she dragged herself away and ducked behind the wheel to start the engine. It was freezing after the coziness of his arms and would take a while to warm up. Each time she climbed in her car and Dean in his truck, it felt like she was heading in the wrong direction. *Don't wait too long.*

CHAPTER FORTY-NINE

Dean lifted the tote into the back of the truck, its lid secured with duct tape. He slammed the tailgate shut and went to the shedrow to make one last pass. It looked bleak, with everything gone. The mats were pulled up and heavy gates removed, all of it locked in a stall. Caroline had spent the last weeks organizing the rest of the equipment, arranging to sell some of it to other trainers — feed tubs and water buckets and extra tack — and then packing the rest into bin after plastic bin. He wasn't getting rid of it all. He'd see how many stalls they got after putting in applications for the new season and go from there.

Caroline followed him, her car packed with what wasn't in the truck or already back at the farm. She pulled in behind him when he stopped at the café, insisting her cappuccino couldn't wait that long even though he'd said she could meet him at home.

Triple Shot was decorated for the holidays, with mini lights and cedar boughs gracing the walls. Faye had their drinks ready because he'd texted ahead.

"Chad's on his way, so better get something for him, too,"

Dean said, and Faye started packing freshly ground beans into the filter for one more hot beverage.

Caroline wiggled her cup from the tray. "I'll go on ahead. I need to say hello to the kids."

"Hang on," Dean called before she reached the door. "I'll get pastries, too. What do you want?"

She shrugged. "I don't know. Surprise me."

Faye was smiling a cheeky smile when Dean turned back to her. "You heard the lady. Surprise her."

He laughed and accepted a Thermos and a couple of bags of treat-filled boxes. "Thanks, Faye."

Dean drummed his fingers against the steering wheel as he drove. Back when Caroline had still been riding with him, she'd switched from classic rock to Toronto's alternative station because Emilie kept giving her songs. He'd maintained the habit when he was on his own, like somehow it eased the fact that they were apart. This was one he recognized, even if he might not be as big a Dave Matthews fan as Faye. *Crash Into Me...* Caroline had certainly done just that.

At the farm, he pulled the truck up to the storage shed and left it there, carrying the coffees and treats to the mares' barn. The yearlings Caroline had started were off now until the new year, so she hadn't been here since the end of October. She and Stacy were at the fence with Ride The Wave, who was fully recovered from his castration surgery. It was the right thing to do but still made Dean a little sad.

Cruze was out with Fargo. *Sure, we'll find Fargo a home.* Caroline said it was still in the works, but Dean wasn't holding his breath. She had the potential to collect retired racehorses like Breyer models if left unchecked, like she was still trying to make up for past wrongs.

It was her suggestion to try the colt with Fargo, and Dean had to admit it was a good one. The older gelding didn't indulge in roughhousing, so the colt had companionship without the risk of getting hurt playfighting. Which meant, the rehoming would probably be put off until Cruze went back to work in February.

Currently, the colt had the tail flap of Fargo's blanket between his teeth and was tugging on it. Fargo pinned his ears, one hind leg cocked, threatening. Of course, if the older gelding kicked Cruze in the knee, the arrangement wouldn't seem so brilliant after all.

Dean pulled a croissant from a paper bag and Cruze dropped the tail flap, ears pricked. He sauntered over to the fence and gobbled the piece Dean tore off. Fargo turned up his nose when offered a taste, but accepted a candy.

"There's Chad," Stacy said, and the three of them headed into the barn.

It was Stacy who had inspired the vet's visit. "Are you sure Cherry's not in foal?" she'd said one day earlier this week.

"She's just fat," Dean said.

"I don't know. She has that look, that fullness through the flank. How far along would she be if she was?"

He'd had to think about it. "Bred the end of June, so five months."

"I think you should have her checked. Just in case, you know. These things happen."

Chad lugged the ultrasound machine in, placing it in front of Cherry's stall. Dean handed him a cappuccino.

"Is this to console me in case I embarrass myself?" Chad asked.

"It wouldn't be the worst mistake," Dean said.

He was trying not to hope. Caroline huddled, arms crossed, her impatience showing. When she'd heard, she'd decided today would be a good time for a visit. Dean thought she was going to bore a hole in Chad's skull, the way she was watching the vet's expression as he palpated Cherry. It didn't take long.

"Yep. She's in foal."

"Yes!" Caroline hopped, bouncing on her toes. She grinned at Dean, looking like a kid who'd been told she was getting a pony for Christmas.

"We'll ultrasound her to check the placenta, given her history," Chad said.

Dean sent the vet off with a pat on the back and a box of treats from the café, then he stood in front of Cherry with Stacy and Caroline, the three of them clutching their coffees and eating the butter tarts Faye had sent. Dean gave Cherry a kiss on the nose and a peppermint. As Stacy put Cherry back out with the other mares, he and Caroline unloaded the last of the equipment from the track.

Dean locked the shed, then turned to her. "Come in for a bit, if you're not in a rush."

Her smile was coy. "I think I can make time."

They rode up to the house in the truck and Caroline closed the gate while Dean gathered the Thermos and the last bag from the café. Gus greeted him as he entered the house, the Golden's lips stretched in a grin, tail swooping.

Dean laughed when Caroline tapped on the door before poking her head in. "You don't need to knock."

"Last time I was here, you were a little tipsy." She hesitated on the mat.

He rubbed the back of his neck. "Yeah, well. Make yourself at home. I'll start a fire."

"I'll take Gus out for you real quick."

"Sounds great."

Torn paper and kindling waited in the hearth, and Dean struck a match. He positioned a couple of smaller logs on top and, when he was satisfied it was burning, returned to the kitchen.

Gus bounded in as Caroline unwound her scarf. She found a hook for her coat and left her boots by the door. "What are you making?" she asked, leaning into him. "Is that Irish coffee? Amazing."

"Is whipping cream out of a can cheating?" Dean opened the fridge and held up a canister.

"Not one bit."

Faye had just the right glasses, showing off the dark mixture of whisky and coffee with its frothy white topping. Dean handed Caroline one of the concoctions and she inhaled, closing her eyes. When she opened them, hands wrapped around the warm beverage, her fingers still pink from the cold, she looked at him with wonder.

"Dean. We're going to have a baby!"

His heart seemed to stop — then it clicked. "I guess we are." Dean grinned and held up his glass. "To Cherry and Ride The Wave. Come on. Let's sit in the living room."

He added a larger log to the fire then realized he'd forgotten the treats in the kitchen, though he wasn't sure how. Faye had put a "C" on one cover in black Sharpie, but Dean double-checked the contents to be sure it was right.

"My own box?" Caroline set down her coffee. "What did you get me?"

Dean settled on the other end of the couch. "You said you wanted to be surprised."

She lifted the lid. "Mmmm... whaah?"

The sound she made was comical, but Dean's heart thudded, too hard and too fast. Caroline gaped, her eyes fixed on the inside. When she reached in, he had just enough reflexes left to catch the box — and the chocolate-raspberry croissant — before it became Gus's.

Caroline balanced the small red velvet cube on her fingertips, the top creaking softly as she opened it. Dean wasn't sure, but he thought she mouthed, "Oh... my..." With something between a snort and sob, she shoved it toward him and whispered, "Put it on?"

Dean pulled the ring free, willing himself not to tremble as he slipped it on her outheld finger, but it was futile. They both stared at it, then he chanced a look at her face.

"Marry me?"

She smiled the sweetest smile and laced her arms around his neck. "Yes."

He drew her in and kissed her. "It's for the best, with the baby coming." He grinned, then wished he could take it back. "I'm sorry. I don't mean to minimize what you've been through, not being able to have kids."

"I said it first. Sometimes you just need to lighten things up. But Cherry's foal was the first one I saw born, and The Wave is my man. Sorry if that sounds weird. I'm never going to have my own, I accept that, so I want to celebrate their baby. It feels like ours, in a way."

She was rambling, but that was all right. "We can talk about it," he said carefully. "Give it some thought. Maybe, if you still want, down the road a bit, we could adopt."

"Someone old enough to learn how to muck stalls," she quipped, then frowned. "That's terrible. I should probably stick to horses."

Dean laughed. He thumbed a tear from her cheek. "We don't have to figure that out right now."

The fire blazed, the whiskey warmed, the chocolate-raspberry croissant melted — and Gus finally gave up on getting a taste and curled at their feet with a huff. Dean had never wrapped up things at the track this soon. Usually he was among the die-hards, slugging it out until closing day, looking forward to his annual ski trip while others headed south. Winter was a time to rest, reflect, regroup. This time, he was already looking forward to next year.

At the beginning of the season, he'd thought this could be his best, the one where he finally outdistanced the demands of his father's memory. In the middle of it, he'd feared it would be his last, that his father was right — he didn't belong in this world. Now he could see it wasn't about who was right and who was wrong. And it wasn't a competition, at least not with his father. Ed Taylor's legacy remained intact. It had begun and ended with him. Dean had neither destroyed it nor enhanced it. Instead, he was building his own, though not *on* his own.

He'd thought he'd be training a small public stable forever, in his father's shadow. Next season's challenge was more than he'd ever imagined, but he couldn't wait. A new hope. A new alliance.

A new generation.

———————————

Thank you for reading! Want a sneak peak of what's next? Check in with Liv and Nate and the next generation of Triple Stripe horses in this bonus content: https://www.lindashantz. com/pages/good-things-come-series-bonus-content

THANK YOU!

Well, this one was a long time coming, was it worth the wait?

I hope you'll consider leaving a review to share your thoughts with other readers. If you're not comfortable with that, even leaving a simple rating helps. I'm so grateful to everyone who takes the time for that show of support. If you'd like to know places you can share, check out my blog post: https://www.lindashantz.com/blogs/news/how-to-support-the-authors-you-love

This book marks number ten in the Good Things Come series, and while I'm calling it the last one, don't worry, I'm not done with these characters.

If you want to see what's up next, grab Chapter One of the as-yet-unnamed book that will start a new series, with those new alliances and the new generation of horses. https://www.lindashantz.com/pages/good-things-come-series-bonus-content

You can also join my Patreon to read as I write. Check it out with a seven-day trial to start, or follow for free. https://www.patreon.com/lindashantz/membership

Stay up-to-date on all my writing news (and see lots of pictures of my horses) by signing up for my newsletter at www.lindashantz.com/writes

If you're on Facebook, join the Good Things Come Readers group: https://www.facebook.com/groups/423653622029344

Thanks so much for taking this ride with me!

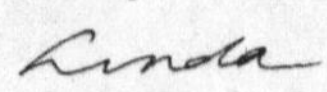

GLOSSARY OF HORSE RACING AND OTHER TERMS

The world of horse racing has its own vocabulary, different from that of other parts of the equine world.

Below are some of the more common terms used in this series, from my experience of over thirty-five years working from tracks in Ontario, Canada, to Florida, USA. In most cases, they are specific to North America but may vary by region.

Exercise:

Back up - to warm up at a jog going the "wrong" way around the track (clockwise). Horse and rider must stay to the outside rail.

Blow out - a short work a few days before a race.

Break off - to start breezing or working, or for a pony to accompany a horse to the starting point (the pole).

Breeze - a timed speed workout at a true gallop where the horse runs without urging from the rider. Also used as a verb. Breezing is done close to the inner rail of the racetrack.

Gallop - daily conditioning; a gallop at the track is a three-beat gait which will vary in speed depending on the horse's training program, Galloping is done in the middle of the racetrack.

Hack - a leisurely walk.

Jog - trot, a two-beat gait, faster than a walk.

Leg up - to assist a rider to mount; also, to bring a horse back into work after a layoff.

Rate - to control a horse's speed (to rate the pace).

Run - what racehorses do in a race. Harness horses race, Thoroughbreds run.

Tack the shed - to walk on the shedrow with a rider up. Can also be called "shedrowing" or "tack-walking." Often done when bringing a horse back into training or during poor weather.

Work - a timed speed workout; also used as a verb. Like breezing, working happens on the inside rail.

People around the track:

Bug (rider) - slang for an apprentice jockey. Apprentices receive lower weight assignments depending on their experience/races won, denoted by an asterisk in the program known as a "bug."

Exercise rider - person who rides the horse for daily exercise. They can either be on salary for a trainer, or freelance.

Gate crew/starter's assistants - people who load the horses into the starting gate and hold the horses until the race begins. They also help teach the horses how to be loaded. This is known as gate schooling and takes place at the end of morning training hours.

Groom - person who cares for the horse, including stall cleaning, grooming, putting on bandages and equipment, and taking them over for the races. Grooming is also known as "rubbing."

Hotwalker - person who walks the horse after training or a race, or on a day off from training. Other duties include holding horses for baths and cleaning up the barn area at the end of the morning.

Jockey - person who rides the horse in races and often for timed speed works in the morning. Commonly called a rider. Real racetrackers never use jockey as a verb or "jockeying" as a career.

Jockey's agent - person hired by jockey to connect with trainers in order to find a jockey horses to ride, both in the morning and afternoon.

Outriders - mounted racetrack officials who oversee proceedings from the time the horses leave the saddling area until the race goes off.

Pony person - mounted person who leads the horse onto the track, through the post parade and warmups, until it's time for the horse to be loaded in the starting gate.

Starter - official responsible for overseeing the horses as they are loaded, and determining when to open the gates.

Racing secretary - official responsible for putting together prospective races and deciding which races will be used.

Trainer - person responsible for overseeing the horse's training schedule, entering races, saddling on race days and making decisions based on all the above, including medications and other treatments. Trainers might be private (on salary for a single owner) or public (paid by a day rate per horse).

Assistant trainer - second in command to the trainer, able to step in to saddle the horse on race days if needed. Daily responsibilities will vary depending on the trainer.

Places around the track

Backstretch - racetrack's stable area; also, the part of the racetrack on the far side of the track (parallel to but opposite of the "home stretch.") Also called the "backside."

Clubhouse turn - first turn after the finish line.

Chute - extension of the homestretch or backstretch which allows a straight start for a race (instead of placing the gate on a turn).

Gap - literally, a gap in the rail that encloses the track which allows horses on ("on-gap") and off (off-gap).

Paddock - area to which horses are brought to be saddled (saddling enclosure) and where the jockeys mount (walking ring).

Shedrow, shed – At the racetrack, a shedrow-style barn has a block of stalls back to back, with a covered (and usually enclosed) outer walkway around the perimeter.

The shedrow (often shortened to shed) is a section of a shedrow-style barn assigned to an individual trainer. It's common to refer to people or horses being "on the shed," which refers to the aisle/walkway.

Test barn – controlled area for selected horses to be cooled out under supervision after a race, after which samples will be taken for drug testing. Normally 2-3 horses are tested per race, including the winner.

Equipment

Blinkers - hood worn with plastic cups to limit a horse's vision and improve focus.

Cantle - the back of a saddle.

Brace bandage - support bandage sometimes used during training. These are a stretchy Ace-type bandage. At the track using boots is rare.

Knot - racing lines (reins) are long, so the rider will tie a knot in the end to shorten them for safety reasons.

Irons - stirrup irons.

Leathers - stirrup leathers.

Lines - racetrack term for reins. They're an inch thick, have rubber grips, and are much longer than riding horse reins.

Neck strap - a loop of leather for added safety - something to grab if a horse misbehaves or if the bridle breaks. During training it is part of the martingale (and so attached to the girth) but in a race it is unattached (and not all trainers equip their horses with them).

Polos - soft bandages used during training to protect a horse from superficial injuries. At the track using boots is rare.

Pommel - the front of a saddle.

Rundowns - bandages applied, normally to the hind lower limb, to protect the back of the fetlock from burning as a horse runs.

Shadow roll - a noseband covered in thick sheepskin (usually synthetic) used to limit a horse's vision and improve focus.

Shank - lead shank, aka lead line, typically made of leather. Chain shank - lead shank with a chain at one end. Paddock shank - lead shank with only a snap at one end.

Sheet - a lightweight blanket. A quarter-sheet is a light blanket (usually wool or artificial fleece) that covers the horse's hindquarters during training when the weather is colder.

Standing bandage - bandages applied after training either to assist in holding topical leg treatments in place or for protection. Most horses are also shipped in bandages. Consists of two parts - an inner "cotton" for padding, held in place by a flannel (non-stretchy) or nylon bandage. Some people call them "wraps."

Race types:

Allowance - a race for which the racing secretary has set out certain conditions, such as the weight the horses will carry depending on their age, sex, past performance.

Claiming race/claimer - a race in which each horse can be bought for a specific price (= tag). The higher the claiming price, the better the quality of horse.

Condition race - after a horse "breaks" its maiden (wins its first race) they can be entered in a series of races with specific conditions, such as non-winners of a race other than maiden or claiming, non-winners of two races other than maiden or claiming, non-winners of three races. Completing each step is known as running a horse through its conditions. Once they've accomplished that, races become more competitive and harder to win.

Condition book - booklet published every two weeks which lists prospective races trainers can enter.

Conditions - the criteria of a race, including distance, type of track, weights to be carried, purse money, restrictions (place of birth, sex, age).

Graded stake - a selected group of stakes races given a rating (one, the highest, through three), depending on the prestige of said race. Called Group races outside of North America.

Maiden - a type of race in which horses who have never won a race run. A race can be "Maiden Allowance, Maiden Claiming or Maiden Special Weight" depending on how good the horse is expected to be. Also, a horse who has yet to win a race. A horse winning its first race is said to "break its maiden."

Stakes/stake race - race for which nomination and entry fees are paid (also known as "added-money" races for that reason). They generally attract a higher class of race.

Terms that didn't quite fit elsewhere:

Ankle - what racetrack people call the fetlock joint, the joint between the hoof and the "knee."

Century home - historical designation in Canada for a house that is, you guessed it, over a hundred years old.

Cross - to "take a cross" is to cross the lines (reins) over each other so the rider holds both lines, making it easier to control the horse. Called a "bridge" outside of racing.

Doing up - daily ritual performed by the groom after training each day and after a race that involves hoof care, application of leg treatments (liniment, sweats, poultice), bandaging and grooming.

Form - a horse's past performance; also short for The Daily

Racing Form, a newsprint publication with the past performances of all horse racing in an area on a particular day.

Knee - carpal joint, anatomically equivalent to the human wrist.

Layup - a horse resting from the track or rehabilitating from a track injury.

Longe - British spelling more commonly written as "lunge" in North America. A training exercise in which the horse travels in a circle on the end of a twenty-foot line while the handler pivots in the centre.

Long-lining - also known as ground driving; when the handler walks behind a horse, steering with long lines. Often used in the starting process.

Pony - racetrackers refer to anything that is not a racehorse as a pony, regardless of size. Track ponies help escort horses from the paddock to the starting gate and also help with morning training. Also called "pony horse," "stable pony."

Rub - to groom; to care for a racehorse.

School - to train.

Start - to introduce a young horse to saddle. Usually a sixty-day period where the horse will progress to learning how to gallop. Also known as "breaking" though it is normally a very slow, gentle process.

Tag - claiming price.

Toque - a knit hat humans wear, typically in winter.

Thoroughbred Life stages:

Sire - father; "by" the sire.

Dam - mother; "out of" the dam.

Foal - from newborn to weaning time (aka suckling).

Weanling - from weaning time (5-7 months old).

Yearling - in North America, from January 1 following the horse's birth until the next January 1, regardless of actual birthdate.

Filly - female from birth through age four.

Mare - female five years and up; when used for breeding becomes broodmare.

Colt - male from birth through age four or until castrated.

Horse - male five years and up unless castrated.

Stallion - male used for breeding.

Gelding - castrated male of any age.

This list is in no way complete. If I've left out words you think would be beneficial to include, I welcome your input!

ACKNOWLEDGMENTS

Wow, so many people who jumped in to read this one at various stages in the process! It always amazes me that everyone catches something different, and sometimes I learn things, too! Any errors or inconsistencies that remain are my own.

Adeline Halvorson, who read chapter-by-chapter once I tamed the messy draft.

Bev Harvey who saw it next.

Kirsty Davis who was thrown in the deep end of my very horsey world!

Nathalie Drolet, Ariana Feldberg, June Monteleone, Mary Hathaway, Juliet Harrison, Andrea Harrison, Cathy Campbell and Allison Litfin (who has been reading for me since the very, very beginning!).

Thanks to my patrons on Patreon! Your support is so wonderful. A special nod to Judi Evans for cheering me on! Your emails (and your eagle eyes!) meant so much.

I'm sure I'm forgetting someone, and I apologize for that. If you're reading this, thank you, too.

If you're interested in joining my review team for future books, email me at linda@lindashantz.com

And last but most important, thank you, Lord. You are my only hope.

ABOUT THE AUTHOR

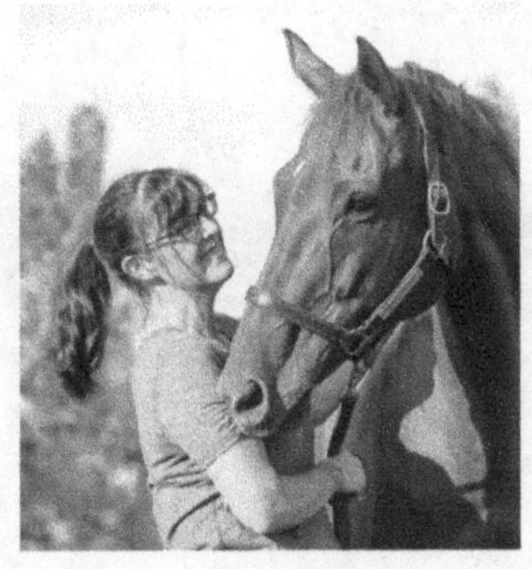

I began working at the racetrack before I finished high school, and after graduating the following January, took a hotwalking job at Payson Park in Florida. Once back at Woodbine, I started grooming and galloping. While the backstretch is exciting, I found I was more at home on the farm — prepping and breaking yearlings, nightwatching and foaling mares. Eventually I started my own small layup/broodmare facility, and in the last few years I've transitioned into retraining and rehoming. Somewhere along the way I went back to school and got a degree. I should probably dust it off and frame it one day!

I live on a small farm in Ontario, Canada, with my adopted off-track Thoroughbreds and a young Border Collie. If you like my covers, check out my artwork at www.lindashantz.com

Author photo by Kyley Woods Photography, used with permission.